Nova Roma
De Itinere in Occasum

Anderson Gentry

CRIMSON
DRAGON
PUBLISHING

Printed in the United States of America
First Printing 2021
ISBN 978-1-944644-07-9
E-book ISBN 978-1-944644-08-6
Library of Congress Control Number 2020945901

Fiction-Alternative History,
History-Ancient Rome, History- North America

Crimson Dragon Publishing
Willow, Alaska
www.crimsondragonpublishing.com

Contents

INTRODUCTION

"There was once a dream that was Rome. You could only whisper it. Anything more than a whisper and it would vanish... it was so fragile. And I fear that it will not survive the winter."
– Richard Harris as Marcus Aurelius, in Gladiator
(Universal Pictures, 2000)

Without Rome, there would be no Western civilization.

During the days of the Roman Republic and later, the Empire, it was accurately said that 'all roads lead to Rome.' Rome gave us the first truly modern roads, on which to move the first modern armies. Rome had the first modern sanitation, modern trade, and the Roman Republic was in place for five hundred years—approximately twice as long as the republic I live in now, the United States, whose founders used the Greek and Roman republics as models for their own. But the Roman Republic ended tragically, with the rise of the Roman Empire.

The fall of the Roman Republic and rise of the Roman Empire under Augustus Caesar is a subject that has been written about, analyzed, fictionalized, folded, spindled and mutilated in a thousand different ways, by a thousand different writers. The fall of the Republic had its genesis in the second Roman Civil

War, when the forces of Julius Caesar moved on Rome. The bulk of the Roman Senate fled south, led by the Roman consul and general Gnaeus Pompey Magnus. We all know how matters in Rome unfolded after that; Julius Caesar assassinated, the Second Triumvirate, Mark Antony's body paraded through the streets of Rome, and Caesar's nephew and heir Octavian becoming in essence the first Roman Emperor.

But in this work of fiction, I've tried to come up with a slant on the second Roman civil war that is a little different, one that I do not think has been done before.

Alternative history depends on a single twist, a point in time in history where one event happens not as we know it but, in another way, with another outcome. In this work the event is the flight of Pompey Magnus and the Senate from Julius Caesar. Instead of Greece, I have Pompey Magnus and his supporters amass a fleet of ships to carry them to Spain, where Pompey had properties, and then—in a rather unabashed *deus ex machina* to achieve the scenario I wanted—a freak storm blows Pompey, the Senators, their families and troops to the place we call South Carolina.

Consider for a moment the implications of this on both sides of the Atlantic.

First, in Rome. Unopposed, Caesar enters Rome, as in our timeline, but there is no second Roman civil war; almost everyone opposing Caesar is gone. But Caesar was known to suffer from health issues, most likely the result of battle injuries in his youth. He may well have not lived long after seizing dictatorial control even without the acts of Brutus, Cassius and the other assassins. As he had no son, the ambitious Octavian may well have been his heir in any reality.

But it is in the New World that this story is focused. Think about the implications of landing a Roman expedition on the shores of North America in 49B.C., in a land then populated by early Indians of the little-known mound building culture of pre-Columbian America. Imagine the impact of Roman technology, Roman society, Roman government and—most importantly—Roman arms on those people. When Europeans first landed in the New World in our timeline, they had the overwhelming technological advantages described in anthropologist Jared Diamond's excellent *Guns, Germs and Steel*—not least of those was the first. Republican-era Romans, on the other hand, have advantages but they are not so great as to be overwhelming. Unlike the Spaniard's cannon, the Roman gladius is something a pre-Columbian Indian would understand as a superior version of something he might craft himself. The two societies would have to deal with each other on something more like an even footing.

But the story wouldn't stop there, of course. Imagine, as their history unfolds, the continuation of a Roman Republic in the New World—a Republic where no Caesar arises, a nation founded by the likes of Marcus Porcius Cato and Marcus Tullius Cicero. Imagine the influence a Cato would have on that founding–Cato the Stoic, who modeled his life after the virtues and ideals of the earliest days of the Republic, the virtues and ideals in place before the Marius/Sulla civil war which indirectly led to the rise of Caesar.

Imagine a new Republic begun with the standards and ideals of the old but surviving and growing half a world away from the old, in a place where the Empire not only never rises but never falls, in a new world where the Dark Ages never happen, where the people do not lose nearly a millennium to starvation, ignorance and disease —and where the new Romans will one day look back across the sea and decide, after enough time has passed, to go back, to see how old Rome fares.

That is the scenario in the Nova Roma series.

For those interested in the history of ancient Rome in our timeline, I strongly recommend several works.

First of all is Livy's *History of Early Rome*, for an excellent work on the founding of Rome and the rise of the Republic. Livy was a scholar who knew Rome and Roman society as few others, and his insights on the founding of the Republic are revealing.

For a later history, read Edward Gibbon's excellent *The History of the Decline and Fall of the Roman Empire*. Gibbon's work chronicles what happened to Rome well after the events of the second Roman Civil War from which this story takes its genesis, but it remains one of the best examinations of why Imperial Rome fell into disarray and was, eventually, overrun.

G. Suetonius Tranquillus' *The Twelve Caesars* is a great work produced by someone who, like Livy, actually knew old Rome, who walked the streets and knew the culture, the people.

For an excellent illustration of how the Roman army worked on campaign in the era of the Republic, read Julius Caesar's *The Gallic Wars*. Caesar figures only marginally in Nova Roma, but he was a brilliant tactician and a canny politician, which made him a very dangerous opponent to our timeline's Pompey Magnus and his Senate supporters. His account of the campaign in Gaul is well worth reading.

Finally, if television appeals to you, catch HBO's stunning miniseries *Rome*. It plays around with the history some, but the attention to detail is outstanding, the character development is very good, and the storyline is well developed. The series excels in one area, namely that it does not only portray the lives of Roman nobles but also the common people, the plebs, the soldiers, merchants and artisans of Rome.

Once, all roads led to Rome. Now, Rome stands as the source of all roads that led to modern Western civilization. In fiction and in fact, Rome excites the imagination as few other nations ever have.

To Dawn
Empress of my heart

Nova Roma
De Itinere in Occasum

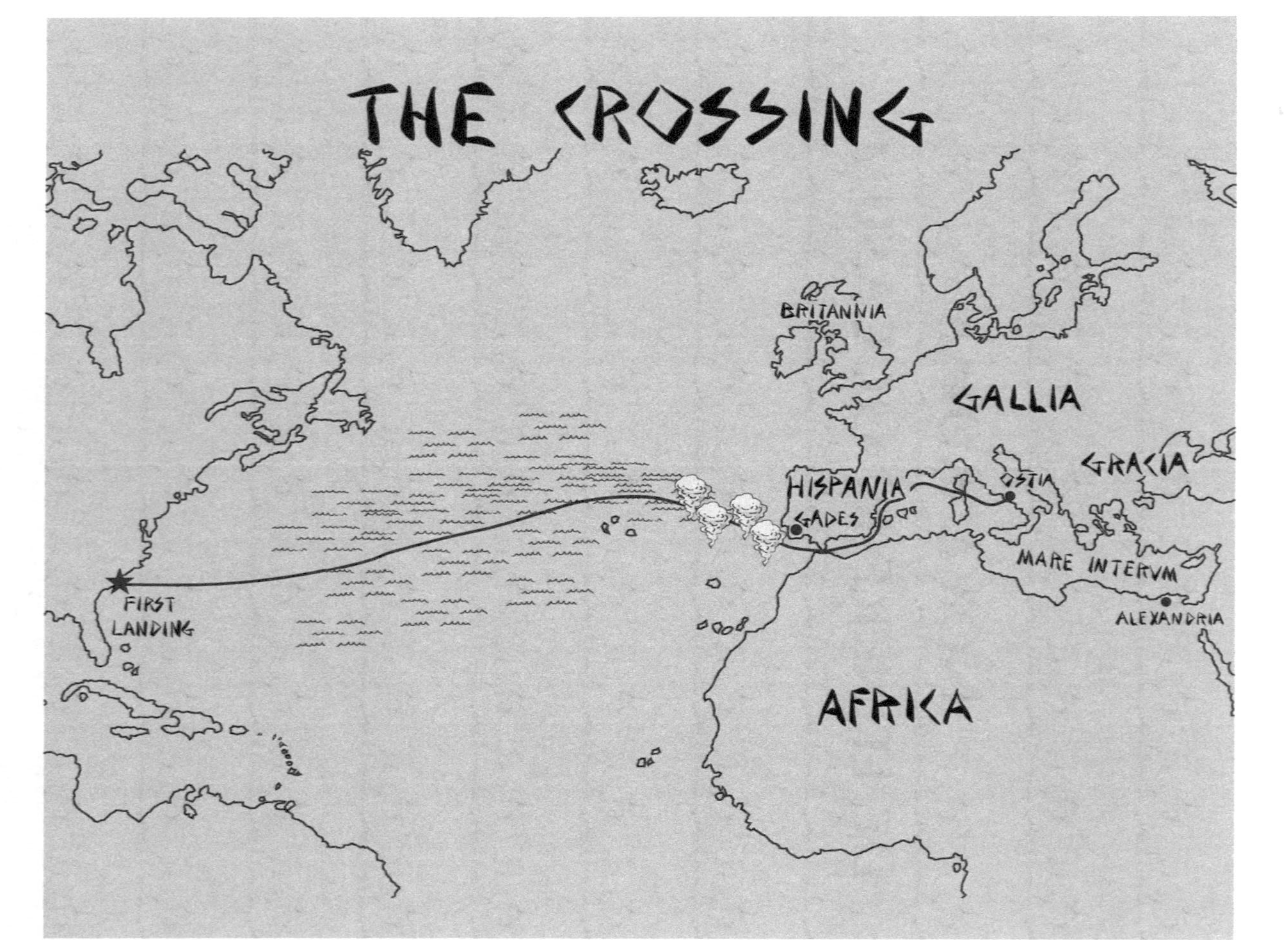

THE CROSSING
BRITANNIA
GALLIA
GRACIA
HISPANIA
GADES
OSTIA
MARE INTERVM
ALEXANDRIA
FIRST LANDING
AFRICA

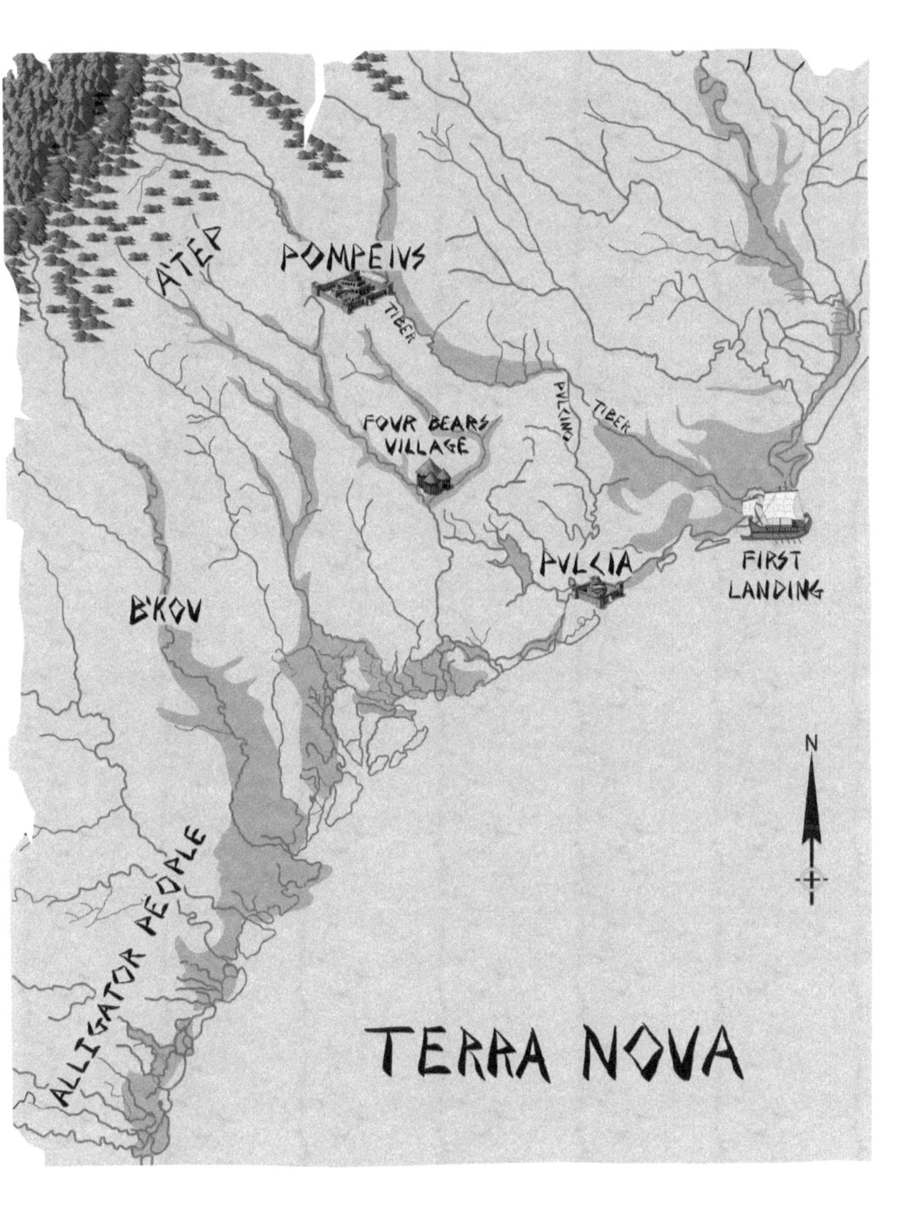

A'TEP
POMPEIVS
TIBER
FOUR BEARS
VILLAGE
PVLCINO
TIBER
PVLCIA
FIRST
LANDING
B'KOV
N
ALLIGATOR PEOPLE
TERRA NOVA

PROLOGUE

Rome

It was a lovely late winter evening, with the cool mild
air typical of Rome at that time of year. The show in *Theatrum
Pompeium* was entertaining; the actors were portraying some
event that had taken place during a trial of an accused murderer
several days earlier. Despite the best efforts of the actors and their
outrageous antics, Gnaeus Pompeius Magnus, commonly known
as Pompey Magnus, general of the Roman Army and former
consul of Rome, was not amused. The news from the north was too
dire.

Pompey was a heavy-set man with broad features and thin,
graying hair which he kept cut close to his head in a soldier's
fashion. Well into middle age but still physically powerful, he was
regarded as a great hero, from the campaigns of his youth in Italia,
Africa and Hispania as well as his clearing the Mediterranean
of pirates. More recently he had formed part of the triumvirate
that effectively ruled Rome, along with Julius Caesar and Marcus
Licinius Crassus, but now Crassus was dead, and Caesar...

Pompey looked past his fifth wife, Cornelia Metalla, to see
Marcus Porcius Cato watching the show with a sour look on his

face. He regarded Cato the Younger; the Senator was younger than Pompey, long-faced, thin and wiry where Pompey was built like a bull. Cato was rarely cheerful at the best of times; his Stoic inclinations saw to that. With the news that day had brought, however...

"Caesar," Cato was muttering, barely audible to Pompey's aged, war-battered hearing. Cato was shaking his head. "Caesar, he who would be a king."

Pompey had bragged that he could raise an army by stamping his foot on Roman soil. He had stamped that foot, and four legions awaited his command on the field of Mars, outside the city. But Gaius Julius Caesar had crossed the Rubicon and was heading towards Rome herself. Caesar had but one legion, but that legion was the fabled Thirteenth, battle-hardened veterans of the Gallic wars to a man, and to a man fiercely dedicated to Caesar.

Pompey was nervous. The very gods themselves seemed to walk with Caesar.

At fifty-six, Pompey was still strong, still vital. He was the grand old oak of Roman arms, a great hero, but he sensed his time had passed. The ascendancy of Caesar was at hand.

He was not at all certain his army was a match for that of Julius Caesar.

The evening ended with applause from the throngs in the massive theater, paid for by Pompey himself. He had devoted his life to the Republic, serving as general, governor and consul, but now his service looked to have been for naught.

The play was ending. The crowd erupted in laughter and applause, and many turned to where Pompey and Cato sat in one of the higher boxes. Shouts of "Pompey Magnus" echoed from the marble walls; he had built this theater at his own expense, and the Roman people favored him for it.

Pompey stood up and wrapped his robes tighter, waving to acknowledge the applause. "My dear," he said softly, extending his hand to Cornelia. She stood, smiling; she was a quiet woman, but not shy. Her confidence in her husband was absolute, which at the moment shamed him a little.

"We meet tomorrow morning," Cato reminded him. "This issue must be decided before the next day is out."

"It will be," Pompey agreed. "It will be."

"It had better be," Cato complained. "We face a bitter choice, Pompey. I tell you..."

"Not here," Pompey snapped. He waved a hand at the crowds around them. "Tomorrow, Cato. Tomorrow will be soon enough. Go home. Sleep."

Cato frowned, staring at Pompey from hooded eyes. He was a tall man, spare, dressed in a simple wrap of gray linen that hung down over narrow, calloused bare feet, quite unlike Pompey's rich robes of orange and gold. Cato took his personal Stoic philosophy seriously, to the point of eschewing most creature comforts–even shoes. "Yes," Cato agreed at last, his tone still sour. "Tomorrow." He nodded his farewell to Pompey, bowed politely to Cornelia, and wandered off through the crowd.

Cornelia wrapped her arms around Pompey's left arm and squeezed gently. "What meeting tomorrow?"

"Nothing you need concern yourself about for now," Pompey said, not wanting to worry his young fifth wife; he loved her very much. "I will let you know if you need to make any preparations." He sat back down to wait for the crowd to thin out. Cornelia sat down beside him.

Cornelia's smile faded. "I'm not some empty-headed shepherd girl, you know. My father was a consul of Rome just as you are."

Pompey looked straight ahead, frowning, saying nothing.

"It's Caesar, then," Cornelia said.

"Yes," Pompey admitted. He smiled, still looking straight ahead. "You know, I remember when he was just a boy, no more than sixteen. He had this fire about him, even then; did you know he was captured by pirates when he was just a *principale*? The pirates asked him if they should demand twenty talents ransom for him, and Caesar, that impudent pup, told them they should demand no less than fifty."

"He was an enemy of Sulla. When Sulla managed to make himself Dictator, he very nearly had Julius executed, since he was Marius' nephew; I wonder sometimes if Sulla's example was what set Caesar on the course he's on now. If Cato is right, and he really does want a crown, then... I shall have to..." His voice trailed off, sadly, as they got up to leave the now nearly empty theater.

"You shall have to fight him. You have four legions outside the city, do you not?"

"Four legions of green recruits leavened with a few veterans," Pompey muttered. "I have four legions to throw against Caesar and his battle-hardened men, who are marching even now from Gaul."

Cornelia was not about to let the matter drop. "I know you are meeting to discuss Julius Caesar marching on Rome. Should I prepare the household to move? Will we leave the city to Caesar?"

"I don't know," Pompey said. He headed for the theater exits, now that the crowd had mostly thinned out, for the walk home. "We'll decide tomorrow— myself, Cato, Cicero, and some of the others. I don't think the Republic can survive another civil war. I never thought I'd see two in my own lifetime. There has to be a better way. No man should be above the law. Sulla himself was elected Consul three times—the law allows once. Once! What good the law if the nobles can bend it to suit themselves?"

"You are beginning to sound like Cato," his wife teased gently.

"I sometimes think I should listen more closely to Cato."

"I think," Cornelia said, "that I will start the servants to packing."

Pompey said nothing.

They walked home through the streets, the bustling, thrumming, vibrant streets of Rome. We are going to have to leave, the thought kept running through Pompey's head. He was greeted by a scarred, one-armed old veteran who saluted, clumsily with his left arm. "General Pompey!" the man shouted, his voice and bearing a trifle unsteady.

Pompey's practiced eyes swept over the man, taking in his ragged tunic, his unkempt hair, his dirty, unshaven face. Pompey also noted the legion tattoo on the man's shoulder. He pressed a coin into the old soldier's hand. "Salve, soldier. Get yourself something to eat."

The soldier looked at the silver denarius in his hand—enough for a hot meal, a drink, a bath, even a bed for the night. His face brightened. He saluted again, shouting: "Very grateful, sir!"

Pompey smiled, slapped the old soldier on the back, and walked on.

"He's likely to just go on a binge with a jug of wine and a prostitute, you know," Cornelia gently teased.

"He served as a soldier of Rome," Pompey said. "I think that entitles him to a jug of wine if he chooses, my dear," Pompey teased right back; he wisely didn't mention any prostitutes. He was no stranger to married life, after all, and knew all too well how to avoid the pitfalls.

Cornelia smiled and patted her husband's arm. The couple walked on through the twilight.

Next morning

The meeting was small; Pompey and Cato were joined by Marcus Tullius Cicero and Metellus Scipio, Pompey's father-in-law. The four men met in Cicero's house, attended only by a pair of Cicero's personal servants. None of the other Senators were to be brought in; not as yet. The servants brought in cups of sweet fruit juice with ice—a luxury of considerable expense—and withdrew to leave the men to their planning.

The discussion had already gone on for over two hours. "Greece," Cato said, for probably the hundredth time that morning. Cicero agreed with him, but Pompey was not convinced. Scipio wavered between advocating for Greece and suggesting a half-dozen other destinations.

"It has to be Greece," Cato continued. "Greece is sufficiently distant from Rome that Caesar cannot easily follow us, not with his entire army. We can regroup there, raise more legions..."

"And what of the four legions we already have here in Rome?" Pompey demanded. "How can we, with four legions, evade Caesar with one? Is it not more difficult for us to move than he? You are not a soldier, friend Cato; you do not understand the difficulties of marching such a large body of men over that distance. They need to be provisioned, we will need supply trains, wagons..." His voice trailed off as he began to mentally compile a list of what would be needed to move his army to Greece.

His musings were not allowed to continue. "You say I am not

a soldier, but I have led men in battle, Pompey," Cato snapped. "I have not seen as many battles as you, to be sure, but I am not ignorant of military matters. I commanded a legion in Macedonia, do you remember? Why must we flee his one legion when you, Pompey Magnus, control four right in the neighborhood of Rome itself?" he demanded. "You have four to one odds!"

Pompey let out a dramatic sigh. "I have four untried, unblooded legions, Cato. Four legions of men who have had elementary training but have never smelled the stinks of battle. Caesar has one legion, but it is the Thirteenth. The Thirteenth of Gaul, of Alesia. The conquering Thirteenth. They beat Vercingetorix, they swept all of the Gallic tribes before them, even outnumbered ten to one, twenty to one! My four novice legions would be no match. There are some veterans in the ranks, true, some of the officers, some of the senior legionaries have joined the Evocati, but not enough. Not enough."

"They are soldiers of Rome," Cato pointed out.

"And so are the veterans of the Thirteenth."

"He can move faster than we overland, it's true," Cicero said. "But can we go by sea? There are ships available at Ostia. What if we move our legions to Greece—or to Alexandria—by sea? Have we enough ships?"

"I'm not certain," Pompey mused. "Perhaps..." He did the calculations in his head; triremes and some larger quadriremes were available, but were there enough for four legions? Pompey had more than a little experience with ships, from chasing pirates; four legions, some hangers-on, the Senators, their families and a few servants; if they could get the right sort of ships, thirty or thirty-five ships would do. The extra people would be a burden, but the members of the Senate that were with him, they and their families would have to go as well. They could hardly leave them in Rome to face Caesar's anger.

If there were enough ships, should they use them to flee Caesar? To Greece?

Or somewhere else?

"No," Pompey said suddenly. The thought came to him like a blinding flash of light. "No, we will not go to Greece. Nor to Alexandria. We will use ships, but we will not go east." He pointed to the map that Cicero had laid on the table they sat around. "We will go west. I campaigned in the west in my younger days, do you all not remember? I have properties and coin in Hispania. We can raise men there as easily as in Greece. Caesar will not expect us to move in that direction. We need to take the initiative from him. For once, we need to make Caesar react to us."

"How will we pay these legions you plan to raise?" Scipio wanted to know. "Do your own resources stretch so far?

"We will take the treasury gold, of course," Pompey said. It was as though the plan had sprung, fully formed, into his mind. "We will take the treasury gold, our four legions, our allies in the Senate, our families—and we will take ship at Ostia. Prepare yourselves, my friends, prepare your families. I want to leave for Ostia in five days."

"So soon?"

"I would leave sooner," Pompey answered Scipio, "but we need to send orders to have every available ship from every port sent to Ostia to meet us; we need to gather provisions for the legions, and we need to prepare to move the Treasury."

Cicero raised a hand. "We should consider the effect our abandonment of Rome will have on the plebs. It will not be viewed favorably; it will make our return difficult."

"If we can raise an army to defeat Caesar in the field," Pompey said, "We can worry about that when Rome is once more ours to return to. If we cannot... Well, then we will have few worries after that, neh? Come, my friends; we have much to do, and not much time to do it. I will see to the legions. Cato, please see to arranging transport for the treasury. Cicero, arrange transport to Ostia for our families. And Scipio, draft correspondence to arrange for the ships. Are we agreed?"

The others looked doubtful, but Pompey spoke with great force; it seemed the old soldier was once more in his element. His recent uncertainty was gone now. The old soldier saw a clear course of action ahead.

Cato finally broke the silence. "I agree," he said. "Hispania, then." Cato was not a polished speaker, but his opinion carried great weight among the other Optimates. Cicero and Scipio looked at each other, then nodded. The plan was set.

Ostia, ten days later

The Ostian docks were ablaze with activity. Various freighters, naval triremes and quadriremes were pulled up to the docks. Soldiers loaded gear aboard, shouting sailors brought in provisions and filled water casks.

To Pompey Magnus' left, three sweating drovers wrangled a small herd of squealing, enraged pigs aboard a small freight hauler. To the right, a centurion oversaw the loading of several cavalry horses. Pompey knew several other ships had loaded goats, chickens, even a few ducks; the only way to have meat on a voyage like this was to take it aboard on the hoof.

Nearby, legionaries lugged heavy chests aboard a wide-hulled cargo ship under the watchful eye of two centurions and a white-robed Senator: the treasury gold. Raising an army would be impossible without it.

Footsteps sounded on the dock behind him. Pompey turned to see Marcus Tullius Cicero approaching, a wide grin on his face.

"I tell you, Pompey, I never would have believed it," Cicero exulted. "Who would have thought, in all the world, that we could assemble forty ships so quickly!"

"The treasury is loading," Pompey said, his satisfaction evident. "The legions are on ships. Using the legionaries as oarsman was a brilliant idea, Cicero; we never would have put together enough ships to move the better part of two legions without it. And the two we are taking are formed from the best of the four I had raised. All the veterans of Africa, Greece and Gaul will come with us, along with the very best of the new men."

"That is a wise choice," Cicero agreed.

"The Senators that are going, their families and households are loading as well. We will be able to leave Ostia for Hispania by noon. Caesar will not expect this; no, he will not expect this," Pompey chuckled.

"I must say, I didn't expect it myself," Cicero said. "Forty ships. Extraordinary, General! Extraordinary."

Cato approached them; his expression carefully neutral. "The loading is almost complete. I don't like the look of those clouds to the east," he pointed over Pompey's shoulder.

Pompey turned and regarded the approaching high clouds with a practiced eye. They were gray clouds, whipped out into long trails by a wind high in the sky. The sky was growing darker behind them. "They look nasty," he opined, "but they won't amount to much. A bit of wind, a bit of rain. Nothing to worry about." He slapped Cato in the back in a rare display of good fellowship.

"Come on, my friends. Let's get on board our ship. Let that little bit of a storm blow us towards Hispania." Pompey was satisfied, for the moment. Caesar would enter Rome to find it mostly undefended, the key members of the Senate gone, and the treasury empty.

That would do, for the time being. He had the flower of the Senate with him. He had the Treasury gold. He had two legions of men. Pompey knew he could raise more troops in Hispania, feed and equip them, return to face Caesar with an army at his back. Rome would be saved. He would reap the glory of being its savior.

He was wrong.

Pompey Magnus headed for the big freighter that his wife, sons and daughter were already aboard. He walked up the gangplank, nodded to the ship's scrawny, bandy-legged Spanish captain, and went below.

Behind him, a gust of wind rattled the freighter's linen sails. The first few drops of rain were falling as the first ships left the docks. Pipers piped a cadence, oars dipped into the water, and the first ships moved off into the Mediterranean, heading west.

PART ONE
THE NEW WORLD

CHAPTER ONE
THE STORM

Pompey Magnus led the exodus from Rome on the kalends of March in the first year. Forty and one ships set forth from Ostia bearing the better parts of two legions of infantry and several cavalry horses. A large portion of gold was aboard as were the Optimate Senators and some family members. Some various civilians also found their way aboard.

All ships set forth for the port of Gades in Hispania where Pompey Magnus had properties and coin to raise further troops. The goal was to oppose the invasion of Italy by would-be tyrant Gaius Julius Caesar who was invading from the north and had even then crossed the Rubicon under arms against Roman law. Caesar had the loyalty of his Gallic legions which accompanied him, and Pompey knew it necessary to raise more arms and men to defeat Caesar.

This journey to Gades did not succeed as planned. What became of the traitor and lawbreaker Caesar was never known. The fleet of ships, having departed Ostia in good order, were instead caught in the teeth of a storm mightier than any previously known, and taken away to a place no man had suspected to exist. Those lands, this Nova Terra, were passing strange lands, inhabited by strange natives and even stranger flora and fauna. What unfolded from the arrival of Pompey and his party, is the ongoing subject of this record.

—From Gnaeus Pompey Novus' New World Diaries

The Mediterranean

In the center of the Mediterranean, south of Greece, a mass of cold air flowing south from eastern Europe met the warm air masses over Judea and Syria. The result was a swirling mass of high winds and rain as the warm air dumped whatever moisture it had into the sea.

Moving west, the storm quickly grew in size and strength, fueled by the hot air over Egypt. When it made landfall in Italy, the storm met the Alps on the north and a high-pressure air mass over Italy, which served to funnel it westward. This channeled the swirling mass into a torrent of air, blasting westward, driving heavy rains before it.

In the Atlantic, a massive tropical storm was forming just west of what would later be known as the Ivory Coast. When the two storms met, the result would be a once-in-a-millennium event, a maelstrom of indescribable proportions, which would drive anything at sea helplessly before it.

It was this storm that awaited Pompey Magnus and his company as they set sail from Ostia.

Nearing Gibraltar

Bamil Barca was an adequate ship captain, but Pompey did not like him personally; the scrawny, wiry little Spaniard was too sure of himself. And one thing he was sure of today: He did not like the following wind that was blowing large, dark clouds in their direction.

Barca's ship was not one of the Roman triremes that hauled troops. It was a freight hauler, a large converted grain ship; Barca made his living taking valuable cargoes from port to port, from Judea to Alexandria to Ostia and anywhere else there was gold or silver to be had. When the call had gone out from Rome for ships, Barca had been in Ostia delivering a load of mixed cargo from Alexandria and had seen the opportunity to line his purse with some Roman coins.

Pompey considered Barca little more than a barbarian. The little shipmaster shaved his head but let his beard grow, like some hairy Gallic chieftain; he wore a leather jerkin stained black with sweat and dirt that he had apparently lived, eaten and slept in for several years, and he chewed continually on sticks of some Eastern spice he had picked up someplace or other. He was also strangely evasive about how and when he came by ownership and command of his vessel. But his ship was large, one of the largest freight-haulers Pompey had ever seen; and had actual separate cabins for passengers. So, Pompey, Cato and Cicero had placed themselves and their households on board Barca's ship for the journey to the port at Gades.

Barca stood at the stern, watching the gathering clouds. Pompey stood beside him, listening idly to the oars splashing in the increasingly choppy waters of the Mediterranean. Cato and Cicero had gone below decks. The rising seas caused them both to fall ill. Pompey was made of sterner stuff. Chasing pirates on the Mediterranean in his younger days had made him an adequate sailor.

The freighter captain looked around at the armada of ships surrounding them, then spat into the sea. "I tell you, General," he said for the thousandth time, pointing at the following storm clouds, "I don't like the looks of that. I've been at sea for fifty years, and I've never seen the like. Coming out of the east, too? A storm sent from the gods, that is."

"If it is," Pompey snapped, "then the gods are blowing us in the right direction. Who are we to question that? It seems to me that the gods favor my plans and wish to help us get to Hispania quickly."

To Pompey's disgust, Barca stepped aft, hauled up his filthy jerkin and urinated off the stern into the sea. "You're paying," the little man said over his shoulder, "and I won't turn down good Roman gold. I just hope we can take all these damned ships into Gades before that storm hits. It will be here by nightfall, or I'm an Egyptian."

"The wind is freshening. Perhaps all ships should make sail, run ahead of it."

"This wind freshens too much, it will rip our sails off," Barca complained. He finished urinating, shook himself off, and let his jerkin drop. "Oh, very well," he said, not willing to withstand Pompey's stare. "I'll pass the word—all ships to make sail."

"I hope all these ships can stay within sight of each other," Pompey muttered. A gust of wind whipped spray off the ocean into his face. "Keeping station will be an unpleasant job in this mess."

"Keeping alive, that will be the thing," Barca snorted.

A nearby trireme

Legionary Titus Caninus counted himself lucky not to have been assigned as a rower; his shoulders were simply too wide to fit among even the *thranatai*, the top row of oarsmen on the open deck. Instead he was posted as a lookout and message-passer, stationed at the bow of the ship to watch that the trireme kept well away from other ships and to watch for signals from the other ships of the armada.

Caninus was a huge bull of a man, hairy as the great dog his name implied, and scarred from a life spent as a soldier. Caninus had seen action in Africa, Greece and Gaul, including the battle at Alesia, and was well-known for his combative skills; be the weapon gladius and scutum, bow and arrows, pilum or bare fists, Titus Caninus was a warrior to contend with.

He suffered now from a headache brought on by too much wine in a boisterous celebration in port the night before, and his left eye hurt, having been blackened in a brawl during that same debauch. The damned pig of an Aventine collegium thug wouldn't be eating too well for a while, not with the broken jaw Caninus had given him in return.

The wind had grown fierce. As the sun set slowly into the sea ahead of them, the waves grew larger, and the oarsmen struggled to keep the ship on course. The triremes, quadriremes and smaller ships had reduced sail to run ahead of the wind.

Titus Caninus grabbed for the low railing as the ship lurched into the trough of a wave. He laughed as the sea broke across the trireme's bow, drenching him. "Come on, Neptune," he shouted into the gale. "Is this the best you've got? My grandmother had more wind than this!"

Julius Gracchus, the trireme's commander—the trierarch ¬–

stumbled past, shouting orders to the *thranatai* to tie themselves to the benches. "Damn you, Caninus," he barked at Titus. "You'll curse us all. You can't speak so to the gods! Would you have us all marooned on some distant shore?"

Caninus laughed again. "The gods are frightened old women! Neptune can suck my cock if he can't produce a better storm than this."

"Be careful," Gracchus warned, "what you wish for, Great Dog."

Pompey's ship

"By the gods, this is getting ugly," Bamil Barca complained. He had lashed himself to one of the ship's steering oars and had his first mate lashed to the other. The wind was grown truly fierce now.

"That rock," Barca shouted at the wind-racked and rain-soaked Pompey Magnus, who had managed to stay on deck. Pompey managed to turn where he had lashed himself securely to the ship's single mast to see where Barca was pointing. He'd seen the great massif before; it marked the point where ships left the sheltered Mediterranean for the larger, wilder Atlantic.

"Can we turn north?" Pompey shouted at the scrawny little ship captain.

"Not a chance," Barca called back over the howling wind. "All oars are shipped in. Sails are folded. All we can do with a wind like this, Roman, is to run before it."

"How long will this blow?"

"Who knows?" Barca laughed. "Days? A week? Go below, Pompey Magnus. There's nothing you can do up here. Only the gods know where this storm will take us."

Barca watched as the Roman general and consul carefully

untied the rope that held him to the mast and made his way below, where his wife and son waited.

The ship captain's demeanor didn't show his worry. He had learned long ago that the key to maintaining control of a ship was to never let your crew see when you were worried, or frightened. Barca was both, but he turned an impassive face to the world.

His first mate was not as practiced. Barca stole a glance at the man, who clung to the left-hand steering oar. Tulla Szabo was plainly frightened, his normally swarthy face pale with fear.

Barca was frightened. He was more frightened than he had ever been in a lifetime spent plying the trade lanes and ports of the Mediterranean. This was not a storm like he had ever seen before; the entire Roman fleet was being driven helplessly to the west. What lay beyond the gates to the Atlantic and the lanes north to Hispania, the Gallic ports and Britannia, no man knew. Barca was afraid to find out. Were they trespassing into the realm of unknown forces? Unknown tribes of savages? Gods? Monsters? No man knew.

He watched his ship with a trained eye as he clung to the oar. He noted how the bow flexed as the waves broke over it, listened to how the planks of the hull groaned as the ship mounted the waves and plunged into the troughs. He watched the masts, rocking in the screaming wind. The deck was clear of clutter, the only men exposed to the weather were the ones essential to keeping the ship in one piece. They were doing as well as could be hoped, all told. Barca hoped the other forty ships in the fleet were doing likewise.

The screaming wind drove the Roman fleet relentlessly past the rock of Gibraltar, into the open ocean, racing to the west, into the unknown.

A trireme in the fleet

Servius Valerius Merulus fought to stay upright as the trireme rocked mercilessly, climbing one mountainous wave to crash again into the trough of another. It was the second day of the storm, and the wind showed no sign of abating. The trireme's captain said the fleet was scattered all over the ocean, but he had sighted at least three of the ships.

All in all, it was amazing any of them were still afloat.

Servius was struggling to fill brass bowls with a slop of barely cooked goat meat and onions, brewed in a huge kettle in the trireme's bowels. A line of legionaries doubling as oarsmen swayed in line, each waiting for a cup of foul water and a bowlful of stew.

Servius was small, slight, with no beard anyone could detect; the crew figured the volunteer cook's age for no more than fourteen, mostly due to pale skin, beardless cheeks and soft voice. Servius' pale blonde hair was cropped into a boy's ringlets, but gray eyes under fine blonde brows were sharp, even calculating, far beyond the face's apparent age. Servius called to the next legionary in the queue.

"Come on," a surprisingly strong voice snapped. "Come on, Lucius. It's a good stew. The goat died happy."

"I wish I would die," Lucius replied, his face a pale green. He paled as Servius slapped a ladleful of stew into his brass bowl. "I can't eat."

"You have to eat," Servius said, "or you'll die, and they will tip you over the side. Or maybe we'll eat you."

"Everything I eat goes over the side anyway."

"Eat," Servius insisted. "Next!"

Farther forward, the trireme's captain and first mate were inspecting the inside of the hull near the bow. "Leaking," the first mate observed, quite unnecessarily. "Between these seas and the wood soaking through, we'll be taking on more and more water."

"Organize bailing and pumping parties," the captain ordered. "Neptune knows, the legionaries aren't needed to man oars in this mess. These ships should be made of sterner stuff; cedar is light, but it leaks."

"Oak would be good," the first mate agreed. He turned to issue orders to one of the ship's crew, who ran off to gather legionaries to man buckets. "Heavy, but strong. Well-tarred, it wouldn't ever leak. At least not like this."

"Keep her afloat," the captain said. "Every ship in the fleet will be struggling with this, just as we are. Keep her afloat, and at least we'll see where this wind from Neptune's ass takes us."

"We'll be lucky if half the fleet survives this."

"I'll be satisfied if we survive it."

Pompey's ship

Pompey Magnus had never felt so helpless in his life. He watched as his beloved Cornelia lay hopelessly sick as the ship heaved in the sea. He listened as the wind screamed outside, driving his fleet farther and farther west.

It was the third day of the storm.

Every day Pompey forced himself to struggle up the narrow ladder to the upper deck. Every day the raging sea looked the same, heaving, angry, monstrous. Every day Barca grew a little quieter and, to Pompey's trained eye, a little more worried.

Pompey had looked in on Cato and Cicero earlier in the day. Both of them were miserably seasick. Conditions in the freighter's tiny cabins were well past horrific; passengers laid in their own filth, and rats ran wild in panic through the vessel.

"Where are we?" Pompey's older son, Gnaeus Pompey, managed to ask. The boy was almost twenty-five, a stout young man, an experienced soldier, but not a sailor; the younger Pompey had suffered like his stepmother from endless nausea in the storm.

"I don't know," Pompey answered. "Nobody knows. Is Claudia all right?"

Gnaeus looked at his young wife, who tossed miserably in a bunk. "As well as can be expected."

"When will this storm end?" Cornelia demanded; her voice weak. Pompey did not answer her. No answer was possible.

Pompey rose to struggle to the upper deck again. The storm continued unabated, he knew the ship was being slashed by wind and rain, but the foul air in the cabin was more than he could take. He made his way above to find Bamil Barca once again—or perhaps still—lashed to the right-hand steering oar. The man had not, to Pompey's knowledge, left that post since the storm began. Credit due for that, the Roman general supposed. He moved carefully to Barca's side; his iron-hobnailed sandals reasonably sure on the wet wood of the deck.

"How are we doing?" he shouted over the wind.

Barca turned to him and grinned, revealing yellow, stained teeth. "Aside from the wind, the rain, the leaks, the sails ripped away, most of my crew vomiting over the side, and your legionaries below laying in puddles of puke? Aside from this damned storm that threatens to blow us off the edge of the world? We're doing just wonderful, General; it's a lovely day for a sail."

Pompey found himself laughing unexpectedly. The man had sand; there was no denying it.

"I told you, General, I've never seen the like," Barca shouted again to be heard over the storm. "We must be leagues and leagues past Hispania by now. No one has ever been this far."

"I wonder where we'll end up when the storm blows out."

"Somewhere new," Barca said. He shrugged. "Somewhere nobody has seen before."

Suddenly worries of Julius Caesar were far from Pompey's mind. "Yes, I suppose we will see a new place. I wonder if we'll have to pay a ferryman to get there?"

Barca laughed again. "You already have, General. Your good Roman gold clinks in my pockets even now."

Pompey slapped the Spaniard on the back.

"Food will be the problem," the little captain said after a moment.

"Food?"

"If we don't hit some land where we can re-provision, we'll end up eating each other before we can get back to Hispania. Most of the goats will be gone, your men's supplies of dried meat and fruit will be eaten. You brought horses, yes?"

Pompey nodded. "Not many. Maybe twenty mares, ten stallions, ten geldings," he said, thinking. "Somewhere out there, on one of the other ships, assuming it hasn't been lost already."

"We may end up eating them," Barca said. "We may end up eating the hay you brought to feed them." He held up a hand in the driving rain. "At least water isn't a trouble."

"We should fill every available container while the rain holds," Pompey said. "It may grow hot and dry heading back."

"We've thought of that," Barca said, a little sharply. "We've been in storms before, you know."

Pompey nodded; suddenly aware he was being fussy. He gave the Spaniard an apologetic smile.

"Go back below, General," Barca said once again. "Try to get some sleep. We can do nothing but ride this out, then worry about what to do next."

Pompey nodded slowly, and then once again headed back to the narrow, smelly passageway below decks.

Mid-Atlantic

The storm had blown now for over a week. The scattered Roman ships were barely able to stay in contact by visual signals; the fleet was scattered over leagues of heaving, tossing ocean.

Triremes and quadriremes kept their oars in, their rowers idle, knowing it was no use to do anything but run before the relentless wind. Several ships had gone down to the endless deeps, sunk by sprung planking, hulls shattered by the raging sea, or simply the collapse of their wooden frames. Most hove on, sails tied tightly to the masts, decks soaked, with only essential personnel above decks. Steersmen fought to keep their ships faced into the waves.

Below decks was a hell. Passengers and crew lay miserably seasick. Vomit and human waste fouled the decks. Fever took away some of the weaker Romans, while others huddled miserably, suffering hot and cold flashes, sweats, and aching bones.

Food was running short, even with most of the people sick. The last goats and sheep were slaughtered on the ninth day. Dried meat there was, but the lack of exercise and nausea made it impossible for many to eat, and the endless drenching in saltwater quickly turned preserved food inedible.

One large cargo ship carried the expedition's horses. One fine stallion stumbled in his stall as the ship rolled into a trough and broke a leg; a centurion assigned to oversee the care of the animal used a dagger to cut its throat, crying tears of rage as he did so. The horse was cut up for stewing.

The storm blew on and on.

Nights were the worst. There were no stars to guide by, no glimpse of the moon to give an indication of direction. The ship's captains all thought they were still headed west, but nobody knew for sure; days dawned gloomy and dark, with only low, dark clouds obscuring any sight of the sun. No land was in view anywhere, nor were any other ships. The expedition of Roman ships, originally bound for Hispania, was lost in a vast, raging wilderness of water.

On the fourteenth day, the wind began to die down. The fifteenth morning dawned ugly, but the wind was down to a manageable level, and the sun broke weakly through the clouds, dead astern. The surviving ships began to slowly gather together, to form a center. Sails were unrolled, and oars finally extended and put into use.

At the center of the loose formation was the freighter carrying Pompey Magnus.

Pompey's ship

Pompey Magnus was hungry, but not yet starving. His years of soldiering had accustomed him to short rations. With the weather moderating at last, Bamil Barca had finally relinquished the right-side steering oar; Pompey did not think the man had slept ten hours in ten days. He stood now, wavering slightly, next to Pompey on the deck near the bow of the ship. The sea was still tossing, but the wind had moderated. Things were, for the moment, at least tolerable.

"I make it thirty-four ships," Pompey said. Barca nodded agreement. "Six lost." Pompey had known one moment of unbelievable relief when the ship holding the Treasury gold had appeared out of a lingering fog bank. A miracle, really, to have lost only six.

"Look there," the little ship captain pointed. "Those birds, flying out of the west."

Pompey followed Bamil's pointing finger to where a line of five large birds, brown and white with absurdly long bills, flew just above the water.

"Those birds came from land," Barca said, "ahead of us somewhere." He turned to his first mate. "Send below to the oarsmen, set the second-slowest cadence. We make for the west. The others will follow us."

He turned to Pompey Magnus and yawned hugely. "There is land in that direction," he insisted. He tottered, half-dead with fatigue. "I'll bet my life on it. I may be betting my life on it."

"Should we turn east for Hispania?"

"Not unless you want to starve," Barca replied. "How long to tack back to Europe in this mess? How long will the oarsmen last on no rations? We're out of food here, General, and I've no doubt the other ships are as well. If we want to live, we have to have food, and there is land in that direction." He pointed.

"You should be asleep," Pompey told him. "Go to your cabin before you fall down. I am sure your mate can handle the ship for a while."

"I believe I will, General."

The ships gathered in, moving into a tighter formation as they slowly rowed west. Pompey realized that they were utterly lost; whatever land lay ahead of them was liable to be their new home, for better or for worse. Six ships were missing, but Pompey saw the ship carrying the horses also present in the formation, maybe a mile behind.

"We have no idea where we are, do we?"

Pompey turned to see Cato and Cicero, both of them in the open air for the first time since the storm began. Cicero still looked a trifle green, but both men had managed to wash and change into fresh clothing.

Pompey turned away, facing west again. "No. We have no idea where we are, except that no one has come this way before us. Europe should be to the east, but how far have we come? How many days have we been lost, driven before a storm the likes of which no man ever saw? Folly, pure folly to try to re-trace our steps now, not with land close at hand."

Cato startled Pompey by laughing. "Suddenly," the Stoic said, "concerns of Julius Caesar and a second civil war seem somewhat unimportant, neh?"

Pompey once more startled himself by grinning at Cato. "My friend," he said, "You have a talent for stating the obvious. But you're right; whatever may happen in Rome, will happen now without us."

He knew a moment of exquisite pain, suddenly realizing the meaning of the morning's revelation. Never more would they see Rome. Never again to walk its streets, its markets, never again to sit in the Senate, breathe its air in the Forum…

"All this talk be damned," Cicero barked. Cato and Pompey stared at him. "For whatever it's worth, in this time and place, we are Rome. We three, the other Senators, and the legions we have with us. We may be lost, but Romans we are and Romans we will remain." He pointed west. "So, there is land out there? We will build a new Rome. A new Republic. And this time, we will protect it against men who seek a crown." He looked at the others, his eyes blazing. "Am I right?"

"You are," Pompey said softly. "We are Rome." Cato only nodded. It was a theme that would become very familiar to all of them in the months to come.

Next morning

It was Legionary Titus Caninus who sighted the thin green line of land the morning of the sixteenth day. "Land!" he roared, bringing everybody but the oarsmen onto the deck in an instant. The cry was echoed from ship to ship, carrying across the formation.

The captain of the trireme Caninus served on slapped the big man on the back. "I'd offer to award you a talent of silver for being the first to sight land, Caninus," he laughed, "but silver may be no more than excess weight to us now."

"I'd not turn it down regardless, sir," Caninus said. He put one foot on the rail and peered intently ahead. Around them, oarsmen on all ships were picking up the pace.

By late afternoon they were within sight of the beach. A narrow strip of sand bordered the water, with large trees growing down close to the shore. Just to the north, a large river emptied into the ocean. The sea was calm now, with evening growing close, and the sun cast its light from low in the west, making the land look a brilliant green. The Romans looked at the forest and saw building materials, new houses, game for eating, wood to cook with, land to be cleared for farms.

Pompey's ship was the first to touch the beach. Gnaeus Pompey Magnus, Consul of Rome, was the first to drop over the side of the ship, to wade up onto the beach of the new land. "Nova

Terra," he breathed to himself. "Nova Roma." He knelt, picked up a handful of sand and kissed it.

For the occasion he had donned full uniform, with bronze breastplate and helmet; his polished, ivory-handled gladius hung at his side. The air was still and hot, even in the evening, and the humidity was oppressive, but Pompey wasn't about to worry about that. Events of great import were underway, and he had to pay the gods their due; a certain amount of decorum was necessary.

He looked up at the skinny brown face of Bamil Barca, who looked down at him from the freighter's rail.

"Begin landing," Pompey said. "Bring our people ashore."

He looked into the trees. "It seems we are home," he said to himself. He stood and took a step forward; his sandal caught on a piece of waterlogged driftwood almost buried in the sand, and the Consul of Rome was sent sprawling.

He sat up, looked at the row of faces watching him from the ship, and laughed.

Nova Roma: De Itinere in Occasum

CHAPTER TWO

THE LANDING

From the day Pompey Magnus strode ashore he knew he and his were utterly lost to Rome and all civilized places. The very trees were different. In that country the familiar species of Europe were present, but their form was changed. Oak, cedar, pine, all were present as were other, unknown types.

The land on which Pompey first set foot was the poor land along the coast known to the natives in those parts as the low country. The natives of that land called themselves the B-Kou, which means "the People" in their language. Pompey and his party began to call them and the members of the related tribes Novans, as they were found in this new land to which they were brought by the storm.

These people proved more primitive than Gauls, Celts, Teutons or even Britons, but they had good knowledge of the land and its creatures, of which knowledge Pompey Magnus proposed to make use.

—From Gnaeus Pompey Novus' New World Diaries

On the beach

The fleet beached with only an hour or two before sundown, so Pompey Magnus assigned priority to unloading what livestock had survived. The outlook there was not good; of the horses, sixteen mares, nine stallions and six geldings survived. What chickens, goats and sheep had been brought along had long since been eaten. The only remaining livestock was a small drove of pigs, nine sows and one ugly old boar. The horses and swine were brought ashore; the horses were watered, rubbed down and tethered in a small clearing where the grass grew waist high. The starving animals set to with a will. The swine were placed in a hurriedly constructed pen under some oaks.

Pompey, Cato and Cicero stood on the shore as the sun set over the forests to the west, watching the legionaries scramble off the ships.

"Our families are offloading now," Cicero reported. "The legionaries are setting up some tents back in the trees for us."

Pompey nodded.

"It's hot," Cato complained. "Humid, too. I wonder how winters will be here."

"I suppose we'll find out," Pompey said. He slapped at his forearm suddenly and frowned at the small spot of red left on his skin. "These insects will be a problem."

A legionary appeared in front of the three nobles and saluted. "Report, young man," Pompey ordered.

"Sir," the legionary began, "We have sent patrols out in the immediate area. One of them found this, sir." He held out a small object.

Pompey turned the object over in his hands, examining it. It was clearly a knife, but not made of iron or bronze; it appeared to be made of some kind of stone, probably flint. The stone blade was broken off a thumb's length from a nicely crafted wooden handle, which explained why it had apparently been discarded.

"Stone," Pompey mused. "A stone knife. I have heard of them, but never in all my days have I actually seen one. Is there no iron, brass or tin in this land? Or are the people here so primitive that they don't know how to work metal?"

"Perhaps it is a ceremonial tool of some sort," Cato offered.

Pompey scowled at the knife. "Where was this found?"

"It was found along a small stream a league inland, sir. There were some scattered bones, as though a beast had been slaughtered there some time ago. There were some animal tracks along the bank of a small stream as well, sir—looked like goat tracks, but narrower, somewhat. Maybe a small deer of some kind."

"So, there are people here," Cicero said, looking over Pompey's shoulder at the knife, "but primitive ones. Savages."

"Tell your centurion that I want watches posted through the night," Pompey ordered. "We cannot assume these people will be friendly."

The legionary saluted again and trotted off, his iron-hobnailed sandals throwing up spurts of sand on the strip of beach.

In the woods

Two young men were watching the Romans land. They had easily evaded the Roman patrols and watched, carefully, from a thicket as the Roman leaders conferred on the shore.

Both men were smaller and slimmer than most of the Roman legionaries. They were well-muscled, though, and strong. They had skin of dark reddish bronze, sharp features, and long black hair.

One wore fringed leather vest and leggings over a breechclout of deerskin; the other, only the breechclout.

"Are they gods, do you think?" one of them whispered. "They wear strange things, and that one had a long knife that..." he paused, struggling for a clever metaphor, "...that shines like water in the sun."

"No," the taller of the two, the one wearing the vest, replied. "They are men. Did you see the old one slap the mosquito? There was blood on his arm. I do not think gods bleed. I don't think gods use canoes to travel on the water, either, no matter how big their canoes may be. No, they are just men—strange men, but men."

"We have to tell the People about this," the other replied. "We have to tell Four Bears."

They backed slowly away from the strange newcomers and stole away through the darkening woods. There was a small trail nearby, visible in the gathering dusk only to them, and down this trail the two young men broke into a run, an easy, ground-devouring lope that would see them back in their home village before the moon rose. Teal, the older, taller of the two—the smaller one's older brother—thought furiously as he ran. His younger brother, Kamundi, could only think of jokes. Teal knew that the People's councils would have to know about the strange people landing on their shores, and quickly.

On the beach

Night fell rapidly as the sun sank behind the trees. Pompey Magnus met with the surviving legates and his senior staff; one legate had gone down on a trireme shattered by the storm, but three of the legion commanders stood before him now.

"I will want patrols at first light," Pompey ordered. "The Seventeenth has the most surviving cavalry, yes?"

He looked at Lucius Germanius, the commander of the Seventeenth Legion, who nodded. "Sir, that is so," Germanius said. "We have forty men schooled in use of the horse; of course, we do not have enough horses for them."

"Yes," Pompey said. A yawn forced its way out; the day had been long, and Pompey was feeling his age. "There are six geldings; they are of least value to us. Send two men to patrol north, two south and two west. Each group will ride out for three days, then return. Their objectives are to find any local towns or cities, and to find a tract of land for us to build on. Clear?"

"Sir," Germanius acknowledged the order.

"How are we supplied for weapons and armor?"

"There we are in good order," Pompey's son Gnaeus spoke up; he had been busy as the light faded, surveying men and equipment. "Even in the storm the men did well seeing to their personal clothing and equipment. We can equip three full legions with armor, gladii, scuta and pila. Food, Father, that will be the stumbling block. I have arranged for hunting parties to go into the woods this morning, but with what remains of the legions, the surviving Senators and families, we have almost four thousand to feed."

"The legionaries will have to work as hunters, then," Pompey said. "And this land along the coast, from what I can see it isn't of much use. It is much too low, swampy, and wet. We will need farmland, and if there are people here, we will need to see what kind of crops they are growing. We brought no seed grain, no farming equipment, only what engineering tools a legion takes to war—this was not meant to be a colonizing expedition."

"We shall have to make do, then," one of the legates growled. "If there are tribes here, they can show us how to farm and work this land—or we can take their towns and supplies by force."

"Let us hope it does not come to that," Pompey answered the man. "We will have to live among these people. Tomorrow, survey your men, any with skills at hunting or trapping, give them what they need and set them to work. The same for any that know fishing; the sea is here, and there is a large river just to the north. We have to feed all these people."

Several heads nodded in assent.

Pompey looked over the legates. They were resolute, their morale seemed good enough. He had chosen them well; they were all veterans. "Time enough to worry about that tomorrow. See to your guards, then sleep, all of you. Tomorrow will be a long day."

The legates left the tent promptly. "Gnaeus," Pompey called to his son before he could duck outside, "If you'd remain a moment."

"What is it, Father?"

Pompey motioned to his son to come closer. The younger Pompey noticed one of the Senators had remained behind, a tall, rather ascetic-looking man in worn Senate robes.

"Gnaeus," Pompey the elder said, "I want you to oversee rebuilding and refitting our legions."

"As you wish," the younger Pompey said, visibly pleased.

"To that end, I want you to have a liaison on the Senate, one of the members who will work with you to gain resources and allocate men and materials as necessary."

Pompey Magnus motioned to the tall, slim man, who stepped forward. "I believe you know Senator Marcus Junius Brutus?"

Next morning

Pompey awoke slowly, at first confused by his surroundings. His bed was not rocking under him; white linen, not cedar planking, was overhead. A gentle wind rippled the cloth of the tent. The air smelled strange, of foreign plants and soil.

He sat up and stretched. Cornelia rolled over and slept on, still exhausted from the journey. It was early; Pompey could tell the sun was only just up by the length of faint shadows in the tent. It was warm already, warm and humid.

He heard shouting from outside the tent. He strode to the tent's entrance and stuck his head outside. "Legionary!" he called to a man rushing past. "What gives?"

"The swine!" the man barked. "Escaped!" He took another step, remembered himself, saluted, shouted "Sir!" and rushed off.

Pompey dressed hurriedly and went out into the heavy, humid morning. Two centurions and several legionaries were conferring near the swine pen; the centurions came to attention and saluted as Pompey approached.

"Apologies, sir," one of the legionaries said. The man was sitting on the ground, rubbing his head. "I was assigned to watch the swine. The old boar, he got out through the fence—ran right over me, sir. Knocked me out. When I woke up, they were gone."

"I will have him punished, sir," one of the centurions began, but Pompey cut the man off with a slice of his hand in the air.

"No," Pompey said. "Punishing this man will do no good. Swine are difficult enough creatures to keep at the best of times, and these are hardly the best of times. Young man," he said, addressing the young legionary who was now struggling to his feet, "rest yourself, then if you wish to make amends, track those swine and see if you can recover them."

The augurs were not promising. Without the fast-breeding pigs, feeding the people suddenly became more complex. To make matters worse, Pompey felt a headache coming on. He stomped off to find his son Gnaeus.

He found Gnaeus in a much better mood. "Father!" the young man greeted Pompey. "Good news here, at least. One of the freighters had a small cargo of seed wheat and barley, so we will have grain to plant after all, as soon as we find suitable ground. It will be a few seasons before we have grain to spare for bread, but we will have it."

"That is good news," Pompey agreed. "I take it you heard of the pigs?" Gnaeus shook his head, so Pompey explained quickly. "The good with the bad," he concluded. "So—what think you on reorganizing the legions?"

"I lay awake most of the night thinking of that," the younger Pompey said. "We took ship with two full legions, but we find ourselves now in a new land, and we will have to build a new Republic from the ground up. Most of our legionaries are recruited from the plebs, and they have other skills. We will need farmers, blacksmiths, shopkeepers, brewers, scribes, stonemasons, all manner of tradesmen. Finally, we lost all too many ships along the way."

"All too many," Pompey Magnus said. He felt the losses keenly, not least of all his daughter and younger son Sextus, left behind in Rome but at least (presumably) alive. He knew he was responsible for every man, every ship lost in the storm.

"Yes," the younger Pompey agreed, and bowed his head for a moment in respect. He looked up quickly; respect was all well and good, but there was work to do. "But with that the case, I think we need to reorganize. The old Marian model won't work here. We need smaller, lighter, more agile units, at least until we rebuild a new capitol and can start increasing our population. It's a new world, Father."

"Very well. What do you propose?"

"I propose to survey the surviving legions and release any men with valuable skills from army service to take up their old trades, and to reorganize no more than two short legions of a thousand each, organized into five cohorts of two centuries each, led by our remaining veterans and long-service soldiers. Hopefully that will be enough to withstand any people that are already living here."

"Sound thinking," Pompey the Elder agreed.

"Senator Brutus has agreed to organize the released soldiers and allocate what resources we have. The man is a moneylender and a bit of a scoundrel, but I think he will manage the task well enough. I will take charge of reorganizing the army."

"Cato and Cicero have been speaking of reconstituting the Senate," Pompey Magnus said.

"How many Senators survived?" Gnaeus wanted to know.

"Aside from myself, Cato, Cicero and Brutus? Metellus Scipio is here, with his wife Aemilia. Titus Annius Milo survived, as did Cassius Longinus, Tillius Cimber and Servilius Casca. Cassius' wife died on the journey. The others either left families in Rome or had none to bring."

"So, nine Senators in all," Gnaeus mused. He looked around. "And a few thousand soldiers, all to rebuild a new Rome."

"But bear in mind, son, that these wetlands along the coast are no place to build a town, much less a new Rome. I plan to move inland as soon as possible. Cato and Cicero agree."

"I know," Gnaeus Pompey said. "Our scouts have already left to explore the area. As you ordered, two of them rode out to the south, two to the west, and two to the north. They have orders to look for any local people, as well as better ground for us to settle on."

"Good." Pompey examined his son keenly. "There is something else, isn't there?"

"There is." Gnaeus Pompey looked distinctly uncomfortable.

Pompey Magnus scowled. "Must I wait for it?"

"Father," the younger man stepped closer and lowered his voice, "This was a military expedition. The Senators brought their families, and there were some other hangers-on, but there are no more than two dozen Roman women among a company of almost four thousand, and over half of the women are already married. It will be a problem." Gnaeus' own wife, Claudia Pulchra, had survived the journey, but only just. Now, on the beach, Pompey knew his daughter-in-law would be recovering her strength.

"It may well be, but it will be a problem for another day. We have bigger nuts to crack at the moment. There are people here; no doubt there are women among them."

"As you say," the younger man agreed, but he looked doubtful. Pompey Magnus chose not to pursue the matter further; instead, he made for his tent, to see if his own wife was yet awake.

A village to the west

The chief Nagi Hilasgiyona—Four Bears—was forty summers in age, healthy, and strong. He was tall for the People, broad-shouldered; he looked at the world through jet-black eyes under heavy black brows. As was typical for his people, he had a broad face, high cheekbones, and long, straight black hair, which he kept tied in two braids.

He made his breakfast as usual, on a few pieces of jerked

venison and a mush of ground maize, but that was the only usual thing about this morning. Unusually for a man of the People, he breakfasted alone. His wife, Pale Eyes, had died in childbirth several summers before, taking the infant with her, and now Four Bears lived in his circular wooden house by himself.

Four Bears laid his breakfast bowl aside. He stood up, stretching, and walked off down the main lane of his village. The village was larger than usual for the People, but typical in other regards; a central lane running through a circular layout of low huts made of wood and woven bark. In the center of the village was an open area where the village's people tended to gather; around the perimeter there was a shoulder-high palisade of logs. To the north, on a series of low hills, lay the mounds containing the People's ancestors.

The B'Kou –Four Bear's tribe, one group of the People—lived in a series of such villages through the low country along the coast and into the low hills rising away from the swampy lowlands. Their "cousins," the A'Tep, lived in the foothills of the mountain range to the west. The People traded oysters, fish and lowland game to the A'Tep for maize and venison. To the south lived the violent, warlike Alligator People, who were well known to the B'Kou but who were not always friendly; there had been war with them in the time of Four Bears' father, and even now relations with them were tense at best. To the north there were few people for several days' walk, until one entered the territory of the Tahona, who dwelled in deep forests and hills.

Now word came of new people, who seemingly sprang from the sea. Pale, tall people, who came from the east in giant canoes with the wings of birds, and who wore shining clothes and bore strange tools.

Four Bears found his steps taking him to the dwelling of old Owl, who was far and away the oldest member of the People. Owl had seen the passing of five wives and four of his eight children. Many of his grandchildren had white hair now and Owl alone of all the People had lived to see his grandchildren's grandchildren. He still lived alone in his round hut, maintaining his own fire and making tools to trade for meat and grain.

At the entrance to Owl's low, circular hut, Four Bears coughed once, as was the custom of the people. Hearing Owl's answering grunt—the old man's hearing was uncannily sharp—he went inside.

"I thought you would come before now," the old man greeted Four Bears.

"Then you know why I am here," Four Bears replied.

"You wish to speak of the newcomers, the people that came from the sea."

Four Bears nodded agreement.

Owl got up slowly. Nobody in the tribe, not even Owl himself, remembered how many summers the old man had seen. He was skinny, his face deeply wrinkled, and his white hair hung past the middle of his back, but his black eyes sparkled merrily from beneath shaggy white eyebrows. The People revered him for his wisdom and his unprecedented survival, and he returned their reverence with humor, well-crafted arrowheads, spear points and knives, and advice. It was that advice that Four Bears sought now.

Owl poured Four Bears a cup of water. He offered a pipe, and when Four Bears accepted, Owl gravely filled the pipe, lit it, and passed it to the chief. With this ritual of hospitality complete, the old man sat down, facing Four Bears across the low pit in which the coals of Owl's breakfast fire still smoldered.

"The People have seen many strange things," Owl began. When Four Bears nodded, he went on. "When I was a boy, the old hunters still spoke of huge hairy beasts that used long noses to strip branches from trees to eat, and of great cats with teeth like knives. My grandfather was one of the first to come to the low country here, along the sea, and he was one of the first ancestors to be placed in the burial mounds."

He paused to light a clay pipe of his own with a brand from the fire pit. After a deal of puffing to get the pipe going, he continued.

"So now something new has happened. I remember when we first met the Alligator People that live to our south, there was confusion and much fighting. Young men like our nephews Teal and Kamundi brought us the news of the people moving north into our grounds, and there was trouble. We did not speak to the Alligator People before fighting them. There is much bad feeling between our peoples even now." He paused and regarded the glowing coal in the bowl of his pipe. "We should talk to these new people before the young men among us start to fighting them."

Four Bears nodded. He had been thinking much the same thing.

"You have good sense, Four Bears," Owl said. "You should speak to the new people."

"I had thought to do so."

"One of the People should stay with them for a time," Owl said.

"One of the young people? Youths learn more quickly, and one of the People will have to learn the newcomer's language."

"Yes," Owl nodded. He looked directly at Four Bears, his eyes sparkling. "A girl, I think. The orphan girl Adsila has no family to look after her, she is bright, attentive, and very pretty—

and Kamundi tells me there are very few women among the newcomers."

Four Bears started up in surprise. "A girl? Adsila? I had thought to take Teal to..." Owl cut him off by holding up a hand.

"These people Teal and Kamundi described, they have many things the People do not. Great canoes that go on the sea, long knives of some new type, they were even seen bringing large new animals ashore. There are many of them, and they bring many strange new things. We can either make them friends or enemies."

Four Bears grunted in assent. Owl went on: "So, how to make them friends? There are few women among them. Who is closer to you than your own family? Adsila is a bright girl, pretty and strong, but she has no family here but the People. Were she to find a young man among the newcomers..."

"A bond of family," Four Bears mused. The idea had some appeal.

"And if you took Teal, or Kamundi, or some other young man along as well, he and Adsila would be drawn together, being of the People alone among strangers. Adsila should go to them herself, and you should maintain close contact with them and with her."

"You make too much sense at times, old man," Four Bears chuckled.

"I have spent too many summers dealing with people that have no sense," Owl replied. "Maybe the newcomers will prove to be good people and will become friends. Maybe we will end up fighting them. But we should start by talking to them."

"I will do that." The People had no 'good-bye,' no expression of parting; when one was finished speaking to another, he simply left. Four Bears did so and went to look for the girl Adsila.

To the north

Lucius Decimus Meridius had been First Spear Centurion of Pompey's Ninth Legion; in the hastily reorganized Nova Roman army, he would now hold that post in one of the two new legions. Today, though, he commanded only himself and one other, Legionary Marcus Claudius. Mounted on two fine geldings from what remained of the expedition's horses, the two were bound north on a scouting expedition.

Meridius had thought to save time by riding up the beach instead of through the heavy forests and swamps that infested the area, but that idea fell short after half a day when the two Roman soldiers encountered the mouth of a huge river. Now, on the second day, they were making their way slowly up the river, looking for a place to cross.

"I tell you; this new land was brought forth from Pluto's arse," Marcus Claudius said for the tenth time that morning. "I don't know which is worse, the heat, the humidity, or the insects." He slapped at his arm.

"The gods sent us here for some purpose of their own," Meridius told the legionary, again for the tenth time that morning. His patience was beginning to wear thin. "It's not our place to question them."

"Bugger the gods," Claudius said under his breath.

Meridius chose to ignore the legionary's comment. He looked around. The woods were beginning to thin out a little as they followed the river upstream. "I think we're getting out of these swamps. The air feels clearer."

"Yes, sir," the legionary responded, his tone a tad surly. "Maybe we'll be able to cross soon and head north." He removed his helmet and rubbed a hand across his stubble of black hair. "I'd be just as happy if..." His remark was cut short as an arrow flew past his head.

"Archers to right!" Meridius barked. Both Romans pulled their mounts to the right, drew their swords, and charged through a thin line of brush into a small clearing.

"There!" Claudius shouted. "You two! Halt!" He kicked his horse after the two small figures racing for the trees on the far side of a small clearing. Meridius charged after the legionary, horrified to see that the man was chasing what looked like two mere boys, whirling his gladius over his head. One of the boys made it to the shelter of the trees where the mounted Romans could not easily follow, but the second stumbled—Meridius was relieved to see that Claudius used only the flat of his sword to knock the lad down before reining to a halt and leaping from his horse.

"Brat!" The legionary seized the boy by his stained leather tunic. "I should beat you to within a fingers-breadth of your life! Loose an arrow at soldiers of Rome, would you?"

"Hold," the centurion commanded; only one word, but Roman discipline was deeply ingrained in both men. Claudius stopped his harangue.

Meridius dismounted and stepped closer, examined the wild-eyed boy where the legionary held him. He was a small, skinny lad, maybe fourteen years in age; his skin was dark, reddish in hue, his hair long and black. Even in his obvious youth, he had sharply chiseled features, high cheekbones, and a nose that might almost have been taken for Roman. He babbled in some foreign tongue.

"He doesn't understand a word you say, you know," he told the legionary who still held the boy in a grip of iron.

"True enough, I suppose." Claudius held the boy higher,

examined him closely. "Never seen the like before, sir," Claudius said. "Have you?"

"No," Meridius answered. He sheathed his gladius and looked around. "There may be more of them nearby. Let him go, Legionary Claudius. We have orders, and no time to waste."

"As you say, sir," Claudius agreed. He dropped the boy and gave him a sharp whack on the behind with the flat of his gladius to speed him on his way. "We move on, then?"

"We do," Meridius said. "Best put some distance between us and this place. Those two may bring their whole tribe back looking for us."

The landing site

Senator Marcus Junius Brutus had assumed responsibility for the treasury gold that even now was being carefully lifted down, bag and box, from one of the beached freighters. Pompey Magnus stopped to speak with Brutus for a few moments to satisfy himself that the man's security precautions were adequate; Brutus had detailed a centurion that Pompey knew to be trustworthy to take charge of the gold and had authorized the man to select twenty legionaries as guards. Satisfied, Pompey moved on down the beach to inspect the unloading.

He came across the freighter captain Bamil Barca, who was organizing the unloading of his own ship with a great deal of shouting and profanity.

"Salve, Consul," the captain greeted Pompey with an impudent grin. "The unloading, it proceeds apace, neh?"

"It does," Pompey agreed. "That river to the north—do you think we can make use of it to move inland?"

Barca scratched his chin. "Who knows? With a river, one can

never tell. It may be as wide and smooth as the Appian Way, and open to freighters for leagues inland. It may be torturous and filled with sandbars."

"How do we find out which, then?"

"Not with my ship. She is too big, draws too much water. Maybe send one of the smaller triremes up the river to see how far it can go. I hear tell there are people in this new land, eh? Maybe see what kind of boats they use, if any."

"Sound thinking."

"So, Chief, when do you think I can re-provision here? I can refill my water kegs from the streams nearby, but I'll need provisions. I would as soon be on my way."

Pompey was taken aback. "On your way? Where?"

"Home, Chief."

"Home? We have no idea where we are, Captain. How will you get back?"

Barca shrugged. "We came west to get here, more or less. We go east, we hit Europe maybe, Africa maybe. Either way I know how to get home to Ostia from there."

"You're taking a huge risk with your ship," Pompey pointed out. "Not to mention your crew."

Again, Barca shrugged. He made a point of looking up and down the beach. "Can't see any place to spend your good Roman gold here, Consul," he said.

"We will build a new Republic on these shores, Captain," Pompey told the man. "We will need men of enterprise. There will be all manner of trade up and down this coast in time, you and yours could become very rich."

"Trade, you say," Barca snapped. "In time, you say. Sorry, Chief, but there is trade in the Mediterranean now. There are active ports there now. All I see here are sand and trees. No, I'll go home, with as much of my crew as will come with me. With all you people staying here and naught but provisions to load, we can stay at sea for two, three months. We'll make it."

"You'll provision on your own, then," Pompey said. "I'll spend none of our resources on this... this fool's errand."

"As you wish, Boss," Barca agreed. "Two of my boys are in the woods hunting now. I'll keep them at it. We'll dry some meat, load up with water, stock firewood. Your cargo is almost all off, anyway."

"See that you get it all."

"No problem, Chief. You paid in gold. I won't cheat you. Bad for business."

The wiry little man returned to shouting obscenities at his crew as Pompey Magnus stomped off up the beach in a fury.

To the west

Centurion Gracchus Agrippa was wondering about his choice of companions for the ride west.

Legionary Titus Caninus was a man of undoubted courage, a veteran of many battles, and a fighter born. But he was also a talker born. Legionary Caninus kept up a non-stop stream of commentary as the men rode west, each on one of the army's priceless horses. Caninus had an observation for everything: the heat, the humidity, the insects, the trees, the small deer that abounded in the forests, the larger deer that seemed to gather in clearings, the birds, and the possibility of women in the local villages. He wasn't a complainer—no, never that—but while his commentary was good-humored, it was also endless. When he wasn't observing some new fact about their surroundings, he was recounting some anecdote from his not-inconsiderable store of army stories.

"Legionary Caninus," Agrippa said at last, when the soldier stopped for a moment to draw a breath.

"Sir?"

Agrippa reined in his horse to face the younger man. "I swear, Legionary, every local within a league must be able to hear you. Has your long service taught you nothing about passing through hostile country unnoticed?"

"Just trying to be pleasant, sir," Caninus pouted.

"Fine—try to be pleasant a little more quietly."

"Of course, sir." Caninus barked and gave his centurion a salute that was exaggerated just enough to stop short of insubordination. "Sorry. Sir," he said in a stage whisper. "More quietly. Yes sir."

"You really do bark like a dog," Gracchus said, shaking his head. He kicked his horse and moved off.

"Sir," Caninus said after a few more moments. The two soldiers had ridden into an open, marshy meadow.

"Yes?" Gracchus rolled his eyes. "What is it?"

"Look yonder, sir. A few points south of west. Smoke, sir."

Gracchus looked. Not one, but several thin threads of gray smoke wafted skywards.

"Thin," the centurion noted. "More than one. Cooking fires, I'll wager. A village—perhaps a town."

They were only lightly armed; both men had their gladii and Caninus carried an archer's short bow and a quiver of arrows for hunting, thanks to which they had dined on squirrel at their mid-day halt to rest the horses. But they had no armor, no scuta, no pila.

"Should we have a look?" Caninus prompted.

"Yes," Gracchus said at last. "Cautiously. Quietly."

They circled around to approach the village from downwind and tied their horses to saplings before drawing their swords and covering the last few yards afoot. They arrived quietly at the edge of a small clearing to see a dozen or so round huts of wood, a small field of waist-high plants of some crop plant or another, and six of the locals standing, staring directly at them.

"Sons of Dis," Gracchus swore softly.

"I was quiet, sir," Caninus whispered. "Quiet as an open grave, me. Quiet as a dead man. Quiet as..."

"Shut up," Gracchus ordered. "Or we may be dead men. Back away slowly."

Swords held ready; the soldiers backed away. The natives, two young men, two women, and two small children of indeterminate sex, watched them go without moving.

When the brush once more concealed them, they made for the horses. "Ride on," Gracchus ordered, and they kicked their horses into a canter to the west, where a series of low hills rose before them.

By late afternoon on the second, uneventful day, Gracchus and Caninus had reached the hills, and found them pleasant and cool. The country was open woodland interspersed with grassy meadows. Large-dark-bodied deer with yellow rumps were abundant in the clearings, while smaller deer with white tails bounded away from their horses in the woods and brushy places. Caninus loosed several arrows at the smaller deer with no success.

Towards evening, they rode into a large open area. "Look at those hills!" Caninus said, pointing to four medium-sized, gentle prominences covered with grass. "Lush as Venus's tits, they are. Let's go have a look, sir?"

Gracchus looked around. No people or buildings in sight. "May as well." He set off at a canter, with the legionary following.

"Now this," Gracchus said when they surmounted the tallest of the four hills, "this is a place for a town."

The four hills were laid out in a rough rectangle, encompassing perhaps three hundred hectares, perhaps more. Knee-high grass covered the hills and spread out into the river valley, forming an enormous meadow bounded on three sides by hardwood timber, on the fourth by a low valley with a good-sized river meandering through it. To the west, a range of low mountains was barely visible. From the hills, the land sloped down gently, gently, to the river perhaps a league distant.

"You have the right of it, sir," Titus Caninus congratulated the officer, "except for one thing. This is not a place for a town. This is a place for a city. It will be easily defended; good water and good farmlands are all close at hand. This is the place, sir, or I'm a Macedonian whore."

"We camp here tonight," Gracchus announced, ignoring Caninus' last remark. "Tomorrow we go back to the shore. Pompey Magnus will want our report of this place."

On the beach

Late in the afternoon of the fourth day, Pompey Magnus was lying on his cot in his tent with a thundering headache. He felt feverish and had no appetite. He was rubbing his temples with both hands when his wife Cornelia came in and spoke softly.

"Dear," she said, "your scouts have returned."

With a groan, Pompey sat up. "Very well," he said. "I'll be out in a moment."

He held his head in his hands for a moment, then collected himself and stepped out of the tent. "Report," he ordered.

Sick or not, the news cheered him.

The pair of scouts ordered north followed the great river upstream and crossed some leagues upstream. The river—the soldiers had whimsically named it the Tiber, which Pompey found curiously appropriate—wound upstream into open, hilly country. When they crossed and stuck north, they found higher country, woods and fields. They had seen several native villages but had only encountered the locals closely once. "Only a couple of boys, really," the centurion said. "No harm done."

The pair sent south had found a large, open harbor at a place where another large river and several smaller ones reached the sea. "A harbor to match the best in Europe," the centurion commanding the pair said, "or I'll be stripped and whipped, sir."

"Better than Ostia, then?"

"Vastly so, sir. Easily defended, too, unless I miss my guess. There is a great island in the mouth of the harbor just waiting to be fortified. Several smaller islands lay within the harbor itself. We saw little sign of people about, only some smoke in the distance here and there."

But the best news came from the pair sent west. "We actually ended up somewhat north of west, sir, unless I miss my guess, Centurion Gracchus Agrippa reported. "We found some low hills, with larger hills to the west. I believe, sir, we found an ideal place for a settlement. Good fields, good water, no native villages nearby." He went on for some time.

"Well done, Centurion," Pompey said when he finished. "I

think you may well have found a site for our new Rome. See to it that the legates are notified—we move west as soon as possible."

The day before, a trireme had rowed several leagues up the Tiber, which another scouting party had determined to be the same river that ran past the four hills, and found a wide place with low banks. Beyond that the way was not passable by the ships, but heavy goods could be unloaded there, within a reasonable distance of the four hills where Pompey planned to build a town. "We'll send the Senators, the civilians and the heaviest equipment up the river," Pompey decided, "and the legions can march, carrying their personal gear. Centurion Agrippa will lead us."

Pompey called to his son Gnaeus, who stood nearby, listening. "Call Cato, Cicero, Brutus, and the others," he said. "Tonight, we plan. In two days, we move."

Gnaeus Pompey saluted his father, an enormous grin on his face, and rushed off.

Pompey Magnus went back into his tent and had a seat on a camp chair. In an ordinary campaign there would be records to keep, troop's pay and rations to worry over, and battles to plan. None of that applied here, in this new world.

The Consul of Rome and senior general of the Roman armies in the new world leaned forward and cradled his aching head in his hands, allowing himself a moment of weakness in the solitude of his tent.

We will have to have food, he told himself, mentally compiling a list of all the weights that lay so heavily on his shoulders. *Food, shelter—I wonder what the winters will be like here? Arms we have in plenty, but hardly anything for farming. I wonder if we can reforge our swords into plowshares?* He barked a short, sharp laugh at the thought, in spite of his fever.

Hunting won't supply us for long. One of the scouts mentioned seeing planted fields, we'll have to find a way to trade with the tribes here for whatever grain they grow. We have some wheat and barley, but all the crops from that will have to go back to seed for several years. Horses—at least we can breed more horses, but we have no oxen to pull freight. And swine—who knows where those swine have got to by now?

There are deer and birds here, but that' s not enough to feed an army. One of the legionaries had brought in a great bird, something like the big grouse of northern Gaul and Britannia but much, much larger. Pompey was impressed but entertained no notion of being able to kill enough to feed the legions. *Maybe we can capture some, tame them, breed them?*

There's no telling how the natives will react to us, Pompey's mental dialogue went on. *When we build shelters, we should build a stout palisade wall around out town, with a walkway for archers and lookouts. We shall have to see to our defense as well as our provisioning. And Gnaeus is right about the other; as soon as the men know where the native villages are, they will be looking for women. Men will be men, there's no stopping that, but the native men won't like it. Bound to be trouble over that.*

Maybe we can find some way to convince them to form an alliance. There are bound to be factions within the tribes here, there always are. We have weapons, training, knowledge they lack. I'd bet a bushel of gold they've never seen anything like soldiers of Rome before.

Another thought occurred to him. *With almost no Roman women here, our men will have to find wives among the natives. In two or three generations, what will we be? What will our sons and grandsons be? Romans? Novans? Some mix of the two?*

Whatever else, he told himself, *we will have to make sure that Rome survives here, if not in the skin and hair of the people, then in their hearts. There is more to Rome than her people. There is more to Rome than buildings, statues, and fancy speeches in the Senate. Rome is more than a place. Rome is the soul of the people. Rome is the hope of the future.*

It is the heart of Rome that we must keep alive here, in this new world. That, above all else.

With that realization made, Pompey Magnus moved to his field desk and began to plan the move west.

That last morning on the beach, Pompey Magnus stepped out of his tent to find Bamil Barca waiting for him.

"We're all ready to go, Chief," the wiry little Spaniard said without preamble.

"Well," Pompey said. He was feeling weak and feverish, more so than the night before, but he forced a smile. "Good fortune to you, then."

"*Gratias*, Chief," the little captain said. "Listen, I should say… Well, the gods don't like me to leave on a bad note, eh? Bad luck. These folks that are staying here with you—they have a bit of luck themselves. You, Pompey Magnus, you are a good man. You'll take good care of them."

"I thank you," Pompey said, surprised.

Barca nodded. "Good luck, Chief."

He walked off then, to board his ship. An hour later Pompey Magnus watched from the beach as the freighter, the only ship to leave the new land behind, made sail and disappeared into the east.

Pompey and his company had no way of knowing it then, but that was the last anyone on either side of the Atlantic ever saw of Bamil Barca, his ship and his crew.

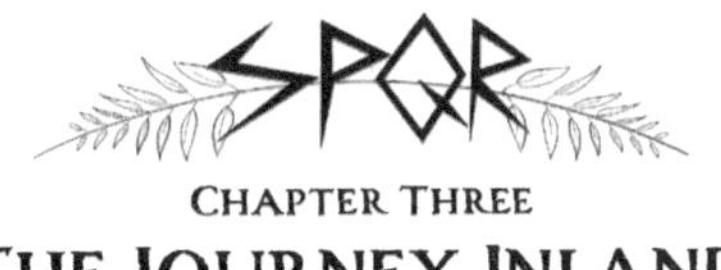

Chapter Three
The Journey Inland

The land west of the shoreline proved much more hospitable and the terrain and climate more amenable to a permanent colony. Pompey Magnus determined to move all of the Romans present inland to a site selected by a scouting party and there, to build a town, to become the new Rome in this new world.

To that end the bulk of civilians moved by river whilst the legions and youths capable to march traveled overland. The journey was one of perhaps one hundred and twenty-five miles in a straight line. The difficult terrain of that region disallows a march of a straight line by even the most disciplined of legionaries, and in that time, there were no roads anywhere in this country, so that the legions must march through swamps, marshes and forests at the route step.

This made the journey inland difficult until, at some distance from the ocean's edge, more open country was encountered, and the marching became somewhat more easy and disciplined.

> *—From Gnaeus Pompey Novus' New World Diaries*

On the beach

The new people were even stranger close up. Four Bears watched for a while from the brush, with the girl Adsila cowering behind him.

Teal and Kamundi had described them well enough, but their strange ways were still astounding. Four Bears goggled at the size of the huge boats, and watched in amazement as two men thundered past, mounted on the backs of two large animals. Many of the men bore long knives, carried red shields and marched together in rows.

It was all very strange.

Finally, Four Bears spotted an older man, clad like the others in gold and brown, with a long knife sheathed at his waist. He wore a strange hat, made of some hard wood or stone, with a crest of black feathers. That, at least, was familiar; the headdress of a chief, no doubt. As Four Bears watched, the man shouted orders at some of the others, who hurried to obey.

Yes, that was definitely the chief.

Four Bears took Adsila's hand. "Courage, girl. We go now."

He put on his hard face, to reveal no fear or uncertainty, and pulled the frightened girl behind him to meet the chief of the new people.

The chief turned to face Four Bears as he strode down the beach. Two of his men rushed forward to their chief's side; one of them started to draw his long knife, but the man stopped him with a gesture and a sharp word. *He is brave,* Four Bears thought. He looked at the man's eyes and saw courage there. That was not all he saw; he has the swamp fever, Four Bears thought sadly. Few men his age survived the fever carried by the air of the low country in summer. The People were accustomed to it, but the fever killed many visitors.

Four Bears marched up to the man and held up a hand in greeting.

Pompey Magnus regarded the native carefully. He was obviously a man of some importance among his people. He was not a young man, and his bearing and confidence spoke to his status as clearly as if it was written on his face, and who else would come down to the beach to meet them? Who else would walk up to him openly, obviously seeking some sort of parley?

The girl with him, now that was another question. She was too young to be the man's wife. His daughter, maybe? Who was she, and why had the man brought her along?

"Fetch my wife," Pompey said to one of the legionaries that had rushed to his side. "And tell the others to stay away; I don't want this man provoked. Juno knows how many more of them may be hiding in the woods."

The native of the new land, of Nova Terra—the Novan—spoke one word. He continued to hold up his right hand, palm outward, and spoke the word again. A greeting?

Pompey repeated the man's gesture, but the word was incomprehensible. No matter; Latin would do for now, assuming the man was at least as smart as the average Roman. "Salve," Pompey said in greeting.

"Sal-vey," the Novan chief repeated, pronouncing the word carefully. He thumped his chest and spat out a stream of syllables. His name, apparently.

"Nazzey? Nasi? Nasi Hisa..." Pompey attempted, but the Novan's rapid-fire speech was too much for him.

The Novan grinned suddenly. He held up four fingers, and

then did a very credible impression of a bear standing upright, waving paws and growling.

"Four Bears!" Pompey burst out. "Your name is Four Bears!"

"Nagi Hilasgiyona," the man said, nodding. "Fow-er Be-ars," he pronounced carefully.

Pompey pointed at the Novan and pronounced, carefully: "Na-gee Hi-las-gee-yon-eea."

The chief nodded. He pointed at Pompey.

Pompey thumped his leather breastplate as the Novan had done. "Pompey Magnus," he said slowly.

"Pom-pey Mag-nus," the man repeated. He motioned the girl forward and pointed to her. "Adsila."

"Adsila," Pompey repeated. He smiled at the obviously frightened girl. Slowly, tentatively, she smiled back. Introductions were repeated a moment later when Cornelia arrived on the scene.

After another exchange of gestures with Four Bears, Pompey turned to his wife. "I think he means for the girl to stay here with us," he said. "If I understand him right, he wants her to learn to speak our language."

"Juno's mercy, Gnaeus, she's just a girl." Cornelia scowled at Four Bears. "What is this savage thinking, leaving this poor thing all alone with strangers? Look at her—she's terrified!" Cornelia went to Adsila and knelt beside her. "You will stay with me. Do you understand? I will care for you," she told the girl, punctuating her remarks with gestures. Impulsively, she hugged the girl.

Adsila smiled tentatively. She put a hand on the Roman woman's robe, amazed at the fine cloth. For a painful moment Pompey was reminded of his daughter, left behind in Rome.

"Four Bears," Pompey said, "I think we have a bargain." He held out a hand.

Four Bears looked at the offered Roman hand with some confusion. His people had no concept of a handshake, but the response seemed obvious. He reached out and took the stranger's hand and was mildly startled when the chief shook his hand, up and down, twice before releasing it.

"We will take good care of her," Pompey assured the Novan chief. He illustrated that remark by placing a fatherly hand on Adsila's shoulder.

"She will be the first bridge between our peoples," Four Bears announced, knowing the new people would not—yet—understand him. He nodded to Adsila and spoke to her briefly: "Learn their words. Learn their ways. You will teach the rest of the People about the strangers from the sea. I will be back to see you before a hand's worth of days are passed." He nodded to Pompey, turned and walked off into the trees.

"Husband," Pompey heard Cornelia ask. "You are not well, are you?" She moved to Pompey's side, placed a hand on his cheek. "You're burning up."

"I do feel feverish," Pompey admitted. "It will pass."

Cornelia looked skeptical but said nothing more.

The morning passed quickly. Soldiers gathered gear and rations to march west, while a few of the few civilians, merchants and other hangers-on boarded triremes with a contingent of legionaries to man the oars. The triremes cast off to beat their way upriver.

Servius Valerius had been left alone since the landing; one of the few civilians in a party consisting mostly of soldiers and nobles,

Servius tended a cook fire and passed out stews and soups to any that wanted them, all the while bemoaning the lack of bread.

With the move west at hand, Servius started no cook fires on the last morning.

"Come on, boy," a passing legionary said. "You'll be walking west with us. Bring no more than you can carry and follow me."

"I'm already packed," Servius answered, picking up a large woven bag and slinging it over one shoulder.

The legionary grunted and stomped off towards the river. Servius followed.

"How far do we have to go?"

"Don't know," the legionary replied. "We march until General Pompey says to stop. Then we stop."

"What then?"

"Build a town, I suppose." The legionary glanced back at Servius. "You're a young lad, and not a bad cook. It shouldn't be hard for you to make yourself useful."

"Maybe I'll open an inn."

"Better to break up some land for farming," the soldier grunted. "Have to have food before you can serve it."

The legions formed for the march in a clearing near the river. The sun beat down, hot as always, and the air was heavy, humid. Most of the legionaries were wearing only belted linen tunics and sandals in the heat, but each had his gladius, scutum and pila. Gods help any native that decides to start a fight, Servius thought, surveying the columns of Roman soldiers.

"Fall in at the rear, boy," a soldier snapped. "Back there with the other civilians."

Servius headed towards the rear of the column. From the river, sounds of shouting drew attention to five of the smaller triremes, loaded with the nobles and heavy gear, already headed upriver.

From the front of the column, a leather-lunged centurion bellowed "For'ard, march!"

For the first time, the soil of the New World shook under the iron-shod tramp of a Roman army on the march.

The column headed upriver, to the northwest, towards their new Rome. Pompey Magnus walked at the head of the column, sword at his side, black-plumed general's helmet on his graying head. He was, however, beginning to wish he had taken passage on one of the triremes with his wife. His head felt about to split open; he was feverish, and a racking cough plagued his every breath.

Marching beside him, his son, Gnaeus Pompey, was visibly distressed.

"Father," the younger Pompey said for possibly the tenth time, "it is not too late for me to call one of the ships. You should not be marching—you look about to fall over."

"I'll be fine," Pompey snapped. He shook his head in annoyance and coughed again. "Just a touch of fever. Once we get away from these lowlands, it will clear."

"At least let me get you a horse."

"No. The scouts need the horses. I will not have us marching blindly into unknown country. I was marching at the head of armies before you were born, son. I will march at the head of a few more."

"As you wish, father." The younger Pompey went on looking worried but held his silence.

The column wound upstream in route step. With no road or even a path to follow, the disciplined Roman synchronized marching was impossible. The best the legionaries could do was to stay in column as the army tramped along through meadows, woods, marshes and sometimes, outright swamp.

At intervals, Pompey Magnus or his son would spy a Novan, standing like a statue in an open area some distance from where the column would pass. The natives took no action but merely stood watching gravely as the army marched by.

"Haven't seen a weapon yet other than a bow," Gnaeus Pompey commented to his father. "They look to be hunters rather than soldiers. Small comfort, but still."

"They want us to know they are watching," Pompey Magnus grunted in reply, his face sweaty and pale. "Otherwise we'd never see them. This is their land, boy, don't forget that. They know every path, every trail, every hidden way."

"So, there could be legions of them out there," Gnaeus muttered. He cast a wary look at the trees.

"If we are fortunate," his father said lightly, "they'll stay out there."

On the river

"River," Cornelia said in Latin, making a sweeping motion from the deck of the ship at the expanse of water.

"Riv-er," Adsila repeated.

"Tree," Cornelia said, pointing at a huge tree overhanging the near bank.

"Tuh-ree," the girl replied.

She had an odd accent, Cornelia had noted. Not so much an accent as a way of speaking, she reminded herself.

Cornelia went to the water barrel set on the deck, dipped in a cup, and brought it back. She put a finger in the cup. "Water."

"Water?" Adsila said, her face an eloquent study in confusion.

How can they have two words for one thing? One when in a cup, one when flowing?

"Water," Cornelia insisted. She waved her hand at the river, from past the bow of the ship to the stern. "River."

"Water?" Adsila stepped to the rail and pointed over the side. "Water?"

"Yes," Cornelia agreed.

"River," the Novan girl said, copying Cornelia's sweeping gesture.

"Yes!"

They use one word for water to drink, but another for the flowing water.

Adsila grinned suddenly in understanding.

"You are a smart little thing, aren't you?" Cornelia said. Adsila's grin faded in confusion.

"Never mind." Cornelia stamped her foot on the deck. "Ship," she said.

"Tsip," Adsila doggedly repeated.

Beneath them, oars beat the water into foam, driving the trireme upstream. Behind them, the other four triremes of the convoy followed.

Towards evening, they passed a Novan village close by the banks of the river. An excited uproar came from the natives, and two young men pushed a watercraft into the water and paddled out to inspect the newcomers. The watercraft was very simple, just a hollowed-out log with points carved in each end, but the natives handled it well. They bore no weapons and made no hostile moves but merely paddled through the formation, closely inspecting the big Roman ships. When that was done, they returned to the village.

"Well, that was interesting," the leading ship's commander

noted. "Let's get around a bend or two, out of sight of that village, and drop anchor for the night. If we stop anywhere close to there, half the legionaries will be swimming to the village looking for women."

Four Bear's village

The long, winding column of Roman soldiers marching through the swamps and marshes of the low country had not gone without notice.

Young hunters and warrior society men of the People shadowed the movement of the legions. Once the army's direction was determined, runners went to the People's cousins, the A'Tep, to inform them of the strangers headed towards their country.

While this was going on, an envoy from the B'Kou went south to talk to the other neighbors, the warlike Alligator People.

The village of Four Bears was off the line of march, but young men of that town trekked through marsh and meadow to join in the observation.

On the second morning of the stranger's journey away from the coast, a council of village chiefs and war chiefs gathered in Four Bears' village to discuss the matter. Four Bears arose early that morning, breakfasted and met in his house with two young men just returned from inspecting the stranger's landing site.

"They left men, perhaps twenty, at the site to guard what was left behind," the older of the two reported. "They are cutting trees and dragging them to an open meadow not far from the beach, and moving what they have there."

"It looks as though they intend to start a town there?" Four Bears asked him.

"It could be, but it looks more like a camp."

Four Bears nodded. "The low country is not good for people not used to it." He remembered his last meeting with the newcomer's chief Pom-Pey, and the fever that sparked from his eyes. "If they are to stay here, they will want to move as many to the hills as they can."

A boy poked his head through the deerskin hanging that served for a door. "Four Bears," he piped. "The chiefs are gathering in the house of Owl."

"Good," the chief said. He stood up and followed the boy outside.

It promised to be a lovely morning. It was too early for the heat of the day to settle in. Four Bears strode quickly down the village avenue, thinking rapidly as he went.

The question goes beyond just the villages of the People, and even beyond those of our cousins the A'Tep. If our young men are already angry, what of the Tsalee nation over the mountains to the west? They have many, many towns, many young men with more muscle than brains.

Four Bears was certain the newcomers did not know of the mountains that lay to the west. He was equally certain he did not know of the many towns of the Tsalee. The People did not often meet with the Tsalee; the way through the mountains was not easy. But on occasion, emissaries from the People would cross to the west to meet with them on matters of importance. Young men from the Tsalee would occasionally cross to the east looking for trade or, sometimes, for wives.

The Alligator People will not react well to this many newcomers, but they should not yet know of them, unless some of the strangers have already gone south into Alligator country. But what of the people to the north? There are many villages between here and the great lakes to the northwest, and that is all good country. Even old Owl does not know much of the people that live in that direction.

It was the warlike Alligator People to the south that worried Four Bears. They were a vicious, warlike people led by a cabal of war chiefs, and any pretext was enough to mobilize the young men of that tribe. Four Bears hoped they would not find out about the newcomers for some time.

He was angered when he arrived at Owl's hut to learn that an emissary had already been sent south to inform them.

"I do not think it wise to alert the Alligator People yet," Four Bears objected. "It is too soon; the Alligator People are too quick to war. Some of our young men already talk of attacking the newcomers, and we do not yet even know how well they fight."

"Two of them attacked two youths of the People in a village to the north," another chief pointed out.

"I think there is more to this than the youths of the northern villages are telling us," Four Bears scoffed. "I spoke with my wife's cousin, who lives in the village. The boys had gone hunting, and he heard one of them mention having loosed an arrow at the strangers first. Were either of the boys wounded? No! One of them came away with a sore backside, which his father made sorer still when he learned what they had done. And now we talk of attacking the strangers and their new weapons over the injured pride of a boy?"

"No one has spoken of attacking them," another chief objected.

"No one should, if the People still have any sense," old Owl said, his first comment in the gathering. All eyes turned to the old man.

"I have seen these people for myself. Their great boats with wings and many paddles, their long column of soldiers with shining weapons, it seems there are as many of them as stars in the sky. And people talk of attacking them? We already have one of the People among them, learning their words and their ways. We should be doing more of this; they obviously have knowledge of things we do not." Owl gestured angrily. "Too many fools are too quick to fight. The Alligator People, with them it is always 'fight, fight, war, war!' I say it is better to talk, talk, first, then war, war, only if there is no other choice."

"So, some young men among the People talk of attacking the strangers. Young men think with their balls. Mature men think with their hearts. Is it only the oldest man of the People that has learned to think with his head?" He slapped the crown of his head with one gnarled hand and sat down with a disgusted grunt.

White Oak of the A'Tep, the senior chief of a village in the hills not far from Four Bears' own and leader of the Red Blanket warrior society, spoke next. First, he inclined his head to Owl, a gesture of respect. "Old Owl has many years," he said. "Many years and much wisdom. No man here can deny the rightness of his words." Four Bears rolled his eyes at the man's pomposity; White Oak ignored him. "But even as we seek to speak with these new people, with their chief Pom-Pey, we should be gathering our men together. We may be wise to seek peace with them, but did they not come to our lands, in great numbers and bearing weapons? Four Bears tells us that he saw only one woman among them. Is not that another sign that they are a war party?"

"I have met Pom-Pey," Four Bears objected. "Of all of us here I am the only one who has looked into his eyes. I do not think he came here to make war. I do not know why he is here with his soldiers, but if he was here to make war, why did he not kill me when I went to talk with him? Why did he summon his woman, this Cor- Neelya, to care for the girl Adsila?" He turned to White Oak. "These are not the acts of man looking for war."

"I am not looking for war," White Oak snapped. "I am looking for prudence. I think it wise we gather our men and be prepared for whatever action these new people take. I simply do not wish the People to be taken unawares. And whatever my friend and cousin Four Bears says about the Alligator People, they are strong, they are practiced in the arts of war. We know them. We know they can fight. And we know there is bad feeling between us and them. If it were to come to a war with the new people, the Alligator people will either be fighting alongside us, or they will wait their chance and attack us when our attention is elsewhere."

Four Bears had to give the Red Blanket leader that point. "I concede," he said, "that there is wisdom in White Oak's words. We should be prepared." He put on his hard face and turned to look White Oak directly in the eyes. "But we should not attack the new people first. If there is to be war, let others start it."

On the trail

The marching column camped in a clearing near a clear stream the first night. Most of the soldiers did not bother with tents or makeshift shelters. The night was clear, the men were tired, so they wrapped up in cloaks and slept wherever there was space on the ground.

Gnaeus Pompey had seen that a small tent was brought along for his father. He saw to raising it himself, and even arranged bedding for the senior Pompey with his own hands.

Pompey Magnus spent the evening in council with the two

new legion commanders and retired late, dizzy with fever and exhausted.

The next morning, he was unable to stand.

Gnaeus Pompey had four legionaries build a makeshift litter from two saplings and a spare cloak. The four legionaries carried Pompey Magnus through the morning. At mid-day, a centurion approached them. "You men return to your cohorts. Four others will take the General's litter this afternoon."

The four refused. "It is our honor to carry the General," one of them said. "We are assigned by Pompey the Younger himself. If he asks, we will step aside. If not, we will not."

The centurion nodded gravely and left.

Pompey Magnus alternately moaned and raved throughout the day. That evening the column reached the clear space on the river where the triremes were unloading materials and crews; the ships would be moored there for the time being. Cornelia Metalla, on learning of her husband's illness, raced to his side, dragging the Novan girl Adsila along.

Pompey was abed in his small tent, lucid but weak when his wife arrived.

"I knew you were ill," Cornelia scolded him, but gently. "You should have come with us on the ship."

"It doesn't matter," Pompey groaned. "Have to walk from here anyway." He looked past his wife to where Adsila stood quietly. "And how is our guest?"

Cornelia motioned the girl forward. "Salve," the girl said softly. "Salve, Pom-Pey Magnus."

"Salve, Adsila," Pompey said gravely. "And how are you getting along?"

Adsila's small face registered a moment of hard thought. "Ver-y well. Thank you."

"She is bright, isn't she?" Pompey said to his wife.

"Bright, and very sweet," Cornelia said. "The legionaries on the ship, you would think they were all her uncles, and she their favorite niece." She smiled at Adsila. "She has no family, you know. That is why that chief, Four Bears, brought her to us."

"No family, eh?" Pompey said. "Well, no longer. Come here, girl," he motioned to Adsila. "It's all right. Come here."

Shyly, Adsila approached Pompey. She laid a small, cool hand on the old soldier's brow, her face screwed up in a study of concern.

"Yes, yes, don't worry about that," Pompey said. He took the girl's small hand in his own knotted, callused one. "Cornelia, ask Gnaeus to step in, please?"

When all that remained of Pompey Magnus' family was present, he intoned gravely, "Adsila, girl of Nova Terra, I, Pompey Magnus, in the eyes of Jupiter, Mars and Juno, adopt you as my own daughter. Your name henceforth will be Adsila Pompeia Atella." He smiled at the girl, knowing she did not yet understand. "With all that lovely black hair, I'm at a loss to think of a better cognomen."

Gnaeus Pompey stood for a moment, thinking of his younger sister and brother, Pompeia Magna and Sextus Pompeius, left behind in Rome. He was surprised at his father's sudden adoption of the Novan girl—but then, he thought, in a new land, we must adjust to new things, learn new ways.

He smiled at the girl. "Little sister," he said, trying the phrase on as he would a new cloak.

He found he rather liked it.

"She will be the first," Pompey Magnus said.

"The first?" Cornelia asked. She was hugging the startled girl, her eyes bright with tears—tears of happiness, mixed with tears of grief for the children left behind in Rome, children not hers by birth, but loved as her own.

"The first new citizen of Rome here in this new world," Pompey said. He lapsed into a fit of coughing.

"She won't be the last," the younger Pompey asserted.

Nearby, Cato and Cicero were in an impromptu council with Marcus Junius Brutus.

"Oh, yes," Brutus was saying, "all the Treasury gold is secure. It's still on the ship I came upriver on, and under guard. Once we have a place to store it, we can certainly detail soldiers to move it. But that doesn't answer my point."

"I understand your point," Cato said, not without some exasperation. "I simply don't agree with you. The gold may be of little use now. In fact, I will go you one better, Brutus, it's of no use to us now. It won't build us houses or grow us food. The local tribes probably wouldn't even know what it is, so it's of no use in trade, at least not yet."

"But it will be of use in the future," Cicero snapped. "What, Brutus, do you think we will live in the woods and fields forever?"

Brutus looked around and lowered his voice. "We may be closer to that than you think. Look you at that tent, where Pompey Magnus lays sick. It is as he said: Pompey stamped his foot on the soil of Italy and raised an army, and that army followed him right off the ends of the earth."

"It's not so much that they followed him," Cato pointed out, "it's more that the wind carried them off, as it did all of us."

"Even so," Brutus insisted. "What if he dies? These legions

follow him. They are here because Pompey Magnus commands them. Not the Senate, not Cato, for all your incorruptible reputation, Cato, they do not follow you, or Cicero, or myself, or anyone else here left from the Senate. They follow Pompey, and if he dies, what is to stop them from scattering to the four winds in search of whatever native cunni presents itself? All the riches of Rome, Egypt and Gaul are of no use to them here! Not when compared to a stewpot filled with venison and a native woman to warm their beds."

Cicero started to protest, but Cato held up a hand. "He has a point, my friend. What if—gods forbid—something happens to Pompey? His son is here, and he has commanded troops. And don't think for a moment that the men don't know that the tribes here may possibly be hostile."

Brutus looked doubtful. "I still say it all depends on Pompey. Let the man live as a tyrant if we must, as long as he lives—I tell you, at all cost, Pompey must live."

"Still, we must plan for the chance that he does not," Cato mused. "The legions follow Pompey, you say, and you are right, no one doubts that. But if something were to happen to Pompey the Elder..."

"...Might they follow Pompey the Younger?" Cicero asked.

"They may indeed. He has the name. He is young, but he has led men in battle before. The legions know this."

"Then we must hope that is sufficient," Brutus said, "to hold the men together. Without the soldiers, we have no chance of building a new Rome here."

Cato stared at Brutus, wishing fervently he could disagree.

Next day

The next day dawned bright and warm. Pompey Magnus, weak, drawn, and semi-conscious, was once more ensconced on his litter, carried once more by the same four legionaries. The soldiers carried the general's litter proudly, heads held high, marching in grim, tight-lipped silence. Pompey's family trailed behind, followed closely by the remaining members of the Senate.

To Cornelia, the procession felt uncomfortably funereal.

The going was faster as the swampy low country gave way gradually to open woods and grassland. The Romans arrived at the four hills late that afternoon, just as the sun was lowering towards the low mountains in the west. The legionaries carried Pompey Magnus to the top of the tallest hill and gently lay his litter down. They saluted and walked gravely off. Pompey's family and the remaining Senators gathered around.

Pompey Magnus extended a shaking hand and felt the tall grass blowing in the breeze next to his litter. "Good land," he managed to say. "Good land." He turned his head and saw the fields of grass, the woods, and the river flowing to the north. He saw yellow flowers in the fields, and birds flying overhead. "Cato?"

"Here, Consul," Cato said softly.

"Build our new Rome here. Here, on these four hills."

"We will."

Pompey Magnus closed his eyes and smiled. "Four hills, not seven. But it will do. It will do."

The Consul of Rome died that night in his tent, surrounded by his family, including the adopted Novan girl, who shed tears of grief as real as any of the others; the old man had shown her more kindness in their brief time together than anyone in the village she had grown up in. The next morning the legions built a massive pyre and burned Pompey's body in the Roman tradition, on top of the tallest of the four hills. As the flames from the pyre roared into the sky, Marcus Tullius Cicero said, "Of his ashes, the new Rome will be built."

"Not Rome," Cato said suddenly. The others stared at him. "Not Rome, I tell you," he said again. "Pompeius. We will call the city Pompeius."

Nobody objected. "Pompeius it is, then," said Cicero.

CHAPTER FOUR
THE NEW LAND

Less than a month transpired from the landing until Pompey's party reached the four grassy hills upon which the Rome in the new world would be built.

To the lasting and intense sadness of all members of the expedition, Pompey Magnus, Consul of Rome and general of the Roman armies, died of an unknown illness in the first night spent on the four hills upon which the town was later built. Senator Marcus Porcius Cato proposed the new capital be named Pompeius in his honor and without dissent, it was made so.

Building began immediately with timbers and tools scavenged from the ships that brought Pompey's party thither and with timber and stone gathered from the rich lands surrounding the town of Pompeius a-borning. The local Novans provided initial assistance in the form of corn and other vegetables for planting, however the good relations with the neighboring tribes did not last. Among the Novans were warlike factions that were determined to make trouble. Those people were soon to make their presence felt.

>—*From Gnaeus Pompey Novus' New World Diaries*

Pompeius

Early on the morning following Pompey Magnus' funeral, Cato and the other Senators gathered the entire Roman community together on the site of the funeral pyre. Cato stood on a wooden crate one of the legionaries had lugged over. He smiled as he looked at the gathered legionaries, Senators, the few family members.

They didn't have time to mourn Pompey, but they did have time to honor him by starting to build his city. Cato spread his hands theatrically and gestured at the open grasslands surrounding them. "Now, the work begins."

Tents covered the three smaller hills of what was to become the city of Pompeius. The largest hill was reserved for the first buildings of the new city: the Senate, an open expanse for the Forum, and houses for the surviving Senators. The city would eventually expand to cover all four hills, everyone felt certain, but for now, the tallest would be their home, not only for the view, but for at least one other reason; "It's the most easily defended," Gnaeus Pompey pointed out.

Senator Marcus Junius Brutus had assumed responsibility for overseeing the construction, and the others gladly let him take that task on. His plans were based on Rome, but were not Rome; the new city will be built in a series of circles around the four hills, and on the plan, in the spaces where the four series of circles met…

"Parks?" Cato had asked when first viewing the plans.

"Parks," Brutus answered. "Green places, with trees, brushes, grass, walking paths. Pompeius will be our capital, neh? Let us not just make it a place for commerce. Let us make it beautiful. Let us make it a place where people will choose to come to live. We have it in us to build a shining city on these hills, to make the natives see how Roman ways are better than their own."

And so, the work began.

The first day began simply; legionaries cut stakes from trees along the river bottoms, and under the direction of two men identified as having some skill in architecture, laid out the foundations of buildings and where the first rings of city streets would lie. One man with training as a stonemason rode out to the nearby hills with an escort of two cavalrymen to find a source of stone for foundations and, more importantly, to build a furnace so that the four trained smiths—a stroke of luck there—could start reforging some of the town's precious stock of steel into construction tools and farming equipment.

Several parties were dispatched downstream on one of the triremes to oversee breaking up most of the beached ships from the journey across the Atlantic. Some of the timbers in those ships would be waterlogged and damaged, but most was valuable, as were the iron bolts and spikes used to hold the ships together. Canvas sails would make additional tents. Even oars would be useful. The ships also carried tools and supplies for their own maintenance, and every tool, every bit of iron was now precious.

The few ships that would remain intact were ordered south with skeleton crews, to investigate the large harbor that the scouts had reported.

By the evening of the first day, Cato stood in the gently waving grass on the top of the tallest of the four hills and looked at the stakes defining what would become the new Senate.

Everything we do here, he mused, everything we do in the

building that will rise on this spot, will define this new land. We cannot afford to repeat the mistakes of the old Rome.

We must keep the best of the old, and only the best. But there were problems in old Rome.

He looked around. All around him, men were moving down the hill to their tents, their makeshift shelters. He could hear the men laughing as they walked; the usual banter of soldiers, but, to his amazement, Cato heard none of the good-natured complaining usual for the army.

No, the men seemed almost... lighthearted.

What weight has been lifted from them, Cato wondered, that makes them so cheerful?

He knew a moment of self-examination. In spite of a grumbling belly, in spite of legs still sore from the walk inland, in spite of a back that ached from sleeping on the ground in a rude tent, he felt...different. What weight has been lifted from me?

Footsteps behind him: he turned. "Cicero," he said.

"Cato." Cicero was clad in a robe nearly as plain as Cato's, a little worse for wear, but the man was smiling. "We're off to a good start, it seems."

"You feel it too," Cato said.

"Eh? Feel what?"

Cato extended his hands, turned slowly in a full circle. "All of it. What is it about this place? The land, the sky, the trees, the water, all of it seems... new, as though it is as things were when the earth was freshly made. My friend, dear Cicero, what place have the gods brought us to? We set sail for Hispania and a storm blows us away from Rome, away from Caesar, away from Europe, to this place no man ever imagined. We find ourselves here in an empty land, peopled with savages. How is it that we feel so..." He searched for a word.

"Free," Cicero commented. "Freedom is, after all, a man's natural state. It is his natural power of doing as he pleases, until restrained by power or law."

"Free," Cato agreed. "In Rome, every man knew his place. A thousand years of traditions, of roles, of rules, every man knew where he belonged—and knew he would never move beyond what his father was, or what his grandfather was. What if... what if the gods brought us here to change all that?"

"Change it? How?" In all the memory of civilized people, things had always been as Cato described.

"The cord of our history has been broken, Cicero. This is a new land. A free land. Why not make it a land where each man is judged for his own self? Where each man is free, not to do what his father did before him, but what he chooses? Where each man is free to advance by virtue of his own work, his own skill?"

"Cato," Cicero laughed, "you're talking complete and utter chaos!"

"I do not advocate an anarchy," Cato said. "The Senate will be needed more than ever. There will still be trade agreements to be negotiated with the tribes. There will be disputes to resolve, and in time I do not doubt there will be war. We will still need to have laws, rules, order. But we can do both, Cicero. We can make this a land for free men, and a land of order. Remember when Sulla flouted the law to make himself Consul, again and again? Let us make a nation of laws, Cicero, a country where no man is above the law—where there will be no flouting of the law by nobles, no dictators, no Sullas, no Caesar. As you just now pointed out, man's natural state is freedom to do as he pleases, until restrained by power or law. I maintain that it should be the latter, not the former, and that we should take steps to ensure it stays that way. Laws, not men."

"Next, I suppose you'll want to make a record of all these laws."

"It would be the rational thing to do," Cato agreed. "And, friend Cicero—I can think of no one better suited to the task than you. Old Rome had a constitution, after all, ignored as often as not. Let us make ours more robust."

Cicero stared at the younger man; his eyes wide.

Then he laughed.

"You make more sense with every word," he said. "So, the cords of the old order are to be cut, even as our connection with the old world was cut by the storm. Very well, then—so be it."

Four Bears' village

"I tell you, Four Bears, it is a thing to see. They are cutting trees as we cut reeds to weave for baskets. They use their great beasts to drag sledges of stone to the top of a hill, in the open, not in the forest. Out where anyone can see! They pile up low walls of the stone and build their houses of wood on top of them. In the center of their town they are building a large lodge, all of stone. What for, I do not know."

Four Bears looked at his 'cousin,' Lost Fox of the A'Tep. Like Four Bears, Lost Fox was a village chief. His village lay in the low hills in the west, above the lower forest country favored by the B'Kou. The two tribes were more than allies, but less than one people; trade and intermarriage were common, but each people retained a distinct identity.

"And their new town is between us?"

Lost Fox took a drink of water from a clay cup. He had arrived that morning, after a brisk jog from his village; he was ten years younger than Four Bears, a tall, slim man built for running. "Yes, almost exactly between our two peoples. Do you know the four great hills along the upper reaches of the river to the north of here?"

Four Bears nodded. "Great beauty in that area. Good hunting and fishing."

"Well, that's where they are. Right in between your people and mine."

"How many of them?"

"More than ten of our villages," Lost Fox said. "And their great beasts that labor for them."

Four Bears remained silent, thinking.

"There's more," Lost Fox offered.

Four Bears raised an eyebrow in query.

"They are building a palisade around their town," Lost Fox said.

"Nothing of note there. Most of our own villages have a palisade," Four Bears pointed out.

"Not like this. Our town palisades are as high as my waist, maybe as high as my neck. Their palisade is made of the trunks of mature trees, on end, and is at least two men high. The tops of the trunks are sharpened." He motioned a point with his hands.

"Preparing for war?"

"I can see no other reason."

"We know nothing of the country they came from," Four Bears mused. "Perhaps such things are normal there."

"Then they come from a place where war is common," Lost Fox said, not knowing how accurate his statement actually was. "The war chief White Oak has a good point, cousin—they are almost all men, like a war party. Almost no women are among them."

Which reminded Four Bears: "Has the girl Adsila been seen?"

Lost Fox nodded. "A girl of the People was seen with them. Always in the company of one of the few women among them. A tall woman."

"Cor-Neelya," Four Bears remembered. The daughter or wife of the chief Pom-Pey; Four Bears wasn't sure which.

"Can you take me there?" he asked Lost Fox.

"Certainly," Lost Fox said, eyes wide. "You would speak with them?"

"I have already spoken with Pom-Pey Mag-nus," Four Bears told him. "I looked in his eyes. I do not think he intends to make war. He took Adsila into his own lodgings. What sort of man would do that, if he intended to make war on her people?"

"Very little these people do makes any sense," Lost Fox said.

Pompeius

A shout rose as two Novan men walked out of the trees and approached the infant town. "Natives coming in!"

Following the death of Pompey Magnus, Gnaeus Pompey had emerged as the default leader of the re-organized First and Second Nova Roman Legions. The remaining Senators met quietly and approved the change; so far, the young man seemed to be up to the task. The young General Pompey, now wearing his father's black-plumed general's helmet, hurried now to the outskirts of the town a-building, to see two Novans walking through the outlying structures towards him.

Gnaeus waved a legionary over. "I recognize that one," he said. "He's Four Bears, the one that brought the girl Adsila in. Fetch her, my stepmother, and whatever we have by way of refreshments. Water, I suppose. Quickly!" The legionary pounded off.

Four Bears and the other Novan approached Gnaeus, who strode forward to greet them. "Salve," he said, extending his hand.

"This is a greeting among them," Four Bears explained to Lost Fox. He took Gnaeus Pompey's hand and shook it, repeating "Salvey." Lost Fox did likewise.

There were a few moments of awkward silence until Cornelia showed up, with Adsila in tow. The Novan girl was passably fluent in Latin now and was able to serve as an interpreter.

After another round of introductions, Four Bears inquired through Adsila as to the whereabouts of Pompey Magnus and was saddened to hear of his death. "He was an honest man, and I think a good man," he told Lost Fox. "This Nay-us is his son. Hopefully things will still go well." He was cheered to hear of Pompey's adoption of Adsila, however, and pronounced her new name carefully, committing it to memory: "Adsila Pompeia Atella."

"Ask him about the wall around their town," Lost Fox pressed Four Bears. "Ask him if they prepare for war."

Four Bears put the question through Adsila.

"We want nothing but to live in peace with all the people here," Gnaeus Pompey answered through the girl.

"Your men all bear weapons. There are almost no women among you. You build a wall around your town. This speaks to us of preparing for war," Lost Fox said, gesturing at the partially completed palisade as he spoke.

"We were at war," Gnaeus replied after Adsila softly translated, "when we came here. The people we were at war with have not and cannot follow us here. That war is over."

"More people like you?" Four Bears asked.

"Romans, yes," Gnaeus admitted. That caused Four Bears and Lost Fox some confusion until Adsila explained that Roman was the newcomers' name for themselves as a people.

"And they cannot follow you; not to make war here, among us?"

"We do not yet fully know how we came to be here," Gnaeus admitted. It took some time, with Adsila softly translating, but he described what he could of the conflict in Rome, the armies in Gaul heading south across the Rubicon, fleeing Julius Caesar, the fleet of ships bound for Hispania, and the great storm that brought them to this new land.

"There are more of them across the sea," Lost Fox breathed. "If they could come here, why could more of them not come as well?"

"I don't know," Four Bears replied, softly, to Lost Fox alone. "It is hard to understand all this. Lands across the sea, great cities, all of it, it seems impossible."

"And yet, here they are, these Romans," Lost Fox said.

"We have to talk to our councils about this," Four Bears said. He turned to Gnaeus Pompey. "Some of our young men are angry," he said, "about your new town. They are angry that you build your new town here, without speaking to anyone that lives in these lands. They are angry that you took this place for yourselves."

"Let them be angry, then," Gnaeus snapped. "We will have to live among you somewhere, and there is no village near here. We take no one's land. This land," he stamped his foot, "was empty."

"Your men scour the forests for game. They have taken many deer, many turkeys"—Adsila did not know how to translate that, there was no Roman word for the great birds— "and many fish from the rivers."

"We have to eat," Gnaeus said, "just as you do."

Four Bears held up a placating hand. "Yes, all men must eat," he said. "The People may be able to help. You have only a small piece of ground for crops. Do you not grow maize to eat?"

Adsila translated "maize" as "plants," which was confusing for a few moments until Four Bears gestured towards the plot of broken ground where the small stocks of wheat and barley were planted. "Ah—yes," Gnaeus said. "Grain. But our supplies are very small." He knew, of course, that the natives had food crops; scouts had seen them.

"Perhaps we can trade food for some of your tools," Four Bears said, "or something else of value."

"Perhaps," Gnaeus allowed. To himself, he thought, *if you want to trade for weapons, you will be disappointed.*

"That would be a good thing," Lost Fox agreed.

"In ten-days' time," Four Bears said, emphasizing by holding up two hands, "We will return, and bring you some of our food crops, so that you may see for yourselves what we grow here. Then we can discuss trade."

Gnaeus nodded agreement. "A sound idea," he said. "Ten days it is, then."

Four Bears and Lost Fox turned to go. As they were walking down the hill, two Roman scouts thundered past on two of the legion's small stock of horses. The Novans stood, open-mouthed, until the Roman cavalrymen disappeared into the woods near the river.

"That," Four Bears said in amazement, "is something I would like to try."

In Pompeius, later that afternoon, the Senate met in the unfinished Senate building in the middle of the town. So far only the stones of the foundation had been laid, but the Senate's business wouldn't wait.

Gnaeus Pompey was there, although his status as Senator was uncertain; his father had held that rank, but Gnaeus had not. Still, he was now general of the Roman army in the new world, so his presence was essential.

Marcus Tullius Cicero was present, as was Marcus Portius Cato, Marcus Junius Brutus, and the other five surviving Senators.

"A small basis on which to start to govern," Cicero commented. "Three hundred Senators there were in Rome. And now, just this small band of us, to build a new Rome?" He shook his head.

"Unfortunately, we must govern with what we have, not with what we would wish for," Cato said.

The Senate's first order of business was organization. It came as a surprise to no one present when Cato and Cicero were elected Consuls by acclamation, following which Gnaeus Pompey was appointed Senator and also elected as Tribune of Plebs, a post which would no doubt cement his authority over the army, as well as securing their loyalty.

"We will eventually have to enlarge the Senate, of course," Cato told the assembly, "as our population grows."

"Bloody little chance of that, with no women about," Gnaeus Pompey said in a harsh stage whisper, eliciting chuckles from the small group.

"A problem," Cicero smiled at the tribune, "that will no doubt sort itself out, as we begin to trade with the natives."

"What will we be, then?" Brutus asked, his expression sour.

"Will we be absorbed by these people? Will our sons and daughters cease to be Roman?"

Cicero stood up. "If I may speak?" he asked formally.

Cato nodded. "if there is no objection, our brother Cicero has the floor," he said.

The Senate fell quiet. Cicero's reputation as an orator was well known and well-deserved.

Marcus Tullius Cicero walked to the center of what was to become of the Senate chamber. He stood there, neither a large man nor an imposing one; he was neither tall nor broad, his face was plain, square-boned and unremarkable. Cicero stood as though he was addressing a Senate of three hundred as in old Rome, not the small, ragged band of refugees the Optimates had become. Somehow, it didn't matter. When he took a pose to speak, all of that didn't matter; the Nova Roman Senators knew they were watching a master perform.

"O conscript fathers! Brothers of the Senate," he began. "It is a long and strange journey that has brought us from our beloved Rome to this new land. Those of us who have been abroad once fancied a trip to Greece, Macedonia, Africa or Spain to be a long journey. How ridiculous those walks abroad seem to us now, who have crossed an unknown expanse of ocean, driven by a storm sent by the very Gods themselves! And yet, here we are. The fact of the journey cannot be denied, nor can it be denied that there will be no return to Rome."

"We have left the city of Rome forever behind, but we are Romans. And I ask you, brothers of the Senate, what is it to be Roman?"

"Does it mean merely to have a certain shape of nose, as does our good friend Brutus?" The Senate laughed as Cicero pointed; even sour Brutus chipped off a sheepish grin.

"Or does it mean to wear a certain kind of robe, or to cut your hair in a certain manner, or to shave your face in a certain way? No, I say; there is much more to Rome, to the Roman people, than that, and that fact was never so apparent as it is here in this place."

"In the past, people from conquered provinces have gone on to become Roman citizens. Were their children not as Roman as any of us here?"

Several members looked doubtful.

"In a new land, we must learn new ways," Cicero insisted, unconsciously echoing Gnaeus Pompey's thoughts of a few days earlier. "We are few, and the natives here are many. But we are Rome, even without the city; we Senators gathered here, in this new, unfinished building in a strange land, *we are Rome.*"

"We will build this town, which I foresee will grow into a city, Pompeius it is and shall be as our capital, but as a people we will always be Romans. Look at the people, the lands about you, populated by people more primitive than any Gauls, Teutons or Vandals we or our ancestors have ever encountered. More primitive even than the Britons! And we come among them now, for whatever reasons the Gods sent us across the ocean to land here among them, we are among them, as Romans. Here, in this new land, we are Rome."

"My brothers, one of the natives of this new world already lives here, in our new Roman city, among us. The girl Adsila was adopted in accordance with Roman law by Pompey Magnus before his death and lives here now as Adsila Pompeia Atella. She will very likely marry a Roman, and her children, no matter what color their hair, no matter what color their faces, they will be Romans, because here in this place, we are Rome."

"In time, our town Pompeius will become a city." He held up a hand before his face. "I see it as plainly as I see my hand before me. Pompeius will be a city, even as Rome is a city. There will be towns, and they will be Roman towns. There will be a port in the harbor we know lies to the south of where we landed, and it will be a Roman port. There will be farms in the countryside, and villages where drovers and tradesmen will live and work, and there will be roads between them, even as there are in the old world, and they will be Roman roads here as there, because we here, in this town a-borning, we are Rome."

"As we grow, as our roads move ever farther into this new land, people will move on them safely, without worry, because they know they will be under the protection of Roman arms. In time the natives will join our army, will learn Roman discipline and Roman ways. They will do so because they see we are strong, but in so doing they will see how Rome offers not only strength but cleanliness, and order, and safety. Rome, my brothers, offers civilization. Even in Europe, Rome was our shining city on a hill; all that was decent, all that was civilized, all that was orderly in our modern world springs from Rome. All roads in Europe lead to Rome, and one day the roads in this new land will all lead here, to our Capitol on Pompeius. In time our roads will cross this land, perhaps even to another great ocean and even beyond that, and no matter what tribes we meet, we will show them Roman ways and Roman arts, and from sea to sea this will be our people's land, because here in this place beyond the sea, this place no one imagined possible, we are Rome."

"What will our children be, you ask, Brutus? Our children's

children? What can they be, other than Roman? Who is to decide, O brothers, but us? It is what we do here now, in this new Senate, in this new town, in this new land, that will define what we will be, what future generations here will be. It is a heavy task, a heavy responsibility, but by the very blood in our veins, we will do it—we can do it—and why? Because we are Rome."

"And what is Rome? A city? It is that, to be sure. But there is more to it than that. The city is the bones of Rome, but the people are her blood. Rome is her people. Not only those of us here, in the Senate. Rome is all of her people. The solders that fight for her. The bakers that make bread for her table, the butchers that cut meat, the carpenters and masons that make her buildings, the magistrates that keep order in the streets, the innkeepers that serve wine and food, the merchants that shout the virtues of their wares in the Forum. Rome is all that and more. And, my friends, we have all of that here with us. Rome herself has come here with us, here to this new world, because we are Rome."

Cicero sat down, as his colleagues' applause threatened to shake loose the very stones of the new Senate.

"Well said," Cato congratulated him. "Well said. I could not agree more." He turned to the Senator that had originally put forth the question. "And you, Brutus?"

"I could not disagree with my colleague Cicero after so heartfelt a speech as that," Brutus said. "Indeed, he hit to the very heart of it."

"Well, then," Cato said, "Let us get to it, then."

Near the river

Titus Caninus was off duty and looking for something to do.

Having spent the night before standing guard, and with no

brothels or inns in the new town to occupy him, he decided to pass the afternoon with a walk along the river. It was the first free time to himself he had managed since the landing.

"Not that there's much to do in any case," he muttered as he stumped along through the grass along the river everyone was already calling the Tiber. "May as well help the others run up the barracks."

At least the air here, up country, was clearer, and the insects fewer and less annoying. The late summer foliage was dark green, the grass beginning to pale. Caninus saw a rabbit bounding away, flashing its white tail, and wished he'd brought a bow.

"What's that?" Ahead, on the riverbank, just beyond some tall plants that bore large, brown heads of some sort, Caninus saw a long pole cut for fishing. The pole flashed back, then forward, casting some sort of bait into the water. "Who's up there?"

A head popped up. "Servius Valerius."

"Ah." Relieved—he had brought no weapons aside from a small knife—Titus headed to the stretch of bank where the boy was fishing. "Any luck, then?"

"Some." The boy had three large fish on the bank.

Caninus had a look; the fish were not like any he had seen before, but would no doubt be good to eat; they were heavy bodied, green with a large dark stripe the length of their bodies, and a large mouth. "The kitchens will be pleased with you today."

"I suppose so. Not much else for me to do here." Servius looked at Titus, eyes calculating. "You're Titus Caninus, yes? The soldier that first spotted land while we were lost at sea?"

"That's me," Caninus agreed.

"I thought so." Servius patted the grass. "Sit down, if you like."

The legionary did. Might as well watch the boy fish for a while.

The sun was warm, and the day was still. Caninus was toying with the idea of laying down in the grass for a nap when the boy spoke up again.

"How long do you think it would take to build an inn?"

"What, by yourself?" Caninus laughed. "Forget it. Wait until you're a little bigger." He remembered the boy now; he had eaten some of the lad's stews and soups while the legions were still on the beach, preparing to march west. "You're a good cook, I'll give you that, but building yourself an inn, that's taking ambition to a fault, that is." He counted off points on his fingers: "It's not just building an inn. First, yes, you have to build it." Second finger. "Then you have to stock it—not just food, but drink." Third finger. "You have to be able to manage rowdies and troublemakers, because you'll have them." Fourth finger: "And here, now, who is even going to buy food from you? And with what? All are eating in the communal kitchens now."

"I'm stronger than I look," Servius said. "And believe it or not, I've run an inn before. The communal kitchens—that won't last. the Senate will want to establish commerce again, soon enough."

"You? A boy like you, ran an inn? Go on. Where?"

"In the Aventine, back in Rome."

"I lived just near there," Caninus objected. "I've been in every eatery, inn and whorehouse on the Aventine hill. I don't remember any bare-faced boy running any inn."

Servius shrugged. "Well, I did."

"What was it called, then?"

"Do you remember the Black Horse? Near the river?"

"Well," Caninus said, "But I remember the owner being a woman. Can't say as I ever saw her, but I've been in the place."

"Do you remember her name?"

Titus Caninus frowned, his face registering a caricature of Deep Thought. "Merula? S. Merula, something like that."

"Close. Servia Valeris Merula."

"Some relation of yours, then? Mother? Sister?"

"No." Servius grinned. "Come on, Legionary Caninus, you can't be that thick."

"You?"

"Me," Servius—Servia—agreed.

"Jupiter's balls!" Caninus burst out. "And here you let everyone take you for a boy?"

"Would hardly do to let them know the truth, when I was trying to get on board the ships, neh?" Servia laughed. "I convinced one of the freighter captains that I knew how to cook, and so he let me sign on to handle the galley."

"Why did you leave Rome? With your own inn there and all."

"My father used to talk about the war between Sulla and Marius, the state the city was in—murdering, raping, looting. The Aventine is rough enough as it is. I didn't want to stick around for another civil war. I heard about the Pompeian faction fleeing to Hispania, and figured, well, why not?" She raised her hands. "I bloody walked to Ostia and got myself on that ship. And so, here I am. It's not Hispania, but I'll make the best of it."

"Here you are," Caninus said happily—one more Roman woman in the new land raised the odds from impossible to nearly improbable, and it seemed he had his nose in the tent flap already. "An inn, eh? Well, I suppose even a small town could use an inn." He looked at Servia keenly. "Could be that I might have some time to help you build one."

"That thought," Servia smiled, "had occurred to me."

Ten days later

Cato stood alongside Gnaeus Pompey and watched the group of five Novans approaching the open gate in the nearly complete palisade.

Construction was going well. The released legionaries had included several trained stonemasons, carpenters, and even a few with experience in civil engineering. A drainage system was in place, and a few cisterns were built to catch rainwater. A rainy spell a few days earlier had the cisterns almost half-way full, and rude wooden pipes were carrying water to the soldier's barracks, the small houses of the tradesmen and the modest 'villas' of the Senators.

The Senate building was nearly complete; the mason had found a supply of good granite nearby, but the decision was made to only build with stone to about the height of a tall man, and finish the rest in wood, of which there was an ample supply. A few ambitious types stretched canvas awnings out in what would become the Forum and one or two were already hawking fish from the river or birds from the forest.

"I wish you would have sent for me, or Cicero, when they came before," Cato chided the young general.

Gnaeus Pompey shrugged. "They were only here a few moments."

"It's going to be tense for some time," Cato predicted.

"Very likely," Gnaeus agreed. He was in full uniform for the occasion, complete with his father's black-plumed helmet and ivory-handled gladius. Cato wore his white and red Senate robes.

"Here we are," Cornelia Metalla announced. Both men turned and inclined their heads to greet Pompey Magnus' widow and adopted daughter.

"Good morning, Consul," Adsila Pompeia Atella said to Cato. "And good morning to you, my brother," she greeted Gnaeus.

"Good morning, my dear girl," Cato said. "Your Latin has improved a great deal."

"Gratias," Adsila said.

Cornelia put a hand on the girl's shoulder and smiled. "She is amazing, isn't she? If all of her people are as bright as she, they must be a remarkable people indeed."

"We're about to find out. Adsila, do you know any of the men approaching us?"

"In front is Four Bears, Consul. I think you have met him. Behind him is White Oak, the A'Tep war chief, and Hawk, the leader of the farming society. And behind him—oh!"

"Yes?" Cato followed her gaze as the Novans drew closer, all of them carrying several woven baskets but one, and that one... "Sweet Juno," Cato breathed.

The Novan fourth in line was the oldest man Cato had ever seen. Could he be a hundred years old? Cato would not have been surprised. The old Novan walked with the aid of a stick, but he stumped along strongly, his head held high. His long hair, arranged in two braids that fell down to his chest, was snow white, and his face was not just wrinkled but grooved, lined, heavily marked with age. His black eyes glittered brightly from under shaggy white brows, though, showing a keen intelligence. In the late summer heat, he wore a leather clout and leggings over leather moccasins, with his skinny chest bare, the lines of ribs plainly revealed.

Adsila said something in her native tongue, shook herself, and began again in Latin. "That is Owl," she said. "He is the elder of the People."

"Which people?" Gnaeus asked.

"All of the People," Adsila answered. "Of all the People, B'Kou, A'Tep, Tsalee, Alligator, all the people. He is the oldest anyone has ever known; even he does not remember how many summers he has seen. Only he has lived to see his grandchildren's grandchildren."

The Novans had arrived and were laying their baskets on the ground in front of them. Four Bears and Owl approached.

"Please tell them I greet them as Consul of Rome," Cato asked the girl, "and tell Owl I greet him particularly, out of my deep respect for his position as elder. We Romans revere age and wisdom. His presence here does us great honor." Cato stepped in front of the old man and bowed, deeply, and Owls' eyes sparkled in amusement.

Adsila translated, stumbling for a moment over the term "Consul," before deciding to translate as "tribal chief."

"We greet you, Cato," she translated the Novan's reply in return. "In the name of the B'Kou and our cousins the A'Tep, we greet you all. And I, Owl, elder of the B'Kou, thank you for the respect you show one who is no chief, but merely an old man." Cato eyed the old man, who had spoken; his voice was strong and confident. What a marvel he is, he thought.

"We have brought these things to show you," the man called Hawk said. He indicated a basket full of a multicolored grain, large kernels, much larger than the familiar wheat or barley. "Maize," he said.

Another basket contained some sort of elongated, yellow vegetable. "Squash," Hawk said.

Another basket contained some small, pale nuts. "Hickory nuts."

The list went on: Walnuts, chestnuts, persimmons, cattail roots, and more.

"We grow corn and squash," Hawk explained through Adsila, "in fields, around each village. You can grow them here, too. The rest we gather in the forests and marshes." He looked through the gates into the town, listened for a moment to the clatter of building. "You already know about the deer, the wapiti, the turkeys in the forest."

"There are new animals in the forest, as well," Owl said, talking quickly enough that Adsila had trouble keeping up with the translation. "Animals as heavy as a big deer, but with short legs. They dig in the dirt for their food." He made a distinctive grunting sound.

"Our swine!" Gnaeus burst out laughing. It was not surprising that the swine, like the humans, left the swampy lowlands along the coast for higher, dryer ground.

"There are small ones among them," Owl said. "Many small ones."

"They will breed quickly," Gnaeus said. "We brought them here from across the sea, but they escaped us. You are welcome to hunt them but be careful; they can be dangerous." Gnaeus knew that if the swine went feral, there was no way either Roman or Novan could kill or capture all of them.

"They are good to eat," Cato agreed.

Four Bears spoke up. "We brought these things to you as gifts, to share among your people. You have things we would like to learn; how you make your tools, how you build your houses of stone and wood. We would like to learn how you tame these beasts, these 'horses,' and if you will be breeding more of them."

"You have things we would like to learn as well," Cato said.

"You know the land and its creatures. You know the other tribes around us. There is much we can learn from each other."

"It will be a good thing, for our peoples to learn from each other," old Owl agreed.

The war chief, White Oak, stepped in front of Gnaeus Pompey and spat out a few words. "He would like to see your..." Adsila began, "I am... I am sorry, brother, I do not know the word." She pointed.

"Gladius," Gnaeus Pompey told her. He looked at Cato, who nodded. After a moment's hesitation, he drew the glittering steel blade and handed it to the war chief.

White Oak examined the weapon carefully.

It was much like a long knife, but not chipped of flint or carved from antler or bone. White Oak knew this was something different, something utterly unlike anything he had seen before. The blade was long and heavy, but the handle, of some polished white material that felt vaguely like bone, balanced it well. It was beautiful, and it was deadly; manifestly the weapon of a warrior.

He ran a thumb along the honed edge, tapped the blade and asked a question. "He wishes to know what it is made of."

"Steel," the young general said.

"Where do you get steel?" White Oak wanted to know. "From some animal? A tree? Does it come from the earth? I have never seen anything like this."

"It comes from the earth," Gnaeus said, "but... it is difficult to explain. We hope to begin making it here soon, and if we do, we will let you see a smith working."

White Owl tapped the blade again. "We should like to have some of these," Adsila translated his words.

After another nervous glance at Cato, Gnaeus evaded the

question. "We have barely enough to equip our own." That was patently untrue; the reorganization of the legions had resulted in a surplus of weapons, with many of the legionaries having returned to their trades. "Perhaps, after we begin making tools here, and we know each other better."

White Oak was examining Gnaeus Pompey keenly. "Perhaps," he said. With one last, longing caress of the blade, he handed the gladius back to Gnaeus, who reseated it in its sheath with a sharp click.

Four Bears broke the uncomfortable pause with a sudden burst of words. "We would like to see your new town," Adsila translated his speech, "If you permit it."

"We do indeed," Cato said. "By all means, a tour of Pompeius is in order. Would you all like to follow me? We can start with the Senate building and the Forum."

Cato and Gnaeus Pompey led the Novans through the bustle of the construction to the top of the tallest of the four hills.

"The very stones of the earth," Owl breathed when they arrived at the Roman Senate building.

Roughly cut granite made up the bulk of the large, round building, from the foundation up to walls about twelve feet high. The balance was cedar wood, almost all salvaged from some of the ships that had been brought upriver and stripped for their lumber. Two carpenters were hanging heavy wooden doors, and Cato noticed that, unlike in Rome, these doors were all wood. No iron straps held the planks together; instead, laths of wood formed an X across the vertical planks and wooden pegs held the whole thing together. It was a good compromise for the metal-poor colony.

The circle of the foundation was a good hundred feet across. Broad stone steps led up to the main doors, which led into a small entryway that led inside to the main Senate chamber, as yet unfinished. Above the stone, carpenters were making a dome of wood with broad shutters that could be closed against weather or opened to allow fresh air and light inside.

"This is where our Senate will meet," Cato explained.

"And it has no other purpose?" Four Bears wanted to know, "other than to serve as a meeting place for your councils?"

"Not at all," Cato said. "In old Rome, the Senate was the center of Rome's daily life. News was announced on the steps. The Forum," Cato indicated the large open area in front of the Senate steps, "was where much of the trade in the city took place. Business deals are negotiated and concluded here. Merchants sell goods here. The Senate and the Forum are the beating heart of Roman society," he finished by thumping his chest.

Adsila had some trouble with the translation; Novan culture had no concept of business or sales, but the gist of it got across. Four Bears stopped in front of a stand where a young man was selling baked fish "fresh from the Tiber."

Cato admitted the fish smelled good; the boy had obviously gotten his hands on some salt from Brutus' party down on the coast, through what means Cato did not know. Since the Novans were frankly interested, Cato purchased each man a share, paying with a sesterce. Four Bears was fascinated by the silver coin but could not see how it was any fair trade for something good to eat; the coin did not seem to have any possible use.

The tour went on, past the small houses of the Senators, past the army barracks and the small huts built by the various civilians and hangers-on, before making the way back to the town gate.

"I thank you for showing us your home," old Owl said gravely though Adsila.

"We were glad to have you," Cato said. "We should like very much to visit your town as well." Beside him, Gnaeus Pompey barely suppressed a squawk of dismay.

"Summer draws to a close," Four Bears said, "and our people prepare for winter, but I am certain the councils of the People would make you welcome."

"Soon, then," Cato agreed. The Novans did not say good-bye, but simply turned and walked off.

"Well," Pompey the Younger said, "that went as well as could be expected."

That evening, 'well' changed dramatically to 'worse' when two mounted scouts appeared back from a patrol with Novan girls riding behind them on their horses.

At mid-day the following day, Gnaeus Pompey had the two dragged before him in the small wooden building in which he had installed his rather Spartan headquarters.

"What the bloody hell were you two thinking?" he roared at the men, whose faces paled in fear even as the General's grew more and more florid in rage. "Never mind, I'll tell you—you were thinking with your balls, weren't you? You men aren't six months from Rome, and you run off after some native cunni without a thought of what relations with these people are like right now!"

"Sir," one of the soldiers began, "it's not like that, we…"

"Shut up!" Pompey shouted. "I don't give two hairs off Pluto's ass how it is! I don't care if each of those girls is Venus given flesh, do you hear me?"

He sat down in his rude camp chair with a grunt. "Do you

know who I had to entertain this morning, with some linguistic assistance from my sister?"

"No, sir," one of the legionaries admitted.

"Well, soldier, let me tell you," Gnaeus ground out. "While you two were waving your cocks for these two native girls, I had five very angry young men in here protesting the theft of one man's intended wife."

"Wife?" The taller of the two legionaries looked thunderstruck.

"Intended wife, yes, soldier," the General snapped. "Amazing, isn't it, that people here actually arrange marriages and expect their intended ones to follow through, neh?"

"I swear, sir, she never mentioned anything about a marriage."

"Oh, shut up," Gnaeus repeated. "You wouldn't have heard her if she had, unless she whispered it to your balls." He rubbed one hand over his face. "So," he wondered out loud, "what am I to do with the two of you? I should have you both flogged, but I never gave any orders against fraternizing with native girls—oh, I assure you that will change, and bloody fast, too! But I can't accuse you of disobedience, and if we flogged soldiers for thinking with their cocks, there wouldn't be ten unmarked backs in all the legions of Rome."

"It's not like that at all, sir. We want to marry the girls, sir," one of the soldiers dared. "And the five men—where are they now?"

"Oh, I sent them off," Gnaeus said. "The rejected husband-to-be, he wanted to fight you for the girl, although why he'd want her back now is beyond me. I wasn't about to make things worse by letting this savage be cut up by a soldier of Rome, so I sent them on their way. Can't say as they were happy about it, but hopefully they won't return with their entire tribe to lay siege to the town."

On the coast

Early on a steamy, hot morning one of the surviving ships, a middling-sized freighter, sailed into the large harbor. The *Neptune* was accompanied by two triremes, each carrying a token force of soldiers, many of them archers and slingers. The ship's captain, Quintus Pulcio, stood on the ship's raised afterdeck, examining the enormous haven.

"Smoke, two points off to port," a lookout called. Captain Pulcio followed the man's pointing hand and saw several fine tendrils of gray smoke in the early morning light.

"Cooking fires. So, there are locals here after all." Pulcio looked farther into the harbor. "By the gods, what a place! You could lose a thousand ships in here."

The anchorage was ideal for the trade that would hopefully one day work this coast.

The ships had passed a small island entering the harbor. Two more were visible now, one a large, lightly forested strip of land between two arms of the harbor. Pulcio pointed at that one. "Make for that island," he ordered. "Signal the triremes to follow us."

"The island, sir?" Pulcio's first mate asked.

"The island." Pulcio pointed at the threads of smoke. "There's a village yonder. They will be on or near the water, I'd bet a dozen denarii on it. The Senate wants an outpost here, but I have no intent of leaving them in a position they can't defend easily. No, that island looks fine."

There was no good beach on the island large enough for the *Neptune* to ground on, but the smaller triremes easily beached on a sandspit on the sheltered north side. The freighter anchored just offshore. Captain Pulcio had a small boat lashed to the back of his ship, an innovation of his own that had proved useful in the many tiny ports and fishing villages in Africa and the Mediterranean. He had the boat lowered and went to shore.

"There is a small stream for water," the tribune in charge of the legionaries informed him as he splashed ashore. "There are no signs of game, but we'll build small boats to get to the mainland to hunt, and we have some nets for fishing."

"We'll have to float your equipment to shore here," Pulcio told him. He looked up at the sun. "Still early—we'll have it all offloaded by nightfall."

The tribune looked around. "I suppose we'll have to give this place a name," he mused. "If the Senate really wants to keep an outpost here. Probably be a town here one day." He pointed. "We'll build our outpost there, I think—on the end of the island facing the harbor mouth."

"Of course, there will be a town here, it's a lovely harbor. Room for a thousand ships. Well, at least the name, that's obvious," Captain Pulcio said.

Soldier looked at sailor, one eyebrow cocked in an unspoken question.

"Pulcia, of course," Pulcio barked. "I brought you here. I found the site. Why not?"

Tribune Marcus Lucanus shrugged. "Indeed. Why not? Very well, Pulcia it is."

Four Bears' village

The councils of the People were informal affairs, with no fixed members and no set agendas; instead, the group of senior chiefs and any others with specialized knowledge gathered together when a crisis was at hand or a particular problem needed solving.

Four Bears had spoken through the girl Adsila with the

Roman chief Cato, and was impressed with their council, which he called a Senate. He had his doubts about how well such a structured group would work among the People.

He knew more serious doubts as he looked across the fire at Man-Ready-For-War, war chief of the Alligator People. His name was also his title, given by tradition to the senior war chief of the fierce people who lived in the swamps and marshes to the south.

Everything about Man-Ready-For-War's appearance was calculated to intimidate. His face was painted black, his yellow teeth sharpened to fangs. He wore a heavy tunic and leggings made from the hide of an alligator's back, with the large, heavy scutes facing outward. A small, round traditional shield of hardwood was strapped to his left forearm. Scars seamed his exposed arms.

Four Bears knew from hard experience that the alligator-skin suit would turn most arrows or even a knife, unless you were lucky enough to hit the narrow spaces between scutes.

Man-Ready-For-War was accompanied by his sons and sub-chiefs, Sharp Knife and Long Tooth. They were painted and dressed in the same way as their father. Heavy wooden war clubs with sharp spikes of fire-hardened bone hung at their sides. They had left their long bows of ironwood outside the lodge where the councils met.

"It is a mistake," Man-Ready-For-War was saying, "to offer to trade with these Romans. They are few now, and we are many. Now is the time to fight them."

"I have seen their weapons," White Oak said. "I have seen their gladius, made of steel. You would not be so quick to want to fight, Man-Ready-For-War, if you had seen this weapon of steel."

"They could be ours," Man-Ready-For-War insisted. "They

may trade food with you. They may trade farming tools with you. They will never trade weapons with you. And I have seen this town of theirs. My sons and I hid in the forest three days, watching this town and these people. Do you know there are almost no women among them? Do you know two women of your villages have already left their homes to join with their soldiers, betraying their own people in doing so?"

Four Bears exchanged an uncomfortable glance with White Oak. They had not known the Alligator People had this information.

"How long," Man-Ready-For-War continued, "before more of their soldiers come to our villages looking for women? How long before they are taking our wives, sisters and mothers?"

"It was a mistake to let this continue as long as it has," Long Tooth added. "Now the wall around their town is almost done. Now it will be harder to strike at them."

"What do you propose to do?" White Oak asked.

Man-Ready-For-War sat up straight. "They send hunting and fishing parties forth from their walls. We will lie in wait for some of them, and we will kill them. They will know that it is not safe to leave their town. They will withdraw behind its walls. When they do, we will surround them. When hunger and thirst weakens them, we will burn their walls, burn their town, and kill them."

"The Alligator People will act, with you or without you," Sharp Knife snapped. "Some of your young men are already angry about these Romans hunting the deer and wapiti. Some of them already worry about their wives and sisters. Some of them will fight with us, whether the chiefs of the B'Kou and A'Tep wish it or not."

Four Bears knew this was probably true. The chiefs of the People were advisors, not rulers. The tribe had no codes of law,

only loose and undefined traditions for behavior, mostly having
to do with marriage and relations between families, clans and
tribes. Each man was free to follow his own whims, his own wishes,
and if some of the young fools among his tribe wanted to follow
the Alligator People into war, there was nothing he or anyone else
could do to stop them.

Nothing good will come of this, he told himself.

Beside him, White Oak could only think of the shining steel
of Gnaeus Pompey's gladius. He wondered how it would feel, to
swing one in his own hand.

Nova Roma: De Itinere in Occasum

Chapter Five
Skirmishes

It became apparent that the Novan tribesman were practiced in their own ways of war, but that their tactics were inadequate for dealing with Roman arms and soldiery. The Novans, however primitive, were and are a clever people. They rapidly adapted to the superiority of Roman steel and armor and found numerous ways to make themselves bothersome.

Gnaeus Pompey, having succeeded Pompey Magnus his father in command of the re-organized legions of the Nova Roman army, determined to bring what force he could to bear on the warlike factions of the tribes. The difficulty in determining which of the tribes were warlike and which were not was considerable, as were the difficulties encountered when Roman soldiers would on occasion make off with women of those tribes of either faction, usually not without willing co-operation of the women themselves.

This was a source of concern to all parties involved. It was a disciplinary matter for the Roman army, and a source of outrage for the Novans, especially the young men among them, always those most prone to war.

—From Gnaeus Pompey Novus' New World Diaries

Pompeius

Gnaeus Pompey looked on in anger as a gray-haired surgeon worked to remove an arrow from a cavalryman's thigh.

The man had been part of a patrol Pompey the Younger had ordered along the river to the west. Several such patrols, mounted on some of the few horses available, went out each day.

"How goes it?" Gnaeus looked up to see Cato and Cicero had come to the barracks to see what was what.

"Consuls," he greeted them. "The surgeon thinks he can remove the arrow, but the man will probably have a limp, assuming he does not contract blood poisoning. He will be a soldier no longer."

"How many does this make?"

"Three killed and five injured, in the last ten days," Gnaeus Pompey snapped. "All in the heavy timber along the river upstream of here, except one man killed while hunting in the woods to the south. At least," he said, wincing at the thought but knowing it to be true even so, "we have lost no horses. We cannot afford to lose even one of them." Three of the town's mares were known to be carrying foals, one of the few pieces of good news the colony had gained lately.

Gnaeus brought up a point that had been much debated in the last several days, as the summer was giving way to autumn. "I say again, Consuls, we should mount a punitive expedition on the savages. We know where at least two of their villages lie." He didn't add the one fact everyone was keenly aware of; they knew of the two villages because now, no fewer than five Novan girls had been talked into accompanying Roman men out of those villages and into cohabitating with them in Pompeius.

"We don't know if the Novans attacking our troops come from those villages," Cicero objected. He was growing weary of making that point. "Our soldiers describe their attackers plainly; faced painted black, wearing what looks like the hides of crocodiles. Did the chief Four Bears fit that description? Or the old man Owl? No, and neither does anyone in either of the two villages."

"Do I dress in my Senate robes to go to war?" Gnaeus snapped. "Did my father?"

Both Consuls stared at the young general. Neither had a ready answer.

"The army follows my orders," Gnaeus said. "I will send cavalry and a cohort of infantry upriver, a reconnaissance in force. If the savages choose to attack a larger force, let them try." He looked at Cato. "We will not attack any villages unless the people of that village set upon us. Is that satisfactory?"

"Nothing about this is satisfactory, General," Cato said. "But it will do."

The force set out the next morning. A century of the Second Legion marched forth from Pompeius, accompanied by four mounted scouts. They moved down the hill and followed the river upstream, west by northwest.

Upriver—the next day

There were six warriors; enough, so Man-Ready-For-War had told them, to handle the usual small scouting parties the Romans sent out. Five of them were of the Alligator People, while the fifth was Stone Gazer, a young man of the B'Kou whose stalk of a white-tailed doe had been wasted by a Roman archer, who had struck the animal down and carried it off.

Sounds and smells of the river bottom forest were nothing new to any of the six young men. Nor were the sounds they heard now: The obvious tread of the Roman's large riding animals, their 'horses,' pushing through the thick undergrowth along a high bank overlooking the river.

Alligator People and B'Kou alike knew the strengths and weaknesses of the men mounted on horses. Their heavy armor and helmets would turn most arrows, but a shot at leg, arm or neck would strike flesh. Their horses were fast, far faster than a man could run, but only in open country. The tight forest hemmed them in, made them vulnerable.

Two of the Alligator warriors were in the trees, bows at their sides. The other four men waited on the ground to exploit any opportunity the archers gave them. If they could pull one of the Romans from the back of their horse and steal the animal, that would be a great prize to take back to their people.

One of the Alligator warriors in the trees saw, briefly, the flash of the red crest of a Roman helmet through the brush.

A gust of wind swirled the first dead leaves of autumn through the brush, masking the faint swish of Roman sandals in the wet litter of the forest floor.

In the tree, the Alligator warrior raised a hand. The others watched.

The Roman on the horse drew closer. He handled his horse cautiously, stepping it slowly over the ground, watching the brush ahead and to either side as he rode. But, as Romans always seemed to do, he failed to look up.

Closer, closer. The wind blew another rattling gust.

The Alligator warrior closed his hand into a fist.

Two arrows shot out of the brush.

Centurion Lucius Decimus Meridius was fortunate. One arrow glanced off his helmet. The second grazed his left arm, leaving a bleeding gash but doing no real damage. "Archers to the left!" he shouted, and then all Hades broke loose.

Meridius drew his gladius and booted his horse into the attack. The arrows had to have come from a small rise covered in brush, about sixty feet away. "Follow me!" he shouted to Legionary Lucius Pilus, mounted on the patrols' other horse. "Attack to left front," he shouted over his shoulder to the infantry.

Another arrow hissed overhead, yet another sailed past him on his right. A yelp to his rear told him Pilus was struck, but he ignored it for the moment: he was on the enemy.

A skinny man with a face painted black leaped at him with a wooden club, howling. A backhanded swipe of Meridius' gladius took the man's arm off. The savage fell into the weeds and was trampled under the flint-hard hooves of the cavalry horse as it charged past.

Meridius saw another Novan to his left. He pointed with his gladius and was relieved to see Legionary Pilus thunder after the man; evidently, he was not seriously hurt. Pilus didn't swing his gladius but threw it, spinning end over end. The blade sank into the fleeing Novan's back, knocking him to the ground.

While this was going on, the infantry were charging forward, moving left and right to envelop the enemy position. Another Novan was caught in the pincer. The man fought, swinging his war club viciously, striking one legionary in the throat and another in the arm before falling to the stabbing swords of several Roman soldiers. Another burst from a patch of brush and charged, howling, but his attack met nothing but the bosses of Roman shields and the points of Roman swords.

"Hold!" Centurion Meridius shouted. "Listen!"

All could hear the obvious sounds of at least one man fleeing, moving away from the river.

Meridius saw his counterpart, Centurion Quintus Longinus, who commanded the infantry. "Follow us as best you can," he shouted. He saw Longinus raise his sword in reply. "Pilus," Meridius called, "are you wounded?"

"Naught but a scratch, sir!"

"Good. Follow me!"

The cavalrymen booted their horses and set off after the fleeing Novans.

The going was difficult at first, through heavy brush and brambles, but the undergrowth cleared away from the river and soon both horses were galloping into a clearing, coming in sight of a small Novan village just as two fleeing Novans dove into a low hut.

"Halt," Meridius called.

"Sir," Legionary Pilus said, "they're right there…"

"Let the infantry catch up," the centurion ordered. Minutes later, the first infantryman charged into the clearing. "Line of battle," Centurion Longinus ordered, after a moment's quick briefing by Meridius.

"On command, we advance into the village. Fire the buildings. Burn everything. Any natives that run, let them go. If they surrender, take them prisoner. Any that resist, cut them down. For'ard—MARCH!" the order was bellowed, and the line of infantry marched into the village behind their shields.

Four Bears' village

"An entire village burned!" White Oak shouted. "All their stored food for winter taken! Nine men killed and six wounded, one of those not likely to live!"

The hour was late. The sun had set long before, and still the council of the People argued.

Owl looked up from the fire. He had his hard face on, revealing nothing. "And why? A young man of the Alligator People was among the dead in the village, White Oak, as you saw yourself. Four more dead Alligator warriors lay near the river, just down the path from that village. Do you think the Romans attacked with no reason?"

"How do we know those men were not defending the village?"

Four Bears looked at the war chief. "I know your wife's brother was among the dead, White Oak," he said, "and we grieve with you. But it would not be a good thing to rush to war now, until we know what happened."

"Was it a good thing to let them burn a village and take its supplies? And what of the young girls who have abandoned the People, to go live among these Romans? What of them?"

"What of them?" Four Bears asked. "Young people will do as they do. Only one of them was promised to another."

"And when her intended husband went to protest, to fight the other man in honor as is his right, this Pom-Pey that you say is your friend, he turned our man away! The People cannot stand for the theft of our game, our land, and our young women! We cannot let this stand, Four Bears. These... Romans, they presume too much."

"It is all as I said," came a voice from the shadows.

The council of the People turned as one toward the voice.

A dark shadow emerged from the night, shifting in the smoke, resolving slowly from the darkness into a malevolent shape, looming over them, a figure of deep shadow in the dancing firelight.

Man-Ready-For-War.

"Now," the war chief of the Alligator People said, "Now, you are ready to listen."

Pompeius

"Food," Cicero said to the convened Senate. "It all comes back to food."

"It is beginning to tell on the army," Gnaeus Pompey admitted. "They march more slowly and have to rest more often. There are no more deer or turkey in the region, and none of our crops will yield anything for eating for another year, at least. We must have gathered everything edible in the woods for miles around."

"One small comfort," Brutus said with a wry grin. "It matters little now that the swine escaped. They wouldn't have been enough to feed us in any case, and now we do not have to feed them."

"Nights are growing chilly," Cato said. "We all feel it. We have no idea what a winter here will be like. Will it be like a winter in Ostia, or in Cisalpine Gaul? Who knows?"

"Adsila knows," Gnaeus Pompey said. "It is cold, but not terribly so. Rivers seldom freeze. Snow is rare but not unknown."

"Well, that will comfort us in our starvation," Cato snapped. His growling stomach was making him testy.

"At least there is plenty of firewood."

"And plenty of salt, should we need it to cure meat," Gaius Cassius Longinus added. A month prior he had conceived an idea and sent a party off to the landing site to start producing salt from the sea water. Their labors had been great, and so had the results, especially since they worked in an area not hunted and fished out by the hungry legions; they worked hard, ate well and even managed to send fish and meat back to Pompeius along with the barrels of salt.

"We have two options, as I see it," Gnaeus announced. "One, we can send legions afield to raid the natives for food." He held up a hand as Cato started a spluttering objection. "I do not advocate it, Consul. In fact, I think it unwise; it is simply one of two alternatives. The other: We disperse. We throw ourselves on the mercy of the natives, and scatter among their villages."

"Neither seems likely," Cicero objected, "after the latest round of skirmishing. Two more legionaries dead, two crippled in the last ten days alone."

"I do not think the natives would make us welcome," Cicero agreed. "So that does not seem a likely option, either."

"And that's another thing," Gnaeus began, only to be interrupted by a cry from outside the Senate building.

"Brother! Brother!" a girl's voice, raised in excitement. "Brother!"

"That's Adsila," Gnaeus Pompey said. "What could she want?"

"Listen," Cato said.

A dull roar sounded from outside. The Senators looked up at the high walls under the ceiling, where wooden shutters were drawn back to let the cool autumn air in. It was a bright, sunny afternoon out, but now the light from outside was dimmed, as though a heavy, dark storm cloud had passed over the sun. The dull roar grew, swelling into a thunderous tumult.

"Brother!" Adsila crashed through the door of the Senate, her face alive with excitement. "The Mijiji! They are here!"

"The what?"

"Birds!" Adsila shouted, remembering the Latin word. "Many, many birds! They are here!"

The Senators ran outside.

Overhead was an impossible sight, a massive flock, swarm, a multitude of birds, like the rock doves of Rome but slimmer, with long tails. The sky was black with them, and the wind of their wings blew down on the faces of the Senators as the throng passed overhead. Birds, plump, round-breasted, full-bodied! As far as the eye could see, birds!

Gnaeus Pompey ran for the barracks. "Nets," he was shouting, "bows, nets, by Diana's sweet round ass, grab rocks! We must take as many as we can! Turn out the town!"

Pulcia

The great flock of birds had passed Pulcia as well, but the masses of fowl had not passed directly over the island, staying further inland instead. The legionaries assigned as hunters had gone ashore one night and netted a few hundred of the fat birds as they roosted, but they were an incidental addition to the diets of men living well on a good, if somewhat monotonous, diet of fish and venison.

Marcus Lucanus made it his habit to walk the entire shore of the island each day at sunup, to make sure no natives had slipped onto the small spit of land by night. The legionaries had dug some stone and floated large trees from the mainland to build a stout fortification around their small camp on the eastern end of the small island, but caution would have to be the order of the day until more men and ships could be brought down.

"It's going to rain later, I think," he heard a legionary say one cloudy, damp morning as he walked back inside the camp. A breakfast of fish baked over an open fire beckoned, but Lucanus had little appetite for it. A layer of gray clouds hung low this morning, echoing Lucanus' state of mind.

"Natives coming in!" a shout was raised from a small watchtower on the landward wall of the fort.

Three native dugout boats were approaching swiftly from the west. That in itself was no particular threat, as the slim, light native draft were fast and easy to handle. Lucanus ordered the legionaries in the fort to stand to and assemble on the beach.

"You, you, and you," he pointed to three men once the soldiers were in ranks, scuta and pila very much in evidence for the natives to see. "Duck over to the other side, make sure they are not sending a fleet of boats in behind us."

"Sir!" the three saluted and trotted off, their iron-hobnailed sandals kicking up spurts of sand.

Minutes later, the tiny fleet of three native craft beached. One man got out, a tall, wiry man, wearing an odd tunic and leggings of what looked like crocodile skin. He had painted his face black, and a nasty-looking spiked club hung from a thong at his side. The other men in the boats looked to be similarly attired and equipped.

"Well, aren't you a pretty one," Lucanus muttered.

With a grunt, the savage stomped up the beach to where Lucanus stood in front of his rank of soldiers. The entire contingent of the fort—a hundred men—was present, minus one in the tower, three sent to the other side to keep watch, and several soldiers and sailors manning the one trireme that stayed behind in the harbor.

Lucanus noted the trireme's crew was alert; even now a few oars deployed to move the warship slowly closer to the beach.

Lucanus met the Novan's glittering black eyes. He stared back, his own gray eyes looking calmly from under the brow of his helmet. Suddenly the Novan grinned, fiercely, revealing long, stained yellow teeth. He jabbed Lucanus in the chest and surprised him by speaking one word in Latin: "Roman."

"Yes," Lucanus, said slowly, nodding. He repeated the gesture, poking the native in the chest. "Novan."

The savage shook his head and spat out a stream of syllables. He rapped on the heavy scutes of his reptile-armor tunic and repeated the phrase.

"Your word for crocodile, I imagine," Lucanus said, examining the man's tunic with a professional eye. Looks like good protection against the Novan clubs and flint knives, he thought. Maybe even arrows. But against a well-cast pila or a gladius thrust? No chance. Unconsciously, not even realized he was doing so, he laid a hand on the grip of this sheathed sword.

Lucanus watched as the Novan turned and barked what sounded like an order to the man in the front of the boat he had climbed out of. That man picked up two objects and tossed them.

Marcus Lucanus watched the two round objects sail towards the Novan standing before him. Time seemed to slow as he saw the two round things sail through the air; they were a dull gold-brown, dented and dirty but the shape was unmistakable. The Novan caught the two objects, dropped them on the ground in front of Lucanus and, with a last contemptuous look, strode back to his boat.

As the Novans pushed back from the beach and paddled

away, Marcus Lucanus stared down at the two Roman legionaries'
helmets lying at his feet.

The heads were still inside them.

"But all my men are accounted for," he muttered as he bent to
examine the heads. "So, where did you boys come from?"

Lucanus became aware of this second-in-command, Optio
Flavius Petrocidius, looking over this shoulder.

"Bugger me," Petrocidius said. "I know that lad there." He
pointed at one of the heads.

"So? And who is he?"

"Lucius Porcius, sir. Thirteenth Legion. I served with him in
the Thirteenth in Gaul. When I was finished with my term I came
home, and old Porcius here stayed on, stayed with the Thirteenth.
I re-mustered as an Evocatus under Pompey's colors before we
took ship. Old Porcius here, solid Thirteenth Legion man and solid
Caesarean, he is." Petrocidius laid a finger on his crooked nose.
"We had a brawl about it once. Bastard son of a whore broke my
nose."

"Wait," Lucanus said. "Wait just a moment. Are you saying
this man wasn't on any of the ships that came east with General
Pompey?"

"Not him, sir. He'd have cut out his guts before joining
Pompey. He would have been with the Thirteenth when they came
south out of Gaul."

Lucanus started down at the dead Caesarean's head. Things
in this new land had suddenly become more complicated.

Pompeius

The villas erected for the Senate members were tiny, made
of wood and wattle rather than marble, but they kept out the rain

and wind. Cato quickly discovered he had a knack for producing workable furniture from bits of plank, rough wood from the timbering operations and rawhide thong from deer hide. He had managed to fashion a sleeping pallet, three chairs and a rude table for his small house, and was beginning to feel almost comfortable. His own lodgings, if they were not noble in aspect, at least commanded a noble view, being as they were near the top of the tall hill. From his one small window Cato could see the meadows surrounding the new town where they ran down to the river, and over that to the forest on the far side.

Cato had long been one for living modestly, as a tenet of his personal Stoicism. The little house was beginning to feel, if not quite like a home, at least like a place that was comfortable and familiar.

Cato was sitting in his tiny "villa"—a shack in all but name—when Cicero rushed in, his demeanor unaccountably excited. "Cato!" he shouted. "I have it!"

"Well, let us hope the physicians have a treatment for it, then," Cato said in a fit of uncharacteristic sarcasm.

Cicero, ignoring the attempt at humor, produced a rolled scrap of parchment. He thrust it at Cato. "Look at this. This is, I think, the form our new Republic should take."

"That didn't take you long," Cato said. He unrolled the rough parchment. "An outline only, I see?"

"All I felt I should do on my own," Cicero replied. "We should collaborate with some of the others to fill in details, but this is the basic form. The Senate as a whole will have to agree on a more complete document that will define the constitution of our new government."

Cato regarded the outline. "Two branches of government?"

"And the courts," Cicero agreed. "So, there will be three branches, in actuality. But the Consuls are elected by the Senate, and I envision they will be able to be recalled by the Senate."

Cato read on.

The two Consuls, when elected by the Senate, actually left that body during their four-year terms to head up a new branch, the Consulate, responsible for the army and dealings with other nations. Consul's terms were staggered by two years, so that an election would be held bi-annually. Reduces the chance for conspiracy, Cicero had recorded in a small marginal note.

The Senate took the familiar Roman form with one exception; Senators could be proposed to that body by Consuls or by a sitting Senator, but had to be confirmed by a vote of the full Senate. As in old Rome, the Senate remained responsible for legislation, appointing Magistrates, but the Tribune of Plebs...

"This election of Tribune," Cato asked, "to be elected by all serving soldiers and veterans of the legions?"

"Two Tribunes," Cicero pointed out. "Two Tribunes to sit in the Senate. The first is the Tribune of Mars, the second the Tribune of Plebs. Both with veto power over the Senate. The Tribune of Mars represents those who pledge their lives to protect Rome. The Tribune of Plebs represents the common people of Rome; artisans, craftsmen, tradesmen of all sorts."

There was more: Magistrates to be appointed by the Senate for the city of Pompeius, and as other Roman towns grew, a Chief Magistrate to be elected by the free tradesman of that town.

The country was to be divided in time into provinces, each governed by a Proconsul appointed by the Senate. The area of the first landing and the environs of the city of Pompeius were defined as the province of Rome.

The last provision struck Cato again. "This definition of rights of the free Roman," he asked. "This is to apply to all free men? Roman and Novan?"

"To all citizens of our new Rome, yes," Cicero asked. "To all men of Nova Roma. There is no reason to doubt that, in time, the tribesmen hereabouts will seek to join us, and if they do, they should be able to seek and obtain citizenship. And what's more, they should be free men, always. We brought no slaves with us on this journey, Cato. You have owned slaves and I have owned slaves, but let us leave that institution behind in Rome."

"The other Senators won't like that," Cato said.

"Let them hire servants if they need them," Cicero snapped. "One of the problems we had in old Rome was the lack of jobs for the plebs; farmers, manufacturers, tanners, butchers, anyone who needed servants or assistants bought slaves instead of hiring free men. Remember you the trouble that caused? Remember the jobless men flooding into Rome, looking to draw a corn ration because there was no work in the countryside? I remind you, Caesar made good use of it in his demagoguery."

"He did at that," Cato admitted.

"One more thing I will insist on," Cicero said, "and I am hoping you will agree. The ceding of dictatorial powers by anyone, Senator, Consul, anyone, must be strictly proscribed by law in our constitution."

"Not even in an emergency?"

"Especially not then." Cicero frowned. "Emergencies are all too easy to engineer, Cato. No dictators. Let us have no Sullas, Cato. Let us especially have no Caesars."

"I do agree," Cato said. "Let us hope the other Senators will as well."

To the south

While Cato and Cicero discussed the form of the new Roman Republic, another remnant of the old was struggling to survive in the new world.

On the beach, several leagues south of the great harbor where the settlement of Pulcia lay on its narrow island, a large Roman quinquireme lay wrecked, its hull shattered on a large rock outcrop. No one remained near that ship now. Of the one hundred and ninety-six men and thirteen horses originally aboard that ship, only forty-eight men and nine horses remained. The forty-eight consisted of seven cavalrymen, two centurions, and the remainder of the ship's crew.

The two centurions led the group. Both men were battle-hardened veterans of the Thirteenth Legion. Both had fought in Briton and Gaul. Each had, at one time or another, saved the other's life. Each had engaged in acts of conspicuous courage that brought them to Caesar's personal attention, which had resulted in him assigning them to lead a detachment of cavalry to trail Pompey Magnus and the Senate.

And both were more bewildered now than either had ever been.

Centurion Titus Pullo and Centurion Lucius Vorenus rode at the head of a bedraggled, starving column of Romans, straggling in a roughly northwesterly direction. Scouts on horseback ranged ahead, riding back to the column periodically to report.

Neither of the centurions had any real idea where they were going. But they had a very good knowledge, gained of hard experience, of the vicious crocodile-skinned warriors they were trying to leave behind.

"Two days," Pullo noted. "Two days since we've been attacked. I count that as a good thing."

"Unless they are massing to wipe us out completely," Vorenus griped. "These sailors—we'll never make soldiers of them, even if we had arms for all of them." Almost all of the losses had been among the ship's stranded crew. Only two soldiers had been lost, although four priceless horses were dead.

"Maybe we've left their territory. We're out of the swamps, at any rate."

"Not much chance of finding out where Pompey and the Senate fled to now," Vorenus observed.

"There's a bright side," Pullo said. "At least Caesar can't have us flogged for failing in carrying out our orders to follow them."

"For all we know that storm wiped Rome off the face of the earth. Maybe all of Italy. Maybe all of Europe. Who knows? Who could have imagined a storm like that, or an impossible land like this one?"

Pullo used the end of his soldier's cloak to wipe his forehead. "One thing for sure," he complained. "There isn't a civilized Roman town, village or person to be found in this entire misbegotten land."

The column moved on, climbing slowly into more open country. The air cleared as they slowly climbed, and gradually the outline of hills appeared to the west.

"Cleaner country," Vorenus observed. "Dryer country, at any rate."

"Humid as ever," Pullo said. "Nearly so, anyway."

"Have to find a spot to camp soon."

The Roman cavalrymen rode on through the steamy heat, with the stranded sailors straggling slowly behind. Hunger was beginning to tell on the men; rations had long since run out, and the danger of savages attacking left little opportunity for hunting. When Vorenus suggesting breaking the march early to make camp and allow for some foraging, Pullo quickly agreed.

One of the sailors had some skill at hunting, as it turned out, and within an hour of the halt he and two companions dragged a large, brown-furred deer back to camp. The cavalrymen and sailors set to with a will and were seated around fires chewing on hastily cooked meat when a shout went up from the one man on sentry duty.

"Native!" he barked.

"To arms!" Pullo shouted.

"I think he wants a parley," the sentry called back.

Pullo and Vorenus walked to the small rise in the clearing where the men were camped. A small, skinny man with long black hair was standing by the sentry.

"Looks different," Vorenus said as the centurions approached.

"He does," Pullo said, sotto voce. "All the others painted their faces black and wore that crocodile skin armor. Bet you a sisterce this man's from a different tribe."

As they approached, the native held up his right hand, open, his empty palm facing the Romans. After exchanging a glance, the two centurions did likewise.

"Roman," the native said, pointing at the sailor assigned to sentry duty. He pointed at Vorenus. "Roman," he repeated, then again, pointing at Pullo.

"Well, isn't that interesting," Pullo said. "He knows us as Romans."

"Interesting, yes, but how?"

"Obviously, Vorenus, we are not the only Romans here. He's

met Romans before. Pompey's party, who else could it be? They would have been caught up in the same storm as we."

"And what do we do about it?"

"Our orders were to follow them, and report back to Caesar where they had gone."

Vorenus looked sour. "Easy enough to say," he snapped. "Hard enough to do. How are we to get to Caesar to report?"

The native spat out a stream of syllables, all the while gesturing towards the west, then the north. "A'Tep," he said, thumping his chest. "A'Tep," he repeated, pointing west. "Roman," he said again, this time pointing north.

"Romans to the north, his tribe to the west," Pullo translated.

"That would be my guess," Vorenus agreed.

"I think he wants us to come with him," the sentry said. "Before you two got here, he was making motions like this;" the man mimed putting something in his mouth with three fingers, "and motioning towards the west."

"Promising us food if we come with him."

"Looks like," Vorenus agreed. He turned to look at Pullo. "Pompeians to the north of us, and we're a small party. But it seems we have allies now."

"So, we go with him, then?"

Vorenus nodded. "Lost or not, we're Caesar's men. Any other Romans here have to be of Pompey's party. Let's go with this man now, try to figure out what's happening here, and let the gods decide what happens next."

"Agreed. It looks like our best chance for the moment."

It took several days to work out the arrangements, but once each party learned a few words of the other's, an agreement was struck. The word spread quickly among the tribes. Alligator People, B'Kou, and A'Tep, all knew within a matter of days.

The People now had Roman allies.

CHAPTER SIX

FACTIONS

In the autumn of the first year the Senate and General Pompey learned that the original party of Pompey Magnus was not the only party of Romans blown to the new world by the great storm

The other Romans would be discovered to be a small party sent by Julius Caesar to track Pompey Magnus and the Optimate Senators, and they indeed did so, even off the ends of the known world, as their ship was caught up in the same storm as the others. Their actions on arriving in the new world divorced them forever from Nova Roma, however well they may have thought they served their far-distant master.

While this was going on, the Optimate Senators were not idle. A new Republic took form in Nova Roma that very autumn, The new Republic was to be similar to the old and yet very different in some ways, which would prove to make it more ideally suited to not only the Roman but, in time, the native inhabitants of the new land. But first, there was the matter of the hostiles among the natives to deal with, and their Roman allies made that task more difficult.

—From Gnaeus Pompey Novus' New World Diaries

Pompeius

As that autumn slid into a cool, damp winter, the Nova Roman government began to take shape.

After what seemed an interminable interval of arguing, debating, deal-making and compromises, the Senate finally met to have a final vote on the form of the new constitution. Once the Senate convened and a quorum was confirmed, Cicero read the particulars of the new governing documents.

"As we have all—finally—agreed, the government will have four parts," he began. "The Consulate, the Senate, the Council of Plebs, and the Magistrates." Unrolling a large sheet of rough parchment (in fact a cured, scraped deer skin) he began to read.

"Since I'm sure we are all familiar with the particulars, allow me to summarize the form of the constitution."

He coughed once, and then eyed the assembled Senators. A lot of haggling had gone on to bring them to this point. Satisfied that all attention was on him, he rattled the parchment and continued.

"The Consulate will be in charge of the army, foreign affairs with the tribes that surround us, and all matters that involve two or more provinces. There will be a Consul and a Lesser Consul, elected by the Senate, each of whom will serve overlapping terms of four years. When the Consul leaves after his term, the Lesser Consul ascends to Consul and a new Lesser Consul is elected. The Consul and Lesser Consul will, every two years, appoint a Tribune of Mars to represent our soldiers and veterans in the Senate."

"After serving a term in either office, Consuls are forever barred from seeking a Consulship again."

Cicero noticed a few raised eyebrows at that. He and Cato had both held Consulships in the old republic, and yet both held that title again now; and none present had forgotten Sulla, who had gotten himself elected Consul again and again, in open defiance of the law.

"You and Cato both hold Consulships now," Servilius Casca pointed out. "How does that resolve?"

"We have agreed to surrender our Consulships on the day that the Senate chooses a new Consul. The first Consul will be elected for only two years, so the terms will be staggered as planned."

"Will you disqualify yourselves from the election?"

"We had not considered that," Cicero admitted. "But as the consulship in old Rome was not deemed as disqualifying here, in a new land, our interim service as Consuls here and now would not disqualify us, as we have not served in that capacity under the new constitution. I cannot speak for my friend, colleague and brother Cato, but if the Senate insists, I will withdraw my name from consideration."

"I doubt anyone would require that." Casca nodded, satisfied.

Cicero continued:

"Each province will be governed by a Proconsul, and by a Provincial Council of Plebs. The Provincial Council of Plebs will be responsible for all legislative matters within the province. The one exception will be the province of Rome, which contains the capital city of Pompeius, which will be governed directly by the Senate."

"The Senate will be much as it is now; Senators may be appointed by a Consul or Lesser Consul, and must be ratified by a two-thirds vote of the entire sitting Senate. There is one new item; each Provincial Council of Plebs will also elect one Senator to represent the interests of their province. That Senator will serve until recalled."

"Assuming we ever have more than the one province," Marcus Brutus said in a harsh stage whisper. Cicero silenced him with a glare before going on.

"The second deliberative body will be the Republic Council of Plebs. Each province will be represented in proportion to their population, with one Councilor for each ten thousand citizens, with a minimum of one per province. This will, of course, make the initial meeting of the Council of Plebs rather small." There was a round of polite laughter at that remark. "Each Councilor will be elected by the citizens of the provinces and will serve one four-year term, following which he is barred from serving in the Council again. The Council of Plebs is also responsible for electing one of their members to represent them in the Senate as Tribune of Plebs."

"Legislative matters may originate in either the Senate or the Republic Council of Plebs, but must pass by majority vote of both bodies before becoming law. The coining of money, the standards for coinage, and all spending by the Nova Roman government is the responsibility of the Senate."

"Finally, each Provincial Council of Plebs will appoint magistrates and judges to settle legal matters within their borders, with each appointment subject to veto by the province's Proconsul. The Senate will appoint a Chief Magistrate and a Chief Judge to arbitrate disputes between provinces or to settle matters that involve more than one province, again, such appointments to be subject to veto by the Consul."

"Citizenship: All members of the crew and all passengers of any ship that accompanied Pompey Magnus here to Nova Roma have all rights and responsibilities of citizenship. Any child born to one or more parents of such are likewise citizens of Nova Roma. Any tribesman or other local who swears an oath of fealty to Nova Roma, demonstrates conversational ability in spoken Latin, and has a useful trade will also be considered a full citizen of Nova Roma."

Brutus raised his hand. "I would speak on this," he said.

"Senator," Cicero conceded the floor.

Brutus stood. "In old Rome, we Optimates steadfastly opposed the extension of full citizenship to the people of the provinces. Do we now truly propose to extend to these primitives the full benefits of Roman citizenship?"

"We do," Cicero said. He and Cato had expected the objection in formal session; Brutus and Cassius had objected to the measure during the crafting of the constitution.

"Justify that," Brutus demanded.

"When our ancestors came to the seven hills of Rome from the ruins of Troy," Cicero replied, "they did not remain insulated. Romulus, when he founded the city, took in as full citizens any of the people of the area around the seven hills. Freedmen, slaves, all were brought in as citizens."

"Granted," Brutus agreed.

"This is not Rome, friend Brutus," Cicero continued. "We are truly beginning anew, as did Romulus. We are building not just a new city for those of us come here through the storm, but for our children, and for their children. We are building a nation, Brutus, and to do that we have to have citizens. We cannot crouch here behind city walls, isolated from the local people. We must establish commerce with them. We must expand, not just outside the walls but across the land, north, south and west. To do that we must be able to travel safely, under protection of Roman law and Roman arms. To do that, we must expand Roman influence. We have not sufficient troops to expand by force. We must expand by trade. We must expand by expanding our citizenry; to do that, we must grant citizenship to all Novans who wish to accept the rights and responsibilities of citizenship."

Brutus looked doubtful. "I know not where this will take us," he said, "but I withdraw my objection. For now." He sat down.

Cicero turned his attention back to the parchment. "Slavery is permanently barred. Assignment of dictatorial powers is permanently barred." Those two provisions had been the subject of much debate. In the end, leaving the Senate almost completely in the hands of the nobility and giving them exclusive control of currency was the price Cato and Cicero paid to have slavery outlawed.

As previously agreed, the proposed Constitution was posted in the Senate chamber for ten days, following which there would be a vote to ratify. Given the deal making and negotiation that went into the document, all parties expected it to pass handily, Brutus and Cassius's concerns regarding citizenship for the Novans notwithstanding.

Cato was leaving the finally completed Senate building when Gnaeus Pompey stopped him. Cato noticed that the young general already had Cicero in tow.

"Salve, General," Cato greeted him. He looked at Cicero curiously; Cicero shrugged. "What is it?"

"We must talk, Consuls," Pompey the Younger said quietly. "Somewhere quiet." He looked back into the Senate chamber, where the few Senators were still milling about.

"My villa is nearby," Cato said. "Such as it is. I'm afraid I can offer you nothing to drink but water."

"Water is fine," Pompey said, "although you'll soon wish for something stronger."

They walked swiftly through a light drizzle to Cato's small house. The wet weather had made the streets sloppy and muddy. Cicero stepped as lightly as possible, detouring around the most obvious puddles and hoisting his Senate robes fussily away from the ground, while Cato squelched through the mud with a resigned air. Gnaeus Pompey splashed along with a soldier's indifference.

"What think you of the new proposals, General?" Cato asked as they walked.

Pompey the Younger looked thoughtful. "I approve of the army and the veterans having a voice in the Senate, of course," he said. "All too often our veterans are forgotten once a war is fought and won. I wondered at first about denying the possibility of a dictatorship, but I remember my father's tales of Sulla and Marius, and then we have our example of Caesar, so I suppose that's for the best."

"What is there that the army will not like?" Cicero was always concerned about the loyalty of soldiers.

"As far as I can see, nothing," Pompey answered. "Having the army answer to the Consulate cements their loyalty to the government and not to any individual general—one would hope. Of course, soldiers must serve their commanders as well. Might it be difficult to expect them to have loyalties in two directions? What if a rogue general appears, even as Caesar has done? Which direction will the troops turn?"

"We cannot know that until it happens," Cato said. "Hopefully never, and if you can organize the army so that they serve Rome as a nation, and not any one person or persons—ah, here is my charming and expansive villa now. Please do come in out of the wet." He led the man inside his dwelling, a villa in name but in reality, scarcely more than a shack.

"Well," Cicero said once they were finally behind closed doors. "What is this all about, General? Why all the secrecy?"

Gnaeus Pompey didn't waste any time. "It is as we feared. There are other Romans here. Two of my men were scouting in the hills to the south. They saw a party of Roman cavalry on a hillside, accompanied by a party of Novans."

Cicero and Cato looked at each other. "Are you sure about this?" Cato asked.

"All too bloody sure."

"Who could they be? And what were they doing?"

"Who they are, nobody knows. My men did not try to get close enough. But there were two centurions among them, judging from the helmets and as to what they were doing—it looked like they were teaching the Novans how to form a line of battle."

"That's not good." Cicero looked thoughtful. "It does explain the delivery the—what does Adsila call them, the Alligator People? The delivery they made to our man down in the harbor."

"Two Roman heads, complete with helmets," Pompey the Younger affirmed, "and verified by the optio as Caesar's men."

"So, Caesar did have us followed."

"Of course," Cato snapped. "Of course, he did. But those men, they are just as lost as we are now. The question is—where is their loyalty? Not to Rome in this new world, it seems, but still to Caesar, or they would have sought us out. They will combine with the natives against us!"

"That hardly seems likely, since the Alligator People have evidently killed two of them."

"We aren't on the best of terms with the tribes at the moment, or I'd ride out to talk with them," Pompey pointed out. "True enough the skirmishing seems to have stopped for the moment, but that's probably just the season. The tribes have to prepare for winter, just as we do. They have to lay in food, cut wood."

"And probably a greater variety of food than we," Cicero complained. The Romans had taken advantage of the two great flocks of birds—Mijiji, Adsila called them—that had passed over, but the resulting winter diet was monotonous. Everyone was growing heartily sick of pigeon.

"The point is, in spring, we can look forward to more activity."

"And if they are being trained in warfare by Roman soldiers, we can look forward to a much greater competency in their warfare."

"That's what I'm afraid of, Consul."

"What is your recommendation, General?" Cicero wanted to know.

"For the moment? I do not see as we can do anything. Only my senior legates know anything about this, the men who saw the Romans have been told to keep quiet if they know what's good for them. I think they will. But it's only a matter of time before word gets out. I have mounted patrols out regularly; those men will be seen again."

"Announce it to your troops," Cato said. "Spread the word. Cicero and I will tell the Senate, and we'll have newsreaders announce it yet today. The secret won't stay kept, so best get it out in the open."

"As you wish," Pompey agreed.

"And General?"

"Consul Cicero?"

"Is it possible to step up patrols in that direction?"

"It is," Pompey agreed. "And I will order it done immediately."

In fact, when the next morning dawned bright, clear and cool, Gnaeus Pompey decided to lead a scouting party himself.

The young general had appropriated one of the stallions for his own use, a fine, large-boned animal with a deep brown coat. He ordered the animal saddled and selected five more men to accompany him on five more of the town's precious horses.

The scouting party left the town through the now-complete gates an hour after sunrise. General Pompey set the pace, urging his horse into an easy trot across the grassy hills, heading south by southwest, farther into the hills.

"Gladii and light armor only," Pompey had ordered the men. "Pack gear and rations for three days. Any of you with any skill at archery, bring bows for hunting. I propose to travel light and fast, cover a lot of ground and see what we can find out about these countrymen of ours."

Trotting at the head of the group, Gnaeus was enjoying the morning. Finally, he told himself, a chance to do something besides squat in that hut that passes for a headquarters, within the city walls. The morning was lovely; it was easy to forget the importance of the mission. The sun shone brightly from the east, and the sky was the most brilliant shade of blue Gnaeus had ever seen. What a marvelous land this is, he thought. What a nation we can build here, if we can just get through these first years.

A flock of great birds—turkeys, Adsila called them—flushed away from the patrol as they crossed a large meadow. Once the soldiers left the immediate area of Pompeius, they started seeing game; deer in the open areas, more turkeys, even quail. At midday the soldiers stopped for an hour near a large stream that was a known tributary to the Tiber, there to eat and rest the horses. While sitting in the grass chewing on a hard biscuit of ground maize and considering a strip of dried pigeon, Gnaeus noticed a large bird landing in a large tree overlooking the stream.

"An eagle," a nearby soldier noted. "Good omen, eh?"

"I've never seen an eagle like that before," another legionary said through a mouthful of biscuit.

Gnaeus examined the bird. It was dark, almost black, but its head and tail were a striking white. It watched the river from sharp yellow eyes behind a hooked yellow beak.

"Nor have you ever seen the great birds they call 'turkey,' Gnaeus chided the soldier, "or a deer with a white tail, or flocks of pigeons that blot out the sky. Why would you expect the eagles to be the same?"

"True enough, sir."

"Still, as you say, a good omen," Pompey the Younger opined. "Maybe the eagles of our new legions should have black bodies and white heads instead of being all gold. It's fitting, neh? A new symbol for a new land."

Break finished, the soldiers took to their horses and rode on.

The tributary's course upstream led them more or less west by southwest, the direction the young General wanted to go in any case, so they followed it for the sake of making the return trip easy to navigate. Gnaeus ordered flankers out to examine the countryside a mile or two to either side of their line of march, but nothing was seen the first day other than birds, trees and sky. Towards evening, a low meadow near the stream beckoned;

Gnaeus thought it looked to be a good place to spend the night. He held up a hand to stop the mounted men.

"We camp here," he announced. "Everyone stays together, near the stream. Sentries will be posted all night."

The men began to dismount. They unsaddled the horses, brushed them, and picketed them in the meadow to feed. The hungry animals immediately set to the tall, lush grass. After tending to their gear, the legionaries started fires to roast the venison they had taken earlier in the day.

Night fell quickly.

Gnaeus Pompey rolled up in his cloak near his own fire. The evening was growing chilly, but not as yet unpleasantly so.

He sat up suddenly. A bird of some sort was calling in the woods: *Tsuk-will-willow, tsuk will-willow*. Over and over again. Pompey listened, fascinated.

What a strange and magnificent place this is.

An A'Tep village

Four Bears only infrequently made the journey into the hills to visit the B'Kou's 'cousin' tribe, but the message received to request a council was too important to ignore.

He and three other B'Kou chiefs had made the journey to this village on this very day, arriving towards evening. The council convened just after the evening meal. Four Bears wished fervently that old Owl was there to lend the wisdom of his unfathomable years to the discussion; that wish was redoubled when he saw the malevolent shape of Man-Ready-For-War seated at the council fire, along with his two sons and two other Alligator warriors.

"We have allies," the Alligator warrior leader said without

preamble. He waved a hand over his head, and two figures Four Bears had not seen earlier came forward into the firelight.

One was tall, taller than any of the People Four Bears had ever seen, and built like a bull wapiti, broad-shouldered, thick-necked. His short hair was as black as that of the People, but his skin was pale. He announced his name. Four Bears muttered the strange syllables to himself, committing them to memory: "Loo-shus Vo-Renus."

The other man was short, almost as dark as one of the People, had barely-visible stubble of brown hair and—amazing! He had brown hair on the lower half of his face, across his upper lip and on both cheeks, running from in front of his ears down to cover his chin. Four Bears had never seen a Roman shave, and so had assumed their faces were normally beardless, like those of the People.

The short man also announced his name, and Four Bears repeated his mnemonic ritual: "Tie-tus Pool-Oh."

Both men wore the gold and brown of Romans, and both men had a stiff brush of red bristles running from ear to ear across the top of their strange headdress. Four Bears was alarmed to note that both were armed with the long steel weapons, the 'gladius.'

"These Romans," Man-Ready-For-War informed them, "are the enemies of the other Romans in their town to the north of here. Their chief was at war with Pom-Pey when they crossed the sea in the storm that blew even here. They came to find the other Romans and tell their chief where to look for them, so he could crush them in a great battle. We learned this after making war on them ourselves, thinking them to be of the same as the Romans to the north. They fought bravely and killed several of our warriors. Once we sought parley with them, we learned the truth."

"And that truth is that we approached them for parley, not you," a village chief of the A'Tep said softly. Man-Ready-For-War snarled at the A'Tep chief but did not challenge the statement.

"Pom-Pey is dead," White Oak informed them. "He died of swamp fever, months ago."

"It makes no difference. His son leads their army now. The chiefs that followed him are still here. They are still enemies of these men's great war chief, Caesar."

"What is this to us?" Four Bears asked.

"They are sworn enemies of Pom-Pey and all of those who came to our lands with him." He nodded to the shorter man, Pool-Oh, who was learning the language of the People. He spoke slowly, haltingly, but managed to be understood.

"We are of Rome," he said. He pointed north. "Pompey and his are of Rome. But we are enemies. Our war chief is the great Caesar. We are sworn to his service. He is sworn to destroy Pompey and all who follow him."

"So, you bring your war here, among us, who have done nothing to you," White Oak snapped. "Why should we not kill you all?"

"We can teach you," Pool-Oh said, "to fight them. To fight like Romans. We cannot make you these," he tapped his gladius in its sheath, "not because we are unwilling but because we do not know how." That last was not entirely true; Pullo knew of one man among their cavalry whose father had been a blacksmith, and who knew the basics of working iron. But who knew if there was any iron in this land to work? "We cannot make you weapons, but we can teach you to use the weapons you do have."

Four Bears pointed at Man-Ready-For-War. "His people are great warriors already." He saw White Oak nod; any warrior society man had to admit that, however unpleasant they were, the Alligator People knew how to fight. "Why do we need to learn your ways?"

Pool-Oh looked confused; his repertoire of the People's language was limited. Man-Ready-For-War answered instead.

"I have spoken with these men," he said. "Their strength is not only in their weapons of steel and bronze. They have discipline. We fight each of us alone, a man against a man here, another against another there." He motioned to either side of the fire as he spoke. He then clenched his two hands together into one hard fist. "But the Romans, they fight as one. All of their men fighting as one man, in a great, unbroken line they call a 'rank.'

"That is not how the People have ever fought," White Oak objected. "Neither yours nor ours. We and our cousins are hunters. When we have to go to war, we use our bows and our knowledge of the forest. When you Alligator People go to war, you use your great strength, your cunning, your courage, and most of all speed, to strike like lightning. It is too much to expect our warriors to stand up in lines and hack at others, especially when we have clubs of wood and knives of flint and they have shields and long knives of steel."

Titus Pullo looked sideways at his counterpart. "I think I'm getting the gist of what they are saying," he said softly in Latin. He glanced at Man-Ready-For-War, all too aware that the painted war chief was learning Latin as fast as Pullo was picking up their language—and Pullo was renowned in the Thirteenth for his facility with languages, due to his long service in Briton and Gaul.

When it came to languages, Pullo had accused Vorenus of being as 'thick as a Briton's skull,' and Vorenus had to admit the truth of it; he had no talent for picking up new tongues. "Well?" he snapped. "What are they saying?"

"Mostly arguing over whether they need us or not."

"Bugger their arguing." Vorenus pointed at an Alligator warrior nearly as tall as himself, who was seated silently by the fire. "Tell that man to stand up."

Pullo did so, interrupting the discussion. All heads turned to watch as Vorenus, with a flourish, unsheathed his sword and threw it on the ground in front of the warrior. "Now tell him to give me his club."

Pullo fumbled for the words, but the Alligator warrior seemed to get the idea. He unhooked his spiked war club and tossed it to the ground at Vorenus' feet.

Centurion Vorenus picked up the club and examined it briefly. He motioned to the other man, who picked up the gladius and held it cautiously in one hand.

"Now," the veteran of Briton and Gaul, the veteran of Alesia, the centurion of Rome, barked at his counterpart in Latin. "Tell him to attack me."

Pullo didn't get the chance. Man-Ready-For-War, his face split in a vicious grin, snapped one word. The savage dropped into a crouch.

Vorenus stood casually, watching the native warrior as he clutched the gladius clumsily in two hands. He turned his left side towards the savage, turning slowly but not moving from his place as the man began to cautiously circle.

Suddenly, with a screech, the savage sprang. He leaped directly over the fire; the gladius raised over his head in both hands. He intended a vicious, two-handed swipe downwards at the Roman's head, but...

Vorenus stepped quickly under the blow and smashed the butt end of the native war club into the man's gut. He spun as the man landed and drove an elbow into the savage's face, shattering his nose. The Alligator warrior fell to his knees, blood running over his mouth and chin. Vorenus kicked him to the ground and slammed one sandal on the wrist of the hand still holding the sword. He raised the club for a fatal blow…

…And then lowered it without striking. Reaching down, he hauled the dazed man to his feet. Only seconds had transpired, and the soldier of Rome had utterly, inarguably defeated a veteran warrior of the Alligator People.

"We know how to fight you," Vorenus snapped at the gaping natives. Pullo translated as best he could. "We have fought your kind before. But you have not fought our kind before. You have never, ever imagined our kind before."

He pointed at the Alligator warrior who was holding his nostrils shut, wincing in pain, trying to stop his nose bleeding. "If you fight Romans as you always have fought each other, you see what will happen. We can teach you how to fight Romans. Now you have seen that it is not the weapons that matter. It is the skill."

Pullo translated as best as he could, adding words of his own: "And if you help us defeat our enemies, the enemies of our chief Caesar, we will stay among you, help you against all of your enemies."

"We have no enemies here," Four Bears objected. He glanced warily at Man-Ready-For-War, who had his hard face on. "At least, no longer. There is no war among us."

"War will come again," Man-Ready-For-War snapped. "War always comes, and it will come to our children and our grandchildren as it has come to us, as it came to our fathers and our grandfathers. Our people have fought yours in the past, and even though we now live together as brothers"—Four Bears fought not to roll his eyes at the exaggeration, things between the tribes were at best tense—"one never knows when new people will arrive, from the sea, from the mountains, who knows? But do not tell me it cannot happen, Four Bears, when you have the proof of it sitting here at this fire."

"We have already learned much from the Romans," White Oak said. "B'Kou, A'Tep and Alligator People warriors have been learning from them how to counter Romans on the backs of their great beasts, their 'horses,' and how to deal with Romans in a line behind their shields. Vo-Renus and Pull-Oh and their men have much to teach us, and with their own horses, they can travel swiftly to discover what the other Romans are doing, where they are going and how many warriors are in any war party they send out."

"What if we fail?" Four Bears asked. "We should talk about that, too. No matter what new tricks we learn, there are many Romans in the town to the north. I have been in their town and seen. There are many soldiers, as many as fleas on the belly of a badger."

"How ever many they have, we have more," Man-Ready-For-War snapped.

Four Bears chose to ignore the outburst. "They all have swords of steel and the large red shields. If they can all fight like Vo-Renus, we should at least consider that we may not be able to beat them."

"The Alligator People have never been defeated in war," Man-Ready-For-War bragged, and Four Bears had to nod in agreement; the conflict between the fierce swamp-dwellers and the B'Kou had ended in a stalemate at best. "Our warriors will open their veins and die in honor before we will admit defeat."

Four Bears thought that to be very foolish indeed—And what will become of your women and children if you do? But he remained silent, his hard face set firmly in place.

"If we lose," White Oak said slowly, "I suppose we will have to come to some agreement on how to live together." As Man-Ready-For-War scowled in utter contempt, White Oak continued. "But the Romans must stop persuading our young women to live among them!"

Four Bears knew a sudden flash of insight then, one so stunning, so real, that he knew it must have been sent from the gods. "If we cannot defeat the Romans in battle," he said, doubting they could even as he spoke the words, "we will live among them, and them among us. Our peoples will become one. Their men will come to live in our villages, and our women in their town. We will each learn the other's ways. Is not that always the way when a war ends?"

"Not with us," another Alligator Warrior barked.

"The Alligator People's blood has never mixed with another tribe," Man-Ready-For-War agreed. "That is our strength."

Your pride is your weakness, Four Bears thought, *and it may yet bring down all of us.*

While the People argued, Lucius Vorenus and Titus Pullo stepped a few paces away from the fire to confer.

"They're wondering what to do if they fail," Pullo said.

"As well they should. There are probably at least two legions under Pompey the Younger, and they are soldiers of Rome just as we are. We are twelve men. Do you think we can teach these savages enough to defeat a Roman army? Brother, we may best be thinking of what to do ourselves if we fail. We can train them, but they are still savages with weapons of wood and bone, to stand against Roman steel. How many tribes of savages did we break in Gaul and Britain? And they were better equipped than these."

"We can hardly join the Pompeians now," Pullo mused.

"Of course not. They will consider us traitors to Rome."

"And from their viewpoint, they would have good reason to. The Pompeians have what remains of the Senate here. Cato and Cicero are with them; Cassius Longinus has been seen, and Marcus Junius Brutus, who Caesar loved as a son until his betrayal. In this place, they are sure and certain that they are Rome," Pullo pointed out, not knowing he was paraphrasing Cicero's speech to the Senate the summer before. "I doubt they will show much tolerance for anyone who has incited the natives against them, and brother, make no doubt, we are doing exactly that."

"So," Vorenus asked, "what do we do if these tribesmen lose a war to the Pompeians, with us among their warriors?"

Pullo frowned. "Only one thing we can do," he said. "If all else fails, play dead. Hide among the corpses until dark and then sneak away."

"And then?"

"Run," Pullo said. "The ocean lies east. The mountains are to the west. If we cross the mountains, we should be safe for some time, at least. Maybe we will even find civilized people there. So, we and our men run west, as though the very Furies themselves were after our arses."

Vorenus nodded in agreement. "Still," he said slowly, "let's hope it doesn't come to that."

Next morning

The two centurions gave their horses a rest and walked out of the A'Tep camp early the next day, with a party of Novans in tow, hoping to work more on massed archery attacks and begin training on siege tactics. Instead, at mid-morning they ended hiding in the edge of a thick patch of forest and watching as a party of six Roman cavalry proceeded at a walk up the creek bottom where they had been working.

"Look there," Pullo whispered. "General's helmet on that one."

"Pompey the Younger, perhaps?"

"Maybe." Pullo examined the column. Only light weapons. "We could charge them—we have twenty warriors with us."

"Not with them all a-horse and us on foot," Vorenus objected. "It would be a massacre. These savages, they aren't ready."

"What to do, then? Talk to them?"

Vorenus considered this. "They must know we are here in this new land. Those damned Alligator people did take two of our men's heads to a party of their soldiers as a threat, when we were still fighting our way through the swamps."

"What could it hurt?" On an impulse, Titus Pullo stepped out of the shade of the trees and stood in the brilliant morning sunlight. As the six Roman cavalrymen shouted and hallooed their horses to face him, Lucius Vorenus motioned for the A'Tep warriors with him to stay here, sighed and joined his comrade.

Pullo raised his hand and shouted. "Ho! Parley!"

Six Roman horses thundered up the slight, grassy rise from the creek and formed a half-circle around the two centurions.

"You men," the man in the black-plumed helmet barked. "I am General Gnaeus Pompey, commander of the Nova Roman legions. State your names and units at once."

By force of habit, both centurions saluted. "First Spear Centurion Titus Pullo, Thirteenth Gallic Legion," Pullo barked.

"Centurion Lucius Vorenus, also Thirteenth, sir," Vorenus said, his voice not as enthusiastic. "Caesar's Thirteenth," he added.

"Caesar's men," Pompey accused.

"We are, sir," Pullo agreed calmly. "I'll not lie to you about it."

"What are you doing here?"

"Out for a walk with our friends, sir."

Pompey the Younger removed his helmet and rubbed his hand through his close-cropped hair. "Friends? Unlikely the two of you should have any, I would think. Where are these friends of yours?"

"In the trees, watching," Pullo said. "At least twenty of them. Good big lads, too."

"Natives?"

"Some native, some Roman," Vorenus lied. All of their Roman troops that remained, along with the surviving sailors, were back at the camp. "Ten more cavalrymen. Maybe a dozen natives." Lies, all lies; Pullo and Vorenus were running a bluff the size of the Tarpeian rock.

It was working. General Pompey looked into the trees, and for a moment looked just a bit uncertain. His eyes, his expression, his body language, all spoke eloquently of his conclusion: Stand-off.

"I don't suppose," he said slowly, "it would do any good to order you men to return to Pompeius with us."

"Pompeius, sir?" Pullo evaded.

"Our town," the general said. "Named for my father."

The two centurions hesitated. All of their training, all of their instincts, all of their inclinations had been hammered into them during years as soldiers of Rome. That training and those instincts shouted at them now, *Obey this man!*

But there was another loyalty, a stronger loyalty. Their loyalty to their own General, the man that had spoken personally to them, rewarded them for their bravery, held them up as examples before their peers, and trusted them on this mission. Their loyalty to Rome was strong, but their loyalty to that man was stronger.

His image was never far from their minds. *Caesar.*

"Sorry, sir," Pullo said. "But we're Caesar's men. Sworn to him and him alone."

Beside him, Vorenus nodded.

Pompey scowled at them. "You realize that if you are taken in arms against us, you will be executed as traitors." He waved to the north. "Rome is here; and is watching you. We have a Senate now. We have two duly elected Consuls. We will be building a new Republic here. What does your loyalty to Caesar mean now? You will never lay eyes on him again. You will never lay eyes on Rome, or Italy, or Europe again. None of us will. This new world, this is where we have to plan our lives now. If this is the path you choose, then you choose a life as hunted men, living among savages for all your days. Not only for you, mind you, but for any Roman men who follow you."

"Understood, sir."

"And your decision stands?"

The two centurions looked at each other for a long moment.

"It does, sir," Pullo said at last.

"You should at least give your men the option we gave you."

"There are some men from the crew of the ship that brought us here," Vorenus admitted. "The natives will know where your town is. We will give the sailors the option to join you, and we propose a complete truce of..." he thought for a moment, "...five days for any who so choose to make their way to you. The soldiers that came with us are all Caesar's men as well. They will stay."

"Very well," Pompey snapped. He looked at the two centurions. "Will you accept some advice?"

"We'll listen, sir," Pullo said. "I won't promise to agree with it."

"Run," the young General leaned forward in his saddle and snarled the words at them. "Run, as fast and as far as you can, and take your fellow minions of Caesar with you. We have two full legions in Pompeius. You and a rabble of savages, you don't stand a chance."

"Noted, sir," Pullo said, his face a mask of stone.

Pompey gave the two a final sneer and pulled his horse around. "Come on," he ordered the five men with him. "Back to Pompeius. We've learned what we came here to learn."

As the six Romans galloped away, Titus Pullo and Lucius Vorenus watched them go. "Well," Vorenus said, "we're in for it now."

"Better forget the training for the day. We should head back, tell those squabbling chiefs to call another council." He nodded towards the six horsemen thundering away down the stream. "That boy general and his legions, sooner or later, they'll be coming after us, sure as the sunrise."

"Best we get after them first, maybe," Vorenus suggested. "One good thing; at least we'll have a chance to get rid of those whining sailors. They wouldn't have fought for us any road. Let Pompey Minor and his lot feed their worthless arses."

"Five days," Pullo mused. "We have five days grace. What can we do with those five days?"

"Plan," Vorenus said. "Train. Make ready whatever weapons we still have." He looked at the sky. "Best if we can avoid any serious fighting until spring, really. They natives aren't anxious to go to war now with winter coming on, at least aside from that crocodile-skin wearing lot, and it would give us more time to get the Novans ready to do the bulk of the fighting."

"The Novans?"

"Of course. A trained Roman cavalryman and his horse are worth twenty of these savages. We'll hold our men until the right moment."

"Good thinking," Pullo agreed. "Let's get back to the village. We've got a war to prepare for."

Part Two
The Novan War

CHAPTER SEVEN
CASUS BELLI

The first winter passed with little martial activity on either side of the conflict. The Novan tradition was similar to the Roman in deferring most military activities until spring, so as the army of Nova Roma went into a winter camp in the town Pompeius, so the Novans went into their villages for the winter.

Fortunately for all in Pompeius the winter in that country proved mild, with cold nights and wet days, but little in the way of snow or freezing temperatures. Food was scarce but there was enough to prevent outright starvation, thanks in no small part to the passage of great flocks of the pigeon the Novans call Mijiji.

Come the spring, martial activity resumed, as General Pompey expected it would. Even as the Novans resumed their harassment and raiding of Roman expeditions, General Pompey ordered a series of distractions to draw the attention of the native warriors away from the town itself. This provided opportunities in several areas: To gain greater access to provisions for

Roman forces while denying them to the Novan soldiers, and to better define the locations of Novan villages. It was during this time that General Pompey also discovered the presence of a reluctant ally among the Novans.

—From Gnaeus Pompey Novus' New World Diaries

Pompeius

The damp, cold winter passed slowly. No snow fell on Pompeius, but it rained, turning the town's paths into freezing mud. Hard frosts turned the churned-up mud into rutted earth hard as iron, making walking easier until the day warmed enough to melt the top layer of mud, resulting in a sort of slime of mud over frozen earth—a recipe for a fall. "It's like walking on a greased tile floor," Titus Caninus was heard to complain. Between bouts of rain, though, were some of the most beautiful, cool, clear days any of the Romans had ever seen, with mild breezes blowing over the town under skies of the most incredible deep blue.

Thirty-one sailors from the ship that had brought Caesar's men to the new world had approached Pompeius to beg asylum, which was granted. From them Gnaeus Pompey learned the true strength of the Roman soldiers in league with the Novans. "Fewer than a dozen cavalry," he reported to the Senate, "which doesn't worry me. What does worry me is what the natives are learning from them." The sailors were, for the most part, assigned to help refit and restore the few remaining Roman ships on the Tiber and at Pulcia.

Between the barrels of salted-down pigeons and fish from both the Tiber and from Pulcia, the people often went hungry but did not starve. Robes hung loose, and bellies grumbled, but that was the worst of it. The town now had several public wells for clean water, and plenty of firewood was at hand, so the Roman standards of cleanliness were met, and the people slept in reasonable comfort, near their hearths.

Clothing was beginning to be a problem. Rudely cured leather from deer and wapiti was growing more common as wraps, and the Senators' white togas were looking distinctly the worse for wear. Adsila assured her brother and adopted mother that there was a plant that grew far to the south, in a large peninsula that projected into the sea. This plant bore large white balls of fluff that the people in that region wove into cloth. "It sounds like a species of Egyptian cotton," Cato commented after hearing a description of the plant. "We'll want to see if we can arrange trade for it, as soon as we can. Maybe get some seed."

"Presuming the natives allow us to establish any trade routes," Pompey the Younger said. He had a point; the most vicious of the Novan tribes lay to the south of Pulcia. "There is that other plant in the area, a species of hemp. We've been making rope with it. I imagine we could make cloth from it. It would make a rough cloth, maybe good enough for tents, bags, cloaks, that sort of thing." He laughed. "Adsila says the Novans call it mokono, and they smoke it. It makes them see visions." He fluttered his fingers in front of his face derisively.

At least the city itself was taking shape. At present it was really no more than a middling-sized town, but the great meadows around the four hills offered plenty of room for growth. The Senate building and the Forum occupied the tallest hill around which the town was built. Main avenues ran to the four directions from the open Forum, one to each of the primary points of the compass. Narrower streets ran in a circular pattern outward so that the layout of the town rather resembled a great spider web. A stout wall of earthworks surmounted by a palisade of oak trunks twelve feet high surrounded the town, with the town's sole gate facing north towards the Tiber. The soldier's barracks lay at the edge, just inside the wall, and in the ring-streets lay the few shops, private dwellings, and other buildings that were starting to spring up.

The "villas"—small houses, really—of General Pompey and the Senators lay closest to the Senate.

Brutus's plans for expansion resided now in the Senate building. In the future, similar webs would grow on the remaining three hills, linked to the first by open avenues and parks. In time, Pompeius promised to be a city of some note. "Fitting," Cicero noted, "being the new Rome, as it were."

Through the winter and spring there had been no more visits from the Novans in the region, and nothing more was seen of the renegade Roman soldiers that were among them. The time passed, slowly, monotonously, but it passed.

It was five days short of the first anniversary of their landing in the New World that the monotony of the past months was suddenly and startlingly ended.

Pulcia

It was the final hour before dawn on a cool, foggy morning in the harbor. The sole sentry in the fort's tower was alternatively yawning and shivering. Visibility was poor. Most of the hundred Roman troops were sound asleep in their barracks.

Six native dugouts approached the island from the west, the Alligator warriors in them paddling hard in the pre-dawn light. Six more approached swiftly from the east, darting out of the river mouth into the harbor. The light, fast boats moved noiselessly—

almost. The slight splash of paddles was enough to alert the lone Roman sentry.

"To arms!" the legionary shouted. "To arms!"

Tribune Marcus Lucanus leaped up from the narrow pallet in the tent he called his own. "To the walls!" he ordered. Around him, legionaries were struggling into armor, pulling on sandals, seizing weapons and shields.

Marcus Lucanus had planned his defense carefully. He knew there were Roman renegades advising the Novans, but he also knew the island was too far from any part of the mainland for any Roman siege weapon to reach. No, the Novans had to land on the island and assault their works directly; Lucanus had planned a few surprises for them.

The walls of the outpost were ten feet high and thick, but they were wood. The Novans approaching from the east drew up to the walls where they came almost to the water's edge and hurled three large clay pots full of bear fat rendered into oil with slow-burning wicks attached. The handmade firebombs shattered, setting the eastern wall ablaze.

Lucanus had expected the use of fire. Buckets of water and sand were at hand, and the legionaries on the east wall were able to douse the flames, and archers on the wall killed two and wounded several more of the natives as they tried to withdraw.

Still, the feint was successful. The approach from seaward enabled the other natives to come ashore west of the fort, just out of archery range.

But not out of range of Lucanus' surprise.

Optio Flavius Petrocidius had taken charge of building the devices, and also for training the men in their use. They had practiced extensively, anticipating an attack from the long western approach. "Target range three hundred!" he shouted. "Come on, you lazy scum, load those things up. Ready, now—loose!"

Two small trebuchets flung forward, each lofting a two-hundred-pound load of loose rocks. Petrocidius had used trebuchet in Greece and longed for ceramic jugs of burning oil to loft at the foes, but for now, rocks would have to do. The trajectory was perfect. The loads of fist-to-head-sized cobbles rained down on the Novans, breaking heads, smashing arms, battering the native warriors to the ground.

Even so, the Novan's alligator-skin armor offered some protection. Even more so:

"They have scuta!" A legionary on the wall shouted. Some of the natives had managed a crude testudo formation with their clumsy wooden shields, but now that the rocks had stopped falling, the natives formed up behind the big wooden barriers and started to resolutely march forward.

Tribune Lucanus had mounted the guard tower, the better to see and direct the defense. "Sons of Dis," he muttered. "They do have Roman renegades teaching them." He gauged the rate of their advance. "There won't be time to reload," he shouted at Petrocidius. "Everyone to the wall!"

Uncharacteristically, the Alligator People had made one critical mistake. Attacking as they were from the west, the early morning sun was in their eyes, and at the same time, illuminated them perfectly for the Roman archers on the wall.

"Hold," Lucanus called. "Let them get in good and close," he ordered. He had his reasons.

At the rear of the Novan formation, several natives where carrying long poles with notches cut into them. On the wall, Optio

Petrocidius saw them. "Those ones with the scaling ladders," he ordered the archers near him. "Take aim at them and stand ready."

The natives came closer under good discipline, their rude wooden scuta up, stepping forward in four solid ranks. They had no gladii, but their wooden war clubs and a few spears were visible.

Five archers drew their heavy bows, sighted along the arrow shafts and waited.

The first rank of Novan warriors stepped forward, as they had been taught. Stepped again. They felt the ground shake oddly under their feet, but before they could react, they stepped again. The second rank stepped forward behind them.

The ground gave way. Two ranks of Alligator warriors were pitched screaming into a long, rectangular pit, landing on rows of sharpened stakes in the bottom.

"Loose!" Petrocidius shouted. The archers released their arrows, striking down the warriors bearing the long poles. The remaining Alligator warriors withdrew to their boats in some confusion and disarray. After a few moments milling around out of archery range, they got back in their boats and withdrew, to the sound of cheers and derisive hooting from the Roman palisade.

"Don't get too happy, boys," Marcus Lucanus warned his men. "They'll be back. And they won't be that stupid twice."

To the west

"That could have gone better." As much as Lucius Vorenus had any sense of humor, it seemed to consist of deliberate understatement.

Vorenus, Titus Pullo and the Alligator People chief Man-Ready-For-War stood on a small rise overlooking the harbor, watching the boats returning. They had seen only some of the action, but they had seen enough to know the outcome.

"Good trick with that pit, though," Pullo observed. "Whoever's in charge there, he's a clever sort."

"They won't try the same thing twice," Vorenus warned.

"That does not matter," Man-Ready-For-War said. He was strangely calm, considering the defeat his warriors had just been handed. "It is as you said. We try a small attack on the fort here, and now we see how they will defend their town there." He pointed west. "So, it was worth those few men. They were not among my best anyway."

"Cold-blooded little shit, isn't he?" Pullo commented softly in Latin, hoping the savage chief had not yet picked up too much of that language. He was afraid he underestimated the man's language skills; Man-Ready-For-War turned his black-painted face towards Pullo, and his face split in a savage grin, revealing sharpened yellow teeth.

"War is killing," he said. "Sometimes the enemy kills yours. Sometimes you kill theirs. In the end it is who kills most who wins."

"You should have seen Gaul."

"You have talked about 'Gaul.' I am not worried about Gaul. I am worried about here, and now."

"Well, that's not a bad attitude to have," Pullo had to agree. "Come on—let's get back to camp. We have to plan our next move."

Pompeius

Lines of communication between Pulcia and Pompeius were complicated and slow, but they existed. Within a few days, word of the battle reached General Pompey in his headquarters.

"It was a probe," he reported to the Consuls the day the

message came in. Three horsemen were establishing a regular path between Senator Brutus' salt-making party on the coast, Pulcia and the capital.

"A probe?"

"Indeed, Consul," Pompey answered Cato. He had found the Consuls seated in the Senate chamber, just the two of them for the moment, discussing farming. "They were testing our defenses, just as they've been doing up here with raids on our hunting and fishing parties. That pit with the sharpened stakes, that was a trick worthy of a Gaul; I have to give credit to Lucanus for that, although I suspect the idea came from that nasty-minded Optio down there with him. Petrocidius is an old veteran, and he's half-Briton, you know. He's fought this kind of war before. The Celts in the northern regions of that island are far more vicious than anything this new world has produced."

"In time, we'll have to stop thinking in terms of half-Roman, and all that," Cicero pointed out. "In a few generations, everyone here will be at least half Novan, probably more so."

Pompey waved it away. "Old habits, Consul, they die hard. And in any case, that won't matter, as long as the standards of Rome hold up. As you yourself pointed out, it's the laws and traditions that make Rome, not what her people look like."

"What we're going to look like is hungry," Cato said, "unless we can get our crops in. We have plenty of maize to plant along with our wheat and barley, but we have to be able to protect it."

"Plant your grain," Pompey said. "We'll protect it."

"How do you propose to react to the attack on Pulcia?"

"I would like to send a full cohort to reinforce Lucanus down there, but that fort he has built is crowded just with the century he has in place, and frankly I don't have a cohort to spare. Still, he's in a good position. Easily defended and hard to approach. I'm more worried about Senator Brutus' salt-making party down on the coast by the landing site. I think we should recall them, and quickly. They are exposed to attack, and we have enough salt for the time being."

"I agree," Cato said. "Can you spare a few cavalrymen to take the order and escort them back?"

"Yes, of course," Pompey agreed. "And, speaking of which, you both will be pleased to know that as of last night we have another healthy foal born to one of our mares. It will take a while, but in time we'll have more horses for farming as well as the cavalry."

"Oxen would be better for farm work, but I don't see any hereabouts." Cato rubbed a slim hand though his thinning hair. "What other plans have you, General? We're getting into spring, and as I recall you expected the Novans to pick up their activity."

"Adsila tells me spring and summer are their traditional times for war," Pompey agreed. "With Pullo and Vorenus out there somewhere whispering in their ears, I'm not sure how much we can count on them holding to their traditions, but they have in at least that much. But I remind you, we do not do much campaigning in winter ourselves."

He looked thoughtful for a moment.

"We already have seen some of the results of that whispering. Lucanus's report stated that they had made crude scuta of wood and advanced in a fairly orderly line of battle behind them. Still no evidence of any weapons of steel or even bronze. They just don't have the skills for it, and odds are long against anyone in the small group of cavalry those two centurions are leading knowing how to make iron."

"You think Pullo and Vorenus are giving them bad advice?"

"Oh, I doubt that. From what I know of them, they are brave and competent men. Back when my father was still on good terms with Caesar, he used to read reports from Gaul. Caesar mentioned those two by name on more than one occasion. He praised their bravery, and it seems their loyalty is noteworthy, too—their loyalty to Caesar, that is."

"No, I think they are giving good advice, I just don't think these natives can do all that much with it. Roman tactics depend on Roman arms. Without steel for gladii and pila, those savages are still disadvantaged in any direct conflict with us. Pullo and Vorenus' training and advice will help, but I doubt it will be enough."

Cicero had a flash of insight: "What would you do, were you in their situation?"

"Raid. Harass. Make myself a bloody damned nuisance wherever and whenever I could. Attack anyone who left the vicinity of the city to hunt or fish. In other words, I would do just as they are doing now."

"I fail to see how you could win a war that way," Cato said.

"You can't. If we were an expedition, you might make it painful enough to get us to withdraw. But we aren't here by choice, and we have no place to withdraw to. Like it or not, we're here to stay."

"So, you don't think they can win?"

"They can't. But we can still lose. I'm going to see that we don't."

"How?" Cicero wanted to know.

"I have a few plans," Pompey grinned, a nasty grin that challenged the most vicious native in savagery. "We have to make them react to us, not the other way around. So, I'm planning, yes. My plans, they have to do with what you two Consuls were discussing when I found you."

"Food?"

"Indeed," Pompey said. "Food. An army runs on its stomach, Consul, and with our cavalry and our march discipline, we can make things very lean for them. We move faster than they do, you see." He stood up. "I plan to deprive them of provisions, and then run their arses ragged chasing my legions around. Then we'll see what tune they sing."

"Things will be very lean for us, if we don't find more sources of food," Cicero said.

Cato looked at his fellow Consul. "You know I agree with you. It would be so much easier if the Novans weren't so hostile. I had entertained hopes, you know... that Four Bears, he seemed a stable, sensible sort. I can't believe he'd have any part of this."

"Spring is coming. I don't know about larger animals, but a few of the farmers among us will be trying to gather and hatch eggs of the local ducks, the large ones with green heads, and also eggs of the turkeys, to hatch them as well. I gather that's a way to start on domesticating them; a newly hatched chick will take the first creature it sees for its mother."

"Juno knows we can't feed this mob by hunting and gathering from the forest," Cato agreed. "We need domestic animals and grain. We need farmers and drovers, fishermen, herds of cattle and fields of grain. We can't go on like we are now, not if we intend to build a city here."

"Adsila says that the Mijiji may be back in the spring. Also, across the mountains to the west, she says she has heard stories of open plains populated by great, shaggy beasts, something like an ox or a bison. Perhaps we can get our hands on some of those in time, raise them like cattle?"

"Perhaps. I know a couple of the men here with some farming experience have tried capturing the local deer, but they are apparently too high-strung to survive well in captivity. Besides, Cicero, trade routes through the mountains, that's some time off yet, I think. And who knows if we'll be able to tame these bison, if that's what they are? Bison in Europe have never been kept as stock, as far as I know."

"All this talk will come to naught, you know, unless our young general succeeds in winning this conflict," Cicero said sourly.

"Yes," Cato agreed. "At this point, everything depends on that."

Cicero leaned forward and peered at Pompey the Younger. "Can you do it?"

"Of course."

"You sound very confident," Cato's tone was sour.

"I am fairly confident. If I learned nothing else from my father, I learned that war is fickle and unpredictable. And in truth, I would like another five legions under arms, and five hundred horse. But we must make do with what we have. And what we have, Consuls, is steel. These Novans have tools of stone and wood. They are vicious, but undisciplined. Like their stone knives, they are hard but brittle. We have steel, Consuls; swords of steel and men of steel. As you said yourself, friend Cicero, we are Rome. We will prevail. Even as we did in Africa and Greece, in Carthage and Gaul, we will prevail."

Four Bears' village

Old Owl condemned the actions, stating flatly that 'young men with more balls than brains' should not be risking the tribes' welfare by starting a war. He refused to offer advice or participate in any planning, and refused to even acknowledge the Romans that had allied themselves to the People.

Man-Ready-For-War and the two Roman leaders had described the fight at the Roman fort in the harbor, near the border of the B'Kou and Alligator territories. Four Bears was shaking his head by the time the description ended.

"How many young men of the Alligator People were lost?" he asked.

Man-Ready-For-War ignored the question, but the shorter of the two Roman leaders, Pull-Oh, understood the People's language fairly well by now. "Thirty-one," he answered.

Four Bears knew that the Alligator People could, if they gathered the entire tribe, field maybe five thousand armed and trained warriors. Between the B'Kou and A'Tep, maybe six thousand more. Pull-Oh estimated there were two or three thousand Romans capable of bearing arms, so the numbers were on the side of the People.

But the Romans have steel, Four Bears reminded himself. And the Romans had unity and discipline, too. Among the People, gathering an entire tribe was seldom possible. Even Pullo and Vorenus, who had lived among them for some months now, did not seem to understand that a village chief or war chief could not simply issue orders; they could only advise or persuade, but each man was free to follow his own wishes.

Four Bears had seen the way the handful of Roman soldiers jumped to Pullo and Vorenus's orders and knew that warriors of the People would seldom be so obedient.

Leaders did emerge among the People, though, especially in times of crisis. Four Bears knew that he was a primary chief among the B'Kou, but he was not a war chief. His cousin White Oak of the A'Tep was taking that role now, and more young men were joining the Red Blanket warrior society that White Oak led, making him in effect the war chief for the B'Kou and the A'Tep for the time being.

And Man-Ready-For-War, of course, held that position among the Alligator People.

Four Bears had never trusted the Alligator People. His father had given up an eye fighting them, and in Four Bears' youth there had still been fighting along the border with the lands claimed by the warlike tribe. For the last five years, there had been a cautious peace. Four Bears knew this was due as much to weariness with fighting as anything else.

But Man-Ready-For-War and his people were again growing restless, and they had a new enemy in sight. Four Bears knew the bitter taste of despair. In their thirst for war, the Alligator People threatened to set the forests afire, and Four Bears knew he was impotent to stop them.

Slowly, he got up and slipped away from the council. No one noticed or tried to get in his way.

Pulcia

Tribune Marcus Lucanus saw the rider approach the beach. The small boat from the fort landed near him. As soon as the messenger was able, he kicked his horse forward, fetlock-deep into the water. He tossed a small packet into the boat, pulled his horse about and galloped away up the beach. In the morning, he would return to take the packet back. Nobody knew where he passed the night, and Lucanus knew if the man was smart, he would never do so in the same place twice.

But the Roman army had a long history of clever messengers,

able to carry dispatches long distances through hostile country. Lucanus wasn't overly worried about the man's neck. No, the tribune commanding the fort at Pulcia was more interested in discovering what was in the packet that even now was being rowed back to the fort.

He unrolled the single scroll in the packet and was not surprised to see General Pompey's handwriting.

> Reinforcements are not possible at this time.
> You are ordered to retain men to hold the fort at
> Pulcia while sending your trireme south along
> the coast, as soon as possible, weather permitting.
> Make a show of investigating possible harbors and
> landing sites along that coast. Map the coast as you
> go and make no effort to pass unnoticed.
> - Gen G. Pompey

"Now, what has that boy got in mind?" Lucanus wondered. "A feint? A distraction? An indirect approach? Whatever it is, I hope it makes sense to someone."

He shouted for the man that was temporarily assigned as trierarch for the ship, which was pulled up on the beach at the moment. "Make ready the ship and select a dozen oarsmen," he told the man. "It seems General Pompey has a job for you."

The trireme set out the following morning. When the winds were favorable it used its sail; when they were not, the oarsman rowed it slowly along the coast. When they encountered a river they proceeded slowly, cautiously upstream for a few leagues, and then returned to the sea. The men slept on the ship, taking care to anchor well away from the shore at night. On several occasions they observed black-painted Novans watching from the beach and once, as they came into a small inlet, arrows arched out of the trees, landing in and around the ship. One oarsman was lightly struck, a stone arrowhead scoring a track along the outside of his leg. The legionary laughed the wound off, wrapped his leg in a clean cloth and went back to rowing.

They went south along the coast for four days, mapping several large rivers and another large harbor, before setting out north for the return to Pulcia, wondering what the whole thing had been about.

A camp west of Pulcia

"The time for talk is over," Man-Ready-For-War had announced, and so the combined warriors of the Alligator People, the B'Kou and the A'Tep began to slowly move east and north, planning as they went. A runner from the Alligator People villages in the south reached them as they made camp on the second night.

"The southern towns will not send all of their men," the runner reported.

"What? Why not?" Man-Ready-For-War barked. "I am war chief, not those tired old women! I called the warrior society men out, who are they to tell them to stay home?"

"They say there are Roman ships along the coast. Their warriors are needed to defend their villages from the men on the ships."

"More Romans?" Man-Ready-For-War's eyes grew large. He shouted for his Roman allies and was relieved when Titus Pullo appeared; he spoke better than the other.

"This man," Man-Ready-For-War pointed at the messenger, "says there are more ships full of Romans landing on the coast to the south."

Pullo's brow creased into a worried frown. "More Romans?" His mind raced. More Pompeians? Not bloody likely. There's been no new storm, not that we've seen. Nobody, whether Caesar commanded it or not, would be insane enough to try that crossing if they had any choice. Who could they be?

"How many ships were seen?"

The messenger didn't know for sure. He described the reports he was given. Only one ship had been seen, but in several places. No one knew if it was the same ship.

"That could have been one ship working along the coast," Pullo told Man-Ready-For-War. "Pompey, he's the war chief for the Romans, he could have sent that ship out to look at the coast."

"Why?"

Pullo thought about the possibilities. None of them seemed good. "He may be looking for rivers that will allow more ships upstream to land soldiers to our south. He may be looking for places along the coast to put soldiers ashore. He may be looking for villages along the shore he can attack." Any of the options seemed to present a very real danger of enemy troops in their rear, which bothered Pullo more than he cared to admit—especially if the troops were Roman legionaries.

"We have the men still watching the fort in the harbor," Pullo said. "They could move south, to protect the coast." He knew Man-Ready-For-War had held several hundred warriors in the area around the harbor, ready to strike the fort. "Those men in the fort aren't going anywhere. There aren't enough of them to come ashore and fight anyone without the walls of their fort to hide behind."

The logic appealed to Man-Ready-For-War. "Yes," he agreed. He turned to the runner. "Go to the upper reaches of the northern arm of the great bay. You will find a camp of Alligator soldiers there. Tell them to go south along the coast until they find this ship, to attack and destroy it. Then go to the villages in the south and tell them I want all of the warrior society men to come north to help us make war against the Romans."

"I will," the messenger agreed, and hurried off.

A group of savages attacking a Roman warship? That will be a mistake, Pullo thought. He had something of a gift for understatement himself.

South of Pulcia harbor

Coming north, the Roman trireme met the freighter *Neptune*, coming south.

"What ho?" the warship's trierarch shouted at the freighter captain.

"Giving the Novans something else to worry about," the freighter captain Quintus Pulcio shouted back, a broad grin on his face.

Pompeius

"Who?" Gnaeus Pompey demanded of the sentry. He sat up in his bed, rubbing his eyes. "It's the middle of the night, this better be important." Beside him, his wife slept on.

"That Novan chief, Four Bears, the one that was here before, sir." The sentry was whispering. "Sorry about the time, sir, but the man just showed up at the gate. We never saw him coming in—like a bloody ghost, he is."

"Give me a moment." The sentry ducked out. Pompey struggled sleepily into his uniform and, after a moment's thought, belted on his gladius and sat his black-plumed helmet on his head.

He poked his head in the room where his sister slept. "Adsila," he called softly, until he saw the girl's eyes open. "Little sister, I'm sorry, but I need your help. Please get dressed and meet me outside." The girl nodded and reached for a wrap.

Outside, the sentry was waiting, holding a guttering torch. Around them, the town slept on. A bird called somewhere outside the walls, and Pompey noted a bat flitting overhead. After a few moments, Adsila came out, dressed in a Roman robe and sandals, and wrapped in a heavy red blanket. "All right," he told the legionary. "Take us to him."

They walked through the sleeping town to the front gate. The other sentry on watch climbed down from the wall and helped the first open the gate enough for the general and his adopted sister to slip through. "Close it behind us," Pompey said. "Don't open it until I say."

"Yes sir," the man said, and softly closed the gate.

Pompey looked at the Novan chief, who stood calmly. He was dressed in a wapiti-skin cloak and heavy leggings against the chill and had the skin of a wolf wrapped around his shoulders. "You know," he told the man, "if it was any other Novan out here besides you, I'd have ordered the soldiers to run him through." Adsila softly translated, and Four Bears surprised Pompey by answering in broken Latin—learned from Vorenus and Pullo, obviously, Pompey thought. The man's Latin had an odd lilt to it–not quite an accent, more like a peculiar speech mannerism that Pompey couldn't quite classify.

"I was your father's friend. I hope you be-lieve that. I am here as your friend, also."

"We'll see." Pompey said. "What do you want?"

"I want to talk to you about the folly of young men," Four Bears went on in his own language—he trusted Adsila's translating more than his own shaky command of Latin. "We are not one people, and even among my own tribe we are not all of us of one mind."

"Go on," Pompey said when Adsila finished translating.

"To the south are the Alligator People, who have sought to lead the rest of the People into war. Some of the young men and warrior society men are listening to them. Not all of us are. I want to talk to you about the rest of us."

"Are you asking for shelter for the rest of your people?" The negotiations suddenly struck Pompey as odd, with the soft, feminine voice of his adopted sister injected between the voices of men.

"No," Four Bears said. "No one knows I am here. The warrior society men would be very angry if they knew I came to talk to you."

"I'm sure they would," Pompey agreed.

"The People are not like you Romans," Four Bears said. "We have chiefs, but a chief does not command, as you do with your soldiers. A chief is only as good as his advice. If he gives good advice, wise advice, people listen. If he does not, they do not listen."

"But not this time," Pompey offered.

"Every man among the People is free to do as he thinks best," Four Bears said. "You know that some young women of the People have looked on your soldiers and found them exciting. That has angered some of our young men, and the Alligator People's war chief has used that to inflame them."

"I admit, I wasn't very happy about it myself," Pompey said. "But I suppose that's easy enough for me to criticize; my own wife survived the trip and is here with me now. Young men and young women will always seek each other out; I see no way to stop it."

"I do not, either, in truth," Four Bears said.

"So, your advice?"

"There will be war between us," Four Bears began.

"There already is war between us," Pompey pointed out. "And it was not we Romans that started it. The only reason I am here at all is because my father trusted you."

"And I, him," Four Bears nodded. "He was a good man, an honest man. I grieve for him still. I hope you believe I am honest too. I hope you will listen when I say you should make war only against the warriors."

"Explain?"

"When this war is over—and I believe you will win, Pompey—your people and mine will live together. We will be one people in time. But if you make war on the women and children of the People, there will be generations of anger, of fear, of mistrust."

"I think," Pompey said, "I'm following you."

"All of the People know that Man-Ready-For-War, war chief of the Alligator People, is inciting the young men against you."

"So, the Alligator People are the real problem here?"

"They have been a problem since my grandfather's time, and even before that."

"I may have to go into the towns," Pompey said. "But I will control the men. We will burn but not kill. Will that be sufficient?"

"It will have to do," Four Bears said.

"Where is Man-Ready-For-War now?" Pompey asked.

Four Bears stared at him. "I am not yet altogether a traitor to my people. I will not tell you precisely where he is. I will tell you he is not close at hand." Four Bears suddenly chuckled. "He is very worried about Roman ships on the coast, far to the south. I will tell you that."

Pompey laughed. "Good," he said. "I'm glad to hear that."

Four Bears looked at him keenly for a moment. He surprised Pompey by holding his right hand out, open. Pompey took the hand and shook. When that was done, Four Bears nodded, turned, and disappeared into the night.

"Come on, little sister," Pompey put his arm around the adopted Novan girl. "I apologize for waking you up, but you see now it was necessary."

"Four Bears is a good man," Adsila said. "I am glad you listened to him. I hope he can help bring peace between our peoples."

Pompey rapped his knuckles on the gate and called for the guard to open up. As the door creaked open, he looked at the girl. "You are a Roman now, little sister. Father adopted you as our law allows him to."

"I am Roman," Adsila said, "and a citizen, as Mother explained. But I am also a Novan. My heart belongs to both people. I hope Four Bears is right. I hope both peoples will soon be one. Then my heart will always be in one place." She clasped her hands together in front of her chest and smiled at the general. "One place—here, in the town named for our father. Do you know, he was the only father I've ever known?" She laid a slim hand on the general's arm and smiled. "And you, the only brother. My father died fighting the Alligator People before I was born. My mother died giving birth to me. I was a useless orphan girl and among the People, no one has a lower status than that. You can see why I have a special appreciation for the ways of Rome, and for the love our mother has shown me."

I will end this was, I will bring our people together–I will make that happen, Pompey silently promised her. *I will do it for you, for our father, for the future of Rome here in the new world and yes—for Four Bears, too.*

The next morning, Pompey's wife Claudia and his stepmother Cornelia looked him over when he came out into their house's tiny courtyard for a lean breakfast of salted pigeon and maize cakes.

"Adsila is still asleep," Claudia said.

"Not surprising." Pompey yawned. "We had a visitor last night. That Novan chief, Four Bears. I needed her to translate."

"Four Bears," Cornelia almost spat the words. Pompey Magnus had liked Four Bears, but Cornelia Metalla, Pompey Magnus's widow, found it hard to forgive the man for (as she thought of it) abandoning an orphan girl to their care.

"He talks sense," Pompey the Younger said. He sat down on a rude bench near the low table, took a chunk of maize cake and regarded it with some distaste. "He wanted to let us know he didn't want this war between our people."

"What does he want?" Claudia asked.

"He is a man of vision; I'll give him that. He sees ahead to a day when both Romans and Novans—at least his sort of Novans— are one people."

"You're right, he does talk sense," Claudia said. "That is how it will have to be, if you want any Roman children running around to build this town into a city."

Something about the way Claudia said children made the young general stop, maize cake halfway to his mouth. He looked at his young wife. "My dear, are you trying to tell me something?"

Cornelia and Claudia exchanged an amused look. "Well," Claudia said, "we know of at least one new Roman citizen who will be joining us."

"Sometime this fall," Cornelia added.

Gnaeus Pompey, general of the army of Nova Roma, tossed his maize cake in the air and let out a whoop. "Now that is good news!" He bounded to his wife and hugged her. "A boy, let's hope. We'll have to think of names. We'll have to... Oh, there are a hundred things we'll have to do."

Claudia Pulchra looked at her husband, eyes shining, but her face very serious. "There is one thing you must do before this child comes, Gnaeus."

"Yes?"

"Put an end to this war."

"My dear," Pompey the (for now) Younger said, "I intend to."

CHAPTER EIGHT
MANEUVERS

During the spring's actions General Pompey determined that the correlation of forces may have favored the Novan, as a great many native warriors were in the field, but the organization of the Roman army certainly favored the latter party. In spite of their Roman councilors, the Novans proved easily led astray by the unexpected appearance of Roman forces in various areas.

By this time the identity of the primary antagonist in the conflict was known. The primary native general was a man of the vicious and now extinct Alligator People, who lived in the swamps to the south of the territory of the B'Kou, who later became Roman citizens. The man's name and his title among his people were one and the same, Man-Ready-For-War, and no more apt cognomen was ever bestowed upon a tribal chieftain. What he possessed in viciousness was however offset by a lack of discipline, and this proved to be a state of affairs that General Pompey and his legates were able to exploit, much to Man-Ready-For-War's sorrow. The first such actions involved

*the surviving ships from the fleet of Pompey Magnus,
and were actions that the Novans had little idea how to
counter.*

—From Gnaeus Pompey Novus' New World Diaries

South of Pulcia

It was a late afternoon on a balmy, breezy day. The *Neptune* cruised slowly along the coast south of the great harbor, sails set. Quintus Pulcio stood on the raised afterdeck, watching the sun sink lower in the sky to the west.

Pulcio enjoyed days like this; they reminded him why he chose his path in life. The trip down the coast had been much like a pleasure cruise, despite all the armed men aboard. The sea was calm. A light breeze kept the pestilential insects of the low-country marches away from the ship, and the spring sun was warm. The oarsmen were idle as the freighter's large linen sail was set to take the ship slowly south. Standing on the afterdeck, Pulcio could hear conversation and the occasional burst of laughter from the rowing benches below. The cedar planking of the ship's hull creaked slightly as the ship rocked in the gentle swells.

"I've never seen such blue," Pulcio said, looking at the sky.

"Nice day to be bait," his first mate commented.

"Yes," Pulcio agreed. "If one has to be blown to a strange land, it may as well be pretty." He looked back at the two men on the steering oars. "Bring us in a little closer to the shore. There have to be fish in there someplace."

"That cove, perhaps," the mate pointed. There was a small bay, where a small stream met the sea, with trees overhanging the narrow entrance.

"Ideal place for an ambush," Pulcio said. "Stay on course; veer us a little bit shoreward, make it look careless. Stay out of range of archers on the beach, though. Make them come out after us."

Quintus Pulcio was fond of fishing. He loved casting nets into new waters, and the waters around these new lands were rich, not only in fish but in oysters and a kind of blue and red crab that proved delicious. A man who knows the sea and knows fishing can never go hungry. Pulcio's small crew was always well-fed, and the people in Pompeius had eaten of their catches, as well.

But they were after a different sort of fish today.

"And there they are," he breathed. Six long dugout boats shot out of the small, almost hidden cove and made for the freighter. Each long dugout contained six men, paddling furiously. White water curled back from the bows of the small boats as they shot towards the loafing freighter.

"All right," Pulcio said. "Get them up here."

Sixteen slingers and ten archers from the First Legion arrived on the top deck a few moments later. The slingers carried bags of round iron shot and larger bags of round cobbles for close range work—iron shot would be at a premium, soon enough.

Pulcio motioned them down. "Stay low, lads. Let them get in nice and close." He turned to the men on the steering oars. "Steer hard away from the coast, now!" He waved at two men standing at the base of the ship's one short mast. "Now!"

The ship's single linen sail rippled and spilled the air. The ship slowed suddenly, and Pulcio shouted, doing a credible job at feigning panic. Several sets of oars ran out and started dabbing at the water. To the west, the six boats of Novans picked up their pace; they were close enough now for Pulcio to see the savage grins on their faces.

He looked at the man in charge of the archers and slingers. "Whenever you're ready, soldier."

"Archers, stand ready," the soldier said. He took a peep over the rail; the *Neptune* had slowed almost to a halt, and the lead Novan boat was only a few dozen feet away. "Ready... now!"

The trap was neatly sprung. At the short range, even from a ship rocking on the sea, the experienced and trained Roman archers could hardly miss. Five Novans were hit in the first volley of arrows.

Fore and aft, slingers let fly with a hail of round rocks—no point wasting iron balls at this range. The long leather slings hurled rocks with enough force to crack a skull or break arms, ribs, and jaws, and this they did, with good effect. Moments later, the Novans withdrew, leaving two boats behind crewed only by the dead and groaning wounded.

"Well, that wasn't so bad," Pulcio observed. "Get that sail set right. Now, we'll go south, see if we can't do it again." His orders, straight from the young General Pompey himself, were to make himself a nuisance along this coast. He intended to do precisely that.

Pompeius

Pompey let a week pass, then two, before deciding the time was ripe for the second part of the plan. Early one morning two cohorts of the First Nova Roman Legion, four hundred infantry, marched out of the city gates, accompanied by two mounted scouts who would also serve as messengers when needed. The cohorts marched into the woods, headed southeast.

Centurion Gracchus Agrippa led the party, and among the second cohort marched Legionary Titus Caninus, who was still grinning at the warm send-off he had received from Servia Valeris Merula the night before. Her status as a woman and her relationship with Titus Caninus had become general knowledge in the town at the same time, which proved a source of consternation for many of the men; Caninus' reputation, though, was such that few felt like challenging him over the matter.

The cohorts marched through forests with spring leaves of bright green, through meadows strewn with wildflowers. Birds sang in the brush and in the trees overhead. Deer and turkeys were seen every morning and evening, and the cohorts managed fresh meat at regular intervals.

On the third day they found the first Novan village.

Both cohorts marched through the town, which they rapidly ascertained belonged to the B'Kou—Four Bears' people. A dozen low huts and a tiny central building comprised the place, which was peopled for the moment only with women and children. The Romans marched through, gathering the inhabitants as they went. This early in the spring the village's stores of food were minimal, so Gracchus Agrippa let the women gather their provisions, then burned the huts. He left them keening in the ruins of their town and marched out, again aiming southeast.

"Aim roughly for the coast," General Pompey had told him. "When you hit the big harbor at Pulcia, proceed inland west and south no more than two day's march. Burn any villages but kill only if necessary. No looting, no raping, no taking hostages. Turn back to the coast after no more than five days."

On the fifth day they met their first real resistance.

A series of thunderstorms went through the night before, rendering the lowland forest wet, sloppy—and quiet. Sunrise, and

Agrippa was watching the men gathered around their breakfast fires when one of the sentries squawked an alarm: "To arms!"

The men scrambled for swords and shields as arrows started to pepper the camp. One man was hit and fell, shouting angrily, with an arrow through his upper arm.

A dozen black-painted Alligator warriors charged the camp at an oblique angle, trying to separate off a few Romans from the main group. Against untrained savages the tactic may have been a good one, but not against disciplined Roman legionaries. The attack was repulsed, and the natives left a dead man behind. But while they were distracted, another group hit the Romans from behind.

One Roman soldier grabbed a burning brand from his own fire and slammed it into the face of an onrushing Alligator warrior. The man fell, screaming, clutching his face. Another legionary ran him through with a gladius, silencing his shrieks of pain. Two other natives rushed the first Roman and knocked him to the ground as the rest of the cohort turned to meet the new threat.

Scuta went up as the line formed, the disciplined Roman soldiers reacting faster than the Novans had any reason to expect. Pila and gladii stabbed outwards, quickly repelling the attack. The Novans retreated behind another volley of arrows, leaving several dead and injured behind.

The soldier who had been hit in the arm was in pain, but able to move. The other, who had been knocked to the ground, had a large red patch on his face that promised a glorious bruise, but he was otherwise unhurt.

"Form up," Gracchus Agrippa called when the last arrows had fallen. "We're moving. No reason to make it easy for them."

"What about their wounded, sir?"

"Leave them. They'll come back for them after we're gone, no doubt."

Within the hour the cohorts marched away. At mid-morning a mounted scout found them; Pulcia was not far off. "You can reach it by nightfall," the scout told Gracchus Agrippa. "Shelter within walls, sir. They've' been busy there. I believe General Pompey sent orders for you in the latest dispatches, they should be waiting for you there now."

"Ride on," Centurion Agrippa told the man. "Inform the garrison commander that we're on our way. He already knows what to have ready."

A war camp of the People

"They are obviously moving towards the fort on the island," Man-Ready-For-War told his assembled sub-chiefs. White Oak sat in on the council along with two of his Red Blanket society chiefs, but it was plainly the Alligator People who directed this reaction to the Roman advance.

"We should have destroyed that fort when we attacked it before," Man-Ready-For-War's son Long Tooth objected. Of late he was objecting to his father's statements and plans more frequently, causing a distinct uneasiness among the black-painted warriors.

"The men at the fort were few," Man-Ready-For-War snarled. "By themselves, hiding behind their walls, they were no danger, even with their great boat with its arrows and rock-throwing devices. But there are many men marching there now, and if White Oak here has the truth of it, they move quickly and will be there by nightfall."

"Snake is our best runner and tracker," White Oak said. "If he says a thing is true, you may rely on it. He says the Romans will reach the fort by nightfall. They will."

"The fort is too small for them to stay there," Man-Ready-For-War said, and White Oak nodded in agreement. "So very soon those men will march out again. Where will they go from there? I think they will go south. Their great boat is still in the south, still looking at the beaches and rivers. They are planning something there. We must go south to meet them."

"You say that because they move now into your lands," White Oak barked at the man. "Until now it was only the lands of the B'Kou that were fought over, only villages of the B'Kou that were destroyed. Now the Romans attack south into your lands, and we must all run to meet them! There are many more Romans to the north. What will they be doing while we run to protect the towns of the Alligator People?"

Man-Ready-For-War let out a derisive snort. "Hiding in their town, behind their walls."

"I think they will not," White Oak answered. "You have not met their war chief Pompey. I have. You have not handled one of their weapons of steel, the 'gladius' that all of their soldiers carry. I have. I say you are mistaken if you think the Romans are afraid of us, especially when two hundred of them march through our lands not a half-day's walk from where we sit!"

"They may not fear us," Man-Ready-For-War was shouting now. "But I do not fear them! We know their numbers, and we are two, even three to their one!"

"And yet they have killed five of us for each one of them we have struck down," White Oak shouted back. "We cannot keep throwing ourselves at them! We must find another way to fight them."

"He has a point," Long Tooth said quietly. "We are like foxes attacking a bear, Father. We are going for his head, where the teeth are. We should strike the bear's hindquarters when he is not looking."

"Which is exactly what Pompey's warriors are doing to us," White Oak added.

"We will fight them the way the Alligator People have always fought," Man-Ready-For-War gritted out through clenched teeth. "We will kill them, the way the Alligator People have always killed enemies. We will win."

White Oak and Long Tooth looked at each other. "We will move on the fort, then?" White Oak asked.

"We will move to the fort," Man-Ready-For-War said. "When the Romans emerge from it, we will be ready. They have to use their boats to move on and off the island. That is when they will be open to attack."

It made a certain amount of sense. White Oak nodded. "It will be as you say," he agreed, but his face was an eloquent picture of doubt.

Pulcia

The island that held the fort at Pulcia blossomed late one afternoon with the tents of the First Legion's cohorts.

"I hate to sound rude," Tribune Marcus Lucanus said to Centurion Gracchus Agrippa, "but you won't be able to stay here long. We simply can't feed all of you, and you won't begin to fit within the walls of the fort if the natives attack us again."

"We won't be staying in any case, sir," Agrippa nodded. "My orders are to touch base here, then proceed down the coast and then inland."

"Impressive how quickly your men knocked those rafts together to cross over here," the tribune said.

Agrippa nodded, looking at the big log rafts that nevertheless had required several trips to ferry almost four hundred men to the island. He grinned. "Don't worry, sir. We'll burn them after we cross back, so the savages can't use them."

"I'd rather you didn't, actually. The smoke would just draw attention, and they have plenty of their own sorts of boats, believe you me. No, when you cross back, tie ropes to them and we'll pull them back. We can use the wood. Cook fires, if nothing else."

"As you wish. One of the scouts will set off for Pompeius in the morning, bearing messages. Is there any message you'd care to send to the General?"

"None," Lucanus said, "except to get this damned war over with quickly."

"Nothing we aren't all hoping for there, sir. I'm sure the General is as well."

"No doubt. Who knew —coming all this way to this strange place, running from a war that old Pompey Magnus thought he couldn't win, and here we find ourselves fighting again anyway."

"We can win this one, sir. We will."

Lucanus looked at the younger man. "You may be right. I hope you are. At any rate—come on into the fort. My men have been capturing some of the big blue and red crabs that infest this bay. They are surprisingly good to eat."

The cohorts from the First passed the night at Pulcia as planned. When morning broke, they breakfasted on strips of dried fish and venison and prepared to cross back to the mainland, to make their way north. The first rafts had crossed to the mainland when the savages struck.

At least sixty black-painted Alligator warriors charged the five rafts and the hundred men they bore, howling like madmen. The Romans had no time to form up, and the fight degenerated into a brawl at close quarters, gladii against war clubs. A shower of arrows from the trees prevented the Romans on the island from retrieving the rafts by the ropes tied to them for the purpose of pulling them back to the island, and so joining their comrades under attack. Only one small boat from the freighter *Neptune* was on the island, and it would only hold a half-dozen men. For the moment the hundred men of the First were on their own.

The Alligator warriors were badly outnumbered, and so sought to slash and run. Ten Romans were struck down, mostly with club blows to chests and necks, while fifteen Alligator soldiers died to Roman gladii. The natives withdrew behind a shower of arrows loosed by their B'Kou and A'Tep allies while the Romans regrouped.

The battle had only lasted a few minutes.

"That," Gracchus Agrippa opined when he crossed to the mainland, "was as good an ambush as any general of the Roman army could have planned." He turned to a legionary standing nearby. "Has anyone counted our losses and the enemy dead?"

"We lost ten, sir," the man said. "Six more wounded, only one can't move. He's already on the raft to go back across to the fort until he recovers. Fifteen enemy dead. One legionary accounted for five of them, sir."

"Really? Who was this man?"

"Me, sir," the legionary grinned. "You remember me. Titus Caninus, sir."

"Yes," Agrippa said. "The Great Dog. Well, good work, Caninus. Best get ready to move now."

"Of course. Sir." Caninus saluted and swaggered off. Agrippa watched him go; the man was a loudmouth, a braggart, and when in a town had a reputation for debauchery, but he was a competent soldier; about that there could be no doubt.

The cohorts re-assembled and marched off, following the coastline south. The day passed without incident. The going was not easy; never easy, down in the low country along the coast that most of the legionaries remembered all too well from the first few days after the landing. Swamps had to be negotiated, creeks and rivers crossed, one legionary was bitten by a creature that resembled a crocodile but that the Romans now knew was called "alligator."

"It's no wonder the black-faced savages took their names from this thing," the bitten legionary commented. "Once the thing gets its teeth in you, you have to kill it to make it let go." He had managed to drive his gladius into the creature's armored head; it was nearly as long as the man was tall, but rumor had it they routinely grew much larger.

The cohorts made camp that night on what Gracchus Agrippa finally realized was a long, slim island that formed a barrier between the mainland and the sea. Camp was made just inside the line of trees facing the ocean with the beach in plain view, so that the pleasant breezes from the water cooled the humid, heavy air somewhat.

Titus Caninus found himself part of a small group of legionaries seated at a fire on a small rise, munching their spare rations and watching the waves roll into the shore. Behind them, the sun had already sunk behind the mountains, and the light was rapidly growing very dim.

"Well into spring," Caninus complained, "and already hot and wet. This low country is no place for civilized men."

"At least the sea breeze keeps the insects at bay," one of the men answered. "I heard from one of the Novan girls in Pompeius that it's the insects that carry the swamp fever, the sickness that carried off old Pompey."

Another legionary chimed in. "I heard an old soldier say once that in Africa, the troops would cover themselves in rendered pig fat to keep the flies off."

"Ugh," Caninus frowned. "I'd rather put up with the insects. Rancid pig fat in that desert heat? I..." He paused, listening. "Did you hear that?"

"Hear what?"

"Quiet," Caninus snapped. "Can't hear anything with you flapping your jaw. I heard a branch snap; I know I did." He stood up and peered into the darkness beneath the trees. Fires were visible to right and left, but farther into the trees there was only the gathering gloom, shadows within shadows. There was nothing moving.

Or was there? Caninus leaned forward, squinting. Was one of the shadows moving?

"To arms!" he shouted. His gladius leaped into his hand smoothly. He fell back to the fire, grabbing up his scutum as men scrambled for swords and shields around him.

A bubbling wail came from the shadows. The cacophony spread, howls from a hundred or more Novan throats spilling into the growing darkness. The Roman legionaries formed a line, backing slowly towards the beach. In the woods, the wailing went on.

And on, and on.

"Stay in formation," Gracchus Agrippa's voice rang out. "Any man steps out of line; I'll have him flogged. Mind the flanks. Stay alert." He moved among the men, pulling the wings of the formation back to form a shallow arc, the convex side aimed at the trees, the ocean at their back.

Still, the howling, yips and wails from the woods went on.

The expected attack never came. Nobody slept that night. When the sun rose over the ocean, the howling faded away.

Gracchus Agrippa sent a patrol into the woods to discover what had gone on and was not pleased at what they reported.

"No more than a dozen men out there, sir," the man leading the patrol reported.

"They aren't stupid, are they?" The centurion looked around to see Titus Caninus standing there, rubbing his eyes. "They know they can't beat us in a straight fight, so they try to wear at our nerves. Wear us out, like, right, sir?"

"It worked, didn't it? And now we start on the day's march down the coast dragging our asses, half asleep," Still, Agrippa told himself, it seems to be working. General Pompey said to get their main body to follow us down the coast. They seem to be doing so.

Pompeius

General Gnaeus Pompey regarded the latest message from the southeast with no small satisfaction. "It's working," he muttered to himself. "It's working."

He stood up, stretched a kink from his back, and walked off to report the news to the Consuls.

"So, you've heard from your men making a demonstration in that southern coastal country?" Cicero asked, after Pompey found them conferring in the sunshine on the steps of the Senate.

"Yes," Pompey agreed, "and it's working." He tapped the message case. "I have the latest reports here. They have burned several small villages. There was an attack when they left the fort at Pulcia, but they repulsed it. They're proceeding south along the coastline now. The freighter *Neptune* will follow at a distance to await their signals."

"Your plan is working, then," Cato asked.

"So far," Pompey nodded.

"And you'll proceed as you planned?"

Pompey's smile turned nasty. "I will," he said. "Their warriors are moving to follow our men south. We've got them leaning the wrong way. Once we get their men all down by the coast, then the next step begins. Our men from the First will be holding them by the nose. Next, we'll kick them in the ass."

South of Pulcia

Two days' march south of Pulcia, the two cohorts from the First set off inland again, into the heart of Alligator territory. They marched steadily west, leaving a trail of burned villages behind them. The cohorts marched swiftly through the low country, marching well into the night, arising hours before dawn to move again. Mounted scouts reported a growing horde of Novan warriors pursuing them through the marshes.

CHAPTER NINE
SETBACKS

General Pompey's plan for the initial spring campaign against the Novan tribes, like most military campaigns, was not executed entirely as planned. No plan survives the first actions without necessary adjustments, and Pompey's plan was no exception.

In the main the diversion was a success, in any case. Two cohorts of infantry striking into the territory of the warlike Alligator tribesmen led the bulk of their warriors south and cast, away from Pompeius and away from the main body of the Roman Army, still encamped in the walls of the city.

While the army at that early point in the history of Nova Roma made up nearly half of the population of Pompeius, almost every man in the city at that point had military experience. Having taken ship with full military kit for almost every man in the expedition, the only surplus the colony had was of weapons. The result of this was such that the entire army could be sent afield in pursuit of the Novan warriors, while the merchants, tradesmen and workers of Pompeius could see to the city's defense.

Pompey planned to put this fact to use.

—From Gnaeus Pompey Novus' New World Diaries

South of Pulcia

Fifteen days of running battles and raids saw the two cohorts of the First once more on the coast, near where a large river emptied into the sea.

Gracchus Agrippa did not like what his orders required of him on the coast, but he had no choice.

"Build several signal fires, one on the north end of our encampment, one on the south," he ordered the centurions in charge of the two centuries of the cohorts. "Plenty of green wood and grass, we want lots of smoke."

The centurions looked at each other. "Sir," one of them said, "that will bring every savage within twenty leagues right down on our heads."

"Half of them are already following us," the other pointed out. "We've lost five men to them in the last ten days."

"Yes," Agrippa agreed. "And it will also bring us some help. Make the fires, make them smoky, and set guards. All men not engaged in essential camp chores are to stand to in daylight. At night, half the men are to be awake at all times. When they sleep, they sleep in full kit, weapons at hand. We can expect to be attacked, in force, if we are here more than a day or two. Fortunately, if all goes well, we should be gone no later than tomorrow evening."

"Where are we going, sir?"

Agrippa managed a grin. "We're going to disappear into the sea," he said.

"We're signaling a ship," the man said, his face brightening.

"More than one ship, to move this lot," the second centurion said. He slapped his counterpart on the back. "Or maybe it's just one big one. Let's get after it, then."

Even as the fires were lit, the legionaries built earthworks reinforced with timbers, two hundred paces wide, shaped in a broad U with the open end facing the sea, anticipating the attack that was sure to come.

The Novans attacked at sunset.

A whistling sound was the first harbinger the weary legionaries had of the assault. "Testudo!" the cry went up, and the soldiers took refuge in the tortoise-like formation under their scuta, but only one volley of arrows came in.

By the time the cohorts recovered, black-faced Alligator warriors had advanced behind their rude wooden shields, nearly to the earthworks. The opposing sides met with a clash, Roman steel and bronze against Novan wood and stone.

Gracchus Agrippa had to force himself to stay a short distance back from the line. He saw, all too quickly, that the Roman advantages in discipline and arms were at least partly negated by the Novan's numbers; the earthworks helped, but the length of the fighting front meant that the Roman troops were drawn up in just two ranks. Half the men were on the front, fighting, at any given moment.

Agrippa found himself glancing over his shoulder at the sea.

The line held the first assault. The Novans withdrew to regroup, leaving their dead and groaning wounded behind. Three

Romans were dead, and several more wounded. Agrippa ordered the wounded moved to the beach.

"Damn, but they are learning," Titus Caninus remarked to the man next to him. He pulled up a swath of long grass to clean his gladius. "That advance would have done any cohort of Roman infantry proud."

"I wish I could say you were wrong."

"If they ever learn to work iron, we'll be in trouble." Caninus finished cleaning his shining blade and slid it back into its scabbard. He looked at the dimming sky. "Dark soon. What will they do next?"

As if in answer, a shout came from off to the left. "Here they come!"

Caninus picked up a pila, one of the few remaining to the cohorts, and balanced it lightly in his right hand. One big native in the ranks looked over the top of his wooden scutum, white teeth showing a savage grin in his black-painted face. *You'll be trouble,* Caninus thought, *so let's take you out at the onset.*

He cast his pila in a low arc. The iron point slammed through the native's wooden shield and into his chest, dropping him to the ground. The other Novans moved in quickly to fill the gap in their line and came on.

"Jupiter's balls, you are learning," Caninus muttered. He drew his gladius and stood, waiting.

The Novans approached the earthworks and broke into a run to cover the last few paces, leaping onto the earthworks and crashing again into the Roman line. In the gathering darkness, Roman and Novan hacked at each other.

Titus Caninus slammed his scutum into a Novan's wooden shield, shattering it. His gladius flickered out from behind his own shield, opening the Novan's belly. He dropped to one knee to let the swing of a Novan war club pass overhead and swung his gladius to take the man's hand off at the wrist as it passed.

Once more, the Novans fell back, unable to break the Roman line.

It was almost completely dark, only a faint light remaining in the sky to the west. After some time passed, the Romans could see the faint flickers of campfires, only fifty to a hundred paces away in the forest. Both sides settled in to wait out a long, tense night.

In the forest

Man-Ready-For-War and his Roman advisors stood on a small rise in the woods, examining the Roman lines as best they could in the faint light of a half-moon.

"Harass them through the night," Pullo said, "just as we discussed. Not with shouts and screams, not this time. We harass them with arrows fired from the darkness. Send single warriors in to attack their guards."

"My men are already preparing," the Alligator People war chief said. He held a Roman gladius, taken from a Roman soldier killed in the fighting, along with his wooden scutum.

Lucius Vorenus still had only a rudimentary command of the Novan's language, but he managed to make himself understood. "Their guards will be alert. They won't be taken easily." It occurred to him that he was in the precise position of a warrior chief of Gaul, a man of the sort that he himself had fought under Caesar's command. The irony was not lost on the Roman centurion. "And when we have defeated these men? What then?"

"Then we move north," Man-Ready-For-War said. "Then we

attack them in their town and drive them away from the lands of the People, forever."

"No doubt the Gauls under Vercingetorix said much the same thing after Gergovia," Pullo said to Vorenus in Latin.

"No doubt," Vorenus agreed. "But we're a long, long way from Gaul, brother."

"And no two wars are alike. Still, bearding the lion in its den..."

Man-Ready-For-War gave a derisive snort, reminding the centurions that he understood more Latin than he let on. "Once their soldiers are defeated, their city will fall. My people have never lost a war. We will not lose this one. Come, my friends, the work of the night has just begun."

The Roman lines

Skirmishing went on through the night. During the first watch, a Novan arrow struck a legionary in the shoulder. Gracchus Agrippa was himself targeted by a Novan archer who loosed his arrow from high in a huge tree, but the arrow struck only a glancing blow along the Roman commander's ribs, leaving no more than a deep scratch.

Titus Caninus was among those woken to take the second watch. He spent a bored, quiet hour staring into the darkness, fighting sleep.

An arrow hissed past, paces to the right. Caninus' gladius leaped into his hand and he shouted an alarm, but no target presented itself. As the legionaries around him grabbed weapons, he took a step up, onto the earthworks.

From under his feet, a shadow rose. Before he could raise a hand in defense, a black-painted hand swung a club. There was a tremendous, sudden explosion of sound and light, and then only blackness.

Four Bears' village

Morning, and Four Bears found his footsteps taking him once more to the house of old Owl. After the traditional rituals of greeting and hospitality, Four Bears broached the subject on which he sought the old man's counsel.

"I am full of dread," he admitted, "over what Man-Ready-For-War has led our warrior society men into."

Owl looked at him keenly. "I know why you worry, Four Bears," he said. "Remember, I was with you in the Roman town. You fear our stupid young men pitting the stone and wood of the People against the steel of Rome."

The old man leaned back against a backrest of woven willow and drew on his pipe, a thoughtful expression on his face. He let out a cloud of fragrant blue smoke and continued.

"You are right, of course. These Romans, it's not just these glad... the long knives of steel they carry. It's not just the shields, or how they cooperate to build their great town. The Tsalee of the west have towns as large as the Romans. The Maya in the south have cities that are much larger. No, it is more than that. They think differently than we do."

"My father used to say, two of the People could work together on a task with no trouble, but three would argue, and four would accomplish nothing for fighting. In my life I have seen nothing to suggest he was wrong. Look how our warrior society men, many of whom fought the Alligator People only a few summers ago, ran to join them now."

"They perceive the men of Rome as the greater threat," Owl

said. "But what they see as a threat, a wiser man may view as an opportunity."

Four Bears found himself chuckling. "You have a way of knowing my own thoughts better than I do myself."

Owl let out a derisive snort. "The thoughts of young men are easy to know." Not many of the People would consider Four Bears a young man, but compared to Owl, all others were but children.

"You are right," Owl continued, "to see an opportunity. Look at how the Romans work together. They think they came to our lands by accident, but I think they must have been sent here by powerful gods, and we would do well to understand them, their ways, and even their gods. What have we to compare with their ships? We have turkeys and dogs, but they have the great beasts they call horses—have you ever before seen men riding on the back of an animal? They think differently than we do, and the Red Blanket soldiers think that we should fight them because of that. But who is to say that we should not instead learn their ways? The young men of the People have always sought wives from neighboring tribes, so the bonds of family have kept all of the People close and allowed us to exchange not just goods but knowledge. With us and the A'Tep it has come to the point where we are nearly one tribe, so that we call them our cousins. Why should it not be the same with the Romans? Remember, that was why you took the girl Adsila to them at the very beginning." Owl diplomatically did not mention that it was his idea originally to place the orphan girl with the Romans.

"So, what will we do now?"

"Wait," Owl counseled. "The Red Blanket soldiers and the Alligator People have no chance to win a war against Rome. They have numbers, but Rome has steel. They will lose. When they do, you go and talk to the Romans again. Find another way."

On the coast

Morning broke on the exhausted soldiers, and revealed a longed-for sight:

"A ship!" the shout went up. And there, a hundred paces off the coast, the freighter *Neptune* lay at anchor. Two large boats were already on their way into the beach.

Gracchus Agrippa lost no time in shouting orders. "Stand to there on the earthworks! If the Novans see this, they'll try to stop us leaving." He ducked as an arrow whistled past overhead. "Never mind, they saw it. Merda! Into line, everyone!"

The boats landed, and a sailor leaped from one of them and ran up the beach to where Agrippa was shouting orders. "We can take twenty at a time," he called to the centurion before an arrow slammed into his shoulder, knocking him down.

"Stay in line!" Agrippa yelled. "Fighting retreat to the beach!"

The Romans retreated in good order, and while the Alligator warriors seemed uncharacteristically reluctant to engage, the B'Kou and A'Tep archers knew no such hesitation, sending showers of arrows into the Roman formation. As the main body of the infantry reached the beach, the reason for the Alligator warriors' caution became apparent as a shout came up from the left end of the line: "Cavalry!"

Impossibly, six Roman cavalrymen charged through the formation, gladii whirling. The infantry fended them off with swords and shields, but two were struck down with deep wounds. One horseman was pinked in the leg by the tip of a gladius blade as he rode through, but the six horsemen sped off in good order to the north, up the beach.

With the horsemen clear, the 'infantry' of the Alligator People charged at last, slamming into the disorganized Roman line, but the freighter was close enough to the beach to cover the retreating infantry with archers and slingers. Arrows and iron shot struck at the Novans and they fell back into the tree line. Under harassing arcs of arrows from the Novan archers, the Romans held the beach long enough to retreat to the ship, which set off at once to the north.

Gracchus Agrippa found the freighter's caption, Quintus Pulcio, waiting for him on the afterdeck.

"That was a near thing," Agrippa told the freighter captain. "Bastards seem to have a never-ending supply of arrows, and there are more of them than I was expecting. Your ship was a beautiful sight this morning. I think we have the entire Novan nation chasing us."

Pulcio laughed. "That was the whole point, neh?"

"Cavalry," Agrippa complained. He took off his helmet and rubbed a hand through his filthy hair, which was matted to his head with sweat. "Fucking cavalry. Only a few, but who would have expected any?"

"You knew there were Romans among the savages."

"Knowing is one thing. Seeing evidence of it, such as their training, and their bearing scuta, crude as they may be, that's another. But having nearly my entire line, two cohorts of trained and experienced Roman infantry, rolled up by a half-dozen horsemen—that's another thing entirely."

Pulcio slapped the centurion on the back. "Well, next time you won't be surprised."

"No, we'll be ready for them. I'll have to have the men make some javelins, maybe some lances to fend off horsemen. It would be good to have some of your archers and slingers along; we have no way to strike at range at all now; our pila are long gone."

"You'll be glad to hear that General Pompey agrees with you." He handed the centurion a scroll. "His latest orders. I am to detach the slingers and archers on my ship to you, and to drop you at Pulcia. You strike inland from there, making your way back to Pompeius overland."

Agrippa unrolled the scroll and read it quickly. "And you?"

"We will re-provision at Pulcia and make our way back south along the coast. It seems we are to continue to serve as a distraction. Make ourselves seen, Set a few fires, that sort of thing."

"Dangerous business," Agrippa observed. "And you're going south with no slingers or archers to defend your ship?

"We have a few other tricks to throw at them," Pulcia said. "Don't worry about the old *Neptune*—she survived pirates in the Mediterranean, she survived that damnable storm that brought us here, she'll survive this too. My men are a rough bunch"—that much was true, the *Neptune's* crew had a distinctly rough-and-tumble air to them— "and they've fought pirates and savages before. We'll be fine."

"Still, it's a dangerous business," Agrippa replied.

"War is like that."

In a war camp of the People

Titus Caninus awoke slowly, as though it was the morning after a long night's drinking bout. His head pounded; his mouth felt full of dirt and ashes. When he tried to move, he discovered his wrists and ankles were tightly bound.

He looked around. He was lying on the bare dirt in a round hide tent. A low pallet lay on one side, and a fire burned in the center of the floor.

"So," a voice said. "You're awake. About time. You've been out a good part of the day."

Caninus blinked. *Latin?* He rolled over and looked up to see a man seated on an upturned section of log, staring at him. The man wore the uniform of a centurion in the Roman army—here, in the Novan's camp?

"So, it's true, then," Caninus said. He ran his tongue around his mouth, trying to moisten it. "There are Roman traitors amongst the savages."

"Mind who you call traitor, boy."

"What shall I call you then, sir?"

The man stood up, and Caninus realized he was a big man, even bigger than Caninus himself. *Formidable in a fight, he is,* he guessed.

The centurion removed his helmet. "Centurion Lucius Vorenus, late of the Thirteenth Gallic Legion," he introduced himself.

"Caesar's man," Caninus groused. "Well, since we're being polite and all—I'm Titus Caninus, legionary of General Gnaeus Pompey's Second Nova Roman Legion."

"Another Titus," Vorenus smiled. "My counterpart shares your name. Centurion Titus Pullo, he is, also of the Thirteenth. He's off parleying with our 'allies,' at the moment. He is better with their language than me."

"Parley? What kinds of allies are yours that you have to parley with them, eh? What are you parleying for?"

Vorenus leaned forward. "They wanted to cut you apart," he

said slowly. "Those motherless scum with the black paint on their faces, they wanted to stake you to the ground and cut you into pieces, slowly. The other ones, they and Pullo are arguing against it." The centurion put his helmet back on and sat back. "Allies or not, I won't see that done to another Roman. Nor will Pullo."

"Kind of you."

Vorenus nodded. "Nothing of kindness in it. Oh, I suppose there's a matter of principle involved; you are a soldier of Rome fighting in good faith, just as we, and you deserve decent treatment. But the arguing point with these people is that your boy general Pompey would serve any of them the same way when captured, were he to find out."

"Very likely," Caninus agreed.

"We will be moving soon; probably to follow that ship north. Nobody quite knows what to do with you." Vorenus shrugged. "I suppose we'll figure something out."

"Ask you something, sir?"

"Go ahead."

"How did you come to this place? And how is it that you're allied to the natives?"

"That's two questions, legionary, but I'll answer. As to how we came here, I suspect the same way as you. Caesar gave us orders to follow Pompey Magnus and the Senate, and report on their whereabouts. When he took ship at Ostia, we hired the only ship left in port and followed. The same storm, I'm sure, brought you and us here, to this place."

He smiled. "As to our allies—well, we were ordered to oppose Pompey. Old Pompey Magnus is dead, we hear, but his party lives on, as do the Optimate Senators allied to him. We are sworn to Caesar, a sacred oath before the gods, which means we are the enemies of the Pompeians. We found Pompey's people have other enemies here, so it was the natural thing to do."

"Romans against other Romans, that can't be natural."

"And how do you think it is back in Italy, now? Caesar will march on Rome—no, he almost certainly already has marched on Rome. Who now is there now to stand in his way? Everyone of consequence that opposed him fled and ended up here."

Vorenus looked at the fire crackling in the center of the low round hut. "I've fought under Caesar for years, in Gaul and Britannia. I was at Alesia when we brought down the armies of Gaul. I saw the king of all the Gallic tribes, Vercingetorix, kneel before Caesar and kiss the eagle of Caesar's legions. What is the boy general Pompey and a few old men in white robes after that?"

"But Caesar's not here," Caninus pointed out.

"No," Vorenus said sadly. "Don't think that hasn't occurred to us. But our course is set now, and all we can do is run it. In honor we can do nothing else."

"And run you might, sir." Caninus observed. "Who knows what lies to the west? Mountains, I hear, and more on the other side."

"If your man wins this war, Pullo, our men and I, we may find out."

"And if you win?"

"We'll see," Vorenus said. He looked at Caninus again. "What is the general's purpose in sending you out, legionary?"

"From what I heard," Caninus said, "he thinks you'll have a harder time fighting in the swamps and marshes in this low country."

"Hah! These creatures with the black faces, they live in these swamps. There is no worse place to fight them."

"I'm not exactly one of the General's closest advisors, sir."

"More's the pity," Vorenus said. "It seems your boy general isn't as savvy as his father was when it comes to war. Maybe we'll put that to some good use."

Titus Caninus did his best to look disappointed. He hoped he was convincing.

Pompeius

"Are you insane?"

To say that the Consuls were displeased with the second half of General Gnaeus Pompey's plan would have been a gross understatement.

"Not at all," Pompey calmly responded to Cato's outburst. The Senate had just concluded its business for the day, and Pompey was seated in the Senate chamber with Cato and Cicero to update them on the progress of the campaign against the Novans. "This plan makes the best use of our strengths."

"It does seem rash. Bringing the entire Novan army, such as it is, right to the gates of Pompeius? It seems very rash indeed, young man."

"Friend Cicero," Pompey explained, "There is only so much we can do in the field. Their villages are spread out, we don't even know how far they range. They have supplies in each village. We have only a rough guess as to how many warriors they can muster. No, if we are to force a peace on them, we have to draw them in, we have to have a decisive—nay, an overwhelming victory. I remind you, time works for them, not for us."

"How so?" Cato demanded.

"Remember, there are Romans among them now. Not many— perhaps a dozen, according to the men from their ship who have found their way here. But those dozen are all experienced soldiers from Caesar's Thirteenth legion, veterans of Britain and Gaul, and they will be teaching the Novans warcraft as fast as they can. And who knows what other skills they possess? If one, even one among them knows how to work iron, and finds them a source of that metal..." He let the thought trail off, knowing what the consuls were picturing: A horde of Novan warriors with steel gladii and iron-edged scuta, bearing down on the Roman town. It was a picture that haunted his own thoughts, late at night. "No, we have to defeat them now, this summer, to force a peace on them."

"And once that is done?"

"Cicero, I'm a soldier, not a politician," Pompey averred. "My father may have known that answer better than I, he having been a consul of Rome himself. But if you ask me, we should offer them citizenship. I remind you, several Novan women live in our town even now—and the men they live with are the object of considerable envy by their fellows."

It was a subject that had arisen before and would again. Cato had no wife to bring from Rome, nor had Cicero, and being soldiers, most of the men on the expedition had been unmarried. Gnaeus Pompey had his wife along, as did Senator Metellus Scipio, and while Cassius Longinus' wife had died on the voyage, the widow of Pompey Magnus lived in the town even now. But there were far too few Roman women to perpetuate any kind of society, and...

"Unless we can bring about a second generation to inherit, all we have done, all we will do here will be for naught."

"And the only way that might come about is to have some of the natives join us," Pompey the Younger said.

"Yes, yes, we've been over this before," Cato interrupted. "We were discussing your strategy for the summer's campaign.

You're using the legions as bait to draw the Novans into the very neighborhood of Pompeius itself."

"Yes," Pompey answered, "and yes, I've thought it through, time and again. I've discussed with the legates and the senior centurions of each legion, and they agree." He spread his hands and smiled. "I know what concerns you both. You heard stories of Alesia, and of any number of other cities put to a siege. And it's true, a besieged city can see terrible hardship. Starvation, disease, you name it."

"And our food stocks are none too generous," Cicero reminded him.

"Granted. But what you do not know is that holding a city under siege is no easier than being besieged. It's also some of the most difficult warfare to learn. I suppose Pullo and Vorenus have some idea of how to carry out a siege; they were probably both at Alesia, which to give Caesar all due credit was a brilliant piece of work. But how easily can they transfer that knowledge to these Novans?"

Cato's eyebrows rose in sudden realization. "You don't think they have the capacity to learn?"

"The capacity, yes," Pompey said. "I have no reason to believe these Novans are any more or less intelligent than a Greek, a Gaul, a Roman or any other man. Not from what I've seen of them, in particular our old friend Four Bears. But what I think they lack is patience. Bringing down a city is a work of months. I don't think they will wait that out. No, they will come here and try to attack the walls. When they are all gathered here, angry, hungry and frustrated, outside our walls, then our two legions will crush them."

"Pullo and Vorenus, and their men?"

"They will make a difference," Pompey allowed. "But not

enough. Not in the time they have. That's why I intend to get this done yet this summer, Consuls; we can't allow them any more time. If they help the Novans to build a real army, we won't stand a chance."

"I still don't like it," Cato said, "but I have to agree with you. We have to conclude this business quickly. If the Novans can see that their best option is to live alongside us..."

"I remind you, Consul, they initiated this war against us. The best way to achieve what you want, the best way to convince them to live with us, is to show them that the alternative does not bear contemplation."

"A Pax Romana here in the new world," Cicero said.

"Better that than the alternative, neh? You yourself said it, Cicero. We are Rome. If there is one thing I know, it is that Rome is all of that which most of the world is not. We must maintain our civilization. We must maintain our standards. We must prevail."

"We are Rome," Cicero breathed. "Yes, you're right about that much."

Cato was less impressed. "You'd better be right about the other as well, young man."

The two consuls left then. Behind them, General Pompey shook his head. "I am growing tired," he told the empty Senate chamber, "of having the same arguments over and over, with the same old men."

In a war camp of the People

Titus Caninus awoke quickly at a shake on his shoulder. Night had fallen some time earlier, and lacking anything else to do, Caninus had curled up on the hut's dirt floor and gone to sleep.

The crude shelter was dark; he could see nothing, but he heard a voice.

"Wake up, legionary." Caninus knew a moment of surprise at recognizing the voice. He had not seen or heard from Lucius Vorenus since his capture. A native had brought him a dish of food about half-way through the day; other than that, he had been left alone.

A stick stirred the fire pit, and a feeble flame sprang up, providing enough light for Caninus to see the centurion, and another with him.

The second man was shorter than Vorenus but broader, darker of skin and broader of face. He also wore the helmet of a centurion. "Titus Pullo, I presume," Caninus said.

Pullo nodded. "Listen fast, legionary, and listen well. We'll be breaking camp in the morning, at sunrise, to move north. Your companions took to a ship, which sailed off, and the war chiefs here decided they want to follow. You, soldier, are the only captive."

Vorenus nodded in agreement. He produced an object that glittered in the firelight; a knife. A good Roman knife, of iron. "Yes," he said. "And the motherless scum want to kill you before we moved on. Pullo and I decided that killing another Roman in battle, on the field, in the manner of war—that is one thing. But standing by and allowing a fellow Roman to be butchered by savages, that's another." He bent and quickly cut through the thongs securing Caninus' hands and feet.

With that done, Vorenus stood, spoke a few words quietly to Pullo, and left.

Titus Caninus rolled over and sat up. He rubbed his wrists and then his ankles, regarding Pullo carefully all the while. "Now what, sir?"

"We wait a few moments. Vorenus will raise an alarm at the other end of the camp. When he does, you will run, as fast as you can. The war chief, he will want Vorenus and I to use our horses to pursue you come morning, but I assure you our pursuit will be among the most incompetent in the history of Roman arms." He grinned. "You should have no trouble making it away from the camp. After that, you're on your own; you have a long ways to go through hostile country."

"Wouldn't be the first time, sir."

"We'll wait here until we hear the outcry," Pullo said, seating himself on the dirt floor. He looked sharply at Caninus. "Were you at Alesia?"

"I was, sir," Caninus agreed. "I was at the gap in the western side of the inner wall, there where the streams flowed through, when the Gauls attacked. We had some tense moments, there in the gap, but the order was to hold that line—and we held it. Gauls coming at us from both sides, thousands of them. I heard sixty thousand attacked us from the Gaul's relief army on the hills to the south, and we held. Damn them, but we held."

"Aye, that you did. Vorenus and I were with the Thirteenth then, on the other side of the city, to the east." He was silent for a moment. "You saw Caesar there and then, did you?"

"I did," Caninus agreed, "on that great black horse of his. He rode back and forth through the battle, shouting at us to hold that line. We did. There was hardly any way to let that man down."

"And yet you joined with Pompey when he and Caesar fell out."

"I did, sir."

"You served under Caesar. You have the measure of the man. What made you turn?"

Caninus thought hard. The centurion had asked a serious

question, one that demanded a serious answer. Titus Caninus knew he was not a man of deep thought, but neither was he a dullard; he knew he had joined the legions Pompey mustered for a reason, but it took him a few moments to put that reason into words.

"Sir," he began slowly, "you are right, of course. I did have the measure of the man. As a general Caesar, he has no peer. But as a king? Sir, I heard Pompey, I heard the Optimate Senators speak, and I have their measure as well. Whatever his intent, no one man should have the power Caesar sought. Only the gods should have that kind of power, and I'm not always so sure about them." He stretched his cramped legs out, knowing he'd be relying on them soon enough. "My father used to talk about the conflict between Marius and Sulla. Two men were then contesting for total control of one city, of all of Rome's provinces, even. Should we not be past that sort of thing by now? Caesar wanted to follow in Sulla's footsteps. Pompey said no, the Senate should rule. I agreed with him. The Senate is far from perfect, the gods know that as well as we, but they are in the main wise men—and better several imperfect men run things that one imperfect man, no matter who he is otherwise. In the Senate, the men's strengths complement each other; their weaknesses are reduced. But a dictator, he rules with no one to check him in his errors." He was a bit surprised at the depth of his own assessment of Roman government.

"You may have something," Pullo admitted. "You may indeed. Still, Vorenus and I—we have a course to run." Shouting erupted from the other end of the encampment. "And now, so do you. Stand up."

Caninus stood up and faced the centurion.

"Now," Pullo ordered, "we must make this look right. Hit me."

"Sir?"

"Hit me. A good blow. This must be convincing. Knock me cold if you can. Oh, come on, I've been hit before."

Caninus grinned suddenly. It wasn't every day you were ordered to knock an officer senseless. "As you command, sir," he said. He drew back his right fist and crashed it into Pullo's jaw.

Pullo dropped to one knee. He shook his head, dazed. "Well struck. Run now, soldier—run away from this camp, run like the hounds of Hades were on your heels."

Caninus followed that order as well. He ducked out of the rude tent and found himself on the edge of an encampment in a dark forest. A sliver of moon was overhead. He looked up quickly—there was Ursa Major, and there, there was the star leading north. North to Pompeius, Servia Merula, and home. He took a step and stumbled over something—his own sword belt with the gladius in its scabbard, his caliga and his helmet. Pullo had obviously left if there to be found. He gathered the equipment in his arms; time enough to put boots and belt on later.

His few hours in captivity had in the end cost him nothing but a sore head and had gifted him with some valuable information about their Roman opponents—information that he knew had to get to General Pompey as soon as possible. After a last look back at the Novan war camp to make sure he was not observed, Titus Caninus raced away into the night.

The Neptune

"This harbor," Gracchus Agrippa observed, "is big enough for an armada. How many ships could you fit in here?"

"Hundreds," Captain Quintus Pulcio agreed. "Maybe more. See that big island?" He pointed at a rocky prominence in the mouth of the harbor. "You could build a fort there that would dwarf the one we've already built inland. It would command the very entrance. With a chain across the harbor mouth, some proper artillery there, some ballistae and a few onagers, not a ship could enter."

"I should think there will be a considerable city here one day."

"I should think you're right," Pulcio said. 'There's another smaller harbor to the south, but nothing compared to this. I'll grant you we haven't explored the coast to the north yet, but this harbor will likely become the center of shipping up and down this coast, in time."

"In time," Agrippa said, "and presuming we win this war."

"And while you are on that topic," the freighter captain said, "are you quite sure of where you want to offload?"

"Quite sure. No reason to go too near the fort at Pulcia; the Novans will no doubt have people watching it, and we'll be going ashore just close enough that they'll see. That's why I want to go in at midday. We're supposed to be seen, after all."

"I fought pirates in the Mediterranean under old Pompey," Pulcio mused. "That's why I was glad to sign up with him on this expedition, even if it did go farther off course than any of us could have imagined. But I have to say this is by far the oddest war, on sea or on land, that I have ever seen or heard of."

"You're not alone," Agrippa laughed. "But Pompey the Younger seems to know what he's about."

At noon, two hundred and ten Roman soldiers went ashore just north and east of the fort at Pulcia. A hundred and eighty infantry were followed by twenty archers and ten slingers from the *Neptune.* The troops assembled into cohorts and made a show of marching inland, heading northwest towards Pompeius.

As they marched, Novan runners headed south, carrying the news to where Man-Ready-For-War and the bulk of the Novan forces were already headed north. The Novan army altered their course to the west to intercept the Romans.

The low country

A faint light was breaking in the east, and Titus Caninus was hungry.

At least thirst was never a problem in this low country. While Caninus was loathe to drink from the water of the marshes, enough small, clear streams flowed that he had no trouble finding clean water. Food, on the other hand...

A small village lay in a clearing in front of the legionary, no more than a dozen wood and wicker huts surrounded by a few small fields of maize and squash. It wasn't the crops that caught his attention, but rather the rack of drying deer meat that stood near one of the huts.

Slowly, he crept towards the huts. There was nobody moving about yet, but Caninus supposed they'd be up and about soon; farming folk, wherever they lived, always seemed to rise early. The rack of drying meat stood just a few steps away. He stood up, looked around, and quickly stepped to the rack. The first piece of meat he stuffed in his mouth and then, chewing, he grabbed several more strips of venison to put in the pouch attached to his sword belt.

He ducked around the back of a hut and found, leaning against a wall, a rude bow and a leather quiver of arrows. He grabbed them up and ran into the forest.

At midday he stopped for a rest in a tiny clearing and used the break to examine the weapons he had stolen. The bow's draw length was too short for his long arms, the string seemed to be of strips of animal gut braided into a fine cord. The bow itself was of willow, not as powerful as a Roman bow, but the arrows were longer and had points of some kind of black stone with razor-sharp edges. He tried a few experimental shots and was able to hit a large knot on a tree twenty paces distant with three arrows out of four. *With a bit of care,* he thought, *I won't go hungry.* He dumped the arrows out of the quiver to examine the lot, and in the bottom of the quiver he found a flint knife with a handle of bone.

He repacked everything, slung the quiver over his shoulder, and pressed on.

Nightfall found him on the bank of a small river. The night was warm, and he didn't know the area, so he eschewed building a fire, instead chewing a chunk of the dried venison and drinking from the river before sleeping in the shelter of a fallen log.

Morning came all too quickly. Titus Caninus rubbed his eyes when the sun woke him, drank some more water, and trudged northwest, chewing on dried deer meat as he walked.

On the march inland the previous summer, Caninus had been in the middle of a long column of soldiers and had not noticed much of the countryside they had marched through. He knew that the lands were wet and marshy near the sea, rising into rolling, wooded hills interspersed with open meadows as you went inland; the town of Pompeius was built in the middle of just such an expanse of grass.

Caninus had crossed several small streams that led more or less northeast, but he knew better than to follow watercourses or trails, as that was where one found villages and towns. So, he walked through the woods, keeping his bearing by the sun as the day wore on.

"Such trees," he marveled quietly to himself as he walked through a stretch of forest. He passed one large, sprawling tree dotted with large white blossoms, tempting him to stop and pick several, but he knew they wouldn't last until he got back to Pompeius and Servia Merula. Another large tree bore a profusion of yellow-green blooms. Several small birds, gray with black caps and bibs and similar to the marsh tits of Gaul, flocked past him into the brush.

As he moved slowly into the low hills that climbed out of the low country, the differences between this land and the Europe that he knew from birth hit him. He stopped suddenly and looked around. "No roads," he mused, "no large towns or cities, no planted orchards or big farms. There's nothing here but a few small trails and scattered villages. These people don't even work metal. Why?"

The trees had no answer, so he moved on.

Chapter Ten

COUNTERSTRIKES

A primary advantage the Roman army had in the initial conflict against the Novans was that General Pompey controlled the initiative. While the training of the Roman renegades Vorenus and Pullo had an effect, the Alligator People war chief maintained overall command and he himself was resistant to the discipline of the Romans, making their impact less effective than it would have otherwise been. The Novan forces were fierce, but also predicable.

With that advantage, the two cohorts of infantry were able to draw the bulk of the Novan army into following them, leaving a good part of the Novan territory unguarded, their families, homes and supplies left unprotected. Their failure to cover their rear areas was not only a disadvantage to them but an opportunity to the forces of Rome, who sallied forth from a town that was chronically short of meat and corn. Pompey knew that the Novans stocks would be easy to capture, which would not only fill Roman stomachs but in so doing, also deprive *the Novan soldiers of forage. Thus, two purposes were served when Pompey implemented the second half of his campaign. An army, like a city, depends on forage, and using food as a fulcrum to twist the odds in Rome's favor was key.*

—From Gnaeus Pompey Novus' New World Diaries

In the forest

The fifth day of Titus Caninus' journey, it rained.

It wasn't an ordinary rain. The morning broke with dark clouds racing in from the sea, driven by a freshening wind. By mid-day the wind had increased to a gale, and the rain came down in torrents.

"Best I stop for the night early," Caninus said to nobody. He had been walking through marshes, but a low ridge laid only a few hundred paces ahead, covered with tall trees. He headed that way and, on the top of the ridge, found a small, abandoned Novan village.

Calling the place a village was, in Caninus' estimation, overly generous. Three circular huts lay in a narrow U shape, with the untended remains of two small fields on the outside of the U. Caninus drew his gladius and circled the place, slowly, moving through the trees, but there were no people about.

Finally, he went into one of the huts.

Inside, it was musty and dark. The heavy rain drummed on the hide roof, which leaked in several places. There was a fire pit in the center of the round hut, but it had been cold for many days. Caninus looked around, but aside from the charred remnants of a few sticks, there was nothing that would make a fire.

Outside, a gust of wind rattled the abandoned structure. The hide flap at the door blew open, allowing entrance of the wind-driven rain. Caninus pulled the flap shut and braced it shut with his confiscated Novan bow.

He passed a boring afternoon. No artifacts in the hut attracted his scrutiny; whoever had once lived here had taken all of their chattels with them when they left. Finally, he fell into a fitful sleep, curled up on the dirt floor of the hut.

Sometime later he awoke with a start. It took a few moments for Caninus to realize what was different; when he did, he sat up with a grin.

"The storm has passed," he announced.

The inside of the hut was pitch dark. Caninus felt his way to the entrance and peered out. There was barely any light to see; plainly the moon had set some time before. A few stars were visible in the sky, and some low clouds still scudded by overhead. Around him, the forest dripped.

In the east, the very faintest first light of morning was visible. Caninus gathered his gear and sat in front of the hut until there was sufficient light to see.

Then he moved on.

Pompeius

The latest reports from the mounted messengers confirmed it; even Centurions Vorenus and Pullo were taken in by the feint southeast into the Alligator People's territory. The two cohorts from the First Legion were carrying on a fighting withdrawal northwest towards Pompeius, with message traffic carried back and forth by their mounted scouts. The cohorts were in good order; three more men were dead and two wounded, but both wounded men were able to move and fight. Forces from the three tribes were in pursuit; the bulk of the Novan forces had been drawn east.

Gnaeus Pompey issued his next orders early the following morning.

Second Legion struck southwest like a thrown spear. Led by Legate Lucius Germanius, the five cohorts of the first marched into B'Kou territory with simple orders:

> Empty all Novan villages. Give the natives a chance to leave peacefully but kill any who resist. Take any adult males prisoner. Burn any supplies that cannot be carried away. Any man who kills anyone not in arms or molests a woman will be severely punished.

It was a plan in two parts; provision the army off the enemy's supplies and destroy the base of support for the Novan forces.

The first village encountered was a small collection of huts, with no more than forty inhabitants. The only Novans in the village were old men, women and children. One old man tried to resist the cohort that marched in even as the other four surrounded the place; he was knocked down, disarmed, and herded to the side with the others. The village huts were burned, their supplies of dried meat and fish taken, their fields of maize and squash set ablaze. When this was done, the thousand men of the Second marched off, leaving the Novans to contemplate the ruins of the village.

Six more villages fell in the next ten days. On the twelfth day, the Second turned west into the foothills as planned, and there they found a considerable town in the approaches to the mountains, an A'Tep town with almost a thousand inhabitants.

Fields of maize and squash surrounded the town. Dogs ran barking on the outskirts, and tamed turkeys fed on the edges of the fields.

Legate Lucius Germanius halted his men a league east of the town to confer with the two mounted scouts that had discovered it.

"Mostly women, children and old men, sir," one of the scouts reported. "A few young men with bows and lances, but they weren't too alert. I don't think they know we're in the area."

"What about the town itself?" Germanius demanded.

"About like the others, but larger." The man climbed down from his horse, scraped a spot in the sandy earth clear with his boot. He found a stick and sketched as he spoke. "It's laid out in a great circle. There's the usual big building in the center, a sort of temple, like, except this one is raised up on a big mound of packed earth, maybe as high as a tall man's head above the ground. The huts near the temple are the largest, I'd wager they belong to the tribal chiefs or whatever passes for the quality among these people." He drew a large circle around the town. "There's a small palisade, but it's only waist-high, and mostly made of sticks and wattle. It looks like it's made to keep children in and animals out, not to protect against attack."

"And their fields?"

"Surrounding the town, sir, except for lanes, sort of paths, like, at east and west. The maize is nearly shoulder-high, sir, and is planted right up to the palisade." The man looked keenly at Germanius; it was obvious what he was getting at.

"That's good," Germanius said, taking the hint. "We can use that." He turned to his five cohort commanders, who were gathered around, listening. "I want the first and second cohorts here with me. Third cohort is to go to the south and take blocking position. Fourth, to the west. Fifth, to the north. Move quickly, move quietly, take up positions at the tree line on the far side of the fields away from the town. We'll give you time to get into position, then on a single trumpet blast, first and second will move into the attack. Remember, control your men; I want no dead women or children, no rape, no looting; we take foodstuffs only. Third, fourth and fifth, you'll move in at the signal of two trumpet blasts and trap any villagers who try to flee. All cohorts will advance in line of battle. Keep low going through the fields so they won't see you until the last possible moment. Kill any armed native who puts up a fight, otherwise, we're herding them, to the west out of the town. Pass the plan on to all of your centurions; I don't want any confusion about what we're supposed to be doing. I will be here with First Cohort. Any questions? No? Get moving."

Three cohorts slipped quietly around through the woods to surround the town. Germanius waited impatiently, tapping his foot, watching the shadow of a sapling in front of him move slowly across the ground. When it gets to that leaf, he thought, then it will be time.

Slowly, maddeningly, the shadow moved. It touched the brown shape of a dead leaf from the great oak he stood under. The legate pointed at the trumpeter next to him. "Now."

A single, shrilling trumpet blast echoed through the forest. He heard the shouts from the two cohorts on the move:

"First cohort, in line of battle! Advance!"

"Second cohort, in line of battle! Advance!!"

Tramp, tramp, tramp. Four hundred men marched forwards behind their scuta, accompanied by warning cries and shouts of alarm from the town.

The two attacking cohorts marched side by side through the

fields on either side of the narrow lane, trampling the maize as they went.

Some Novans fired arrows blindly into the maize, but from the town all they could see was the tall tassels of the plants moving. They had no vantage point, no watch towers to see over the crops. One enterprising man finally figured out to climb the mound of earth supporting the temple and watch from there.

"Romans!" he screeched. "Many, many Romans!"

The few young men left to guard the town, one of the A'Tep's largest and most prosperous, ran to find weapons, even as the women, children and elderly began a panicky and disorganized retreat to the west.

They ran right down the narrow lane into the woods, astride which sat the fourth cohort, Second Legion.

Lucius Germanius followed the first and second into the town, arriving at the palisade just as a dozen young Novan men finally armed themselves with clubs and lances. They charged the Roman lines, howling like madmen, and were just as quickly repulsed, bouncing off the Roman scuta like pebbles off a tiled roof. They fell back into the village, leaving two men behind dead, pierced by Roman pila.

"Sound the second call," Germanius ordered the trumpeter. Two long blasts echoed out through the town. The remaining three cohorts of the legion moved in under a shower of arrows from the town to strike the flanks and rear.

Once the legion was in the town, the normal order of the Roman ranks dissolved into chaos. Shrieking women and shouting men made the very air ring. Roman soldiers fought in small groups and mutually supporting pairs, while the Novans attacked in wild abandon, flailing club blows against Roman armor and, occasionally, against Roman flesh. Several climbed the mound holding the temple and loosed arrows at the Roman troops. Others hid in the huts and jabbed lances at Roman soldiers as they passed, usually only to die under stabs from several gladii when they revealed themselves. While in the town, the Romans were not as easily able to defend against arrows and lances, which cost them several soldiers, but in the end, the outcome was never truly in doubt.

Within the hour the battle was over.

Eleven Roman soldiers were dead, and nine more wounded, only one of those serious. The town proved to be full of stored grain and dried meat, and the live turkeys were a bonus, although any of those the Romans were able to catch were immediately killed for that night's meal. Sixty-two young male Novans were taken prisoner and were assigned to pull travois loaded with the town's goods.

The rest of the town's inhabitants were moved into the woods and held there under guard.

Germanius went and examined the huddled women and weeping children, and on the spur of the moment knew a moment's compassion. "Fire that temple," he said, "and trample the fields flat. Spare their houses. We won't send women and children to sleep on the bare ground, and we don't need them straggling after us, begging for shelter. Make sure you search the place for any weapons, though; pile those in the temple before you burn it. Detail some men to build pyres and burn our fallen."

It was quickly done. By the time the temple was ablaze, it was nearing nightfall.

"Sir," one of the cohort commanders asked him, "will we make camp here tonight?"

"No."

The man looked disappointed, and suddenly an image flashed in Germanius' mind: All the women of the tribe, gathered together, helpless. "No, we won't stay here. That pyre is bound to draw attention, and I'd rather not give the natives time to concentrate against us. No, we'll move on, to the northwest, until midnight at least. Then we'll make a cold camp until morning."

"Yes, sir," the man frowned.

"Centurion," Germanius reminded the man, "make sure every commander remembers my orders. We do no harm to anyone unless they bear arms against us. Do you understand that? No beatings, no rape, no plunder for personal gain. Any who violate orders will be whipped. Once this is over, we will have to live with these people. We need no tales of atrocity spread among them."

"Yes, sir."

In the low country

Novan runners darted east through the forest to where Man-Ready-For-War and White Oak were coordinating the pursuit of the Romans moving towards the Roman city. On receiving that word, White Oak wanted to drop the pursuit. "These Romans are already fleeing," he pointed out. "They are returning to their city. The others raid in our villages and towns."

Man-Ready-For-War pointed at the messenger. "His news is days old. We have no idea where to go to chase these other Romans. Our quarry is in front of us, weighted down with their shields and swords. Now is the time to run them to ground. No, we will continue."

"It is easy for you to say this," White Oak shouted, "now that we have driven them out of the lands of the Alligator People. But now they raid in the lands of the B'Kou and A'Tep, you do not care."

"I care only about finding these Romans and killing them," the Alligator People's war chief said, his voice and bearing radiating arrogance. "When that is done, we will find the others and kill them, and then we will burn their town."

"How many Romans have you been able to kill so far?" White Oak sneered. "And how many of our young men have the Romans killed in return?"

Man-Ready-For-War flew into a rage and ordered all of the Alligator People to continue the pursuit. "We will deal with the Romans fleeing us now," he snapped, "and turn west to fight the others when that is done." White Oak disagreed and took the warriors of the B'Kou and A'Tep on the trail of the Second. Pullo and Vorenus conferred quickly and decided that Pullo and three cavalrymen should stay with the A'Tep and B'Kou to screen their move west, while Vorenus and the remaining four would go with Man-Ready-For-War and his forces. Both of the Roman centurions argued against splitting the forces, but Man-Ready-For-War overruled them.

The Novan forces were split, their supplies going up in smoke behind them, and the summer was rapidly slipping through their fingers.

The B'Kou and A'Tep warriors found sign of the Roman legion passing through B'Kou territory. The inhabitants of the razed villages all reported similar news: "They killed only those who fought back, but they took all the food and burned the crops." The legion had turned west, into the hills, and was raiding into A'Tep country now. White Oak ordered his men to follow.

To the southeast

Titus Caninus knew the country was familiar; Pompeius could not be far off. After ten days on the run, he was beginning to look rather Novan himself. His skin was burned brown by the sun, and he had the roughly cured skin of a deer wrapped around his hips to help obscure his Roman belt and gladius. He had given thought to abandoning his helmet, but in the end, he carried it along, knowing it to be nearly irreplaceable.

There was one respect in which he knew he would never pass for a Novan, and that was apparent one morning as he went to a still pool to drink and contemplated his reflection in the water: Several days' growth of beard now obscured his jaw.

"I wonder why they don't grow beards," he wondered aloud, examining his own hirsute image in the clear water. "We're used to deriding Gauls and such as hairy barbarians, just because we know what a razor is good for. What will we call these folk, then? Hairless barbarians?"

His own voice sounded odd, somehow, out in the woods all alone.

Caninus gathered his possessions, splashed across the small creek that fed the pool, and walked off through the woods. The evening before he had passed a clearing that he thought he remembered from the march inland, the summer before; he headed northwest now, hoping to hit the Tiber. The river would lead him home.

He stopped at midday, built a small fire of dry wood and cooked some of the venison from the deer he had killed the day before. He stamped the fire out and walked on, eating as he went. Late in the day he hid in the brush while a war party of Novans passed by. He carefully counted the men and noted their equipment; these, like others he had seen, bore the rude wooden scuta that the renegade Romans were teaching them to carry and use.

"Heading for Pompeius, no doubt," he muttered to himself. When they had passed, he slipped away, bearing due north to avoid the Novan's line of march.

Two evenings later, Titus Caninus, legionary of the First Nova Roman Legion's first cohort, approached the gates of Pompeius wearing the skin of a deer, his helmet and sword belt, carrying a native bow and arrows, and bearing two turkeys taken late in the day. After establishing his bona fides to the guards at the gate, he was allowed into the city and ushered into the presence of General Pompey.

"Well, now," the young General greeted him, "aren't you a sight. I suppose your cohort presumes you to be dead?"

"I wouldn't chance a guess, sir," Caninus offered, then did so: "I suppose they probably do."

"Well, they should be back here within the next day or so. You spent some time with the Novans, then? Sit yourself down, soldier."

Caninus hesitated—this was a nobleman and a general, after all—before shrugging and planting himself in a low chair across from the table that served the young officer as a desk.

"Tell me," Pompey ordered, "your opinion of the savages as soldiers."

Titus Caninus thought for a few moments, and Pompey noted the expression. *He's smarter than he lets on,* the young general told himself.

"Well, sir, they are smart, there's no denying it. Vicious, but smart. And brave—on the coast, they marched into our lines with only thin wooden shields. We cut down their front line, and they came on. I hit one of their chiefs with a pila, and his men closed the line and came on. We struck down five for every one of ours they struck, and they came on. They coordinate well, too. Their archers covered them very well, as well as any support Roman archers could offer. I imagine that the Romans among them have trained them, but even so, the Novans are quick studies."

"You were captured in battle?"

"I was in their captivity, yes sir," he began. "I was on the line, in the middle of the night. They were harassing us with archery and such throughout the night, so Centurion Agrippa kept half of us awake and on guard at all times. I was on watch, and one of them made a noise to draw me to the top of the earthworks. It was an ambush. One of their warriors was hiding, it seemed as though he came out of the ground itself. Hit me here," he pointed to the side of the head, "and knocked me cold. Good thing I have a hard head, but they dragged me off before my comrades could react."

"They held you as a captive, then?"

"Yes sir. But I was among them for less than a day. The two Roman officers with them, they let me go."

Pompey's eyes opened wide. "They let you go? Why?"

"Sir, the one of them, Vorenus, he said that the Novan warriors were moving out to follow the rest of my cohort. They wanted to kill me before they left. Actually, to be exact, they wanted to cut me apart. Well, Vorenus and Pullo reckoned that if they allowed that, then we'd treat any of their men we captured the same way."

"And they'd likely be right, whether ordered or not. Atrocity breeds atrocity."

"Just so, sir. So, the night after I was taken, they came and told me all this, then Vorenus, he raised a fuss at the other side of the camp. I knocked Pullo out and ran for it."

Pompey laughed. "I've met Titus Pullo. He's a big man, knocking him out would be a trick."

"He did stand still for it, sir," Caninus said, grinning. "Ordered me to do it, in fact."

"To make your escape look plausible?"

"That's how he put it, sir." Caninus rubbed his knuckles. "Hard-jawed man, that Pullo. But a decent man, in the end. He told me that he had no issue killing a man in battle, in the way of war, but killing a helpless captive was dishonorable. Yes, a hard man, but a civilized one."

"You're a hard one yourself," Pompey said. "All to the good, you'll need to be. You have powerful gods watching over you, Legionary Caninus. I expect we'll see big things from you." Pompey startled Titus Caninus by standing and offering his hand. As the legionary took the General's hand and shook, he regarded the young man carefully. The General was no soft child of privilege, at least not any longer; his eyes were hard, his grip strong, his hand tough with calluses. "Take the next two days to rest, clean up and recover yourself. I hear tell you've taken up with our former cook boy suddenly turned into a Roman woman full-fledged, neh?"

"True enough, sir," Caninus grinned.

"Well, don't exhaust yourself with your reunion. Your cohort will be in action again soon enough."

"I'll be ready, sir."

"Yes, I'm sure you will. Very well, soldier—be about your recuperation, then. You're dismissed."

Caninus saluted and left to go find Servia Merula.

The Senate

While Titus Caninus and Servia Merula were enjoying their

reunion in the tiny sleeping room in the back of the shack that served as the latter's "inn," the Senate was debating another issue, this one having to do not with the war but its aftermath.

"Assuming we win," Marcus Junius Brutus was saying, "am I correct, my dear friend, colleague and Consul Cato, that you advocate taking the Novans into our very city? As citizens?"

"If they desire, yes," Cato said. "As our constitution states, we will–we have had that discussion before, I remind you."

"I harbored reservations then, and still do. Could you elaborate on your reasons for that, if you please?"

"Certainly," Cato agreed. "It's not a complicated prospect, nor is it without precedent. Look you at the history of Rome."

"Rome has ever expanded by the use of arms. But have Rome's wars been fought with mere conquest, loot and rapine as their goals? No. Rome's goal was to spread Roman civilization, Roman culture. Roman citizens even now, in Europe, in the old world, live from Judea to Hispania, from Africa to Gaul. The army is the sinew of Rome, the Senate its mind, but the citizens of Rome are its beating heart."

"The old world, you said," Brutus objected. "I concede all you say of the old world. But this new world is different, its people are different. They are far more primitive than any Gaul, Saxon, Briton or Egyptian. The basest Hun of the far east is more advanced than these people, who lack even the knowledge of metal—they make their tools of bone and stone!"

"So they do," Cato agreed again. "There can be no doubt, these people's tools, their towns, their farms, all are far more primitive than any we have seen in Europe. But can you judge a man by the tools he uses? Some may think so. Perhaps you do, friend Brutus. Before coming here to Nova Terra, I may have myself. But no longer. Not after meeting Four Bears, not after meeting old Owl, or their general White Oak. They are men of considerable intelligence; they are men of substance. If it is intelligence you seek as a measure, Brutus, I would place Four Bears alongside any man in this chamber. If it is honor, or integrity, I say the same again."

Brutus considered that briefly before taking another tack. "So, when the war is won, and I am sure our young General will win it—what then?"

"Look at what we have done here already," Cato said, spreading his arms theatrically. He knew he would never be Cicero's equal as an orator, but he was learning a few tricks. "Look at this Senate chamber. Look at the town. Look at our fields, look at the new-fledged merchants even now beginning to think about trading with the natives. We are already building a future here."

"So, I ask you, friend Brutus—I ask all of you—what sort of future do we want? We have a bright start, a new Rome to match, nay, to exceed the old. We have a Constitution, we have a Senate seated, and we have the basis of a new government. But a government is nothing without its people. Here we have the seed, but the seed needs fertile soil in which to grow. The hearts and minds of the people here, they are that soil, and when this conflict is over, the only way our Nova Roma will grow is with their support, with their participation."

"Their participation as citizens," Brutus said.

"I would have it no other way," Cato answered. "I reminded you once, and will again, Rome started in exactly that way. Can we do any less?"

Brutus's normally dour expression turned thoughtful.

Cato continued. "If the Novans are not with us, then for all our grand pretensions, our new Rome is confined to the area around Pompeius. If they are with us, then all of their villages become Roman villages. All of their trading partners become our trading partners. All of their knowledge of the land, the people that live in other parts, will all become our knowledge. In this manner our new Rome will survive here. My friends, I see this not only as our best path, but as our only possible path."

He looked around; heads were nodding in agreement.

"They will elect representatives to the Council of Plebs, then?" Brutus asked.

"Of course," Cato replied, "and the best among them will sit here with us in the Senate."

Brutus stood. "I'm sorry, friend Cato," he said, "but I cannot agree."

"Say on," Cato conceded the floor.

Brutus left his seat and walked to the speaker's platform in the middle of the Senate chamber. "Friends," he said, "Here in this very chamber, only weeks ago, we listened to our esteemed colleague and friend Cicero remind us all how we, here in this new land, are all that remains of Rome. That here, in the new world, we are Rome."

"He was right, of course. But I ask you this: How is it that we came to be Romans? Was it by chance of birth? In part, perhaps, if only that we were fortunate enough to be born Roman. But how did Rome come about?"

"Our ancestors were not ordinary people. From Romulus on, the very gods marked Rome and Romans for something more than the barbarian folk that surrounded them. Rome was forged in the fires of adversity, facing Etruria, Gaul and Carthage. Eight hundred years and more have our ancestors been shaped by great events, leading to the men that stand here in this chamber. True, this is not the hallowed Senate chamber set in place by the early kings of Rome, but a new chamber for a new land, but it is not the building that makes the Senate—no, it is the men within it. These men are the foundation of our Republic. A Republic, I remind you, that a hallowed ancestor of mine created through the destruction of a tyrant. And now, we are to consider allowing the basest savages of all to take part in shaping this new Republic, with no sense of the traditions involved? Of the honor? Of the responsibility? No, I say. We cannot—we must not—allow it."

"Our new constitution allows full citizenship to any native who learns Latin and takes an oath of loyalty," Titus Annius Milo pointed out. "You voted for that constitution, Brutus."

"And I still support it," Brutus retorted. "But nothing in that provision requires us to extend the offer of taking that oath. Perhaps in generations to come, some of the Novans will acquire the learning and the sophistication to serve Rome in some capacity. But now? A stone-chipping savage in the Senate? No."

"Do you have a motion to make, Brutus?"

"I do, Cato. I move that legislation be made barring any offer of citizenship be made to any of full Novan ancestry until the span of three generations have passed, beginning with the founding of Pompeius."

"This motion should wait until we have a Council of Plebs in assembly," Cicero objected. "The constitution says legislation must be approved by both bodies."

"There is as yet no Council," Brutus snapped, "and what of it if there is? Shall we wait on a council of one, drawn from the merchants and soldiers of Pompeius? The constitution allows one chamber to act alone when the other chamber is unable to gather. I invoke that clause now."

The argument was heated; and went on for some time. After the Senator's passions wore down, Cato called the issue to a vote.

"The motion passes," he announced after the simple showing of hands, "by a count of five to four."

Off to one side, still wearing his soldier's cloak, belt and breastplate, Gnaeus Pompey stood up. "I would speak," he said.

"Say on," Cato agreed; he had not failed to note the young General's hand among the no votes.

Pompey stood up and brandished a scroll. "I have read the constitution as well as you, friend Brutus," he began, "and I note that it gives certain powers to the Tribunes, both the Tribune of Plebs and the Tribune of Mars—that latter being me. One of those is a veto power. I use that power now, to veto this motion. Veto, I say!"

"Would you favor us with a reason?" Brutus sneered.

Pompey the Younger sneered right back at the older man. "Have you so much as spoken with one of the people you deride? No? I thought not. Well, I have, and what's more, I've fought against them. I will say this: Few Roman generals could have accomplished what they have, with the weapons they have to work with."

"That proves nothing," Brutus argued. "In fact, it proves my point. It is only the influence of the renegades Vorenus and Pullo that allow them to make any headway at all."

"Only today I spoke with a man who was held captive by the Novans," Pompey shouted. "Only today, that man told me that Vorenus and Pullo are largely occupied with holding these people back! Ask Legionary Titus Caninus, soldier of Rome, if the Novans can fight! Ask any of my men if the Novans can fight, and they will tell you that these people are canny, dangerous, and worthy opponents. And I will tell you another thing; my father knew the Novan chief Four Bears, even as I know him. I tell you he is a smart one. A fine mind, the equal of any—any in this chamber!"

"He is your enemy!"

"If a commander may be judged by the caliber of his enemies, then I will be remembered in our history as a great general indeed. I am satisfied with that. I am also satisfied with the progress of our summer campaign, and I am confident we will prevail. When we do, I would be satisfied as well to sit beside Four Bears in this very chamber, should he choose to do so. No, my veto stands. Citizenship for any who wish it. No less."

"Veto is recorded," Cato said, his voice solemn but a note of satisfaction evident, nonetheless. "The motion is not carried."

The session dissolved in some disarray after that. As he was leaving, the young General Pompey found himself facing the senior Consul, who had a new look of respect in his eyes.

"That," Cato said, "was very well said, General."

Pompey snorted. "Brutus may come from an old and distinguished family, but sometimes he cannot see past the end of his own nose."

"His family is a proud one," Cato reminded the younger man. "His ancestor drove the last kings out of Rome–in many ways, his family founded the old Republic."

"I grant you that. But he seems determined to forestall us starting a new one here."

The two men walked outside into the Forum. From the hill that the Senate building occupied, one could see over the walls of the city to the forest and the stream of the Tiber nearby. The summer day was warm, but the full, oppressive humidity of the region had not set in yet. Overhead, the sky was the brilliant blue so startling when first beheld; it was as though the very heavens themselves were somehow different in the new world.

"Consul," Pompey began, "I didn't say what I did just for Four Bears, or just for his tribe."

"Go on," Cato prompted.

"Look you at those hills. We've enough Novans here in the town, my adopted sister for one, that we have learned a little about what lies beyond those hills. We know this land goes far to north and south, and we know that to the west there are mountains, with great plains beyond that. There are rumors even of cities far to the south, across another sea. Who knows how large this land will be? It is far, far larger than Europe, almost certainly, neh? With villages and towns full of people in the thousands, perhaps tens of thousands or more?"

Cato nodded agreement.

"Our friend Cicero says that we are Rome. Well, he's right. Cicero is an orator without peer, but at the time he gave his excellent speech, we didn't yet know all we know now. There may be thousands upon thousands upon thousands of Novan tribes out there," he motioned toward the hills, "and if our new Rome is to survive and prosper, we have to have them with us. To do that, we need a unifying idea; something that we can show them, by our own example. Our example must be something that is obviously a better, finer way to live than they know now. That example, Consul, has to be just what Cicero said, and more. Not just that we are Rome, but that they can be as well."

"And that can only be achieved if they are citizens."

"Exactly so. This war," Pompey went on, "is just a skirmish, as such things go. What are a few savages with weapons of wood and stone when measured against the armies of Carthage and Gaul?

This contest of arms, Consul, will only be the first step of showing these people the might of Rome. Next, we must show them the civilization of Rome. We have to be the example of what men can do. We are Rome, and we have to continue to be all that old Rome was at her best, not just at her worst."

Cato regarded the younger man. "Gnaeus," he said, "I have to say, I think your father would be very, very proud of you today. You have done the memory of Pompey Magnus proud"

Pompey the Younger bowed formally in gratitude. "In a city named in his honor," he said, "how could I possibly do any less?"

In the hills

Second Legion turned east back towards the city after twenty days, as ordered, leaving a trail of burned villages behind them. In tow were more than a hundred Novan captives, all dragging travois and carrying packs laden with maize, squash and dried meat.

Legate Lucius Germanius was all too aware that a growing number of Novan warriors were pursuing them. He pushed his men as hard as he thought possible; mounted scouts kept track of their pursuers until one of them came face-to-face with three mounted Roman renegades. The scout barely escaped with a nasty sword cut on one arm, after which Germanius kept the horsemen forward of the main body, watching for ambushes.

He was all too aware of the gathering pursuit. In the night, sometimes, the cook fires of the Novans were visible in the hills to their rear. The numbers were beginning to grow.

At sunset on the twenty-third day, Germanius sent for the centurions and optios from each century in the legion. As they walked, he issued orders: "From now on we keep moving every evening until midnight. Half the men on guard at all times during the night, while the other half sleeps. We march again at sunup, every day until we get to Pompeius."

"With the natives hot on our heels," one of the centurions observed.

"That's the plan, you know," Germanius said. "And it would seem to be successful—oh, yes, it would seem to be successful. Let's hope the rest of the young general's plan works as well."

Chapter Eleven

Gathering Forces

The Novans and the Roman renegades advising them understood that, while the bulk of war is fought by the sinews and weapons of an army, a smaller part is fought in the minds of the soldiers on both sides. While the Romans have made use of this in past conflicts, Pompey himself initially underestimated the capacity of the Novans to do likewise.

General Pompey made use of this in wrong-footing the Novan army and rampaging unchecked through their very home villages. But the Novans made use of it as well, in their obstinate refusal to be predictable. An army of Gauls or Carthaginians would have pursued the Roman army to the gates of their city and attacked at once, but the Novans did not. Later, it was determined that part of the delay was due to the disorganized nature of the Novan war parties. Another part of the delay was due to the necessity of gathering such supplies as the Second Legion had overlooked. But during the time taken, the Novans took pains to ensure that the Romans did not sleep too

peacefully behind the walls of the town, nor did they
venture forth without proper arms and preparations.
—From Gnaeus Pompey Novus' New World Diaries

Pompeius

Four days after the argument over citizenship in the Senate, the two cohorts of the First Legion returned to Pompeius. They marched through the town gate on a hot, still, muggy afternoon, and were told to stand down and rest. The soldiers immediately headed for the town's public wells for fresh water while their officers went to be debriefed by General Pompey.

Several men from the first cohort arrived at a well near the forum to find a familiar figure pulling a bucket of water up. "Titus Caninus!" one of them barked. "We thought you were dead!"

"Hah! Julius Salvius, you old bastard, it will take more than a few savages to kill me." He embraced the man, then exchanged greetings with the others. "Just back in from the field, are you?"

"Just now," Salvius replied, "with probably half the Novan army hot on our heels. I expect they are no more than a day behind us; we left some rear guards behind on most of the march, but they closed in tight when we got close to the city. What about you? You vanished in the middle of the night—what happened?"

Caninus pointed to his head. "Took a hell of a rap on the head, is what happened. They dragged me off, and I spent a day enjoying their hospitality before I managed to escape. Knocked one of the Roman renegade officers ass over tip and ran for it." He casually omitted the fact that he was allowed to escape by that same officer.

"And you made your way back here alone?"

"Well, I knew you lot were boarding a ship, no way to follow you. Figured it best I head straight here, better to get back into whatever fighting remains to be done."

"More likely to get back into whatever fucking was to be done," Salvius laughed. "We know about you and Servia Merula. One unattached Roman woman in this whole town, not counting old Pompey's widow, leave it to the Great Dog to sniff her out."

"Was she that came to me, as it happens," Caninus said with a broad grin. "The reason's obvious, neh? All these Roman men to choose from, stands to reason she'd want nothing but the best."

"There will be more fighting, though, no doubt of it." Salvius dipped a wooden cup that hung on a cord into a bucket and drank. "Gah. I do wish there was something better than water to drink."

"No sign of any wine grapes hereabouts," another legionary pointed out.

"Another thing we'll have to find a substitute for," Caninus said.

"Well, once we get the Novans properly subdued, at least there will be some local woman about, and..." Julius Salvius was interrupted by an outcry from the direction of the town gate. "Pluto's ass!" the legionary burst out. "Can't we even have a moment to wash our feet and eat something before someone sounds an alarm?"

Caninus accompanied the men from first cohort to the gate, where the guards were just closing the doors after allowing in a scout on a lathered, panting horse.

General Pompey himself pushed through the gathering crowd a moment later. "What gives?" he demanded.

The scout was already off his horse; he turned to the General and saluted. "Message for you from Second Legion, sir," he panted.

"Very well," Pompey the Younger said. "Someone get this man some water. You there, take his horse, take it to the stables, see that it's watered, fed and brushed down proper." He looked at the panting, sweat-soaked scout. "Sit down, over there on that stack of rails. Catch your breath."

A few moments later the scout had drunk a pint of water and was breathing more normally. "Legate Germanius reports that they are making a fighting withdrawal back to the city, sir. He reckons that more than a thousand native warriors are pursuing them, fewer than half of them are the black-painted ones. No fewer than three mounted Romans were sighted among the pursing Novans. The other Roman cavalry were not seen, sir."

"When does Germanius expect to be back here at the city?"

"No later than tomorrow night, sir. The Novans will be directly behind them. They've been in contact for the last several days. At least, until I left them this morning, that is."

"Excellent. All right, your horse is being fed; I suggest you do the same. Get to the barracks, get some food and some rest. You'll be needing all of your strength soon enough."

Next morning—in the forest

White Oak had slept well for once; a clear, cool night in the forest and a good fire saw to that, and as a Red Blanket society leader he was accustomed to sleeping in the open.

He woke at the first touch on his shoulder. He looked up to see the silhouette of a young man's head against the stars. "What is it?" he demanded.

"The Romans have left their camp, and are moving east," the scout reported.

"Good," White Oak said. He sat up and rubbed his eyes. "Tell the village war chiefs to make ready. Now that all the warriors are finally here, we can attack them at first light."

"It will be a hard thing," the young man said. "I am afraid our bows will do little good."

"Why? What do you mean?"

"The Romans, they march with prisoners of the People surrounding their soldiers. We will not be able to strike them without striking their own."

"They march down the south bank of the river as before?"

"They do."

Footsteps announced the arrival of another in the darkness, and White Oak knew who approached by the heavy tread of a big man in iron-hobnailed Roman shoes; Titus Pullo. The big Roman nodded to the runner and squatted by the remains of White Oak's small fire. The boy smiled at the Roman, showing a flash of white teeth in the night, and then slipped away into the darkness.

"You have heard?" he said.

White Oak nodded.

"I was just out and saw for myself." The Roman never seemed to sleep. "We will have to move quickly to catch up. If we can't slow them down, they will reach their city today."

"Can you use your horses to stop them?"

Pullo shook his head. "There are too many of them, too few of us. You see our horses as great, powerful beasts that seem fast and invincible, but we Romans have been dealing with cavalry for a long time." White Oak's eyes widened at the Latin term 'cavalry' until Pullo explained: "Cavalry, that is, soldiers mounted on horses. There are many ways to defend against men on horses. Every Roman soldier is taught how to do this."

"What do you advise?" White Oak asked.

"We will have to move quickly, to get in front of them," Pullo said. He looked up as the four other village war chiefs that accompanied the war party arrived. "We have to force them to..." He struggled for a moment for Novan words carrying the concepts he needed, deployment, formation, and defense. "We have to force them to move out of the arrangement they march in and into the arrangement they must use to protect themselves. The Novan prisoners among them are bearing supplies of food they will want to take to their city, and so if we confront them in the right way, they will have to adjust to prevent them from running away."

"And then?" one of the other chiefs asked. "We have attacked their lines before, their steel swords and shields. It is not a good thing to do."

"We won't attack head-on," Pullo said. He explained for a few moments, and in the gathering dawn he saw the Novan chiefs' heads nodding. "We must move quickly," he concluded. "On the march we must move quickly and quietly, and when we attack your men will have to respond to orders quickly. These are Roman soldiers, and they will react as a group, faster than you can imagine. They do not need to be told what to do; they are trained to react without thinking, without orders. They see and they do. Speed is the key."

"Our soldiers will move like the wind," one of the village chiefs said proudly. The others nodded in agreement.

"Good," White Oak agreed. "Good. We move, then."

Pullo stood up. His horse was already saddled, and out in the darkness his own three horsemen should be preparing theirs as well. *One thing about these Novans,* he thought as he walked off, *they prepare quickly. Morning comes, they roll over and stand up, and they're ready to fight.*

Along the river

Lucius Germanius wanted to reach Pompeius by sunset; he wanted more than anything else this morning to pass that night within the walls of the town. But the spectacle before him now made him wonder if that was possible.

"How in Hades did they manage to get around in front of us?"

"Has to be four-five hundred of them," he heard someone in the ranks mutter. The man was right; probably five hundred native warriors faced them across a large meadow. They were drawn up in a credible formation, too, although no weapons other than the rude wooden scuta, bows and clubs were in evidence.

"Line of battle," Germanius ordered. "Wedge formation. Second century of second cohort, gather the prisoners and form up around them. We can't afford to lose those supplies."

The legion hastened to obey. Arrows started to arc towards the Roman formation, but it only seemed to be harassment, almost as if...

Germanius' head snapped around. The meadow was shaped like a large inverted U, with the open end facing the river, and was easily large enough for a set battle; the Novans had chosen the location of their stand well. They had their backs to the trees where the forest met the river on the downstream side, while the Romans had just emerged from the woods on the upstream side; the two forces stood now facing each other across perhaps two hundred paces distance. To Germanius' right the forest formed a broad arch, curving eventually back to the river behind the Novan formation.

The Novans stood, impassively. Archers to the rear of their formation continued to plink arrows at the Roman formation, but the distance was too great for the crude Novan bows.

In front of Germanius and his two aides, the Second Legion

had neatly formed into a broad wedge, the legionaries drawn up four ranks deep. To their rear, a small box formation consisting of second cohort, second century guarded the prisoners and their burden of foodstuffs. The left flank was protected by the river, but the right was open.

"Legion," Germanius roared, "advance!"

Centurions echoed the orders. The soldiers stepped off, neatly, behind their scuta, gladii drawn.

Germanius intended to drive his formation right through the Novans, but the right flank bothered him. As he followed the battle line, he sent one of his aides with a message: "Tell Honorious to bend the right flank back some more. Tell him to watch those trees on our right."

In the trees

"Perfect," Titus Pullo breathed. "Just too bloody perfect." He turned in his saddle to look at White Oak. "Hit them now," he advised.

White Oak motioned to a younger man, who drew his bow and sent a flaming arrow soaring into the blue morning sky.

Pullo had laid a perfect ambush, and Second Legion had marched obligingly into it. While the Roman legate was distracted by the Novan formation to his front, Pullo raised a hammer of three hundred Novan warriors and sent it crashing into the Roman right flank. At the same time, the signal of the flaming arrow sent the first formation charging at the Roman front, supported by archers from the tree line.

It almost worked.

Germanius' order to refuse the right flank didn't reach the centurion in charge of that part of the formation in time, but the man was an experienced commander. Alarmed by the war cries of the Novans, he gave the necessary orders to bend his century at a sharp angle to the rest of the formation, partially enclosing his second cohort and the prisoners. The move was accomplished just as the Novans crashed into his line.

Novan wood and stone crashed into Roman bronze and steel, with predictable results. Some of the Novans had lances made from saplings and were able to drive them into the Roman formation, causing some injury, but in the main their war clubs battered uselessly against the Roman scuta, and approaching closely enough to use them exposed their unarmored bodies to attack by Roman swords.

The line bent slightly in the center, where the Novan onslaught was strongest, but held. The native warriors had attempted a four-rank line, as was usual for Roman troops, but the undisciplined Red Blanket soldiers and the village warriors all wanted to draw blood, and so the neat formation rapidly dissolved.

Roman soldiers knew all too well the value of discipline. After several minutes of fighting, the Novans' passion for the battle was wearing down. Several whistles sounded, and the first-rank Romans slipped back through the ranks, leaving the Novans facing fresh troops.

In the center of the main line, a small group of twenty Alligator warriors that had accompanied White Oak's group west were finding their alligator-scute armor fared somewhat better against Roman arms than the bare skin and deer hide garments of their fellows. A combination of discipline, courage and viciousness carried them into the Roman line. Howling like banshees, they crashed through the scuta of the main line and almost made it through the four ranks of Romans to the prisoners before Roman troops in the ranks surrounded them. They went down under the hacking, stabbing gladii of the Romans, but not without leaving three Romans dead and nine wounded.

"To the trees!" Germanius kept the formation moving forward towards the far tree line, hemming the Novans in. By this time the Novan line was disintegrated, each warrior fighting by himself against the monolithic Roman line.

Pullo considered charging at their rear with his three cavalrymen but decided against it. Four horsemen would have been easy meat for the experienced legionaries.

Instead, another signal passed through the Novan line. They backed into the trees and, amazingly to the Romans, simply melted away into the forest.

Legate Germanius ordered a short rest. "We will want to keep moving," he told his centurions and their optios, "so don't let the men get too comfortable. Home this evening! See to any wounded that can move. Improvise litters for any that can't, we'll have some of the prisoners carry them." *We can't afford to lose even one man,* he left carefully unspoken.

"At least the prisoners and the supplies are safe," the centurion in charge of second century announced. "A few slipped away in the confusion, but no more than a half-dozen. The rest will be dividing up their loads. They'll be ready to move again shortly."

"Good. We'll need the food back at the city." Germanius knew that denying the grain and meat to the Novans was as important to the plan as obtaining it for Pompeius, and he intended to see it all delivered safely.

Late afternoon—in the forest

Runners hastily arranged the meeting, at the cost of no small amount of sore muscles and sweat. For the first time in many days, the two primary Novan chiefs in command of the Novan offensive stood face-to-face.

"White Oak," the Alligator war chief snapped.

"Man-Ready-For-War," White Oak replied. Both men were as polite as the occasion dictated, but neither was particularly glad to see the other.

"The Romans you left us to pursue, they are withdrawing to their town?"

"They are," White Oak said. "We fought a battle with them this morning. We killed twelve and wounded more."

"That is a good thing," Man-Ready-For-War allowed. "But we will need to kill many more."

"We have come here to do that. With them all gathered in their town, behind solid walls made of the trunks of great trees. It would have been much easier to take them in the open. Now we must dig them out, and I tell you it will be like digging a badger out of its winter den."

Man-Ready-For-War bared his filed teeth in a vicious grin. "Young boys of the Alligator People dig out badgers for sport."

White Oak chose to ignore the remark. "I have spoken with a man who escaped from the Roman soldiers."

"What did he say?"

"He talked of the way the Romans treated him," White Oak said. "He understands some of their talk, but he pretended he only spoke our language. The Roman soldiers are giving their captives food and water, and treating them well, and this man overheard one of them saying they would release the captives once they return to their town."

"Release them?" Man-Ready-For-War's face revealed surprise;

it was common among the People to keep captives as slaves, or even to adopt them into the tribe if they proved to have some worth. Sometimes they were even killed outright, although that was uncommon. But to release them? That was unheard of.

"Think about it," White Oak said. "They have much of the food from the B'Kou and A'Tep villages. Most of the food in the towns of the Alligator People has been taken or burned, as you have said. Now they are using our people to take it to their town, where they will enclose it within their walls."

"Then," Man-Ready-For-War snapped, "we will have to take it back."

A short distance away, a similar reunion, less acrimonious, was taking place between the renegade Roman centurions.

"Brother," Titus Pullo greeted Lucius Vorenus. The two men clasped hands.

"Your lot retreated to the town?" Vorenus asked.

"They have," Pullo agreed.

"What did they achieve on their sweep west?"

Pullo frowned. He understood now, too late, all too well what the boy general's plan had been. "They swept through every village they could find, and according to White Oak some of them were of pretty good size, up to a hundred or more families. They burned the houses and took the food. All adult males were taken prisoner, but they left the old people, women and children where they found them, unharmed but hungry. And brother…"

"Yes?"

"There was no looting other than taking stored food. There was no rape, no abuse of the women, children, or the elderly. Pompey Minor is keeping a very tight rein on his men." Much tighter, they both knew, than was usual for Roman armies on missions of conquest.

Rapine, taking of women by force and even murder were not uncommon in war; both men knew that. Both had even taken part. The campaign in Gaul had been a long one, and the nature of the conflict had inspired hatred and rage on both sides, with the concomitant atrocity. But this war was different.

"He's thinking ahead," Pullo said. "He's thinking of after the war. He wants to smash the Novan army, but he knows they'll have to live among them once it's over."

"They can hardly return to Rome," Vorenus agreed.

"Nor can we, for that matter." Pullo's face grew long at the thought, even though it was hardly a new one to either man. But there was other business to concern them: "Do you have any idea what Man-Ready-For-War plans to do now?"

"He has spoken with me about it some, but he is not one to seek council. I gather he intends to attack the walls with fire, to harass and annoy, until Pompey Minor sends his troops out to fight."

Pullo looked at Vorenus in dismay. "He intends to face two Roman legions in the open? On an open field of battle?"

"He does, brother. You will have looked at the ground, of course?"

Pullo nodded. They were only a half-hour walk from the Roman town. "The town sits atop one of four hills. It is surrounded, just as White Oak said, by a stout wall of tree trunks, as high as two men. There are now two guard towers, and archers and slingers were seen on the wall. They are well defended, and if Man-Ready-For-War tempts them to come out, they will be in formation atop that hill. The Novans will have to attack up the hill."

"He is quite mad, isn't he?"

"I'm not so sure. I think he's ignorant. He's fighting the war the way he knows how, the way his people have always fought. They do not think in terms of campaigns or even of war as such. Their way of war is not like ours. They won't be up to a siege."

"It will be a bloody disaster," Vorenus predicted. "He won't listen to us. Why are we still here?"

"Our task will be seeing that enough remain to carry on the fight later."

"Perhaps," Vorenus allowed, "if Mars is watching over us very directly. Otherwise…"

Pompeius

Second Legion marched in through the city gates just before sunset. They were somewhat the worse for wear but unbeaten; even the wounded, helped along or carried by their comrades, held their heads high. General Pompey and the Consuls were there to meet Legate Germanius when he finally came inside, after the last of his men passed through the city gate.

"They aren't long behind us," he reported. Pompey looked pointedly at the bandage on Germanius' shoulder. "It's nothing, sir," he said, noting the young commander's gaze. "Glancing blow from a Novan arrow, just an hour or so ago. They kept contact with us the whole way in; skirmishers and scouts, I'd say, although we had a fairly tense battle yesterday afternoon."

"You won?" Cato demanded.

"We did, Consul. Would have been a near thing if they had any infantry worth the name, but they really don't. They can form a line and hold it, but when pressed they start to lose heart. It's the gap in weaponry, sir. They don't lack for courage, but courage won't put steel in their hands."

"You've done a fine job," Pompey the Younger congratulated the officer. "See to your men. I've already made arrangements for dealing with your captives and the supplies."

Legate Germanius saluted and left, his footsteps dragging tiredly in the dust of the city's main avenue as he trailed after his men.

"What do you plan to do with the prisoners?"

"Consul Cicero," Pompey grinned, "I intend to relieve them of the burdens they carry—large amounts of maize, squash, dried meat and other foodstuffs, from the looks of it—and turn them back out of the gate." He motioned towards the trees. "Let their own people feed them. I don't care to kill them outright, and we will need the food for our own people. Obtaining it was a large part of Germanius' mission."

"While depriving the Novans at the same time," Cato observed.

"Indeed, Consul. That was exactly what I had in mind. We now have our forces safe within city walls, with plenty to eat. The Novans are out there with most of their stored food gone. It's happening just as I said; they will come here to try to get their foodstuffs back, and when they do, we'll smash them."

The consuls left, and as was his practice at sunset, Pompey climbed up to the guard post atop the wall by the gate. As he reached the top of the ladder, he heard one of the guards.

"Look at that bastard," the man said, "just standing out there!"

"Where?" Pompey demanded. Could it be old Four Bears back for another parley?

The soldier pointed. A lone figure did indeed stand by the trees just to the west of the river. It wasn't Four Bears, but rather a taller, leaner man, one of the Alligator warriors, judging from his black-painted face and reptile-scute armor. He stood, alone, impassive, arms folded across his chest, staring at the walls of the Roman town. Even at the distance, Pompey fancied he saw an arrogant sneer on the man's black-painted face.

"Fetch my sister," Pompey ordered the guard. "Quick, before we lose the light."

It was growing dim by the time Adsila clambered up the wall, but not quite too dark to see. "That man," Pompey pointed to the black-painted soldier. "Do you know him?"

"I think so," Adsila said. "I have never seen him before, but I have heard White Oak and Four Bears speak of him. I think he is the leader of the Alligator People, their highest chief. He is Man-Ready-For-War, and he will be the leader of their army."

"Their war chief?"

"The Alligator People have only war chiefs. All of their men are soldiers. I have heard Four Bears say they live only to fight."

"Too bad he's out of easy bow range," Pompey snorted. "If we could take him out, I wonder if the whole Novan offense would come apart. He's not stupid, is he? Well, we'll see if he lives up to his name. Come on—let's get down from here. I've got some planning to do."

CHAPTER TWELVE

PREPARATIONS

It took many days for the Novan forces to gather in the region of Pompeius. The soldiers and people of the Roman town could see their fires at night, carelessly built in their camps in the forest around the town. From its commanding position on the hill in the middle of a great meadow, Pompeius could not be approached by so much as a single man without drawing the attention of the archers who manned the walls day and night, so the Novans must gather all of their forces before striking.

Due to the actions of Pompey's soldiers the town had an ample supply of corn and dried meats, mostly taken from the Novan villages. What Novan prisoners the army held were turned out of the city, so that their confederates must feed and equip them.

Fortunately for the soldiers and people of Pompeius, the Novans proved to have little skill in siegecraft, nor did they have the requisite patience, just as Pompey predicted. They did have numbers, and their Roman advisors sought to put that advantage to work.

—From Gnaeus Pompey Novus' New World Diaries

Pompeius

Pompey mounted the wall again at sunrise. To his surprise, the Novan war chief stood once more at the edge of the trees, exactly where he had been the night before.

"Persistent bastard, aren't you?" Pompey muttered, setting the sentries on the wall to chuckling.

"We saw him standing there before the moon set, sir," one of the sentries reported. "The men on watch before us said he stood there all night."

"Look there," another man pointed. "One of the Roman renegades!"

"It is indeed. I wonder what he's up to? No good, I'll wager."

Titus Pullo was not, as the young General Pompey had speculated, up to no good. What he was up to was trying once more to talk some sense to the Alligator People's chief.

"You've been out here all night," he told the Novan. "I think they know you are here now. Shouldn't you try to get some sleep?"

"Are the runners sent south as I ordered?"

"Yes," Pullo said, noting the evasion. "We even sent two of our men on horses with them to some of the farther villages. We agreed to wait to attack the town until all of the people are here, yes? Alligator, B'Kou and A'Tep, all together?"

"We did." The man folded his arms across his chest. Atop the wall of the city, a figure in a black-plumed helmet raised a hand in a mocking salute.

"Come and rest, then," Pullo said.

Man-Ready-For-War shook his head. "I do not need rest. I

taught myself long ago to go without sleep. I have stayed awake for four, five days on war party." Not taking his gaze off the town's wall, he pointed at two scars on his chest, just beside the pectoral muscle, barely visible through the arm holes of the reptile hide chest piece. "The name I bear is not just a name for a man. The name of Man-Ready-For-War belongs to all of the Alligator People, and only a chief who has endured the most difficult tests can earn it. When I was a young man, I had skewers of bone pushed into my chest. I was hauled aloft on ropes attached to the skewers and hung over the smoke of a fire for three days."

"That would take great strength and courage."

"Yes, all of the young men of the Alligator People are taught to show such strength. That was only the final trial of many trials. Before that, I had to run to the great sea to the south and back, without stopping to eat, drink or sleep. I went for days without eating, without sleeping. I killed all of the fierce beasts of the forest and swamp with only a knife—bear, alligator, panther, wolf. I still wear the hide of the alligator I killed in my trials, like all of our soldiers." He tapped the scutes of the alligator-skin armor on his chest. "Of all the villages of the Alligator People, I was the fastest runner, the best fighter, the most cunning planner. When all of the trials were over, only myself and two other young men were left. After we hung over the fire for three days, the three of us fought for the right to bear the name Man-Ready-For-War. With our wounds still bleeding, we went into the forest with a knife and a club, with no food or water. We hunted each other. Only one could come back alive, and that one would be Man-Ready-For-War. I was that one."

Like the Spartans of old, born to war, trained to war. Despite himself, Titus Pullo was impressed. The savage was ignorant in many ways, but he had a discipline of his own, and an iron courage that would do credit to any Roman. *If only we had the time and the equipment to properly form these men into a real army,* he mused, not for the first time.

"You are proud," Pullo told him, "and you are right to be proud. But the Roman soldiers in that town have passed trials of their own. They will be brave as well."

"I have seen," Man-Ready-For-War agreed. "They are brave. But they are not many. When the full force of the Alligator soldiers falls on them, they will be defeated. I will stand here until we are ready. I will show them what makes us great warriors."

Pullo kept his own counsel. He was thinking of Alesia. He was thinking of Caesar. Most of all, he was thinking of the unmatched discipline of the Roman army, to which Man-Ready-For-War seemed to be blind.

He left then, feeling the sudden urge to talk to Lucius Vorenus.

Four Bears' village

As chance would have it, Four Bears' home village had been untouched by the Roman raiders, lying as it did directly south of Pompeius, out of the line of march of either legion. But the messengers of the People's war chiefs assembled knew all too well how to find it, and since Four Bears was still a strong and vital man, he found himself packing to go to the war parties.

A peaceable man by nature, Four Bears had not been on a war party since his youth, but he still had the trappings of a warrior; red paint for his face, a stout bow otherwise used for hunting, a hatchet with a fine obsidian head. With these and a supply of maize biscuits and dried meat, he joined the younger men of the village as they prepared to trek north. As a village chief, it was his place to be among their leaders.

Old Owl stopped him just as he arrived in the center of the town where the war party gathered. The old man gripped Four Bears' arm in a tight grip, his hand surprisingly strong and hard for one so old.

"There will come a time," the old man said, "when a voice of reason is needed. You have good sense, Four Bears. Your father and his father were men of good sense. Men of good sense are too hard to find these days! All these young men, I think they think with their balls. You, Four Bears, walk a calmer path. The Romans are not animals. They are men. If the time comes for the fighting to stop, you will know, and you will be the one to speak to them. Talk sense to them, Four Bears. Lead your people to a better path."

"I will try," Four Bears agreed.

"Do not try," Owl snapped. "Do."

Four Bears nodded. "It will be as you say." He smiled suddenly. "You are a stubborn old man, you know."

"A stubborn old man who grows tired of fools. Go now. Go to this war. Watch your back."

Four Bears nodded again and walked off. The young men of the village were laughing, slapping each other on the back, whooping and brandishing their weapons. Four Bears noted he was the only one who did not already wear the red war paint of the B'Kou, even though no man yet knew when they may be in battle.

Their bravery will be tested soon enough, he thought. He was the oldest man going on the war party and the senior chief present, so it fell to him to lead. He held up both hands until the young men quieted down.

"We go now," he ordered them. "This is a war party. Remember your trials. We walk in file. No man speaks. We move like smoke in the forest. By tonight, we will be at the Roman town. Then we will see how brave the men of this village are."

That brought a cheer. Behind the group, Four Bears saw old Owl scowling at the young warriors. The old man shook his head and stumped off towards his own small hut.

"Aaiieeeee!" a young soldier, barely more than a boy shouted. "It will be Roman blood spilled, and none of ours!" Several of the men started chattering about the goods they expected to take from the Roman town.

"Be quiet! All of you! We march now." His heart full of misgivings, Four Bears led the young men north.

Pompeius

"Jupiter's balls, there he stands still," a sentry said.

Pompey the Younger clambered up the ladder to the lookout tower just recently finished. He was pleased with the tower and its twin, placed on opposite sides of the town, one facing the Tiber, one facing the woods to the south. He was sure they would prove valuable in the town's defense.

But for now, he was bemused to stand and behold Man-Ready-For-War.

He turned to the two sentries just going off watch now, at sunrise. "Was he there all night?"

"He was, sir, as long as we could see. It got right dark when the moon set, and there's not much moon at that. But when we had moonlight, there the bugger was."

"How many fires could you see?"

"A lot, sir," the man said. "Maybe a hundred, just what we could see from here."

"Figure three to four men to a fire," Pompey pondered aloud. "And certainly more back in the forest."

"We'll be ready for them, General."

Pompey climbed back down with the men going off watch. They went off to sleep; he went off to his headquarters, thinking as he went. He had more reason to win the battle that was sure to come now, as each day he saw his wife grow ever more ponderous with the child she carried.

Food was not an issue. There were sufficient supplies in the town to last a month, perhaps two, and Pompey did not expect the Novans to be able to maintain a siege that long. Even with Romans offering counsel, he counted on their patience running out quickly. They will have to attack the town. They can't stay out there forever.

In the forest

Four Bears shared a fire that evening with White Oak, his cousin from the A'Tep.

After the two men shared a meal of jerked venison, Four Bears told White Oak of old Owl's admonition to him the day before.

"He was a brave man when he was young, or so my grandfather told me," White Oak said when Four Bears finished. "He was known as a wise man even in my grandfather's day. Four Bears, do you agree with him?"

"It is not for me to agree or disagree with one that has seen as many summers as Owl," Four Bears evaded.

"Then tell me what a man with as many summers as Four Bears thinks."

"In truth?" Four Bears looked at the A'Tep Red Blanket man over the fire. "I will tell you. I believe in time we will be at peace with these Romans. Their gods must be strong; stronger perhaps than the people in the land across the water to the south, the Maya, those that the Tsalee speak of in their great cities of stone."

"But you brought the men of your village to fight them."

"I did," Four Bears agreed. "And my heart is filled with dread that some of these young men may not return to mothers and wives. I am an older man and a chief; my wife is long dead. It matters little if I return or not. It matters a great deal if the young men return."

White Oak frowned. "But you came with them! You came to fight!"

"It is always the way," Four Bears said, "that people will fight when first meeting. It is not a matter of who is brave or who is not; it is not a matter of who has more food or more women. It is just the way of people—all the people, including these Romans, to mistrust what they do not know. But I tell you, cousin, these Romans are not going anywhere, no matter what we say. Look at their town! Look at their works! They will not leave them. No, I am here to watch over our young men, but I tell you now, if I can see a way for us to live alongside these Romans, for them to learn from us and us from them, then I will work to that end."

"Man-Ready-For-War intends to kill them all."

"Man-Ready-For-War is brave, and a great warrior. When we arrived here last night, he was standing watching the Roman town for the third night. He stands there even now, for the fourth. He has not eaten or slept, they tell me, since he arrived here. He has just watched the Roman town. And he has the support of the Romans Pullo and Vorenus and their men and horses. But cousin, I do not think it will be enough against the soldiers of Rome. I think a better course would have been to make peace when we could, but there has been too much fighting now. There is too much bitterness on both sides now. I see that. So, yes, I am here to fight. But there will come a time for t it to end, and when it does, I will be here for that, too."

"You are a wise man, Four Bears. When the time comes for that—if it does—I will speak in support of you to the warrior society men of the People."

Four Bears inclined his head in gratitude.

White Oak chuckled suddenly. "These Romans, the ones with us, I mean, they do have some strange ways. Ever since they arrived here, they set their men to digging trenches for their wastes. Pullo, he tells us we should do the same. He claims it will spread sickness if we do not."

"They have much experience in this sort of thing. Perhaps they are right."

"Perhaps. I don't think any group of the People this large has ever gathered in one place before."

"Are any of the men digging?"

"They insist on doing things the way they always have. Mind your step if you walk into the forest; you may step in a pile of shit some young buck has left on the ground."

The two men went on talking. Fifty paces away, the two Roman centurions sat around another fire, making plans of their own.

"Make or break," Lucius Vorenus growled. "Another damned siege, and those aren't Gauls behind those walls."

"They don't have a relief army coming to help them, either," Titus Pullo pointed out.

"And we don't have a Caesar. Just a pack of illiterate savages with clubs and stone knives. Pullo, we can't even convince them to dig a proper latrine. There will be sickness in this camp, mark my words."

Pullo nodded; he wasn't optimistic about what was to come. "I've tried to explain the idea of a siege to Man-Ready-For-War. Juno knows I have. He says his people can't wait to starve them out, and to be fair, he may be right. That young general burned a lot of villages, took a lot of their food. These people aren't much for storing food, other than a little maize. No granaries hereabouts, no herds of cattle. It they want to eat, they have to hunt and fish, and tend their own fields."

"So, he wants to attack them straight on?" After a year, Vorenus was finally becoming conversant in the Novan's patois, but Pullo's language skills were still far superior.

"He does. I've talked to him about scaling ladders and so on. We have some ladders, but no time to build siege towers or anything like that. And damned near impossible to build a ballista or an onager, not with the time and materials we have to hand."

"So, we attack the walls with fire," Vorenus snapped. "An act of genius, no doubt about it."

"The town does have walls of wood, not stone. The idea has some merit."

Vorenus stared into the fire, his face set in a skeptical scowl. "Brother," he said after a few moments, "I wonder if we judged this wrong."

"Wrong?"

"Those are Romans behind those walls. Whatever other differences we have, those are Romans. What are we doing here with these people?"

"Our loyalty is to Caesar."

"Caesar is a long, long way from here," Vorenus pointed out.

Pullo looked up, away from the fire, into the darkness beyond which lay the walled Roman town, the first of its kind in the new world. But not the last? No, probably not. "Too late for such musings now, brother," he said. "You heard the boy general yourself. We are traitors to Rome."

"It has been a long, strange road we've traveled to get to this place," Vorenus said. "And I fear we have a long way yet to go."

A dark figure appeared in the firelight, interrupting the centurion's musings. They looked up to see Man-Ready-For-War staring down at them, his face lined, his eyes red with fatigue.

"All of the People are here now," he said. "The Romans in the town know we are here. I will sleep now. In the morning, we begin."

Chapter Thirteen

Battle of Pompeius

Finally, the legions of Nova Roma under command of Gnaeus Pompey drew the Novan tribes in, but their pursuit was faster and more effective than Pompey had anticipated.

Their food supplies destroyed, and their villages put to the torch, the Novans followed the legions back to Pompeius, where the Roman army had once more sheltered within the city walls. A desultory siege began but did not last, as the Novans had no stomach for sustained action and their supplies of meat and grain would not allow a long campaign, so that they must attempt a full-scale assault on the city.

This met well with General Pompey's expectations, and allowed the army of Nova Roma to conclude the conflict on terms best suited to their equipment and training.

The outcome of that battle led to a rather unorthodox conclusion to the Novan war, but in the end, it proved an effective and humane solution to bring an end to the conflict.

—From Gnaeus Pompey Novus' New World Diaries

In the woods

"I wouldn't have believed had I not seen it myself," Lucius Vorenus said.

Before Vorenus, Pullo, White Oak and Man-Ready-For-War stood ten young men, specially chosen for the task of this early, early morning.

It wasn't easy to see the ten men for three reasons. First, Man-Ready-For-War had ordered all fires extinguished. Second, it was two hours before first light, and only the faint starlight allowed any vision at all. Third and finally, the men were cleverly disguised.

"A trick the People use in hunting," White Oak had explained.

The ten young men were all from White Oak's A'Tep branch of the Red Blanket warrior society. All ten of them were conspicuous young men, known for their bravery.

They would need all of their courage this morning.

All ten were wore specially made jerkins made of loosely woven hemp. Attached to the jerkins were tufts of grass, freshly cut grass of the same sort that now, in mid-summer, grew knee-high in the meadows on the four hills of Pompeius. More tufts of grass were attached to the young men's heads. Their faces were darkened, not painted uniformly black like the Alligator warriors but smudged and smeared with soot from cooking fires so that they hardly resembled faces at all.

"Are you prepared?" White Oak asked the men. They all nodded in the affirmative. "You have all you need?"

Each man was equipped with a large gourd filled with oil rendered from bear fat, a bag of shredded bark, and a hollowed-out bison horn containing coals in a nest of crushed wapiti and deer droppings. White Oak went to each man and inspected his kit as the Roman centurions watched.

"You will do well," White Oak told them at last. "Go, then. The Red Blanket soldiers are proud of you."

As Pullo and Vorenus watched, bemused, the ten young men turned and melted into the darkness. "Good luck," Vorenus breathed after them.

At the edge of the tress all ten men dropped into the grass and crawled. Man-Ready-For-War and White Oak had chosen their night well; not even a sliver of moon showed to lend light to the faint movement in the tall grass that marked the men's passage. Moving as quickly as they could and still stay quiet, the ten Red Blanket men fanned out and made for the town's west wall, well away from the gate.

The wall and watch towers were manned, but the night was dark as pitch and in any case, the watchers were nearing the end of a boring watch. Nothing had happened for several nights except for the Novan war chief standing in plain view for days on end—no one had noticed his departure after sunset the evening before— and the soldiers on watch were sleepy.

All ten Red Blanket men reached the wall without incident. They opened their gourds of oil and poured it on the dry wood of the palisade wall. Next, they placed their bundles of tinder against the base of the wall, and finally they removed coals from their bison horns, placed them into the kindling, and blew them into life. Within the space of seconds, fire was climbing the dry wood of the palisade in several places. A cry of alarm went up quickly then.

Sextus Florius was in the watch tower closest to the fire. After shouting the alarm, he grabbed his stout recurved bow and his quiver of iron-tipped arrows. Florius was one of the best archers in the First Legion, and it was good fortune that he was on the wall at that moment. Even as legionaries bearing swords, shields, heavy cloaks and buckets of water ran for the gate, Florius nocked an arrow and watched the area lit by the flickering flames.

There. He saw grass moving. He drew the bow back, feeling the string hum with tension, feeling the muscles in his arm and back pull the familiar pressure. Sighting along the shaft of the arrow, he loosed. The arrow leapt from the bow and struck into the grass, and Florius was rewarded with a yelp of pain.

"Men in the grass outside the wall!" he shouted. "Watch for an attack!" He nocked another arrow and watched for more movement in the grass. He saw the grass moving off to the left, drew and loosed again.

The flames climbed as high as a man's head, but twenty Roman legionaries armed with buckets of water and cloaks quickly extinguished the flames; the fire had not time to burn past the intact bark on the logs, and the rendered bear oil made a poor accelerant. But while this was going on, Man-Ready-For-War made his move.

Forty Alligator warriors ran at the crouch out of the darkness and attacked the fire party. Caught unaware, the twenty Romans had no time to form a line and so were forced to fight individually, hacking with gladii and fending off blows from Novan clubs and hatchets. Three Romans fell dead and two more were wounded, but the Alligator warriors withdrew after ten of their number were killed. Two of those were slain by Roman arrows from the watch tower, as Sextus Florius did his best to support the infantry with well-aimed arrows. His third shot took an Alligator warrior in the left eye. Moments later, he saw an Alligator soldier shouting orders and loosed another shaft that took that one in the throat. Their leader slain, the Novans withdrew, leaving behind six groaning wounded, including the first arsonist that Florius had wounded in the thigh. The Novan wounded were left where they lay. The Romans withdrew within the scorched walls of the town as the faint light of dawn began to brighten the eastern sky.

The sun was a hands-breadth above the trees to the east when one of the Roman centurions approached the wall, leading a small party of Novans. The tall Roman held both hands high, palms open.

The resulting outcry brought Legate Germanius to the wall. "Hold," he ordered the archers who were taking aim. "He's not armed."

"Parley," the renegade Roman shouted.

"Come ahead," Germanius called back. "Just you."

The centurion approached the wall and stood looking up at the legate.

"Which one are you?" Germanius demanded. "Just so I know who I'm talking to."

The man removed his helmet and rubbed his close-cropped head. "Centurion Lucius Vorenus, late of Caesar's Thirteenth Gallic Legion," he said. "We seek only to remove our wounded from the field. You have my word we will take no other action until all of our wounded are moved from the clearing around the town."

"I am Legate Lucius Germanius, commanding the Second Nova Roman Legion. Very well," Germanius agreed. "Agreed. Be about your work."

"I'll signal from the tree line when we are finished," Vorenus agreed. He turned and motioned to the Novans. None of them, Germanius noted, were of the fierce, black-painted sort. *What does that mean?*

The Novan warriors carried their wounded from the field. When that was done, Lucius Vorenus stood at the edge of the forest, unsheathed his gladius, and waved it overhead. Germanius waved back.

"At least the Romans are teaching them something of humanity," an archer opined.

"We'll see—look at that young bastard!"

Maybe thirty paces from where Vorenus had just disappeared into the trees a young Novan warrior stood facing the town, his face screwed up into a grimace. He gestured wildly at the walls then, turning and bending over, raised his breechclout, wagging his bare buttocks at the Romans on the wall.

The archers burst into laughter. Germanius looked at the archer next to him and, still chuckling, asked: "Do you think you can…?"

"I think so, sir," Sextus Florius answered. He nocked an arrow and drew his bow. He gauged the distance, the wind, raised his bow carefully, sighted, and released.

The arrow shot across the distance, nearly a stadium's worth, and struck home in the young Novan's left buttock. Yelping, the young native limped away into the forest as the Romans roared with glee.

"Well struck!" Germanius shouted. He slapped Sextus Florius on the shoulder. "If we ever get around to making wine here, remind me to buy you a barrel."

"Sir," Florius chuckled, "I'll remember. If it takes ten years, even twenty, I'll remember."

In the trees

"You young fool."

White Oak, Four Bears and Titus Pullo watched dispassionately as an older man, a village chief from the medicine society, examined the young warrior with a Roman arrow protruding from his backside. The older man, Clouds-In-The-Morning, was the one with the strongly expressed opinions of young men. "Hold him down," he ordered.

Several grinning men held the youth down. Clouds-In-The-Morning grasped the shaft of the arrow and, as sweat poured out of the young man's head, turned it slightly and, with a swift pull, removed it. Blood ran from the wound, but the medicine chief did not look concerned. The blood was not spurting, and was dark red, not bright. Experience told him that was serious but not life-threatening. "Fold some soft deerskin and press on it until the bleeding stops," he told one of the Red Blanket soldiers that had held the wounded man down. He rummaged in a pouch he carried on at his side and produced a small clay pot filled with a noxious-smelling concoction. "When it stops, smear some of this on it. Make sure it gets into the wound. It will prevent poison from getting into his body through the wound. Then wrap it up in clean deerskin."

"He will heal, then?" White Oak asked.

"He was lucky," Clouds-In-The-Morning answered. "The arrow only punctured the big muscle of his backside. Most of the injury was to his pride. He will fight no more on this war party, though." The medicine chief rubbed the small of his back. "I have to see to the others," he said, and left.

Four Bears picked up the bloodied arrow. "Look," he said. "Look at this. This point—iron, like your knife, Pullo. Look at how finely made this is."

"Good Roman craftsmanship, that," Pullo agreed.

"Iron arrowheads. Swords of steel. And we fight them with wooden clubs." Four Bears dropped the arrow and walked away, shaking his head.

White Oak looked at Pullo. "Man-Ready-For-War was willing to leave the wounded to die," he said. "You went out to retrieve them."

"That's what civilized people do," Pullo told him. "There's more to Rome than steel weapons and war, you know."

White Oak nodded. "There is truth in what you say."

"Then why won't Man-Ready-For-War listen to me?" Pullo demanded. "We should be starving them out. They can't have that much food in there."

"They have food taken from several villages," White Oak objected. "Crops in those villages were trampled or burned. Our people will starve if we don't get that food back. And none of our men here have more than five day's food. The land hereabouts is hunted out. No deer, no turkey, no wapiti are in the area. They have more food than we do. Man-Ready-For-War wants to end this quickly. I think he is right. We end this or we go hungry."

"This isn't how a siege is supposed to work," Pullo said plaintively. He knew he was wasting his breath. The die was already cast. Man-Ready-For-War intended to ram his head against the walls of the town, and there was nothing Pullo and Vorenus could do to dissuade him.

The Senate

Eight members of the Senate sat nervously in the Senate chambers. Technically the Senate was in session, but no business was conducted; the eight men were too keenly aware of what was going on outside the walls where their ninth member, Gnaeus Pompey, was coordinating the defense of the town.

"There goes another one." Titus Annius Milo looked nervously at the ceiling. As the afternoon wore on, Novan archers were sending fire arrows on high arcs into the city, where each one was announced with an outcry. So far, the arrows started several small fires, but each was extinguished quickly.

The effect on the people's nerves was of more import than the fires themselves.

"It's only a matter of time before they hit something that will burn more easily," Servilius Casca pointed out. There was enough of that in the town: Wooden buildings, thatch roofs, piles of wood for cooking fires, piles of wooden rails for building.

Cato was pacing back and forth. "General Pompey has his troops on alert," he pointed out. "He assures me that their fire arrows are crude, and that the high arc they must travel to reach the city makes them ineffective. Most of them aren't even afire when they land."

"And yet you pace like a nervous old woman," Marcus Junius Brutus observed sourly. Cato ignored him; Brutus was unpleasant at the best of times, and these were hardly the best of times.

Cicero wasn't as tolerant. "General Pompey has proven himself," he said. "He has made his plans known to us in advance, has he not? Did you object when he did so? And those plans have unfolded as he said, have they not? The Novan army is out there now, with their rocks and sticks. Our army is here, rested and fed, with bronze and steel. Are you afraid, now, Brutus?"

Brutus looked away angrily. Cicero walked over to him and bent, cupping a hand theatrically behind one ear. "What's that? I didn't hear your reply. What say you?"

"Enough," Cato snapped. "This accomplishes nothing."

"We are accomplishing nothing," Metellus Scipio pointed out. "I move we adjourn. Further, I move that we go forth from here into the streets, arm ourselves with brooms and buckets of water, the better to help with the fire watch."

"Second," Casca said.

Cato stopped his pacing. "Very well. Motion is made and seconded. All in favor?"

It was unanimous. Even sour Brutus raised his hand in support.

"Motion is passed. We are adjourned. To the streets, one and all."

The Senators took the time to remove their worn white and red Senate robes, replacing them with even more worn wraps of plain linen. "We look almost Catonian," Cassius quipped when they reassembled in the Forum. Cato, barefooted as usual and in a robe that was shabby even for his stoic inclinations, frowned. Then he laughed.

The men of the Roman Senate spent the balance of the afternoon running from place to place, splashing waters on the smoldering fires started by Novan arrows.

Evening found Cato facing the young general himself.

"It's been a while since the last arrow," Pompey reported. "The men on the wall can see cooking fires in the trees. I think we've seen all the action we'll see for today."

"What do you think they will do next?"

"I think they will attack soon. To do that, they have to approach the walls. That's when we'll have them."

"You don't think they will try to starve us out?"

"I don't think they can afford to, Consul. We've taken too

much of their food, their supplies. They farm but they don't seem to store much, from what we've seen of their towns. No, they'll hit us, and they'll hit us soon. Within the next few days, unless I miss my guess."

"I hope you're right." Cato ran a soot-covered hand through his thinning hair. "We don't have all that much food ourselves."

"We have enough for a while, and we have some crops planted within the walls. It's odd, but the Novans don't seem to be bothering our fields outside the walls."

"None of the crops are ripe to eat, and I expect they plan to make use of our crops at their leisure."

"That's very likely." Pompey looked sharply at the older man. "You look tired, Consul. The evening watch is set. I'm off to get some rest. I suggest you do likewise. I suspect tomorrow will be a busy day as well."

"General, your words carry much wisdom," Cato sighed. "I believe I will follow your advice."

Cato walked off through the darkening streets, back to the tiny house he jokingly called his 'villa.' There he washed, threw his soiled, stained wrap into a corner, and collapsed into his rude bunk.

Sleep did not come easily. After tossing and turning for some time, he finally rose, lit a lamp and splashed some more water on his face.

He regarded his reflection in the water of the bowl. His face had new lines that had not been there the year before, even after the harrowing crossing of the Atlantic.

"Where will this all end?" he wondered aloud. "When will this all end? What will we be when this is all over?"

Cicero's speech of the previous year still haunted his thoughts.

"We are Rome," he muttered. "Will these Novans be as well? Can we really bring Rome to this new world?"

He knew the next few days would decide the issue.

The next morning

On the wall, Titus Caninus was on watch as the dawn broke, cool and foggy. Caninus always liked this time of day in the new land; he enjoyed watching the sun slowly push through the mists, watching the shadows slip slowly away from the four hills of Pompeius, watching the sun light up the meadows around the walls of the town. In the cool morning the air was heavy and wet, but not as oppressive as it could become in the muggy heat of day. Only the biting insects marred what Caninus thought the best part of the day.

It was a quiet, reflective time most mornings, but it was not to be, today.

"Legionary," a voice behind him said, softly.

Titus turned. "Morning, sir," he greeted Centurion Gracchus Agrippa.

"Good morning, indeed," Agrippa began. "Now, if only..."

Titus Caninus turned his head as the centurion's voice trailed off into a gurgle. An arrow, long and slim with striped fletching, was protruding from Agrippa's neck.

Caninus threw the centurion down on the walkway and fell on top of him as several more arrows hissed past. He took a peek over the wall and saw, in the dim morning light, Novan warriors forming into a line near the trees. "Here they come!" he bellowed.

"Archers and slingers to the walls," came a shout from inside the town. Gnaeus Pompey was, at least, awake and alert.

Caninus rolled off the palisade and dropped heavily to the ground. "Centurion Agrippa is wounded," he called out.

"The surgeons will see to him," another centurion barked. "You—Caninus, isn't it? Get your armor and scutum."

The warriors of the combined tribes, B'Kou, A'Tep, and the fierce Alligator People—advanced from the tree line. The B'Kou and A'Tep, as was their custom, held half of their men back to engage with their bows, while the rest joined the Alligator people. Man-Ready-For-War placed the B'Kou and A'Tep warriors on the left and right flanks of the line; he did not trust them over much to stand and fight.

He held no such doubts about his own Alligator people. Clad in their traditional war tunics of alligator skin, thick scutes outward, they formed a very credible line of battle near the river, facing the town's gate. Beating their war clubs against their shields of wood as they advanced slowly, step by step, towards the town walls, they began a frightful war chant.

Behind them, in the trees, the rogue centurions Lucius Vorenus and Titus Pullo stood close by the war chief Man-Ready-For-War, prepared to offer advice. The rest of the Roman renegades were nearby, mounted and ready for action.

Gnaeus Pompey, meanwhile, had mounted the wall. "Now, this," he said, "this is what we've been waiting for. Get these savages in the open for a proper fight." He turned to the open area around the gate, where soldiers of Rome were gathering. "First Legion!" he roared. "In column! Prepare to march! Through the gate in column, then into line! Quickly, boys, quickly—the enemy is close."

Raggedly but quickly, the First Nova Roman Legion formed into column.

"First Cohort!" Pompey the Younger's bellow rang out over the clatter of armor and weapons. "Prepare to sally! Second cohort, on their heels!"

The gates swung open, and First Cohort, First Legion, trotted out of the walled town. They were halfway into the line formation required for battle when the whistling of arrows in flight came overhead.

"Testudo!"

Shields planted on the ground in the first rank, held over head in the following ranks. Iron or bronze arrowheads would penetrate the Roman scuta if they hit the right spot, but the thicker flint arrowheads of the Novans, sharp as they were on the edges, almost never did.

After a few moments, the hail-on-a-roof sound of striking arrows ceased. "Recover!"

Scuta went down. The cohort finished the move into line smartly, with discipline.

The ground surrounding the palisade had been cleared for a full stadium from the walls. On the palisade, the archers held their arrows; the Novans loosed their handmade shafts in undisciplined arcs, but Roman archers would not.

The Alligator People finally ceased their chant. A low growl came from their ranks, building slowly in intensity.

"They're getting ready to charge," a first spear Centurion opined.

He was proven right a moment later. With a howl, almost five hundred warriors of the Alligator People charged, a wild, undisciplined charge, uphill, directly at Roman lines in front of the city gate.

"Cast... pila!"

The two hundred men of the first cohort cast their pila in sweeping arcs. The heavy spears struck soil and flesh, piercing the Novan's alligator-scute armor, points breaking off, leaving horrible wounds—but the Alligator warriors came on.

The Novan attackers crashed into the Roman line like waves breaking on a boulder. The first rank stabbed forward with their gladii, steel breaking through the thin Novan shields and hide armor while the Novan war clubs battered ineffectively against Roman helmets and shields. But while the cohorts were face to face with the Alligator People, they could not adopt the turtle-like defensive position in defense against arrows. The B'Kou and A'Tep sent another wave of arrows at the legion, and Roman soldiers fell.

On the wall, Gnaeus Pompey was cursing the lack of heavy weapons. *I swear, I will set craftsmen to building ballistae the moment this battle ends.* The tree line was too far away from the town for aimed archery, but not for volleys of arrows, and Pompey had a trick up his sleeve. "Archers!" he called. "I want those natives in the trees suppressed!"

The centurion commanding the archers barked orders. While supplies of oil were barely sufficient, enough had been scraped together to make a few hundred fire arrows. Braziers had been set along the wall; on command, the archers each nocked a fire arrow, bent to light them from the braziers, and resumed their formation.

"Draw!"

Each archer pulled his bow.

"Aim!"

The archers raised their bows skyward. Practiced eyes gauged the stadium's distance separating them from the trees, and practiced arms adjusted their aim.

"LOOSE!"

An arch of fire roared into the trees, starting fires in the grass at the tree line and setting the forest floor litter ablaze in a dozen or more places. Smoke began to obscure the Novan archer's vision, and their arrows went wild.

In the tree line, amidst the swirling smoke, the Alligator People's war chief Man-Ready-For-War watched his warriors batter uselessly against the Roman shields and fall to wounds from Roman steel. They were being driven back, slowly but certainly.

Man-Ready-For-War had been raised as a warrior and was experienced in battle; thanks to advice from the two renegade centurions he knew the Romans had weapons and tactics he had not encountered before, but he had an idea how they might be countered. Their walled town had only one entrance, and the gates stood open now...

As Four Bears looked on, the war chief turned to a boy standing nearby and barked orders.

"Are you sure you want to do this?" Four Bears asked. "This is almost all of your remaining warriors. All the young men of your people."

"They are warriors," Man-Ready-For-War replied. "It is their place to fight." He pointed. "We have drawn their attention to the front of their village. Look how all their men are on the wall and in front of the opening. We have presented them with what they hoped to see, and they have reacted as I knew they would. Now the warriors of the Alligator People will strike. You will see. We need only get inside their walls, and it will be like the spikes of bone we hide in old meat to kill bears; we will bleed them to death from inside."

Close to a thousand young men were hiding in the woods on the south side of Pompeius, led by the sub-chiefs Long Tooth and Sharp Knife. They were, to a man, young men schooled in war, hardened by life in the swamps of the low country. When the runner from the war chief arrived at the two sub-chiefs that served as their leaders, he spoke only one word: "Now."

The Alligator warriors charged, silently, half of them moving around Pompeius on the right, half on the left. Long Tooth led the group moving right, while his brother Sharp Knife led the group to the left. Man-Ready-For-War had taken a trick of Pompey's and used it against him, albeit on a smaller scale. The Roman's attention was fixed on the north side of the city, in front of the sole gate. Nobody was watching to the south.

The Alligator warriors ran on the callused soles of bare feet, with no metal armor clattering, no iron-hobnailed sandals thundering; in eerie silence they charged, rounding the city walls and crashing into both flanks of the Roman First Legion.

Spiked war clubs had little effect on Roman helmets and Roman shields, but the Alligator warriors struck at arms, legs, and exposed necks with uncanny accuracy. A shower of arrows struck into the Novans from the Roman archers on the palisade walls, but the Roman legionaries on the ground were hard-pressed to take maniacal attacks from three directions.

While they rushed to form a box formation, a hundred or more Novan warriors broke through and raced for Pompeius's open gate.

Only one Roman soldier remained near the gate, where he had stayed to see to moving Centurion Agrippa to shelter with the surgeons. Second Legion was forming for battle in the town even now, but his place was with the First, and he hurried to join them. He was running for the gate when the Novan warriors came into view.

There was no time to call for help. Titus Caninus had his gladius, his scutum and a pila. "All any real Roman needs," he said aloud. He took his helmet from where he carried it under his arm, jammed it on his head, and prepared to make his stand.

In building the palisade, the Roman engineers had made the one gate wide enough for four soldiers to pass through, shoulder to shoulder, in column. Titus Caninus placed himself in the center of the open gate. Four Novans had broken ahead of the others, coming at the legionary at a dead run. Titus cast his pila, striking the Novan leader in the chest, killing him instantly. He drew his gladius and went into a defensive crouch behind his scutum.

A few arrows landed near him, but they were random shots from the tree line, not aimed; Caninus ignored them. The nearest warrior was on him. The Roman slammed his scutum forward, taking the Novan's war club on the rim, while stabbing out under the shield with the gladius, striking the native in the stomach. Another came at him from the left; Caninus backhanded with the sword, nearly taking the man's head off.

The rush was on him then. Caninus was forced back into the opening, between the gate doors where they pulled back into the palisade. He struck right, left, took a blow on his shield, a glancing blow on the hard leather armor on his back. Two, three, four more Novans fell to his sword. Blood spattered Titus Caninus' face, but none of it was his. Roaring his challenge, he charged into the body of Novans, gladius striking like a snake.

A black-painted Novan warrior grabbed his scutum and spun Roman soldier and shield both, spinning Caninus around. The Roman lost his grip on the shield and almost fell. He looked up at the Novan, who hurled the scutum away and walked towards him, grinning, even as the other natives backed away to watch. They wore smug looks; obviously the big man was a notorious character.

"By Mars' own balls, you're a big one," Caninus breathed.

The big Novan crouched, still grinning, his war club balanced easily in his left hand. Caninus looked him over carefully, examining the gaps in his crocodilian armor, the grin on his black-painted face, the way his eyes shifted as he moved, the way he moved his feet.

"Legionary!"

Titus risked a look up at the wall, there to see Gnaeus Pompey himself looking down. "Here!" the young general called. He tossed another gladius which tumbled, shining in the early morning sun, to land near Caninus. The legionary shifted his own gladius to his left hand and picked up the second in his right; it was a fine weapon, glittering steel, a longer than normal blade, honed to a razor's edge, a fine ivory grip. *The General's own,* Titus thought.

The Novan leaped at the Roman. Titus spun away from the attack, not to the rear but to the side, striking at the native as he landed. The Novan danced away from the shining blades.

Caninus wasn't about to give the native a moment to rest. He charged the big man, stabbing forward with both gladii. The Novan was fast—very fast. He dodged both blades and managed to catch Titus' left arm with a swipe of his spiked war club.

Blood dripped from his arm, but the legionary had known worse wounds campaigning in Greece, Africa and Gaul. He charged the big man again, and again the big man danced away. *He's left-handed, and always moves to his right,* Caninus thought, *to keep his strong side facing me.* It was an all-too-common failing in combat, being predictable.

Titus Caninus was anything but predictable.

He paused for just a moment; a gladius balanced lightly in each big hand. The other Novans were just standing there watching, confident that their big warrior would finish the Roman and open the path into the city. *Let them watch, then.*

In sizing up his opponent, Caninus noticed the man's eyes, and how they kept flickering downward. *He's watching my feet, to see which way I'll go next.* He decided to test the big native and so stepped quickly ahead, swords held ready. The native dodged away well before the Roman was close enough to strike.

Hah. I have you now.

He rushed the big Novan again, feinting right, and as the man spun away, changed direction and struck to his left, catching the native in the throat with the fine general's blade, in the chest with his own. The Novan dropped his war club and, as Titus Caninus pulled his blades free, dropped bonelessly to the dirt.

The other Novans stood dumbly for a moment, looking at the body of their champion lying in a spreading pool of blood. Caninus spun around to face them, crouching, both gladii at the ready. He snarled at the savages, and was mildly startled to see their eyes widen, and watched them start to back away.

"Well done," Titus Caninus heard General Pompey's voice. He looked around to see the General standing in the gate alongside him, with a full cohort of the Second Legion at his back. He turned to the Romans behind him. "Cohort—CHARGE!" As the cohort charged through the gate and crashed into the Novans, General Pompey grabbed Caninus' arm and pulled him to the side. "Not you," he said. A wide smile bisected his face. "You've done quite enough. Bloody Horatius at the gate, you are—take on a hundred native warriors by yourself, would you?"

"Seemed like a good idea at the time, sir," Caninus grinned.

"Very good, Centurion," the General grinned back, making Titus Caninus' eyebrows shoot up in surprise. "First Spear, I should think. Titus Caninus, isn't it? Better you be Canis Magnus, from now on, I think. Yes, Canis Magnus. It suits you. Keep the sword—it was my father's, but I think you've earned it." He clapped Caninus on the back. "In war, Centurion, men are nothing. A man—a man is everything. Our sons will need heroes here in this new land." He took the issue gladius from Caninus' unresisting left hand. "I'll just take this, if you don't mind—still a few natives out there need settling." He rushed after the cohort that was even now smashing into the Novans sent to attack the gate. His departure left Titus Caninus, for the first time in his life, speechless.

Gnaeus Pompey ran after the cohort of the Second, with the rest of the legion close on his heels. "Close that damned gate!" he shouted over his shoulder as he ran. Behind him, the big wooden doors pulled slowly closed.

The initial attack had been repulsed, and the attack on the gate dissolved, the attackers fled. Pompey the Younger saw the Novans reforming near the trees, preparing for another assault. He ran to the front of the Roman battle line.

"Soldiers of Rome!" he shouted.

"Five hundred years of Roman arms have you within you! Each and every one of you!" He motioned towards the Novans gathering near the trees. "What do those savages have? A generation or two, perhaps? How many among them can name their fathers?"

The legions laughed—laughed!

"Five hundred years of Roman arms—Roman steel! Roman blood!" He remembered Cicero's speech in the Senate. "We, my brave men, are Rome! Here, and now, we are Rome! Your ancestors, the soldiers of Rome that have fought and died for Rome, are watching you now! The lost veterans of Africa, Greece, Hispania and Gaul, all of them are watching us here, today!" He drew the battered issue gladius and waved it over his head. "Form up! Line of battle! This is the day when we win this fight! This is the day when we end this, once and for all. Let's show these savages what Roman arms, Roman soldiers can do!"

"Form up!" a legate echoed the command. The legions formed into ranks, scuta leveled, gladii drawn.

"Legions—soldiers of Rome!" Gnaeus Pompey roared. "Advance!"

The First and Second Legions, in line of battle, moved forward.

The Novans, howling their war cries, charged. The Novan charge smashed into the Roman line, but it was like water breaking over stone.

Roman sandals dug into the earth as the sheer weight of the Novan charge pushed the front-line back a pace, then two; but they held. The second rank lent their strength to the first, pressing against the backs of the legionaries at the front. The Roman line hardened and held. Gladii stabbed at Novan arms, legs, stomachs and chests. The hard-bronze bosses of scuta slammed into Novan faces, broke Novan skulls, but the war clubs of the Alligator warriors drew blood as well. The alligator-scute armor worn by the Novans was lighter than the Novan leather and bronze, and so enabled the Novans to leap high and crash into the Romans, battering Roman shields down enough to strike.

But it wasn't enough.

"Advance!" came the shout. The Roman ranks stepped forward, scuta held up, gladii stabbing forward. "Advance!" and the Romans stepped forward again. The Novans tried to reform their line, but the training Pullo and Vorenus had been able to give them didn't hold up under the clash and roar of battle.

A few paces behind the rearmost rank of legionaries, Gnaeus Pompey saw his chance. "Extend the line," he shouted. "Fourth rank, extend to the left. Encompass their flank!"

The orders were quickly passed on by centurions and optios. As practiced in a thousand drills, the Roman line thinned and extended, step by step.

A whistle blasted. The forward rank of Roman soldiers slipped back through the ranks, falling back to the rear while the second rank took their place. The Novans found themselves facing fresh combatants.

Man-Ready-For-War saw his soldiers being pushed back. The line was failing, and his soldiers had the river at their back. The wings of the Roman ranks were curving around, hemming the Novan warriors into a progressively smaller space. Man-Ready-For-War shouted orders into the trees and, with his last reserve—two hundred seasoned warriors—at his back, he charged at the Roman left flank.

"Refuse the left!" a centurion shouted, and the cohort that had just moved out to the left wing spread out and stepped back, quickly, with the ease of men who had carried out this exact evolution a hundred times. The Novan charge smashed into a wall of scuta bristling with gladii.

Man-Ready-For War ran at the line himself, leaped high, and came down hard on a Roman shield. He struck at the Romans with his war club and smashed two of them down before the edge of a sword caught his arm, laying it open. He dropped his club and, blood dripping from his arm, grabbed at his obsidian knife.

Weakened, losing blood, he slashed helplessly at the Roman shield wall. Around him his black-painted warriors were screaming and dying.

It was a debacle.

The Roman left flank pulled around straight, driving the Novans before them.

Pompey grabbed a legionary to act as messenger; shouting orders did no good now, with the legions fully engaged. "Run to the wings," he ordered the man. "Tell the centurions there to bend the flanks forward." Under the new orders from Pompey, the Roman line began to draw forward on the flanks while the center held fast, to form a shallow arc with the Novans in the center.

The B'Kou and A'Tep archers, seeing what was happening, began to slip away through the trees. Unlike the Romans, no oath held the People in place to fight. The soldiers of the Red Blanket warrior societies would only fight as long as they were well led.

In fact, the very nature of the B'Kou and A'Tep played into the Romans' hands. Novan population densities were much lower than was the norm in Europe. When the Roman army lost a man, or ten men, or a hundred men, new ones were always available. Roman generals were accustomed to raising legions freely, as long as there was coin to pay them.

The Novan warrior societies lived with the fact that if they lost a man, they had to wait for a boy to grow to replace him. Further, every man lost was a brother, or a cousin. That fact held even the most aggressive war chief of the Red Blanket society in check. General Pompey had been careful playing the cards he was dealt. He knew, at some level, that he could not replace the men he lost, and had fought the summer campaign accordingly.

But in the end, he was a soldier of Rome, and fought as Rome had always fought.

The Alligator People were more aggressive than any B'Kou or A'Tep had ever dreamed of being. This made them fearsome warriors in the forests and swamps of the low country, but even they were not willing to stand in the face of Roman steel and absorb thirty, forty, or fifty percent losses.

The result was predictable. "Our young men are abandoning the fight," Four Bears said quietly to White Oak where they watched.

White Oak said nothing. He was watching the battle in the meadow.

"To the river!" Gnaeus Pompey roared. First Legion pressed in on the Novan flank, bending the line still further. The whistles blasted again, and another rank of fresh Roman soldiers pushed their way to the front, anxious for blood. The warriors of the Alligator People found themselves with their backs to the river, with Romans on all sides. Their archery support from the trees was all but gone. One by one, the hardened Alligator warriors began to abandon the fight.

Farther back of the line still, Titus Pullo and Lucius Vorenus sat astride their horses. Their cavalryman, all mounted, sat in a neat row behind them, waiting.

"Do you think we can make a difference?"

Vorenus pointed at the city gate. Even now, a half-dozen Roman cavalry burst out of the town and charged at the left flank of the Novan forces, shouting and whirling swords. "Not now," he said. "They have us, brother. We have lost the day, and we have lost the war. There's no coming back from this."

"We could yet surprise them with a charge at their flank."

"Look at them," Vorenus snapped. "Those aren't savage tribesman. Those are soldiers of Rome." His tone was downcast, but there was still, deep down, a note of pride. "There are nine of us and at least a thousand of them. They'd have us unhorsed in a moment, and a moment after that we'd be standing at the banks of the Styx. No, brother, we've lost, and that boy General will be looking for us as soon as he cleans up those savages."

"Well, we did plan for that." Pullo pulled his horse around. "Follow us, boys," he told the seven cavalrymen.

One of the men looked through the trees at the battle, and then back at Pullo. "Where are we going, sir?"

"Back to camp, gather our gear and as much food and water as we can carry. After that? West," Pullo said. "As far and as fast as we can. Unless you want to stay here and be crucified as a traitor to Rome, that is." He kicked his horse to a gallop, followed closely by the others.

A few yards away, Four Bears and White Oak watched the Roman horsemen ride away.

"Our young men are dying, and see now what your allies are made of?" Four Bears asked. "They use their great beasts, their horses, to flee. You depended on their advice. You went to war based on the advantage you said their help would bring. And now look—look, cousin! They flee!"

"I have heard them talk," White Oak said sadly. "They were worried that the other Romans would kill them as traitors if they were taken in battle. Would we not do the same, cousin, for any of ours that betrayed us to an enemy?"

"Pullo asked me two days ago about the Tsalee on the far side of the mountains. He seemed very curious. I suppose they will go there now, to settle with those people instead."

"The Tsalee are traders and farmers, not soldiers. They will have no luck persuading the Tsalee to take up arms. Perhaps they will go south to raise an army among the Maya."

"Perhaps they will not try to raise soldiers against Rome again." Four Bears pointed at the Roman town, just visible through the trees. "We can see very plainly that the people of Rome have other skills besides war. We can see very plainly that the people of Rome excel at other arts, as much as they plainly do at war. No, Pullo and Vorenus have learned their lesson and acted accordingly. Will we be as wise?" The sarcasm in Four Bears' voice was painfully obvious.

"The Romans certainly excel at war more than do we," White Oak said sadly. "Look—the Alligator soldiers have their backs to the river now and are beginning to flee. The Roman town stands untouched."

"Our soldiers cannot win now, cousin," Four Bears said. "The B'Kou and A'Tep are pulling back away from the Roman fire-arrows. Man-Ready-For-War has lost—for the first time that anyone can remember, the Alligator People have lost a war. I tell you now, cousin, it is time to end this."

White Oak looked at Four Bears. The two chiefs had known each other all their lives; while it was customary among B'Kou and A'Tep to use the polite address "cousin" between members of each tribe, in their case it was literally true; White Oak's mother had been Four Bear's father's sister. The two had played together as boys, hunted together as young men, sat in council together as chiefs, and now faced deciding the way forward for their people.

"You have something in mind," White Oak said.

"I do," Four Bears replied.

"What do you plan to do?"

"I will talk to the Roman chiefs, their war chief Pompey and their tribal chief Cato," Four Bears said, and went on for a few moments. "What better way to end this? If I can offer them a way to end this with no more war, a way to end this that no matter what the outcome, the warrior society men and the others of the People can accept with honor."

"It is a good idea," White Oak agreed. "If they agree, it is probably the best we can hope for now that Man-Ready-For-War has failed. I will have to talk to the other Red Blanket chiefs, but if the Romans agree, I think the Red Blanket society will agree as well. Your plan, if the Romans accept, allows us at least our honor."

"The Alligator People will fight to the last," Four Bears said, "but they have already lost. When the day draws to a close, the fighting will stop. Then I will talk to the Romans."

On the city wall

"Look! Look there! The savages are starting to swim the river!"

An archer pointed. The bowmen on the walls had been standing idle for some time, as the Roman forces were in close contact.

"They are! They are! The Novans are breaking!" another man called into the town.

The Alligator soldiers were, to a man, hardened soldiers of the sort typical to the new world. They were physically tough, inured to pain, heat, cold, famine or thirst. They were experienced warriors and had taken readily to the tactics brought to them by the Roman centurions Vorenus and Pullo.

But nothing in their training could have prepared them for this.

War, to the Alligator soldiers, meant a summer enterprise of lightning raids on unprepared opponents, of stealing food and occasionally women. Nothing in their experience prepared them for the steady pressure of the disciplined Roman legions, the wall of scuta, the stabbing gladii and the heavy, crippling strikes of pila. Most of all, nothing prepared them for the steady pressure of a unified line of soldiers bearing steel, hemming them in, pushing them slowly into the river.

Once the panic set in, it spread quickly. When the rearmost warriors were waist-deep in the waters of the Tiber, they dropped weapons and struck out for the far bank. On seeing that, any Novans not directly engaged joined in.

General Gnaeus Pompey quickly saw what was happening. He looked to the left, where six horsemen rode through the Novan lines, gladii swinging; the Novans scattered before them.

But the rout was not yet complete. A hard core of the black-painted warriors was still fighting, there in the center of the line. Pompey turned to the centurion in charge of the one century held in reserve, a hundred men still behind the lines—just behind the lines. "Form your men," he ordered. "Wedge formation. Now we break them."

The centurion bellowed orders. Pompey shouted for a messenger, sent him to let the cohorts at the front know what was coming.

When the reserve century was formed, General Pompey looked at them and grinned. He drew his gladius, held it over his head, the plain issue blade gleaming in the morning light. "Century!" he shouted. He dropped the sword, pointing it at the gap slowly opening in the front line. "Follow me! CHARGE!"

The hundred men of Second Legion howled like wolves and smashed into the thin line of black-painted Novans, scattering them like dry leaves on a windy day. The young general fought alongside his men, swinging his gladius and shouting like a common legionary. As the battle degenerated into a general melee, He found himself facing a black-painted Novan, a tall, spare man holding a spiked war club that dripped blood—Roman blood.

"You," the Novan said in passable Latin. "You are the one they call Pompey." He was looking at the general's tall, black-plumed helmet crest.

"I am," Pompey agreed. He circled slowly, watching the tall Novan even as the battle raged around them. "And who in Hades might you be?"

"I am called Long Tooth," the man said, "son of Man-Ready-For-War, and I will now kill you."

"Good luck, then," Pompey said agreeably. "You won't be the first to try." He had no scutum, but he did have a pugio, a stabbing dagger, on his belt. He drew the dagger and held it in his left hand, the gladius balanced in his right. Long Tooth produced a knife of black stone with a bone handle to back up his war club.

"Your men fight well," Long Tooth said. "Perhaps too well, better than even your fellow Romans were able to make us understand."

"Too bad for you, then," Pompey said. "Maybe you should have listened more closely to them." He parried a blow of the Novan's war club, taking it on the blade of the gladius. He spun, struck out with the pugio, but Long Tooth danced away. "Did your renegade friends tell you of Gaul? Of Greece and Macedonia?"

"They told us they fought there."

Pompey feinted left and struck right, catching Long Tooth a glancing blow in the ribs, a mere scratch, with the edge of the gladius. "They should have told you those places, and of Spain, and Africa, and all the other places the Roman army has fought and won."

"You will not win this war," Long Tooth said. He leaped, dodged, and slammed a blow into Pompey's ribs. Even through his heavy leather cuirass Pompey felt a rib crack. He swung his gladius and missed. The two men started circling again.

"Look around you," Pompey told him. "We already have won. Your men are fleeing."

Long Tooth risked a glance to his left and right. The Roman was right; second by second, more and more of the surviving Alligator warriors were leaping into the river, fleeing—fleeing! A body on the ground nearby caught his attention—his brother, Sharp Knife, gutted by a Roman sword.

"It is not possible," Long Tooth said in his own language. "No— it is not possible!" He looked back at Pompey, and said in Latin, "I will at least kill you."

He dropped his knife, raised his war club over his head and, howling, leaped at the Roman general.

Pompey crouched, ducked under the swing of the club, and drove his gladius into the Novan's stomach. Long Tooth landed, dropped to his knees, and clutched at his middle. Dark blood poured from between his fingers.

"Not possible," he said, still in Latin. He looked up at Pompey who stood over him, glaring down. "Not possible. My father planned this—my father is Man-Ready-For-War."

The Roman general sheathed his pugio. He took his gladius in both hands, blade pointed downward, and raised it high. "And my father," he told the Novan, "was Gnaeus Pompeius Magnus, Consul of Rome, Optimate Senator and General of the Roman Army. I do this in his name."

"I will see you in the next life, War Chief Pompey."

"And I, you," Pompey agreed easily.

With that he drove the blade down, into the Novan's chest. Long Tooth fell backwards, blood pouring from his mouth and from the wounds in his chest and stomach.

"My father approached your people in friendship," he told the dying Long Tooth as he pulled his sword free. "Four Bears listened to my father. Your father should have listened. You could have avoided all this. You stupid, stupid man, you could have avoided all this!"

He looked at Long Tooth, but the man was past answering.

Around them, the last Novans were fleeing. Archery from the trees stopped. Pompey, suddenly exhausted, waved at a centurion who stood nearby, watching the last Novans swimming the river. "Gather the wounded," he ordered. "See to ours first, then see to any Novans that can be helped. We'll show them we're better men. Send someone for water and biscuits. Pass the word, if Man-Ready-For-War is identified among the dead or wounded, I want to be notified immediately."

"As you command, sir," the man said. "I saw you fight the Novan, sir. That was well fought."

"He as much as threw himself on my sword," Pompey replied. "I suppose he couldn't bear the thought of losing." He slapped the centurion on the back. "It will make a good story for my sons one day, neh? Go on, then—be about your task."

Then, the battle won, he sat, and then lay back in the grass, staring at the summer sun overhead. "We did it," he said to no one in particular. "By Mar's own balls, we did it."

In the forest

"Cousin," Four Bear said, "It is over."

"And we have lost."

"How many of our young men are dead?" Four Bear was having trouble overcoming his own uncharacteristic anger. "How many of our young women have no husbands? How many of our children have no fathers?"

"Too many," White Oak muttered.

"They fought and died," Four Bears was almost shouting now and even more alarming, was not even taking his usual indirect approach to the topic. "They fought and died while we stayed here in the woods like old women."

The B'Kou village chief took a deep breath, trying to calm himself. He looked up and there was the beautiful blue of the sky, there were the green leaves of the trees, stirring gently in the mid-day breeze; the sight was madly, insanely peaceful after the event of the morning. He closed his eyes and let the sun play on his face, finally regaining some of his typical calm.

"Where is Man-Ready-For-War?" Four Bears asked at last.

"He has not been seen for some time," White Oak answered. "He may be dead. His sons are known to have been killed, we know that much." The battered soldiers of the Red Blanket Society had passed that news on as they filtered through the trees, heading home.

"So fall the mighty soldiers of the Alligator People," Four Bears said, "laid low by the soldiers of Rome. Like many before them, I suspect."

White Oak nodded. He, too, was looking at the sky. A small white cloud passed over the sun, casting a shadow on the Red Blanket society chief's face.

"Clouds-In-The-Morning and the medicine society men will need help tending our injured. I will help them this afternoon, but before this day is out, I will seek out the Roman war chief Pompey. I will speak with him. There will be an end to all this." He turned to go.

"The young women with no husbands, the children with no fathers," White Oak said, causing Four Bears to stop and turn back.

"Yes?"

"I think they will have husbands and fathers, cousin," White Oak said. He pointed at the Roman town, barely visible through the trees. "I think their husbands and fathers will be men of Rome. Isn't that the way of war?"

"This one time," Four Bears snapped, "perhaps it is for the best. Perhaps the strong Roman blood will help a people who have grown too stupid."

A league to the north, Man-Ready-For-War stopped running at last. His arm was still bleeding, but his legs were working. He had swum the river among the rest of the Alligator warriors, but when they reformed on the far bank for the march home, their war chief had already slipped away into the forest. The day was lost; the war was lost; he knew he had gambled everything and failed. Even his sons were gone; he had seen Long Tooth fall to the Roman general just before he leaped into the river. Man-Ready-For-War neither knew nor cared what would become of his soldiers; his life was already forfeit thanks to the loss, and he did not care to wait for the tribe to pass judgment on his leadership now.

"I will find new soldiers," he muttered. "I will return to this place, and I will kill them all." He spat in the direction of the Roman town.

His vow made, he tended to his arm. With his knife, he cut a strip of deerskin from his clout. He used a stick to stir up some of the sandy loam of the forest floor, urinated on it, and applied the resulting thick mud to the gash on his arm before wrapping it up in the deerskin.

With that done, he walked off to the west, into the face of the setting sun.

The battlefield

The sun was sinking low in the sky. The wounded were recovered and taken into the city for treatment; the dead were laid out for rites and pyres on the following day. General Pompey was in conversation with his legates when he noticed the two Consuls walking towards him.

"Excuse me," he said to his legates. He strode over to where Cato and Cicero had stopped to survey the red field.

"Consuls," he said, saluting.

"General," Cato smiled. "It seems you've won."

"They're on the run," Pompey agreed. "We've broken the worst of them. It will take some time to dig those Alligator People out of the swamps where they live, but with the cream of their warriors lying dead here on our hills, I think we'll be able to do just that. We lost some men as well, and while every one of ours is precious, our legions struck down five for every one we lost. Unprecedented, Consuls; it is unprecedented."

"I think—Sons of Dis, look there," Cicero pointed down the hill, to where the trees met the river. A lone figure was walking towards them, slowly, his head low—in grief? In shame?

Pompey drew his gladius. Several soldiers ran to intercept the lone figure, but Pompey called them to stop.

He recognized the man.

"Four Bears," he said quietly.

The B'Kou chief walked slowly up to the Roman general. "Salve," he said, startling Pompey.

"Salve, indeed. What do you want?" Pompey asked.

"This must end now," Four Bears said.

"I quite agree," General Pompey said. He sheathed his sword just as Cato and Cicero walked up. "Since we seem to have won this battle—overwhelmingly, I might add—I think it's time you admit defeat."

Four Bears shook his head. "I am sorry. I do not yet—I do not... understand, your tongue well enough." He looked around. "Could we call the girl Adsila here?"

"Here?" Pompey gestured at the bodies littering the battlefield. "I should say not. I'll be damned if I expose my sister to this. We will go to the town gate. Consuls, would you come with us?"

"Of course," Cato said.

Pompey summoned a legionary standing nearby. "Run ahead to my villa and ask for my sister. Escort her to the city gate."

"Yes sir!" The young soldier saluted and ran.

The walk up the hill was awkward. General Pompey led the procession, with Four Bears walking silently behind him, and the Consul and Lesser Consul of Nova Roma bringing up the rear.

Four Bears looked sideways at Pompey as they walked. "You are a sincere man," he said, "and you call Adsila your sister as easily as though she was born to your mother."

"My father adopted her as is his right under Roman law. She is my sister, in every way but birth. And in the time, she has been here I have grown as fond of her as I am of my own blood sister, left behind in Rome."

"That is a good thing," Four Bears agreed. "If you can accept Adsila into your family, then that is a good sign that our peoples can live together."

Adsila herself met them at the gate. With the adopted Novan girl translating, the negotiations began.

"Do you offer terms of surrender?" Pompey asked.

"Our warrior society men are angry and ashamed," Four Bears began, as usual approaching the topic at an oblique angle—an odd habit, and one that Pompey always found annoying. Magnanimous in victory, though, he let the man go on.

"They are angry over losing this battle. I think they are angry at themselves for hearing Man-Ready-For-War's words and believing he knew what was best. They are ashamed for having followed him and for acting out of anger."

"Bloody well ought to be," Pompey snorted.

"But all of the People are proud, Gnaeus Pompey," Four Bears continued, ignoring the remark. "They will not surrender easily. I cannot speak for the Alligator People, and Man-Ready-For-War has not been seen since the battle ended. The Alligator People left alive have all run away to their homes in the south. But I have spoken with my cousin White Oak, who leads the Red Blanket warrior society. I have presented my thoughts to him, and he consents that the warrior society men of B'Kou and A'Tep will agree with what I have proposed."

"And what is that?"

"The Red Blanket soldiers will choose their best fighter. You choose yours. The two will fight, one man against one man, and the winner will decide the war. If your man wins, it will be as I have foreseen. B'Kou, A'Tep and Roman will all become one people. All of our towns will become Roman towns. We will be able then to do this with honor, the honor of an agreement struck and kept. Not as a conquered people."

"And if your man wins?"

"The Red Blanket soldiers say that if their man wins, you must promise to leave your town on the hill and move away to the north. Few people live to the north, and you should be able to find new lands there to call yours."

Gnaeus Pompey turned to Cato and Cicero. "It is for you to decide, Consuls," he said, "but I recommend we accept. We can end this now. This war, this conflict, ended at a stroke."

Cato looked at Four Bears. "We will need a few moments," he said, and as Adsila softly translated, he drew Cicero and Pompey aside.

"General," Cato said, "are you quite certain this is a good idea?"

"I'm positive, Consul," Pompey the Younger said. "I'd bet my life on it. In fact, I will. If we lose, I give my word to open my stomach in penance."

"You're that sure of this?" Cicero demanded.

"Of the man I have in mind? Of course. I'd put any trained Roman soldier against the main run of these Novans, but the man I have in mind, I'd put up against the best they can muster, and wager my life and a hundred gold pieces in the bargain."

"If you're sure," Cato mused. "If we really could end this... And the tribes would join us, with their knowledge of the land and its creatures, added to what we bring from Rome herself, we could build a remarkable nation here. A remarkable nation indeed."

"My thoughts exactly."

A few feet away, Adsila spoke quietly to Four Bears in their own language. "I have lived among the Romans for a year now," she said. "I know them, better even than you. There is much good among them, Four Bears. The way they live, the things they know, the things they can do—it goes so far beyond war. I have heard my brother speak of their plans for their town and their land, and they have not yet done one part in ten of what they plan. Great runs of stone to bring water from the mountains, walls of stone around the town, weaving plants for clothing—I could not begin to tell you all I have heard."

"I know," Four Bears said. "I saw these things, when we were still friends, before Man-Ready-For-War came north and incited our young men to war. Pompey Magnus was my friend. Cato was my friend. I grieve for Pompey Magnus. I hope one day to be friends with his son. I hope to be friends with Cato again."

"You hope the warrior society man of the People loses the fight, then?"

"Do you not think that would be best? The Red Blanket soldiers will choose their best, and he will fight like an angry bear, but he will be fighting all of Rome. You, Adsila, of all the people, you know the ways of Rome best. Do you not think it would be a good thing for the People to join them?"

"I do," the girl admitted.

Pompey the Younger and the Consuls approached. "We accept," the young general said.

"There is a clearing, half a morning's walk up the river, where a small stream joins, it," Four Bears said. "We propose to meet there. The Red Blanket soldiers say they will need some time to pick their best. I presume you will as well. We will not fight with you until the matter is finished, if you will agree to the same."

"Agreed," Pompey said. "A truce until our champions can meet. If your man loses, you join us."

"As citizens," Cato said. "You become Romans, just as we." Beside him, Cicero nodded.

"Yes, of course as citizens," Pompey agreed. "Citizens of Rome, with all that entails. If your man wins, we will move out of your country, find another place to live. Somewhere north, I presume."

"It is done, then." Four Bears said. "When the Red Blanket men have made their choice, I will return to you myself, to choose the day." He turned to go, but Pompey called him back.

"There are Romans among you," he said. "They helped you in the fight against us. Our agreement does not include them, as they are traitors to their own people. We want them."

Four Bears smiled sadly. "I would gladly give them to you, Gnaeus Pompey, but you may not have them, unless you find them yourself. When the battle here turned against us, they took to their horses and rode away. They were last seen running west, as fast as their beasts would carry them."

Pompey snorted. "And in the end, they prove to be bloody cowards. Fine; trouble yourself no more about them, Four Bears, unless they return. If they do, I would count it as a personal favor if you would turn them over to us."

Four Bears nodded and walked away.

As they watched the B'Kou chief walk down the hill, Cato had a question for Pompey. "How," he asked, "do you plan to choose the man to fight for Rome in this duel?"

"That's the easiest part of this whole proposal," Pompey chuckled. "I have the very man for the job. Our own Horatius, Consuls; he is the man who stood down a hundred Novans in the town gate, only this morning."

"Does this Heracles of yours have a name?" Cicero asked.

"He does indeed. He is First Spear Centurion Titus Caninus, now called Canis Magnus in honor of his stand at the gates of the town. The Great Dog, Consuls. He will fight for Rome, and he will win."

Chapter Fourteen

INTERVALS

General Pompey's victory in the battle of Pompeius had several immediate and surprising effects, even before the agreed-upon contest of champions took place.

First, interactions between the natives of the immediate locality of Pompeius and the people of that city increased almost immediately. Many of those interactions were of the most normal, natural and expected kind, when many of the young men of the tribes were slain in the fighting, and Pompeius was peopled almost completely with young, vigorous Roman men. Such is the fundamental nature of human beings everywhere.

Second and most surprising was the reaction of the B'Kou chief Four Bears. While he is mentioned in these pages previously as a man of uncommon insight and wisdom, it was during this period that these qualities came to the fore in the eyes of the Roman people. He was a regular visitor to the city in that time, even passing nights in the house of Consul Marcus Porcius Cato as Cato's honored guest. It was during this time that the true bonds began to form that eventually resulted in Novan and

Roman bonding as one people.

> *—From Gnaeus Pompey Novus' New World Diaries*

Pompeius

Only five days after the battle, with the meadows around the Roman town still showing the effects of trampling soldiers—although, at least, the bodies had been carried away—Four Bears was amazed at one change that had happened already.

He approached the town gates late in the day, having spent most of the day walking north from his home village. The Roman soldiers manning the guard towers recognized him and shouted a message, whereupon the city gates swung open to admit him, unchallenged.

The B'Kou chief walked in. The guards at the gate nodded to him, their expressions carefully neutral and their body language cautious. Four Bears raised a hand in greeting and walked on, heading for the center of town where the Senate building lay.

Going to the Senate required the pedestrian to pass through the town's growing Forum. Now that the fighting with the Novan tribes was ended, and the bodies of the Roman fallen burned and all ceremonial duties completed, the town had gotten back to the business of doing business, and business was booming. "The business of Rome," Senator Cassius Longinus had explained to Four Bears, "is business." Already men released from military vocations by the end of the conflict were setting up shop dealing in a variety of wares.

Four Bears was not terribly surprised to see two merchants had taken on Novan apprentices. The final contest not yet decided, he mused, and already it begins, as I foresaw.

He found the nine Senators of Nova Roma standing outside

the building. They were gathered around the Senator called Brutus, who was holding a large, flat sheet of something that looked like deerskin scraped thin. Some strange marks were on the thin sheet. Brutus was gesturing towards the top of the Senate building, while the others looked from the sheet to where he was pointing and back.

"Salve," he said, approaching the group. His Latin was quite good now, although he still had occasional trouble with concepts the Romans took for granted. He was about to encounter another.

"Salve," several of the Senators greeted Four Bears, but Consul Cato made the point of extending his hand. Four Bears, now familiar with the custom, took his hand and shook.

"Salve," Cato said. "What news?"

"The Red Blanket men are still arguing over who is best to represent them. They have set a series of wrestling matches and races to pick their champion. Every village chief wants his son to be the choice, and every young Red Blanket solider thinks he is the best. They ask your forbearance for another five days, ten at most."

"Of course, of course," Cato agreed, knowing as well as Four Bears that time worked for the Romans. The evidence Four Bears had just seen in the Forum spoke eloquently to that.

Four Bears' curiosity overwhelmed him. He pointed at the sheet that Brutus held. "What is that?"

"Plans to improve and extend the Senate building," Brutus told him, "and to add a second chamber for the Council of Plebs, which will be our second body of government."

"You will have two separate groups of chiefs?"

"In a manner of speaking," Cato said.

Four Bears looked closely at the thin sheet. It was indeed deer skin, scraped very, very thin and dried. Some of the marks were incomprehensible, but on examination he could see that the large figure in the center was the Senate building as seen from above, as a bird might see it—and another picture on the side showed the same building from the front, as a man may see it.

"Amazing," he muttered.

Cato pointed at the sheet. "You can see," he said, "this is the second chamber for the Council. It will be built there," he pointed, "just to the east, in that open space. The building will be pushed out larger on all sides, and we intend to complete the work with all stone, where there now is wood."

"All this will be done if you win the contest, of course."

"Of course," Cato agreed. He looked confident, and Four Bears did not doubt he had reason. He knew all too well the martial skills Rome had at her command. And in his heart, Four Bears had already accepted the likely outcome.

"In time," Brutus said, "and if we win, of course,"—a sly look at that— "Pompeius will expand to cover all four hills. In old Rome, from whence we came, there were seven hills, but four is adequate."

"A city on a hill," Four Bears thought aloud. He looked around. "Already you have built a town the likes of which none of the People have ever seen, and yet you plan for more."

"Who would think otherwise?"

Four Bears nodded and, his message from the Red Blanket chiefs delivered, turned to go, but Cato called him back.

"Where do you go from here?" he asked.

"It is a long walk back to my home," Four Bears said. "I will walk until sunset. Then I will eat, sleep, and walk the rest of the way tomorrow."

"Why not pass the night here? You could just as easily walk back tomorrow, yes?"

"Yes," Four Bears admitted. "I could sleep within your walls, certainly. I have a blanket," he said, tapping a small roll he carried on a thong, tucked under his arm.

"Nonsense," Cato said. "We were about to adjourn here. My house is big enough for a guest, I think, and I can easily arrange a pallet for you to sleep on. Join me for supper, and we can talk the evening away. Friend Cicero, would you join us for supper?"

"Certainly," Cicero agreed.

"Well, then, Four Bears? Will you stay?"

He really did not have to think about his answer, especially since he had planned to spend the night sleeping in the forest beside a fallen log. "Yes," Four Bears accepted.

"Excellent! Allow us a moment here, then, to conclude our business."

Four Bears walked a few paces away and watched the activity in the Forum as the Senate concluded their planning.

"So much goes on," he whispered. A group of soldiers, perhaps ten, marched past in the unique synchronized step that no Novan ever imagined. As he watched the soldiers pass, a large, broad man in a faded red robe walked into the Forum, accompanied by a smaller man in a simple gray tunic. The smaller man carried a wooden box. The small man set the box down, and the larger man stepped up on it, unrolled a thin sheet of deerskin similar to the one Brutus held, and began shouting from leather lungs:

"The Senate will meet in formal session for the next five days, beginning tomorrow morning. Any citizens with grievances will be allowed to speak before the Senate from the hours of noon until the supper hour."

Four Bears noticed the activity of the Forum slowing as people stopped to listen.

"The marriage of Centurion Titus Caninus Magnus, hero of the Nova Roman Army, to innkeeper Servia Merula is announced for the kalends of September. Marcus Porcius Cato, Consul of Rome, has proclaimed a day of feasting and celebration in honor of the first marriage in the new land."

It was fascinating to watch the man speak. As he shouted, he gestured, posed, and thumped his chest. The People were more modest when speaking to groups, but Four Bears had to admire the man's flair.

"Baker Petrus Agricola seeks ten men to accompany him on an exploration party to find farmlands north of the Tiber for the growing of wheat and barley as seed stocks become available. Each man will be paid ten denarii per day, apiece, on completion of the five-day expedition. Men with archery equipment are encouraged to apply."

"General Pompey announces the birth of a young stallion, the first stallion born in Nova Roma. The foal is to be called Bucephalus, after the favored mount of the fabled Alexander."

With that said the large man stepped off the box and walked away. The smaller man scooped up the box and hurried after him. After a few moments, Four Bears heard the shouting start again some short distance away.

"Listening to the newsreader, eh?" he heard Cato ask.

Four Bears turned to face the man he hoped to be able one day to call his friend. "It is a good thing," he said, "to share the news of your people in such a way. The People share news more slowly. Mostly it is the women who gather to talk, and when women gather, the words seem to grow wings."

Cato laughed and slapped Four Bears on the shoulder. "See," he said, "our people are not so different after all."

Cicero joined them. "To supper, then?" he asked.

"Indeed," Cato agreed.

The Consul led them into the Forum, where he stopped at a stall and spoke with the operator. He bought some baked fish the man announced was caught "only that morning in the Tiber," a small basket of maize biscuits, and another of what Four Bears recognized as dried, preserved persimmons. He watched as Cato handed over several small coins to the man, who bowed and thanked the Consul profusely.

When they arrived at Cato's small house, Four Bears had a question. "Friend Cato," he asked, unconsciously copying the Roman's term of familiar address, "your... coins. May I see one?"

"Certainly." Cato withdrew a silver denarius from his purse and handed it to Four Bears.

The Novan chief had seen Roman coins in use but still was unclear on the concept. He examined the coin closely. It had no sharp edges, no scraping blade; it was just a small, round disk of some bright metal, with the image of some Roman man on it, along with some of the Roman symbols similar to those he had seen on Brutus's plans for the new Senate.

"This thing," he said at last, "I have seen you trade these for food, and I presume you trade them for other things as well. I do not see why a man would trade food for this. It does not seem to have any purpose. It does not seem to be good for anything."

"That," Cato said, "will take some explaining. First, let us sit down." He motioned towards the side of the room where several low benches surrounded a table. Cato placed the food on the table and motioned Four Bears to a bench.

When the three men were seated and had sampled the food, Cicero spoke. "The reason the coin has value," he explained, "is partly because of the rare and precious metal of which it is made. That metal is silver," he pronounced the word slowly.

"Silver," Four Bears repeated, committing the word to memory.

"We have coins of gold as well," Cato said. He produced a gold aureus and showed it to Four Bears. "Coins of gold have more value, because gold is rarer and more precious still than silver. Therefore, you can trade a gold coin for more goods than a silver one."

Four Bears shook his head in annoyance. "But why are these coins made? How does one come by them in the first place? Do you make your own?"

"The Senate is responsible for coining money," Cicero said. "The Senate ensures that all coins are made the same, that the metal is of certain purity and that each coin contains the same amount of that metal. Men earn coins—money—by working for other men, or by producing goods themselves that they sell for coins. Then they can use those coins to trade for other things they want, that are made by other men."

"Among the People," Four Bears said, "we simply trade for goods. If I go hunting and kill a deer, I may trade a portion of the meat to old Owl, who crafts the best knives in our village. I may present a tanned deer hide to Clouds-In-The-Morning of the Medicine Society in return for a tea that cures headaches. When a young man takes a girl to wife, he usually makes a gift of tanned hides, tools or weapons to her father."

"It is not so different," Cato replied. "Your work produces things of value. You trade the product of your labor, of the things you do well, to others for the things they do well. Each man has his own skills and talents, and each of those skills and talents have their own value. It is up to each man alone to use his skills and talents to his own best interest."

Four Bears turned the silver coin over in his hand. Suddenly, with a flash of insight so sudden it was almost blinding, he understood. "This... coin, it is not the metal that gives it the great value," he exploded. "This coin is a symbol of the trust between men. It is a great symbol that binds people together in trade and work. This coin represents the work of the baker the newsreader spoke of. It represents the work of you, friend Cato, and you, friend Cicero, in guiding and counseling your people. It represents the work of your soldiers in protecting your people." He stood up, too excited to sit, and began to walk around the small room. "It represents the man who catches fish from the river and the man who hunts wapiti in the forest. A man that works hard may gain more coins, which shows more value for his work. A man who is lazy and sleeps the day away will have no coins to trade for anything he wants, and so will be punished for his laziness. Your coins are a measure with which you reward those who work hard and produce good things, and encourage others to do the same! With all men working to make and produce and gather things for trade, then everyone grows in wealth!"

Cicero and Cato stared at each other. Four Bears had just explained the basics of the Roman economy with a brilliant simplicity that neither of them would have been able to articulate so clearly.

"You hit to the very heart of it," Cicero said at last.

"You have," Cato agreed. "You have indeed."

The next morning

Four Bears breakfasted with Cato in the morning and then,

looking uncomfortable, announced he would walk back to his village. The People had no concept of farewells or good-byes, and Four Bears was having trouble with the idea that it was considered rude among the Romans to simply leave.

Cato escorted the Novan chief to the town gate, stopping to gather up Cicero at his house along the way. Four Bears turned at the gate and nodded to the Consuls.

He felt he had to say something. "You are good men," he announced. "I hope one day we can be good friends."

"That is our fervent hope as well," Cato replied.

Four Bears blinked at the Latin word "fervent" but derived the meaning from context. He solemnly shook hands with the Consuls, turned and walked off.

"Friendship," Cicero said, "is only possible between good men. I think Four Bears is a good man."

"I think so as well. Now all we have to do is ensure our agreement doesn't oblige us to move off to the north."

The three men had talked late into the night, and Four Bears had confirmed a rumor that had been going through the town since the previous year. "So," Cicero said, "what some of the Novans were saying about cities to the south would seem to be true."

"The Maya." Cato pronounced the word carefully. "There may be civilized people here after all. Mind you even Four Bears only knows of them third hand. The Tsalee on the other side of the western mountains trade with them, and know where they live, somewhere far to the south."

"In cities of stone," Cicero remembered the description Four Bears had provided.

"Question is, how civilized are they? The Gauls have cities as well, and one can call them civilized only by applying the word in the broadest possible sense."

"I imagine," Cato said, "that we will eventually find out. For now, we have the advantage of distance and time."

"Time to build an army before we meet them, is that what you're thinking?"

Cato turned to look at the older man. "When we do eventually meet these Maya," he said, "don't you think it best we meet them in a position of strength? We have nothing to lose by it if they are peaceable, civilized and friendly. We have everything to lose if they are not."

Elsewhere in the city

Word of the challenge and Titus Caninus' promotion had spread rapidly through the town. Everyone now insisted on naming him Canis Magnus, which embarrassed him slightly in spite of his usual braggadocio. "Still," he told Servia Merula, "the name was placed on me by General Pompey himself, so I can hardly decline the honor, neh?"

Another result of his new-found fame was that, for the time, he was eating well. Everybody in the town insisted on providing him with the best cuts of meat and fish, 'to build his strength.' With the upcoming duel in mind he exercised a good part of each day by helping construction gangs with carrying foundation stones and timbers. When not engaged in that he practiced with some of his comrades from First Legion. A carpenter crafted some wooden practice gladii, and the new First Spear centurion practiced for hours every day, sometimes until well after dark.

This morning he had breakfasted on a thick steak of wapiti, proudly cooked for him by Servia Merula. When he had eaten, he washed, donned his gear, gathered his pilum, scutum and practice sword, kissed his intended wife and went out through the city gate to the grassy meadow overlooking the Tiber.

He practiced feints, spins and stabs until his friend Julius Salvius approached, similarly laden with gear and practice sword.

"Sir!" the legionary came to attention and saluted, but there was a twinkle in his eye.

"Oh, balls," Canis Magnus spluttered. He wasn't yet used to his new status.

"Mars smiles on you," Salvius grinned. "Venus too, it seems. Let's see if your sword arm lives up to your new status as hero of Rome, shall we?" He drew his wooden practice gladius and crouched behind his scutum.

Caninus went into a similar stance. He smiled inside; he was well rested and well fed. The days of exercise and practice were yielding deadly fruit. He knew he was as good a warrior as he would likely ever be, right now, today.

On the other hand, Julius Salvius was an experienced and skillful fighter as well. He was smaller than Caninus, with perhaps less brute strength, but he compensated for that with lightning reflexes and sheer speed. Caninus had seen him in battle, striking like a snake with stabs of his gladius.

He also knew the Novans relied on the same advantages of speed and agility in fighting the typically larger, heavier Romans.

Salvius moved in quickly. He raised his scutum and slammed at Caninus' shield with the lower edge, simultaneously stabbing low with his wooden sword. Caninus blocked the thrust, pushed Salvius away and recovered. The two started circling. Caninus stabbed out suddenly, almost catching Salvius on the arm, but the smaller man dodged, taking the blow on his scutum.

They practiced through most of the warm, muggy afternoon, and when the sun finally drew low in the sky, walked to the riverbank, shed their gear and leaped into the Tiber with loud animal shouts, drawing laughter from the guards on the tower by the city gate.

Four Bear's village

Four Bears arrived home late in the day, as the sun was growing low in the west. The summer days were long, but Four Bears had made the journey slowly, thinking all the way. The evening spent in warm camaraderie with Cato and Cicero was weighing on his mind.

He went into his small round house, kindled a fire, and sat staring at the flames. He had food in the house but was not hungry.

"I knew they were different," he muttered to himself, "but not how different. Their coins... not even the Tsalee, not even the Maya have ever thought of such a thing. Their coins are such a powerful symbol of trade, of balance. It is a remarkable thing."

He found himself hoping the Red Blanket society's champion would lose his fight.

CHAPTER FIFTEEN

CHAMPIONS

The Novan chief Four Bears had in the end suggested a solution that was simple, elegant and satisfied the honor of all involved. Only the Alligator war chief Man-Ready-For-War did not approve, but his disapproval was noted only by his absence, since he was not in evidence at the end of the battle for Pompeius or at any of the events afterwards. Indeed, he was never seen again. It is not known whether he died unknown in the battle or if he fled following his army's defeat.

Primary in the success of Rome's participation in the arrangement to end the fighting was the soldier Titus Caninus, who was since that time better known as Canis Magnus in honor of his conspicuous courage. His promotion to First Spear was hailed by all who saw his stand in the gates of the city, and his defeat of the Novan champion resulted in him being acclaimed as one of Nova Roma's first conspicuous heroes.

A society a-borning is shaped by extraordinary events and extraordinary people. Nova Roma was fortunate in that the memorable people of its first years included such

figures as Pompey Magnus, Four Bears and Canis Magnus.
—From Gnaeus Pompey Novus' New World Diaries

Four Bears' village

Another five days passed before White Oak appeared outside Four Bears' house. A polite cough alerted the B'Kou chief of his A'Tep cousin's presence. Four Bears called for White Oak to come inside, which the Red Blanket warrior society leader did, in a hurry.

White Oak stood just inside the door and shook his head. Water droplets flew from his long black hair. "It is a detestable day," he announced.

"A bad day to travel," Four Bears agreed. "It has been raining all day. Still, you come at a good time; I was just about to eat. Come sit down, have some stew."

"I will," White Oak agreed enthusiastically; the stew's aroma filled the little round house. Years of fending for himself had made Four Bears into an adequate cook.

White Oak sat on one of the pallets near by the fire in the center of the hut, and Four Bears handed him a wooden bowl full of venison stew. He pulled a large chunk of meat from the bowl and popped it in his mouth. He chewed, swallowed, and then looked at Four Bears. "I have three things to tell you, cousin."

"I expected you came bearing news."

"First," White Oak began, "my thanks for the meal. I do not envy you having to cook for yourself all the time, but you seem to have grown skilled. Have you never thought of marrying again?"

"Perhaps someday. I am content as things are for now. Young men are always anxious for wives, but you and I, cousin, we are no longer so young."

"Young enough," White Oak chuckled. "The second thing: The

Red Blanket society has finally chosen a champion to represent the People in the duel you arranged."

"That is a good thing," Four Bears agreed. "And the third?"

"All of the Red Blanket soldiers want you to accompany the party to the duel. All agree that you are a man of wisdom, and since you proposed this solution, you should be there to see the outcome."

"I am honored," Four Bears inclined his head. "Cousin, we should speak of certain things. If your Red Blanket soldier wins this fight, then I presume the men of Rome will move away to a new place, and we will live as before."

"Yes," White Oak agreed warily.

"But consider what would happen even so. Do you think the influence of these people will fail to spread across the land, no matter where they live? Do you think a people as different as these men of Rome will fail to make their presence felt?"

"You are probably right. They are so different than any of the People, and with the tools and weapons they bear... Every village will want to trade with them. I can see that people will walk a long way to gain a Roman tool of steel."

"And with their horses, they can range even farther to trade with us."

"This is true."

Four Bears poked the fire with a stick. The rain was growing heavier, drumming on the bark roof of the hut. Somewhere in the village, a dog barked. "So," he said at last, "what difference will there really be in the outcome of this duel, either way?"

"You did not mention this when you proposed the idea."

"That was before I spent some time in the Roman town," Four Bears answered, and described the night he passed in the company of Cato and Cicero. He described the news-reader, the Forum, and finally the Roman concept of 'money,' which was so brilliant, so profound, that not even the Romans seemed to completely understand its impact—or perhaps, they were so accustomed to it as a matter of course, that they had long since ceased thinking about it.

"And so, you see," he concluded, "I think now, cousin, that the arrival of the men of Rome has changed us already. Rome has brought great things to our land, and no matter what we would prefer, things have changed forever, and will continue to change. I think it is the destiny of Rome to spread its influence over all the land. The People can either join or be left behind. It is a new time, and we must learn new ways."

White Oak had no ready answer for that.

A clearing near the Tiber

On the appointed morning representatives of both sides assembled in a clearing, several miles up the Tiber from Pompeius. Four Bears arrived with White Oak, old Owl and several others from the B'Kou and A'Tep tribes. Of Man-Ready-For-War, his people and the renegade Romans there was no sign.

The Romans arrived only a brief time after the Novans' party. The B'Kou chief greeted the Romans solemnly. Gnaeus Pompey and one other soldier were mounted on horses, as were the Consuls Cato and Cicero. Four Bears noticed that the girl Adsila was seated behind Pompey on his horse, her body language speaking eloquently of excitement mixed with nervousness. Four Bears correctly guessed this was her first time on a horse.

A group of dozen soldiers in full gear marched behind the

mounted party. At a word from Pompey then went into ranks and stood stolidly still, like statues.

Romans dismounted and exchanged greetings with Novans. Then it was time to begin.

"Our champion," Gnaeus Pompey announced; Adsila translated in a softer tongue. "Titus Caninus Magnus, Centurion of the First Nova Roman Legion." Caninus stepped forward, confident, in full armor, bearing his ivory-handled gladius and scutum. He wore the helmet of a centurion now, with its bright red side-to-side brush of horsehair.

White Oak spoke for a few moments in the language of the People; he spoke adequate Latin now, but the ceremoniousness of the occasion seemed to require his own language. "Our best fighter and wrestler," Adsila translated softly. "Black Wolf, Red Blanket Society chief of the Black River village of the B'Kou."

Titus Caninus regarded the barbarian warrior. He was a big man but lean, well-muscled. As was the manner of his people he wore very little, as was appropriate for the weather; in the warm summer sunshine he was clad only in his clout and fringed, knee-high soft leather boots. His long black hair was tied back; he examined Caninus from confident, jet-black eyes. He held a long club of stout wood with a round, spiked head in one hand, a keen-looking knife of some black stone in the other.

"So," Caninus grinned at the man. "A dog against a wolf. Let's see who barks louder this morning, neh?"

Adsila translated. Caninus' grin grew wider as the savage threw back his head and laughed.

"We ask for a few moments to prepare," Pompey said. "Is that agreeable?"

Four Bears looked at his cousin White Oak, who nodded. "We agree."

Pompey pulled Titus Caninus off to the side. He regarded the big man with a sardonic smile. "I suppose there's little point in my offering you any advice on fighting."

"I never turn down advice, sir," Caninus said. His tone was carefully diplomatic, but his eyes were twinkling. Even after a summer of campaigning, the big man was still looking forward to a good fight.

"Watch his feet. Watch his eyes. If I've learned one thing from fighting these people, it's that they are bloody fast. Stay on your toes."

"I will, sir."

Pompey looked past Caninus' shoulder. Black Wolf was seated on the ground, legs crossed, eyes closed, his face turned skywards. "It looks like our friend is having a talk with his gods before he fights. You may want to follow suit."

"I'll do that."

The young general faced Caninus. He placed both hand on the centurion's shoulders and looked him in the eyes. "Steady," Pompey said. He slapped Caninus on the shoulders and walked off.

Titus Caninus looked up at the sky, so brilliantly blue here in the new world. *It is as though the very sky is somehow different.* A few wisps of cloud drifted over. There was only a hint of breeze, and the morning was warm, but the humidity was within reason. *It's going to be a beautiful day,* Caninus thought. He closed his eyes.

Caelus, Ceres and Mars, he said silently, *smile on me today. Make me swift and strong. My people are depending on me.*

He opened his eyes at a sound from a tree nearby. A tiny bird, gray with a white belly, black cap and black bib, was watching him. He recognized it as one of the birds he saw in the forest on his escape north from the Novan war camp.

The bird looked at Caninus and bobbed its head up and down. "Tsik-a-dee-dee-dee," it piped, and flew off.

"A good sign, that," Caninus grinned. He glanced skyward again, and then looked at his opponent.

Black Wolf was standing, watching him. Caninus walked towards the man. On an impulse, he extended a hand. Black Wolf had some knowledge of Roman ways; he took the hand, shook once, and let go. Then he walked a few paces away, turned and stood, waiting. Caninus adjusted his scutum on his left arm, drew his gladius and waited.

Four Bears held up one hand, palm facing forward. He waited thus until he had both men's attention, then snapped his hand down with a sudden movement. Caninus took that as the sign to begin.

He was quickly proven correct. Black Wolf leaped forward with a distinctly lupine howl, swinging his club. Caninus took the blow on his scutum and spun, stabbing at Black Wolf's momentarily exposed side with his gladius. He missed as Black Wolf whirled away with the grace of a dancer.

"Light on your feet, aren't you," Caninus muttered.

Black Wolf smiled as though he understood Latin—and well he might, Caninus reminded himself. The two men began circling, slowly, looking for an opening. *He's fast,* Caninus reminded himself, *but faster than I only because he wears no armor and bears no steel. I only need to hit him once, make him bleed and he'll slow down. Have to watch that knife of his, though, looks made to cut tendons.*

As through to verify this, Black Wolf dove suddenly at the

centurions' legs, his left arm flickering out with the black knife, seeking Caninus' hamstrings. Caninus slammed the bronze-covered edge of his scutum downward, striking the man's arm a glancing blow. Black Wolf rolled away and leaped to his feet, but he left the knife behind. Titus Caninus kicked it away into the brush at the edge of the small clearing and smiled.

"Pulled one of your fangs, there, wolf," he said companionably.

"I have another," the Novan replied in halting Latin.

"So, you do speak some of the Roman tongue," Caninus chuckled. He stepped, stepped, and then suddenly lashed out to the left, aiming his gladius at the Novan's arm. Black Wolf dodged, spun, and landed a solid blow on the Roman scutum. Caninus struck at the Novan's leg and missed.

Black Wolf started circling again. Caninus watched him from behind his scutum; the savage's eyes kept flickering back to the honed edge of the Roman's gladius. *They don't know how to make steel,* Caninus remembered. *The edge of the sword makes him nervous.*

Black Wolf attacked again, screeching his rage as he landed three fast club blows on Caninus' scutum. He grabbed the edge of the shield to try to wrench it away but was forced to retreat as the gladius flickered forward, directly at his face.

The Roman centurion knew his opponent was strong and fast, but his fighting style was undisciplined, untrained. He relied on speed and intimidation. *A brawler,* the Roman thought, *and considered a great warrior by his tribe, but Roman discipline beat Carthage, the Gauls, and many a tribe stronger than his. The renegades did not yet have time to teach these savages that discipline.*

Act, react. Caninus decided to put the Novan tribesman on the defensive.

He stepped forward, left foot leading, right following, always keeping his scutum up, the edge of the gladius visible on the right, ready to stab forward. Black Wolf kept up the circling, but Titus Caninus moved with him, always advancing behind his red-painted shield of hardwood and bronze, hemming the Novan in. He watched the savage's eyes, his hands, his feet; the man was beginning to grow uncertain.

"Hyyahh!" Caninus feinted forward, driving the bronze boss of his scutum at Black Wolf's face. The Novan leaped backwards and almost tripped as he landed in the low brush and the edge of the clearing. Caninus followed quickly, stabbing with the gladius and catching Black Wolf's left arm a glancing blow with the shaving-sharp edge.

"First blood to me, then," he growled. Behind him he could hear the Novan girl softly translating. Black Wolf grimaced, risked a glance at the blood dripping down his arm.

Black Wolf tried to circle away, but he was caught in a small cul-de-sac in the brush, held in by the Roman shield and the glittering edge of Roman steel. Caninus took one more step forward, flashed the gladius quickly to the side and, as Black Wolf dodged to his right, away from the shining edge, slammed the bronze boss of his scutum into the Novan's face, stunning him.

Black Wolf fell to one knee. Titus Caninus kicked him to the ground, dropped his scutum and held the point of the gladius to the Novan's throat.

"Yield," he said.

Adsila was confused for a moment. She looked at Gnaeus

Pompey, then at Four Bears, before translating the Latin word as "stop."

On the ground, dazed, Black Wolf nodded.

Titus Caninus, Centurion of the First Nova Roman Legion, stood up and slid his gladius into its scabbard. "You are brave, strong and fast," he told the Novan. "With some training, you could be a fine soldier. I give you your life and a place in my century, if you'd have it." He held out a hand.

Black Wolf looked at the pale Roman hand cautiously. He listened as Adsila translated the Roman's language into the words of the People. At the edge of the clearing, he saw Four Bears' eyes open wide in surprise.

He considered briefly. Black Wolf knew he was one of the finest warriors of the People. Fellow Red Blanket society members held him in high esteem, especially after his participation in the campaigns against Rome. His name was feared among neighboring tribes when war parties went into the summer forests; young men of his village sought to test their strength against him in mock combat and invariably failed. Even the Alligator People held him in respect. He knew he was expected one day to be a considerable war chief. But this tall, pale man with his shield the color of blood and flashing silver blade had defeated him as though he were no more than a boy, then offered him mercy and a place among his own... How could he refuse?

He nodded, then reached up and took the Roman's hand. Titus Caninus hauled the Novan to his feet, and then slapped him on the back. "It was a good fight, neh? A dog and a wolf?"

Adsila translated, adding an explanation of the meaning of the Roman's name. Black Wolf chuckled. He spoke in his own tongue, and Titus Caninus listened as the Novan girl converted his words to Latin: "You have shown the wolf to be a pup among your kind this morning. But dogs of the village sometimes run with wolves of the forest. It will be a good thing, for us to learn each other's ways."

Caninus nodded. "Come along, then," he said. "Let's get that arm looked at. Can't have my newest legionary getting a poison of the blood from an untended wound."

White Oak looked at his cousin. "So, it is decided," he said. "We will be as one people with Rome now. Who is to say whether it will be a good thing or not? Only time will tell. But cousin, I think you are right. Rome has come among us, and we are forever changed. Perhaps this way is best. Perhaps it is best we change all at once, in our time, and not over a span of generation, with fighting and ill feeling."

"Time, indeed," Four Bears agreed. He looked over at old Owl, who was plainly pleased with the outcome. "And the one of us who has seen the most time of all, I think he saw this before any of the rest of us."

"And I will see much more yet, I think," Owl said proudly. "Do not make the mistake of thinking I am ready to die yet!"

Four Bears was preparing to leave with the rest of the Novan party when the Roman consuls approached him. The senior Consul held up a hand in greeting. "Salve, Four Bears," Marcus Porcius Cato said, pronouncing his name in accented but intelligible words of the People. Four Bears looked at Cato, this man he respected; he did not want him as an enemy. He had hoped for some months now to have Cato as a friend. Perhaps, now...

The chief of the People held up a hand and answered in kind. "Salve, Cato." He was learning Latin more quickly now and suspected that henceforth he would be learning the Roman tongue more quickly still.

Cato motioned for the girl Adsila to join them. He wanted to make sure there would be no misunderstanding, not today. "Four Bears, he said, "as you have seen, we Romans are governed by a body of wise men chosen from among us. There are, or I should say there will be, two groups that work in concert, but it is the senior of the two assemblies which I wish to speak to you of. We call this group the Senate."

Four Bears listened gravely to the translation, even though by now he understood the Latin well enough. He nodded. He remembered all too keenly the Senate building in the Roman town—an entire building of stone and wood, dedicated to their council! It made good sense, if the people chose men of proven wisdom and good judgment, and didn't sound all that different from the chief's councils of his own people. Based on what he had seen of Cato and the other, Marcus Tullius Cicero, he had to admit the Romans seemed to choose well.

"Now that the contest is decided, we will be one people, as we agreed beforehand," Cicero said. He waited for the girl to translate and continued. "The Novan people of the B'Kou and A'Tep will be Roman citizens and will be represented in the government. The Senate is chosen from among the best, most intelligent, most noble men among the people. We have considered the Novans we have known among you, and Cato and I agree the choice is an obvious one. We would like you, Four Bears, to represent your people in the Senate."

"You will be the first Novan Senator," Cato said, "if you accept."

Four Bears nodded gravely. He and his tribe were essentially conquered people despite the pleasant, face-saving fiction allowed them by the agreement. Yet the Romans offered him a place in their council. The way was clear; his responsibility to the People only allowed one course. He looked at old Owl, who motioned towards the Romans with his eyes, his body language obvious: *Accept, you fool!*

There really was no choice. "I will join you," Four Bears agreed. "If the other Senators will agree to have me."

"Oh, I wouldn't worry about that," Cicero chuckled, abandoning the deep ceremoniousness of the moment now that the offer was tendered and accepted. "We have already discussed this with the full Senate."

"All nine of us," Cato said, smiling.

"The Senate's decision was unanimous. And so, you see, the offer comes from all of the Senate of Rome, Four Bears. It will be as Cato said. You are the first. You will not be the last."

Cato extended his hand. Four Bears was familiar with all the meanings of the Roman gesture now; it was not only a form of greeting but was also used when a bargain was struck. He took Cato's hand and shook it once, up and down, and nodded. "It will be a good thing," he said, "for Romans and for the People."

"For Nova Roma," Cicero agreed. "For the Republic."

Cicero shook Four Bear's hand next. His eyes were twinkling as he looked pointedly at Four Bears' leather vest, clout and leggings. "We'll have to get you a proper Senator's robe," he said.

Four Bears' eyes went wide. "Robe?"

The Forum—ten days later

"Friend and fellow Romans," Consul Marcus Porcius Cato called to the crowd gathered in the Forum. He was greeted with a roar of applause, along with yips and howls from the city's Novan-born inhabitants and guests for the day.

Cato stood at the head of the ten members of the Senate, who stood in a row behind him on the Senate steps. All wore their traditional robes of white and red save General Pompey, who for today wore his uniform, complete with his father's black-plumed helmet and, oddly, a plain, oak-handled issue gladius belted at his side. Behind him stood First Spear Centurion Canis Magnus, similarly uniformed, but wearing his red-brush centurion's helmet and again, oddly, a fancy ivory-handled sword on his hip. Beside him stood his once and former opponent in the duel, Black Wolf, who now wore the uniform and accoutrements of a Roman legionary.

Cato had observed the two soldier's swords earlier and was sure there was a good story behind it, but for now, that would have to wait.

At the end of the row stood Nova Roma's newest Senator, the B'Kou chief Four Bears. He looked hot and distinctly uncomfortable in his new white and red Senator's robe, an extra that Cassius Longinus had found among his baggage.

Cato examined the crowd of people gathered in the Forum. He saw Roman faces, and in and among them, Novan faces. One people now, he thought. What a long, long way we have come from old Rome. It is as though many of the old ways have fallen away from us like leaves in the autumn. But we have kept the best and discarded the worst. The proof of that stands here on the Senate steps behind me. He stole a glance out of the corner of his eye to where Four Bears stood, fidgeting uncomfortably in the heavy linen toga.

The Consul continued. His task this morning was simple; to

present the one man in Nova Roma best equipped by experience, inclination and talent to deliver this morning's oration. "Men of Rome," he called out, "Citizens, countrymen. Please lend your ears to the Lesser Consul of Nova Roma, Marcus Tullius Cicero."

Cicero came forward. Cato bowed to him formally, a gesture Cicero returned before stepping to the low stone set in place for public orations.

"Men and women of Pompeius! Citizens of Nova Roma!"

Another round of applause, cheers and howls greeted Cicero. Grinning broadly, he held up his hands until the crowd settled down.

"Ten days ago, a bargain fairly struck was seen through. Ten days ago, the most elite of warriors of the B'Kou and A'Tep nations met the finest soldier of the Nova Roman army in a contest of champions, a contest of honor, which decided the fates of both nations. That fate was..." He held up his hands and paused theatrically, "...unification!"

He waited for another round of applause and cheering to die down. "As evidence of that unification, I offer you three extraordinary men. First, I present to you the first Novan-born Senator, Four Bears of the B'Kou!"

As Cato and Cicero had coached him, Four Bears stepped forward and bowed. Then he stood very straight, and held up his right hand, palm forward, in the traditional greeting of the People.

"And second, I present to you the very men who competed on the field of honor. Both men fought in the recent unpleasantness on opposite sides, but now they stand together in Nova Roma's First Legion. Those men are First Spear Centurion Canis Magnus and Legionary Black Wolf."

The two soldiers stepped forward. Both men stood at

attention and saluted the crowd. Black Wolf wore his uniform with obvious pride, but in one respect he did not conform with the Roman ideal; long black braids still hung down from under his bronze legionary's helmet. Both men pivoted with a soldier's precision and saluted General Pompey, who gravely returned the military honor.

"Try not to trip, now," Canis Magnus said to his new subordinate *sotto voce.*

"Me? I move like the deer runs in the forest," Black Wolf whispered back in halting Latin. The two men marched back to their place without incident.

Cicero continued: "O people of Pompeius, people of Rome, I look out on you today and I see a people united. I see the people of old Rome there in among you, men and women who made a horrible journey, braving Neptune's wrath running before a storm sent by the immortal gods themselves to bring them to this place, even as I myself and the rest of the Senate—save one—was brought here."

"I see men and women of Nova Terra here today, many here in the city for the first time. I say to you, it will not be your last time, nor will it be the last time for those of us from old Rome to venture among you. Already trading missions are forming, planning travel to the Tsalee in the west, and the Tahona, the people that live to the north. Old Rome was built on trade, and here, the new Rome will be so made as well."

"When you travel abroad, all of you, every one, you will travel with peace of mind, knowing that Roman arms protect your safety. Men like Canis Magnus, Black Wolf and their leader, General Pompey, will be watching, ever vigilant, ever strong, to keep the roads of Nova Roma safe for travel, safe for commerce."

"It is a bright new era we move forward into, together, as citizens of Nova Roma. A nation of law, where no man is above the law, no man can fail to find justice under the law, where everyone is treated as they deserve; that, O Romans, is the legacy we bring to you from old Rome. In old Rome the old order was being usurped; an ambitious man with an army at his back sought to make himself king. That army answered to him and him alone, and you have seen the results of that misplaced loyalty. The Nova Roman army answers to the Senate, to the Consuls of Rome; the reins of power are ultimately with you! The people of Rome, the free people without whose consent the existence of government is not possible. That is the path forward for all of us, from old world or new alike, regardless of birth. That is our future, because, my friends, here and now, all of us together in this place, we are Rome."

The cheering threatened to shake down the very stones of the Senate building, but the morning's events were not finished yet, for now Cicero stood aside and bowing, yielded the podium to Nova Roma's newest Senator.

"I am not a man to speak at such length as my friend Cicero," he said. "But what he has said is true. Wise men can lead a people into a safe and happy future. Wise and prudent men can govern and lead us to a future in which we will be happy to raise our children." His eye caught Pompey's wife, heavily pregnant, standing to the side of the Forum near the Senate steps, guarded by two Roman soldiers lest she be jostled by the enthusiastic crowd.

"Since the time of my grandfather's grandfather, my tribe, the B'Kou, was allied with the A'Tep of the hills to the west. That alliance lasted so long and proved so fruitful that we have come to think of the A'Tep as our cousins, and in many cases that came to be true as well, as young men of each tribe married young women of the other. In time we would surely have become one people, and that would have been a good thing for both."

"Instead, now, for reasons only the gods can understand, the people of Rome came among us. We did not understand them at first, and many of us followed the angry words of Man-Ready-For-War and fought them. That is over now. The Alligator People are defeated for the first time in memory, and Man-Ready-For-War has fled to some unknown place. That evil time is past! It is time for us to learn new ways. It is time for us to be as one with Rome, and for the people of Rome to be as one with us."

Marcus Porcius Cato strode forward and linked arms with both Cicero and Four Bears. "So shall it be," he announced. His voice was loud, strong and sure. "People of Nova Roma! The new era my good friends Cicero and Four Bears speak of starts today."

"It is as the Consul has said," Four Bears agreed. "And so, let us begin."

EPILOGUE

SUMUS ROMA

Pompeius–autumn

Evening, and the town of Pompeius was, finally, at peace. The damage to the city walls was mostly repaired; the small amount of fire damage was put to rights. In the fields outside the walls, crops were growing ripe. The city bustled with activity; as Four Bears had predicted, some Novans were coming to live in the town now that they were officially one with Rome, and even now a few Roman men had gone out to the local villages to live. Four Bears' village had even taken the Roman name of Ursinleus, in their chief's honor. Romans had taken to calling the man himself Ursus Quadrus Tranquilus, for his part in ending the war.

Pompeius had gained one resident of note almost immediately. Within three days of the conclusion of the duel in the clearing, old Owl had packed up his worldly goods, marched alone from his village to Pompeius, and sat himself down on the Senate steps. "In times like these, men must learn new ways," he announced, repeating a theme that was fast becoming a slogan of Novan and Roman alike. "If I am now to be a Roman, then I will live here, in the Roman town. I will wear Roman clothes and eat Roman food."

A small house was provided for him, and he was now a common sight in the Forum, his white hair cut short in the Roman style, his skinny body wrapped in a dark red toga gifted to him by Gnaeus Pompey. He was learning Latin at an incredible clip, mostly by haggling with the various merchants who were beginning to operate in the Forum. Pompey, out of honest affection and respect for the ancient Novan, personally saw to it that the old man wanted for nothing. "It's odd, but he reminds me of my father," he told anyone who asked.

As the air grew cool one particularly lovely evening, Consul Marcus Porcius Cato and Lesser Consul Marcus Tullius Cicero mounted the city wall to watch the sun set over the fields to the west with no small amount of satisfaction.

"Two years next spring, since we came here," Cicero mused. "It feels like it has been longer, somehow."

"It does. But life is settling down." Cato looked out to the grain fields. "Our young General has a new son. The first Roman child in our new world, but I'm sure young Primus Tiberius Pompeius won't be the last. And our crops are doing well. Another year, perhaps two, before we can spare any wheat for bread, but there is plenty of maize to go around. Maize flour doesn't make a bad biscuit, once you get used to it, and if you have some of the syrup the Tahona boil down from tree sap, they are quite good."

"Another item we'll want to arrange more trade for," Cicero agreed. "We already have a few more merchants wanting to go out to open trade routes."

"Actually," Cato reminded him, "that's a chore for the next Consulate. My term as Consul is finished next summer. You will have two more years as Consul, and then those tasks will fall to someone else."

"Plenty of time to strike a trade deal," Cicero said.

"Perhaps."

"It looks like Cassius has the favor of most of the Senate to replace me as Lesser Consul. If anyone will be interested in negotiating trade for something good to eat, it will be he. Brutus is interested in it as well; you know how he can be, if he smells even a single brass obol in a deal, he's in favor of it."

Cato chuckled. "Best I leave that with Cassius and Brutus, then." He looked sideways at Cicero. "And you, old friend? Will you retire after your term as Consul, or return to the Senate?" The Senate was already expanding; the hill-country home of the A'Tep was organizing as the Roman province of Ateppia under the proconsulship of White Oak, who would be sending a Senator to represent his people. In the spring, that Senator would be followed by the first provincial representative to the Council of Plebs.

"Retire? Me?" Cicero snorted a brief laugh. "I'm a young man yet, Cato. Not as young as yourself, granted, but young enough. No term limits in the Senate, you know. I have a good long time yet to help get our new Rome on her feet."

The two stood silently for a while, watching as the sun sank towards the western hills. Birds sang in the meadow, and as the sky grew dim the Consuls saw a small herd of the big deer the natives called wapiti come into the open to feed.

Just as the shadows were about to cover the town, a shout came up from the sentry, one that sent a chill down Cato's back. "Natives coming in!"

Cato and Cicero ran to the southern side of the wall by the gate, to where a sentry was pointing. A large body of people was approaching the town from the river, but they were obviously not warriors.

"Sons of Dis," Cicero breathed. "They're all women and children."

There were perhaps a thousand women, many with babies in arms or toddlers in tow. There seemed to be no boys above older than ten or twelve, and no men at all. All were carrying something, a basket or bundle. Some dragged rude travois loaded with their goods.

They were, manifestly, refugees.

"Soldier," Cato told the sentry. "Run, quick as you can, fetch General Pompey and his sister. I expect you'll find them at their villa with their mother. Hurry!" The sentry leaped down from the stockade wall and pounded off.

Pompey the Younger arrived with his sister and stepmother just as the crowd of women and children arrived at the gate. By now Cato could see that the women's faces were white with ashes, and many of their garments were torn. As a group, they fell to their knees in front of the gates and set up a frightful wail of anguish.

Cato and Cicero joined the young General, Adsila and Cornelia at the gate. Pompey the Younger spoke to the soldiers manning the gate. "Open it," he said, "just enough to let Adsila and me out. No more. Close it behind us and don't open it unless I order you to, no matter what happens."

"Yes, sir," the soldier agreed, and cracked the gate just enough for the young general and his adopted sister to squeeze through.

Cato and Cicero sprang back to the wall to watch. Cornelia climbed after them, in a more dignified fashion but still wasting no time.

"They have sent one old woman forward to talk to Pompey, see?" Cicero pointed out as Cornelia looked over the wall.

The conversation went on for only a few minutes, through the intermediary of young Adsila Pompeia Atella. Then the gate opened to admit a grinning General Pompey and his sister, who wore a look of sternly repressed amusement.

"Well?" Cato demanded once they had climbed down from the wall.

"It seems that the Alligator People, the very ones who started the war against us and incited the other tribes to join them, had never before been defeated in battle. Not in all the history of their tribe." The general of the Roman army was grinning like a large ape.

"And so?" Cicero barked. "Get to the point, young man!"

Pompey the Younger waved at the open gate to the crowd of women. "It seems their own sense of honor would not allow them to stand the loss. To a man, the warriors of the Alligator People—that is to say, every male over ten summers in the tribe—opened their throats in penance to whatever gods they appease."

"Like the Spartans of old, they—come home with your shields, or on them. They got stuck with the latter, it seems. And this crowd?"

"Their wives and daughters," Pompey said, still grinning. "Out of food, and starving. They seek asylum among us. The woman I spoke with, she says that since we won the war against their tribe, their lives are ours now."

He turned to Cornelia and bowed. "Forgive me, stepmother, and you also, sister, but I must be a bit rude for a moment." He turned back to the Consul and Lesser Consul. "Sirs, I believe our problem concerning a lack of women is nearly solved."

"They will not be slaves," Cicero demanded. "Our new laws prohibit it."

"So I told them," Pompey agreed easily, "and they were familiar enough with the concept, since slavery is exactly what they came here expecting. No need for it in any case even though, as I made plain to them, they will still be expected to work if they want to eat, like any other Roman here. I'm sure they all have skills for surviving in this land, and really, they aren't a bad-looking bunch. Do you think they will have any trouble finding places for themselves in our town, which, I remind you, is peopled almost completely with horny young soldiers?"

Cato and Cicero exchanged an embarrassed look. The young General put it crudely, but he had the truth of it. "So, the lands of the Alligator People stand empty," Cicero said. "That, I admit, solves more than one problem."

"That had occurred to me as well," Pompey the Younger admitted. "I'm not sure of what use those swamps will be, but I suppose we'll be finding out. And out there are the very people to tell us."

"Well," Cato said at last. "What are we waiting for? Let them in!"

"Not just yet," Pompey held up a hand. "While I'm sure our men will be very anxious, and while I'm afraid the order will make me very unpopular for the next few days, I intend to order that they be camped outside the walls until they are inspected for weapons, disease, and until we can at least speak a few words to each of them. We have no idea what treachery they may be plotting. But, if there is none, and from the looks of them, I'd say there likely is not..."

"Children," Cato breathed. "There will be Roman children to inherit what we've built."

"Quite so, Consul," Pompey agreed. "Quite so."

On the southern coast

Man-Ready-For-War knew the failure of the Alligator People was not his fault.

His plan would have worked if the soldiers had not fled. When he saw the black-painted soldiers collapse before the Roman lines and flee into the river, he knew that the Alligator People were no longer worthy of a war chief that bore an ancient and honored name.

He thought he knew now, finally, where there may be people that were worthy.

When he was younger, he had accompanied some of the older men of his tribe on trade missions to the Tsalee towns along the great river to the west. The Tsalee were farmers and traders, not soldiers, but they told the young Black Snake—his name before assuming the mantle of Man-Ready-For-War—of the great cities of the Maya, far to the south. The Maya were countless, he was told, living in great cities in deep, wet forests on the far side of a great dry country. Man-Ready-For-War remembered the tales; most of the Mayan lands lay far away, and one had to cross the great river Mesi-Zibi, follow the coast south through the burning lands, stay along the great water where the land bore east, then north into the deep forest. There he would find the Mayan cities. The Mayans would not be happy to learn of the Romans incursion into the lands to their north, and with their numbers, not even the steel and discipline of Rome could stand against them.

Man-Ready-For-War had spent the last three moon cycles moving among the Tsalee, going from town to town and trying to incite them as he had the B'Kou and A'Tep. He was not successful.

The Tsalee seemed more interested in trading with the men of Rome than in warring with them, and finally the Alligator People's last war chief left the Tsalee lands, heading south. If the Tsalee would not go to war with the Romans, perhaps the Maya would.

The Maya were far, far to the south, in a strange land. Man-Ready-For-War was not worried. If Tsalee traders could make the trip, so could he. He still had his strength. His arm was healing. Most of all, he still had his craft, his cunning.

He reached the Mesi-Zibi ten days after leaving the last of the Tsalee towns he visited. He lashed what few goods he carried to a dead log of driftwood and crossed in good order, reaching the far bank a good ways downstream due to the current, muddy and exhausted. His anger drove him on into the swamps on the western side. The country was boggy and difficult, even for a warrior born and bred in the swamps of the eastern coast low country, but anger drove Man-Ready-For-War on: Anger at Rome, anger at his own people, anger at his faithless Roman allies, anger at his cowardly B'Kou and A'Tep neighbors. He moved through increasingly hostile country, making his meals on snakes, fish, bird eggs and other small fare he was able to easily pick up as he went. When he came to creeks and streams, he crossed them. When he came to swamps, he waded through. He had met no people in several days, but after a time some of his warriors' reason returned, and he stopped to spend a day fashioning a new war club from the lower trunk and root ball of a small tree. Spikes of bone completed the deadly device, fixed in place by a rude glue of the boiled skin and hooves of a small deer found dead in the brush.

When this was done, Man-Ready-For-War felt once more able to fulfill his name and purpose, so he moved on.

Two days later, still angry, he found himself facing another, smaller river. The banks were muddy but reasonably solid. The day was hot, the air stifling. Without a look at the water, Man-Ready-For-War waded in, and then struck off for the far bank, swimming powerfully.

He didn't notice the eyes protruding from the water, the cold, black eyes that followed his movements before submerging in a swirl of brown water.

Man-Ready-For-War almost made the far bank.

The old bull alligator was six paces long and weighed as much as eight men. The reptile was almost seventy years old, a massive, armored apex predator that saw any movement as potential prey, even if that movement was a great war chief that made the mistake of entering an unfamiliar stream carelessly.

Man-Ready-For-War felt the movement in the water too late. He gasped as the huge jaws closed around his legs and the weight of the reptile dragged him under. He fumbled for his war club but lost it in the dark water. He managed to seize his obsidian knife from his belt and stabbed futilely at the alligator's armored head before the beast grabbed again, crushing Man-Ready-For-War's legs and hip. The beast pulled Man-Ready-For-War down deeper into the muddy water and, holding the Novan war chief in the iron grip of his massive jaws, began to spin.

Far to the northwest

"Another lake to detour around. I swear," Titus Pullo complained, "there must be ten thousand lakes in this misbegotten land."

"The Tsalee chief in that last little village did say that the lake we were looking for was much larger than any other in this country, did he not?" Lucius Vorenus was a sight now. Mounted on his large gray mare, wrapped in the skin of a black bear, with a month's worth of beard obscuring his face, the big man looked more like a Gaul or a wild Briton than a Roman centurion. Pullo looked no better; his helmet was long lost somewhere on the journey since the battle at Pompeius, and so he wore the skin of a wolf over his head, and more skins wrapped his legs. His horse was a massive roan stallion of mostly Germanic stock, which seemed to be thriving in the new environs.

"He did. Mother of Waters, they call it." Pullo pulled his tattered red cloak tighter about himself and looked around at the heavily forested, flat, wet, cold country. "Their great town is to the north of the Mother of Waters, straight from where it forms a point aimed at the setting sun, he said. Poetic lot, these Tsalee."

Eight men remained now. All nine Roman soldiers had survived the battle, but one had died on the journey across the mountains—a fall from his horse, of all the ways for a cavalryman to perish. At least the group's nine horses were strong and fit. Once crossing the mountains and making contact with the expansive Tsalee League, Pullo, Vorenus and their men had traveled through lush country with plenty of grazing for the horses and ample game for the men. This country here, though, so far to the north...

As the Roman renegades had traveled north, they passed progressively from steppes of tall grass to low hills covered with hardwoods, and then into flatter country with vast forests of pine and spruce. As they moved farther north, lakes and rivers grew ever more frequent. As the autumn progressed, the only consolation to be found in the freezing nights was that the plague of biting insects finally ended.

"There is still plenty of grass for the horses," Pullo had said a hundred times or more, "but I fear what winter will bring."

"We can only see what we will see. Only nine horses, we can always store hay for them." The nine horses were soon to be ten. Pullo rode the sole stallion in the group, and the one mare unencumbered with a rider was obviously with foal. Several more were suspected to be as well; the stallion had been busy, earning it some degree of envy among the Roman men.

At least the Tsalee had proved a friendly folk. Once Pullo had learned enough of their language to get the idea across that they had to go a long ways to escape a determined enemy, the Tsalee had directed them west to the great river called Mesi-Zibi. An amazing river it was, one like no other. It didn't even flow like a normal river, but rather to move as a mass, almost like a huge, brown, moving lake of water.

The Romans were told to follow that river north to its source, then strike northeast to find the huge inland sea the Tsalee described. "North of the western point of the Mother of Waters," they were told, "there is a great town of our people. Tens of tens of hands of Tsalee live there. It is good country. Many fish, many deer. You will be safe there. They will welcome you and your great beasts. The Tsalee can always find a place for strong men."

A light snow was falling the morning the Roman party finally discovered the Mother of Waters and found it another impossible sight of many in the new land. The Mother was not a lake like they had been seeing, but an inland sea—of fresh water!

They followed the shoreline west until reaching the end, then proceeded as they had been told, three day's walk due north, moving out of the flat land around the inland sea into low, rolling hills.

They reached the great town in the early afternoon, as the snow was thickening. Pullo shook snow off the wolf's fur over his head and brushed snowflakes out of his beard. "There we are," he announced. "That has to be it."

On his horse beside him, Vorenus grunted in agreement.

The town was expansive indeed. Perched on a small hill with a commanding view of the flat country around, the town consisted mostly of a disorganized cluster of sturdy wooden huts stood around a large, central structure of some sort. A waist-high palisade of thick pine trunks surrounded the town. Smoke rose from the huts.

The centurions turned at the sound of a horse approaching at a trot. One of their soldiers was approaching, a broad grin on his dirty, bearded face.

"Happy to be here at last, are you, Octavius?" Pullo asked the man.

"Oh yes sir— but it's not just that. Remember I told you my father worked iron, sir?"

"That's right. He ran the smithy in the lower part of the Aventine, is that it?"

"Yes sir. That's what I wanted to tell you. I stopped to look at that rock outcrop we passed a while back— do you remember, sir, that shelf of dark rock with the gray streaks running through?"

"Yes, yes," Pullo said in some irritation.

"Iron, sir. There's iron here. And I'm sure there's more than just in that spot. If there's iron, I can make tools and weapons."

"Can you teach the rest of us to work iron?"

"Of course, sir!"

"Well," Vorenus said, "that is good news. With a skill to trade and even to teach, we'll be well set up."

"A good start, then," Pullo observed. He hunched forward in

the saddle, staring at the Novan town. "Pompey's lot, they have their new Rome in the south. I suppose this will be ours."

"No," Vorenus said. "Two Romes in one land? No, that won't do. Remember, old Romulus had a brother. This town, here at the end of our journey, will be the start of a people named not for Romulus, but for Remus. It will be a counterpart—maybe a counterweight—to those in the south."

Pullo stared at Vorenus. In the years they had campaigned together, he'd never known Lucius Vorenus to be one for philosophizing. Lucius Vorenus was a stolid man, humorless, mostly silent, and considered a bit slow by some who did not know him well. Pullo, who knew Vorenus better than anyone, knew him to be a hardened, canny warrior who kept his own counsel, but a simple man rather than a deep one. Still... "I like the idea," he agreed. "Remus it is, then. Mind you, though— Remus was killed by his brother."

"Things change," Vorenus muttered. "If we have learned nothing this past year, we've learned that."

A shout from the town drew their attention. Several young men and a handful of children were running towards them. None bore weapons, and their faces revealed only curiosity, not aggression.

"Our hosts," Pullo pointed at them. "Let's go see how well we will be received. If we can make them tools and weapons of iron, I think we will do very well here indeed." He turned to the tiny column of Roman cavalry behind him. "We're home, boys! Dismount!"

Twenty years later–Pompeius

A brilliant autumn sun shone down on the white marble city of Pompeius, which bustled with activity.

The Forum lay in the center of the city, on the tallest of four low hills overlooking the banks of the Tiber, and it was in the Forum that most of the business of the city took place. Tradesman of every sort shouted the virtues of their wares. A cart drawn by two huge, shaggy bison imported from the west hauled a load of white marble from the south to some new building site. To the west, granite was being hauled to the construction of three great aqueducts that even now reached into the mountains to bring fresh water to the growing city. Trade was brisk: iron from the north, marble from the south, a curious black stone that burned from the west, crops, fish and beasts from every corner of the growing Republic. Pompeius hammered, shouted and rattled with activity.

Marcus Porcius Cato made his way slowly across the Forum to where the white marble of the newly rebuilt Senate building rose above the shops and public buildings in the center of the city. The Senate was not to officially convene for another day, so Cato was not wearing his white and red Senate robes. Instead he wore his usual simple wrap of undyed cotton cloth, and despite his growing wealth, still walked slowly on bare feet.

Around him the city bustled. Nova Roman citizens mixed with a few tribesmen from across the western mountains, come to the city to trade. Many of them greeted Cato by name; he was well known as one of Nova Roma's founders and revered as a senior statesman.

One thing Cato noticed, as always, was the change in colors from those he remembered from the Rome of his youth. White was still often seen in the people's clothing, but purples and blues were almost unknown; cloth-makers had as yet found no good substitute for indigo in dying cloth. Plenty of white, Cato chuckled silently to himself, because you can always get piss. You still saw robes cut in the Roman fashion, mostly in browns and yellows, but you saw many Novans still wearing their traditional clouts and leggings, while the Novan women tended to cling to their ankle-length dresses, mostly of woven cloth now rather than deerskin. A cluster of inns had sprouted on the edge of the forum closest to the river; the most prominent of these was the Black Dog, operated by Servia Valeris Merula, retired centurion Canis Magnus and their ever-expanding brood of children. There was still no wine, but the local innkeepers were brewing beer from barley and wheat. While the drink had been reviled in old Rome as a brew for barbarians, it was beginning to gain a strong following here. Old Canis Magnus himself had in recent years put on a notable addition in girth due to his fondness for the stuff.

Cato climbed the steps of the Senate even more slowly. His age was telling; a nagging pain in his knees made the steps a trial. But he bore the pain as he dealt with the rest of his life, stoically.

The two men he was on his way to meet were already seated in the Senate chamber, talking quietly. They stood up as Cato approached.

"Salve, Cato," Marcus Tullius Cicero greeted him. Like Cato, Cicero was older now; his once-dark hair was almost completely gray. The younger, thinner man had disappeared into a larger, heavier one; still, Cicero was prospering, even as the new Republic prospered. Cato took Cicero's hand and shook it before turning to the other man.

"Salve, Cato, my old friend," Four Bears said in flawless Latin.

"Salve, Consul," Cato said as he gripped Four Bear's offered hand. He smiled at his friend; Four Bears' election to Lesser Consul two years earlier had been very nearly unanimous, and a month earlier he had ascended to Consul in his turn. *The first born Novan to serve as Consul of Nova Roma!* Cato thought. *Imagine that.*

Four Bears still wore his hair long, but his braids were now iron-gray instead of black. He wore simple Roman-style robes in a deep red, red being the traditional color of good luck and protection among the tribe he was born into.

"Your nephew—he received the funds he needed to start his trading company?" Cato asked.

"He did," Four Bears nodded. "Old Brutus, he is a usurer and a bit of a rogue—during the negotiations he looked at me as though he was wondering where to slip in the knife. But he offered the boy a good rate, and the loan went through with no trouble."

"Good." Cato seated himself slowly, for the thousandth time wondering why they had equipped the Senate chamber with the traditional white stone benches instead of some more comfortable seating. Still, they were there to work, not to relax. "And you, Cicero, I hear tell you are writing again?"

"I am," Cicero smiled. "A work inspired by the events of past years; Treatises on Friendship and Old Age."

"I look forward to reading it," Cato said. He turned to Four Bears. "Consul, you asked us both here to ask us something, I believe."

"I asked the two of you here this morning to ask your advice," Four Bears said.

"Advice?" Cicero asked.

"I have received an emissary from the Tsalee League, on the

other side of the mountains. You know we have formal trading agreements with them. They wish to move beyond trading."

"Move beyond? In what way?"

Four Bears looked at Cicero. "They wish to join us. At least, most of them do; a couple of their groups in the far north are opting out."

"The northern groups that have somehow learned to work iron and are building ships for trade across the great inland seas in that region," Cicero scowled. "The Remans, from the land of the Five Seas. Pullo and Vorenus having their say, no doubt." Word had long since reached Roman ears of the sudden rise in ironworking in that northern region, centered on a rapidly growing city with the Latin name of Terminus.

"No doubt," Cato agreed. "But as long as they confine themselves to the north country, I'm content to leave them alone. They have taken no hostile action against any of our trade emissaries or any villages of ours bordering their lands."

"Exactly so," Four Bears said. He went on: "The Tsalee emissary said, and I quote, 'Any fool can see the gods are with Nova Roma. You move the very stones of the earth to suit you. Our councils have met, and we wish to join you as Nova Roman citizens. We wish to have the paved roads of Rome reach to our lands and to stand beside you as fellow Romans.' They have seen the wisdom of our ways, and who can blame them?" Four Bears laughed. "I can tell you, my friends, I know how they feel."

"This will more than double our territory," Cato mused. "And give us a border on the edge of the great river the tribes call the Mesi-Zibi. It will make trade routes to the Mayan cities in the south that much easier as well." The Mayans were not overly friendly, but they wanted Roman steel and had plenty of gold to pay for it, ensuring a brisk trade. Ships from the growing harbor town of Pulcia made their way to the Mayan territories regularly.

"What are your thoughts, Consul?" Cicero asked.

"Jupiter's balls, how can we refuse?" Four Bears burst out. Cato smiled; the man even swore like a Roman. Cato knew Four Bears was a regular visitor to the temple of Jupiter. Like most of his people, he had long since converted to the Roman religion.

"I'm inclined to agree," Cicero said. "I've heard good reports of the area. The western regions near the great river are supposed to be incredibly rich farmlands. The tribes are already growing traded wheat and barley there as well as maize. You both have very likely eaten bread from the region."

"You will propose the matter to the full Senate then, Consul?" Cato asked.

"I will," Four Bears said.

"I will speak in support," Cato agreed. "Cicero?"

"Of course," Cicero concurred.

"It is good," Cato said, "to see the Republic expand by trade instead of conquest. If only Caesar could see what we have done here!"

"What do you suppose goes on there now, in Rome?" Cicero wondered.

Cato was silent for a moment. Sometimes, even now, after the long span of years, he was overcome with a desperate homesickness. He had long since accepted that he would never again see the seven hills of Rome, never again walk the Appian Way, never walk across the forum to the old Senate hall, never again see the rich fields and vineyards of Italy. But the memory still hurt.

"I suppose," he said at last, "that Rome continues on. With

us gone, with old Pompey gone, I suppose Caesar succeeded in gaining his crown. I fear the Republic may be dead there, in old Rome." He brightened. "But we have preserved it here, my friends, and now it grows."

"It does," Four Bears said. Reaching behind him, he produced a small wooden flask and three fired clay cups. "It is a tradition among my people," he said, "to share a pipe of tobacco when an agreement is made, but in old Rome, I have been told the tradition was to drink to seal a bargain. I know you have not the wine you speak of from your old lands," he said, "but I have here a drink some of the people are brewing from maize. I think you might enjoy it."

He poured the clear liquor into the three cups and handed Cato and Cicero each one, keeping the last for himself. Cato tasted experimentally; the stuff had a bite like fire.

Four Bears smiled and held up his cup. "To the Republic," he said. They all drank.

POSTSCRIPT

There were several items in this book that I had some fun with.

In Chapter Three, Owl, the eldest of the B'Kou, says: "The Alligator People, with them it is always 'fight, fight, war, war!' I say it is better to talk, talk, first, then war, war, only if there is no other choice." He is paraphrasing Winston Churchill, who famously said "I'd rather jaw, jaw, jaw than war, war, war."

Also in Chapter Three, Marcus Junius Brutus expresses his hopes to Cato and Cicero that fate let Pompey Magnus live. He says, "Let the man live as a tyrant if we must, as long as he lives—I tell you, at all cost, Pompey must live." This is, of course, in marked contrast to his tyrant-killing reputation in our timeline. In the epilogue, however, Brutus indirectly and symbolically returns to form, as recounted by Four Bears in recalling a loan negotiation: "Old Brutus, he is a usurer and a bit of a rogue—during the negotiations he looked at me as though he was wondering where to slip in the knife." Marcus Junius Brutus was in fact a moneylender, and it is no stretch to think he would return to that trade when economic conditions in Nova Roma allowed it.

Even more with Brutus: In Chapter Four, after Cicero's 'We are Rome' speech, Cato congratulates him and turns to Brutus, asking "…and you, Brutus?" These, of course, are Julius Caesar's last words (Latin: *Et tu, Brute?*) as he recognizes the man behind the assassin's knife in Shakespeare's *Julius Caesar.*

Chapter Six contains another little Easter egg. In discussing their aid to the Novans, Titus Pullo and Lucius Vorenus are quietly making plans in the event their alliance fails to defeat Pompey's army. In the event of their failure, Pullo only sees one option: "If all else fails, play dead." This is a nod our own timeline's Great White North, specifically to Steve Smith's wonderful Red Green Show. Pullo is unknowingly quoting the Possum Lodge motto, given in rather inaccurate pidgin Latin as *Quando omni flunkus moritati.*

Chapter Eight has the young General Pompey telling the Consuls, "Their warriors are moving to follow our men south. We've got them leaning the wrong way. Our men are holding them by the nose. Next, we'll kick them in the ass." He is paraphrasing a famous saying from our timeline's General George Patton, one of our world's greatest warriors and one of my own personal heroes.

In Chapter Thirteen, after Titus Caninus makes his stand in the gate of Pompeius, Gnaeus Pompey tells him "In war, Centurion, men are nothing. A man—a man is everything." In our timeline, of course, that quote is from another famous general, Napoleon Bonaparte.

And, finally, in the epilogue; on the journey north, Titus Pullo complains bitterly of the number of lakes they have had to detour around. Anyone familiar with the American Upper Midwest will know the area he speaks of, known in our time as the Land of 10,000 Lakes.

A note on style; I chose to open each chapter with an excerpt from Gnaeus Pompey Novus' fictional New World Diaries. Readers may notice he refers to himself in the third person throughout those quotes, as well as noting the rather turgid style in which they are written. This was a standard of writing in these times; read Julius Caesar's *The Gallic Wars* for an even longer and somewhat more tedious example.

As to characters:

Titus Caninus, later Canis Magnus (the Great Dog) was my favorite of all the dramatis personae in this work. His carefree, even joyous spirit contrasts so wonderfully with his other facet, that of the canny, analytical professional warrior; he was a lot of fun to write. And if one of my old Army buddies who bore a similarly canine nickname recognizes himself in the appearance and character of the Great Dog of Nova Roma, then I can only adopt an innocent expression and assure everyone that any resemblance is purely coincidental.

It was a great experience to write in another two of my personal heroes, Marcus Porcius Cato and Marcus Tullius Cicero, but oddly enough it was the B'Kou chief Four Bears who emerged as the most able, natural leader of men in the story, with the possible exception of Pompey Magnus. Unlike Pompey, Cato and Cicero, Four Bears is an entirely fictional character, as are the B'Kou, their cousins the A'Tep, the Alligator People, and all of the pre-Columbian Indians in this book and its sequels. The Tsalee League does have at least some basis in history, as this was the time of the Hopewell culture, which inhabited all of the Mississippi River drainage from the Gulf of Mexico to the Great Lakes, taking in much of the upper Midwest. The Tsalee are based loosely on them. And the Maya, of course, were and are a real people, who live even today in the Yucatan Peninsula, and were building cities in those forests when the Roman

Republic was building theaters and temples in Rome.

In real life Marcus Tullius Cicero was a prolific writer. The work he mentions in the epilogue, *Treatises on Friendship and Old Age*, is a real work of Cicero's from our time; in the Nova Roma world, it probably had a different slant. Cicero was also famed as an orator, and in preparing to write this work— especially Cicero's "We are Rome" speech, I read quite a bit of his oratory. He could be long-winded at times, and the style of speaking common in the late Roman Republic seems terribly prolix today, but it's important to do the old boy credit. And, of course, it was fun to plan and write of an American Republic with Cato and Cicero among the founding fathers.

As to the Novans: In actuality we know little about the ancient mound-builder cultures of the American Southeast in the time period encompassed by this book. Instead of bemoaning the lack of information, I took that as license to craft my pre-Columbian cultures in a way that made for a good story, while remaining, at least, likely. One important note: The layout of Four Bear's village in the early parts of the story is, based on archeological finds, accurate.

Civil War history buffs and South Carolina residents may have also figured out that the Roman fort at Pulcia is on the present-day site of Castle Thunder in Charleston harbor. The larger island mentioned is the site of Fort Sumter. The New World's Tiber is our time's Congaree, which joins the Wateree to form the Santee, which the Romans in this work followed inland.

Finally, the Roman Army. The Roman legions were the first modern military in history. Their technology was not significantly more advanced than that of Greece, Thrace, Carthage, Gaul or any of the other nations they defeated; it was the training and discipline of the Roman soldiers that won battles and conquered nations. Exceptional soldiers were not uncommon; Julius Caesar's The Gallic War record two such, the centurions Titus Pullo and Lucius Vorenus, who competed to outdo each other in acts of valor. That mention was enough to earn them a place in this work, although the role they play here is not quite as sympathetic.

When I read and write of the common Roman soldiers and their commanders, I feel certain that the soldiers of Rome had many of the same gripes, the same pleasures, the same joys and heartbreaks that my fellow soldiers and I knew in the service of my own country, in the United States Army.

To the soldiers of both Rome and the United States I owe my thanks, not only for their service but for my own insights and experience that were of incredible value in producing this work.

About the Author

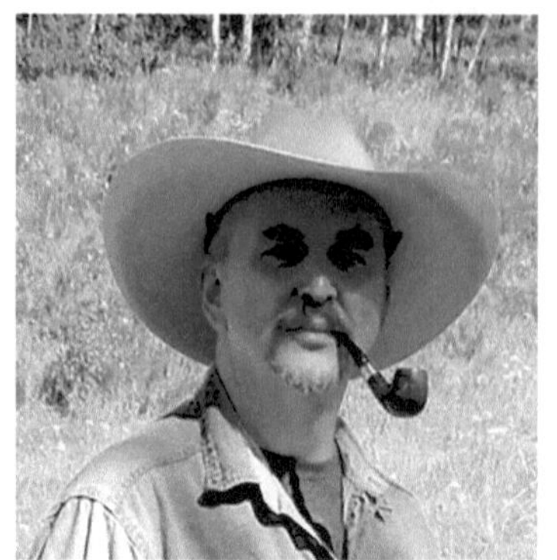**Anderson Gentry** grew up in the hills and trout streams of northeast Iowa's wooded uplands, gaining a keen interest in wildlife, camping, hunting, fishing, and the outdoors.

Gentry served in the U.S. Army in the last years of the Cold War, including service in the Persian Gulf War. Captain Gentry concluded his military career by serving on the staff of the Command Surgeon, U.S. Army, Europe. Along the way, he obtained a bachelor's degree in Biology.

Anderson Gentry's first major novel, *The Crider Chronicles* received a 2005 Preditors & Editors Reader's Choice Award for Top Ten Science Fiction Novel. The Galactic Confederacy series continued with the 2008 release of *Sky of Diamonds*. A spin off work, *Barrett's Privateers* was released in 2008.

His fast-paced, hard-hitting style combines a unique blend of outdoor savvy, real-world military experience, and realistic character development.

Other Books by Anderson Gentry

The Crider Chronicals
Sky of Diamonds
Barretts Privateers

Coming Soon

Nova Roma 2: Quaestu pro Nova Terra

Eighty years have passed since General Gnaeus Pompey and the Optimates of the Senate took refuge on the shores of Nova Roma. In that time, the new Roman Republic has grown steadily and is now ready to explore the great expanse past the Mesizibi. But their goal is not going unnoticed.

To the north, the Remans of the Five Seas Nation have not found life easy. The nation of soldiers and ironworkers rely on the Romans much more than they like and are not content to let the Romans claim the entire continent.

To the south, the Mayan nation is at the pinnacle of their civilization. The Mayan king and his court are looking with great interest at the resource potential of the uncharted lands to their northwest.

Complicating this tumultuous situation are fierce natives who will fight to protect their lands from intruders.

Who will prevail in conquering this vast, wild land?